JANELLE DILLER

THE VIRUS

WORLDTREK PUBLISHING

Published by WorldTrek Publishing
Copyright © 2015 by Janelle Diller
Printed in the USA

This is a work of fiction. Names, characters, places, and incidents either are the product of the author's imagination or are used fictitiously. Any resemblance to actual events, locales, organizations, or persons, living or dead, is entirely coincidental and beyond the intent of either the author or the publisher. The exception to this is where names were used with permission.

ISBN: 978-1-936376-12-4
Cataloging-in-Publication Data available from the Library of Congress.

DEDICATION

To my favorite lover of conspiracies.
You know who you are, sweetheart.

IF YOU CAN BELIEVE THE MEDIA, this story starts with one death and one survivor. But if you believe this, you also have to believe that 9/11 started on September 11, 2001.

Like that first disaster, the initial news blip came on a crisp late summer morning. But it wasn't the earthshaking, glue-you-to-the-TV explosion like 9/11. Life didn't unexpectedly freeze into startling memory shards. Since the death occurred just forty miles down the road from us, Channels 5/30, our local NBC affiliate in Colorado Springs, actually reported it first. By one o'clock, it made the news ticker tape that scrolled non-stop on the bottom edge of the Fox News and CNN screens. That evening, the story led on all three major networks.

Even then, I'm pretty sure most Americans couldn't have told you the next day what it was they were supposed to be afraid of *now*. We'd become a nation that shrugged our shoulders through one scare or another every season. Anthrax, SARS, H1N1—too much shouting dulls the hearing. And we were certainly a nation that had been shouted at plenty.

I would have missed the story entirely except that I happened to be working from home that week, neither of my two current clients desperately needing me at the moment. My high-tech consulting job puts me on the road traveling to client sites at least four or five days a week nearly every week of my working year.

I survive the grind because when I'm home, I'm truly at my house and not stuck on a freeway or trapped in a cubicle with ominously appropriate padded walls.

That morning, the TV was on in the background, but I wasn't paying attention. I'm not a news junkie. Instead, I was clicking through the forty emails that had bred overnight in the cozy darkness of my inbox and trying not to be irritated by Eddy's careless breakfast noises in the next room: coffee grinding, coffee bubbling; cereal pouring, cereal crunching; newspaper rattling, newspaper ripping. Even with all the news at his fingertips, he'd be the last man in America to give up the chance to hold an actual newspaper (or in his case three).

Eddy was an article ripper (never an article clipper) and favored wayward and seemingly random tidbits, his theory being that the media gave us lots of trees to study, but never painted a picture of the forest. Pattern, context, and themes were everything. The individual stories, nothing.

"Did you hear that, Maggie?" His breakfast noises stopped.

"What?"

"The thing about the prisoner."

"I'm doing email." I tried not to sound annoyed. But I was, after all, working and he was, after all, leisurely eating breakfast. "What happened?"

"I think they said a prisoner down in the maximum security prison in Florence died last night. Looks like smallpox."

"Smallpox? Really? I thought smallpox was eradicated decades ago. Anything in the paper about it?"

"Didn't see it if there was."

Which meant there wasn't.

"Sounds like a second prisoner has the same thing but hasn't died yet."

"Weird."

I don't remember if the news anchor used the word "weird" in his five o'clock story, but it's the word I kept thinking of all day. It was weird that someone could die of smallpox, weird that someone in prison could contract a dead disease.

Eddy must have been thinking about it too because late morning he randomly asked, "Isn't there an incubation period?"

Fifteen years of marriage gives you a rhythm. You share the same skin. I knew what he meant even though we hadn't said a word for two hours.

"I mean, how could you be in a maximum security prison and contract a contagious disease that's been eradicated?"

I looked at him, really more at his T-shirt stretched across his muscular arms and back, since our desks sat at right angles to each other in our home office. He had the luxury of the view of Pikes Peak because he camped out at his computer nearly every day of the week doing freelance web design. "It's like chicken pox, isn't it? At least it's somehow related to those horrible poxy things that pop up and fester."

He pulled up his left T-shirt sleeve to look at his ancient inoculation scar. "Mine's gone."

I checked my upper arm too, but my sun- and age-worn skin didn't show a trace of the old peanut-shaped ripples. What decade had it disappeared?

"Think we're still immune?" Eddy sounded curious, not worried. He swiveled around in his chair and faced me. His blue eyes matched the sky outside. A couple of loose black curls fell across his forehead. Usually, he kept his hair trimmed shorter, but I liked it this length.

"I don't think so. With the anthrax scare awhile back, there was lots of stuff about all the other bioterrorist stuff. I think they said the smallpox immunity lasts only several decades."

Eddy raised his right eyebrow—his trademark flirting signal and gave me a soft smile. "That puts you in big danger."

I laughed and jabbed his ribs. "Only if I end up in the federal pen.

He turned back to his web work, which on one of his computer screens looked suspiciously like the Center for Disease Control's smallpox site, and I went back to entering my travel expenses.

Mid-afternoon he mused, "Even if our vaccinations are still good, is this the same virus?"

I turned and stared at his back. He continued to click away at his keyboard. One of his screens still had the CDC partially visible.

He loved to worry. It gave him a reason to clip all those newspaper bits and pieces.

I shrugged my shoulders. "What's the statistic on how many people get the flu every year? Five percent? Ten? I haven't had the flu for fifteen years and I've never had a vaccination. I guess I'm not too worried about the odds." I come from a long line of optimists, Eddy from an even longer line of pessimists. Our children, if we'd been able to have any, would have been interesting.

We watched the news that night, popcorn bowl between us, more attentive and curious than usual, but we didn't learn anything new.

The national newsmongers insisted that we be nervous. For the next week, they led every evening newscast with a panicked twist on the smallpox crisis, all delivered with solemn authority: the government wasn't releasing the name of the prisoner until they could investigate further; the prison officials wouldn't allow an interview with the surviving but apparently heavily scarred other prisoner; the CDC—whose initials the entire nation now recognized as easily as the Federal Bureau of Investigation's—shut their doors to the cameras when asked about the nonexistent supply of fresh vaccines.

The Colorado Springs stations gloried in being at the epicenter of all the attention, although their stories didn't have quite the weight. They interviewed everyone associated—directly, indirectly, and not even remotely connected—with the event: family members of any prisoners, including those in the county jail forty miles away from the incident; any prison guards and family members of any prison guards; doctors who had an opinion about smallpox; local university professors who had opinions about doctors who had opinions about smallpox; someone with an opinion who had a relative who'd died of smallpox decades ago (the opinion ungraciously leaned more towards the long-dead relative than the disease); and even shoppers at the mall who could talk about smallpox as articulately as they could talk about the World Bank's impact on US coffee prices.

I called the shopper opinion story a new low in local journalism, but Eddy reassured me that they hadn't done any pet-related smallpox stories, so the low was yet to come.

Every story held the same subtext: the disease either dealt a gruesome death or left survivors with grotesquely ravaged skin.

All the media cautioned us repeatedly about how this explosively contagious virus spread by inhaling a single airborne smallpox virus particle. Simply talking was enough to spread the particles, although coughing—one of the symptoms—hastened the spread even more dramatically. Computer animations showed full progression of emerging blisters, or pustules, that filled with pressurized milky pus. These blisters didn't break open so much as they tore away from the underlying skin, an extraordinarily painful process. In the final days, the pustules became hard, bloated sacs the size of peas, encasing the body with pus. As the disease progressed, victims lost the ability to speak and grew blinded as the pustules squeezed their eyes shut. Yet they remained alert. Death came from arrested breathing, a heart attack, shock, or an immune-system shutdown.

We had a new plague.

As happens with constant nightly news drum-beating, the public's noise level began to rise. In less than a week, the polls indicated that "sufficient smallpox vaccinations for every citizen" was more important than the quagmire in the Middle East, the deficit, or an inept congress.

The White House issued a statement saying the CDC was working hard to determine ways to bring vaccines to market faster, but it could be weeks before the first ones were ready and months—maybe a year—before they had sufficient immunizations to vaccinate the entire country.

Then came the capstone. CBS broke the story first. The prisoner who died was being held without bond while waiting for a hearing. His name: Abdulaziz al-Sherhi.

In a nation rich with imagination, this name required none at all.

From that moment on, we were putty.

Chapter
02

 I was too weary to imagine anything, even something obvious.

I was a firefighter—my business card said communication specialist—for Zaan, a mega tech company that sold and implemented database technology and business software. That's the geek description. The translation? If your world crossed paths in any way—employee, supplier, or consumer—of a Fortune 50 company, chances were good Zaan had its fingerprints on your life, whether you knew it or not. I wrote memos, created newsletters, led workshops—really anything that helped decode the high-tech world into everyday lives. Along the way I did a lot of handholding. I often felt as much like a corporate therapist as a communication expert. I managed the people directly impacted by the inevitable disruptions and changes the new software brought.

I loved the work since it gave me a window into pockets of countless organizations, which ranged from public school systems to jet engine manufacturers. I got to work with everyone from the Chief Executive Officer to third-shift punch press operators. And I made a difference in their lives, or at least their lives as they dealt with the misery of changing software and the way they were used to doing their jobs.

But I hated the travel.

I hated leaving Eddy week after week. I hated airports. I hated driving a strange car in a strange place. I hated going to Detroit in January and Phoenix in July, and I'd done both too many times. I hated adjusting to multiple time zones within a few days. I hated sleeping in a different bed every week. I was even beginning to hate room service, if you can imagine hating having a pick of the menu, having someone deliver it to your door, and not having to do the dishes.

But I truly did love the work, so I suffered with the rest of it and collected hotel points that upgraded me to suite level in every major hotel chain and air miles I was too tired to use except for the yearly exotic vacations Eddy and I spent our airmiles on. The job took me to off-the-beaten-path places: Strother, Kansas; Keene, New Hampshire; Avery Island, Louisiana. Normal places, too. I just never had a chance to have fun when I got there.

The day CBS broke the story I was in the Bay Area working with Baja Breeze, a trendy retail clothing chain, in the throes of a very messy software implementation. The shipping software wasn't working in the test phase. If we couldn't get it to work, shipping from factories to stores would stop overnight. Not a good thing, regardless of the upcoming Christmas season. My job was more complicated with this client because the CEO was sixty-five. Everyone else was under thirty, and too many of them had exposed navels, cleavage, and unexplained facial metal for my corporate world experience. I could have easily lived with that except that most of their project team, especially their project lead, seemed to be hiring mistakes. They never, ever arrived anywhere on time: for work, for meetings, for individual appointments. And deadlines? Only a suggestion for these folks. It all had an ugly ripple effect on everything else.

They required three times as much effort from the Zaan team and delivered half as much as my previously most miserable client. And frankly, every day they made me rethink whether I really did love my job.

Mid-afternoon, Eddy pinged me on Google Talk. Long before Edward Snowden's revelations about the creepy invasiveness of the National Security Agency, Eddy had insisted enabling the off-the record function on gtalk. Our chats still weren't encrypted, but at least they weren't logged for NSA perusing.

EddytheWebMan: *hey mz m.*

MRiderZaan: Eddio... Whassup?

EddytheWebMan: *did you watch the news?*

He knew better.

MRiderZaan: Nope. What'd I miss?

EddytheWebMan: *more stuff is surfacing on this whole thing.*

I had no idea what "whole thing" he was talking about. My head wasn't anywhere but whether I could calm the masses long enough for the Zaan consultants to work their voodoo with the shipping software—and what I would have to do to finesse the ugly message if they couldn't.

MRiderZaan: What happened?

EddytheWebMan: *two more cases of smallpox surfaced in salida.*

Salida was one of our favorite little Colorado towns because it somehow managed to navigate that ever-shifting thin line between normal and mountain artsy. As an added bonus, it rivaled any place in New Mexico for its fabulous green chili choices, and we'd tried them all. Numerous natural hot springs also dotted the area. Over the years, we'd soaked away countless weekends there as we recovered from weeks that made us weary.

MRiderZaan: You're kidding.

MRiderZaan: Locals? Or do they have Mideast names, too?

EddytheWebMan: *locals.*

MRiderZaan: Weird. Truly weird. So is it a terrorist thing or not?**EddytheWebMan:** *dunno. the talking heads say yes.*

MRiderZaan: In Salida? What's next? A terrorist cell in Mattoon, IL?

EddytheWebMan: *you read my mind.*

EddytheWebMan: *anyway, they're trying to quarantine the town.*

MRiderZaan: How are they ever going to q a whole town?

EddytheWebMan: *dunno. nobody in/nobody out i guess.*

MRiderZaan: Ugh. Aspen season. It'll kill 'em if they miss a season of those tourist $$.

EddytheWebMan: *they're trying to track who all these guys have been in contact with.*

MRiderZaan: Long time to track contacts.

EddytheWebMan: *no kidding. if you were exposed, how many people did you come into contact with last week?*

EddytheWebMan: *…and how would you let them know they'd been exposed.*

MRiderZaan: Couldn't do it.

He didn't say it, but he could have added, "or how many times were you exposed?" I don't let fear govern my life, but a little seed planted itself in my stomach anyway. Who could help that?

EddytheWebMan: *BTW, 7-17 days incubation period. average is 12.*

MRiderZaan: So they could've been exposed before or after the dead guy went to prison.

EddytheWebMan: *yup. but probably after. i think you're only contagious when the scabs appear till they drop off… so unless these salida cases were in prison, they couldn't have gotten it from him.*

MRiderZaan: Were they?

EddytheWebMan: *maximum security and exposed to the smallpox cases there? then out on the streets? don't think so. don't think there's a chance.*

MRiderZaan: Very, very weird.

EddytheWebMan: *yup.*

MRiderZaan: Gotta run. My Breezy friends are whining.

MRiderZaan: … I mean calling.

EddytheWebMan: *later 'gator.*
MRiderZaan: Keep me posted ...
EddytheWebMan: *as always. xoxo*
MRiderZaan: u2
Weird. It was my new word for life.

I CAME HOME TO A STACK OF EDDY CLIPPINGS. Well, "stack" is probably a charitable word since they were randomly scattered in the kitchen, bedroom, bathroom, and my office chair. Being the generous man he is, Eddy always leaves information tidbits for me to peruse since I can go an entire travel week and not even turn on the TV. Not only do I not remember to look for forests; most of the time I forget there are trees out there.

I guess I'm hopeless.

"The one on your chair is the most important one."

"I knew that." Although I couldn't exactly figure out why since it was just a stapled list of Ixquick searched headlines that went back ten or twelve years.

"Something, isn't it?"

I looked at Eddy out of the corner of my eye. It was ten thirty on a Friday night. My flight from San Francisco to Denver had been delayed, which meant I had barely caught the last flight into Colorado Springs. I hadn't eaten since one o'clock in some time zone that wasn't the one I was standing in. I wasn't in an insightful mood.

"I'm sure it is." I nodded encouragingly. "Just help me out with this."

"Count how many articles there are each year."

"I don't know if I can. I'm pretty tired."

It was as if I hadn't said anything.

"Look. I made a little graph at the end."

I flipped to the last page. Ten years ago, people were panicked about bioterrorism because of an anthrax scare. Ninety-two articles showed up that contained "smallpox" somewhere in the content. As anthrax became old news, bioterrorism references dwindled. The next year only sixty-eight articles referenced "smallpox." The number of articles dropped to fifty-six the next year and forty-seven the following. The last few years, posts about smallpox became almost nonexistent.

This year, 846 articles or posts popped up on on Ixquick—Eddy's least worrisome search engine du jour—prior to September first, "In other words," Eddy, ever the gentleman, leaped to my conclusion for me, "there were more articles or posts written about smallpox from January to the end of August than were written the year of the anthrax scare. All before this prisoner died."

He poked hard at the paper. "Plus, look at the headlines. In the past, the search engine pulled up these articles because they referenced smallpox. This year, smallpox showed up in the titles. I've highlighted them."

He was right, for whatever that meant: next to zero highlighted headlines on the earlier pages, lots of highlighted headlines on the most recent pages. My insides did a jolt when I spotted a number that hinted about where the world still held live smallpox vials. Others noted at how little true security surrounded these labs, including a series of very ugly headlines about how a lab near Washington, D.C., "lost" a smallpox vial.

"So for some reason, this was becoming an issue before it was an issue?"

Eddy just nodded and gave me his look.

A week with a messy client and six hours of awful travel had left me in my usual Friday night zombie state, I was too tired for this discussion.

I love this man. I've loved him since some university chemistry class we both took before the beginning of time. Believe me, the real chemistry in that class didn't happen in any test tubes. But I discovered too late that along with his genetic predisposition to pessimism, he's also paranoid. Pathologically so.

"Eddy." I couldn't think clearly at the moment, and I knew I'd be bested by his latest conspiracy theories. Web design work aside, he spent way too much time on the Internet, or "doing professional research" as he preferred to have me refer to it. "Isn't it possible that it's just a bigger deal again for some reason? Maybe there was an outbreak in some third-world country. Or maybe with all that ISIS stuff, they're worried about what's cooking in those Middle Eastern labs. Turns out they would have been right about that one."

"Look at the titles, Maggie."

I skimmed the first page:

Smallpox: Apocalypse When?

Dead Disease Rises again: Smallpox Vaccination Must Be Revived

W.H.O. Panel backs Gene Manipulation in Smallpox Virus

Smallpox Vial Goes Missing in CIA's Backyard

Smallpox: Without immunizations, the REAL bioterrorist threat

Smallpox Immunization for Life? Think Again

White House Has New Concerns about Smallpox Readiness

Test of Experimental Smallpox Vaccine Begins

Bioterrorism Researchers Build a More Lethal Mousepox

Russia, Iran, and North Korea Admit to Secret Stash of Smallpox

White House Urges Shift of Focus in Preparing for Smallpox

Not 50, not 40, not even 20; Try 10 Years of True Smallpox Protection

Time's Running Out: Rebuild Vaccination Supplies or Risk Smallpox Epidemic

Eddy's eyes shifted over my face, trying to read my expression. "Do you see it Maggie? Do you see the thread?"

I wanted to make him happy, but I was too tired.

"It's all about immunizations. It's not about the disease. It's about getting vaccinated." He took the sheaf of papers out of my hands and paged to the headlines from earlier years. "Then look at these article titles." His finger ran down the list, stopping at the highlighted lines: "Less Lethal Cousin of Smallpox Arrives in US"; "Smallpox Worry Misplaced"; "Forget Smallpox; Anthrax Has Greater Potential for Death and Destruction"; "Smallpox Vaccination Program Halted Amid Safety Concerns."

"Do you see the shift? Before the message was that smallpox wasn't that big of a scare. Now there's a panic about getting immunized. And all this before that al-Sherhi guy is ever a blip on the news radar."

"Maybe it's a slow news year." I meant it to be a joke, but it landed flat.

"Something's going on here. I don't know what it is. Yet."

I wanted to tell him that what was going on here was that he needed to get his medication adjusted, but I didn't. First of all, he wasn't actually taking any drugs for his paranoia, and second, I'd used that little joke years earlier and we had a two-day fight about it. I knew when to keep my mouth shut, although I sometimes couldn't follow my own advice.

So instead, I kissed him on the cheek and told him I was headed to the shower and then to bed. He could join me either or both places as long as he didn't bring up the subject of smallpox.

Fortunately, even in his bleakest moments, Eddy could be easily distracted.

Chapter
04

THE ZAAN PROJECT TEAM FIGURED OUT within about six hours that Keri, the Baja Breeze project manager, wasn't kept for her project management skills. Her entire first day on the project included a two-hour lunch where she went AWOL.

Women like her made it harder for women like me.

It didn't matter though. The Zaan team was stuck with her and her non-existent project management skills.

That week, I'd barely gotten settled into my guest cubicle when Michael de Leon, the Zaan project manager, stopped by. "How's the shipping software going?" The crisis from the previous week was always my first question in the new week.

"It's a red herring." Michael shook his head. I liked Michael. If he'd lived in Colorado Springs, he would have been a regular at our dinner table. As it was, Eddy had never met him.

"So you can get it fixed by the time we go live with the rest of the software?"

"Piece of cake." He paused and then grimaced. "Well, not piece of cake, but very doable. The real problem is that Baja Breeze is way behind on their data conversions. They want someone to blame for a delay." Michael was a transplant from the Philippines. His soft brown skin and charcoal eyes somehow matched his slightly sibilant speech. "Better us than them, right? Anything to divert the shareholders' attention."

"So will it impact go-live?"

Michael laughed. "Of course. They were supposed to have cleaned up their customer information and be ready to convert the data into the new system by now." He paused, then sighed. "Maybe they're at thirty percent."

"You want some help documenting that?"

"An email draft would be nice." He smiled. I loved those white teeth.

I got it now. He hadn't just happened by. He wanted some help but even though this was exactly my job responsibility, it wasn't his nature to be bold enough to ask. Which was another reason that thirty-two-year-old vamp got away with her miserable project management style.

"I'll put something together. Give me a couple of bullet points, and I'll translate it."

"Thanks."

This was my job. I put out fires on both sides. I finessed messages. As one client told me, I was good at turning chicken shit into chicken salad. I think it was a compliment.

I plugged away for the rest of the afternoon. The agony of working and living in different time zones is that regardless of the time you wake up, you're held to the time zone you're working in. And the Zaan style is that there's no such thing as an eight-hour day. By 6:00 p.m.—seven Mountain Time—I was totally fried. I'd been up since 4:00 a.m. to catch my flight and then worked an eight-hour day once I got to San Francisco. The glamour of travel had disappeared within months of my arrival at Zaan.

I closed down everything I was working on and checked email one more time. Before I could hit the X and be gone, Eddy pinged me on gtalk.

EddytheWebMan: *hey mz m. u there?*

I debated a minute. I really wanted to get to the hotel and crash.

But it was Eddy, so I put off packing up for another five minutes. I opened my spreadsheet again so I could at least multitask.

MRiderZaan: Yup. Whassup?

EddytheWebMan: *you still at work or at the hotel?*

MRiderZaan: Work. Just getting ready to leave, though. What's up?

EddytheWebMan: *had an interesting conversation today.*

MRiderZaan: Yeah?

EddytheWebMan: *ran in to cindy marshall at costco.*

MRiderZaan: ...And?

EddytheWebMan: *turns out she finally married that guy she's been living with for a hundred years. they're living in salida these days.*

I waited for the next comment since this one didn't seem to expect a response.

EddytheWebMan: *u there?*

MRiderZaan: yes

EddytheWebMan: *salida, mz m.*

EddytheWebMan: *where those 2 guys contracted smallpox so randomly.*

MRiderZaan: Ohhhhh ... was Cindy worried they'd been exposed?

EddytheWebMan: *not anymore...but she said there was real panic in the town at first. she told me some pretty amazing gossip.*

MRiderZaan: Yeah?

EddytheWebMan: *call me ... how long?*

MRiderZaan: I'm leaving as soon as I close down my computer. My brain's fried. Give me 20 minutes.

EddytheWebMan: *ttyl*

Talk to you later. What I really wanted to do was check in, order room service, have a glass of wine, and go to bed. But we'd talk because that's what we did every night. This time we'd actually have something new to talk about.

MRiderZaan: xoxo

EddytheWebMan: *u2*

There's something wrong with your life when the night manager of a hotel knows your name before you register. I certainly wasn't famous, and I didn't frequent the place because I was local and sly. Unfortunately, I traveled to this man's city and stayed in his hotel way too many times.

"Welcome back, Mrs. Rider."

"Hey, Tony."

We mechanically went through the steps of checking in while we small-talked.

It was always the same conversation. I was from Colorado; he loved to ski. It didn't matter that the season wouldn't start for almost two months.

Once in my room, I kicked off my shoes, ordered a Caesar salad and tortilla soup from room service, and then dialed home.

"Hello?"

"Hey. It's me."

"I'll call you right back." Eddy distrusted any cell phone conversation. "What's your room number?"

Another sign of the times: Eddy had my Sheraton number on speed dial.

A minute later, my hotel phone rang.

"So what's the gossip?"

"Cindy said they locked down the whole town during the quarantine. They had government agents going door-to-door with flyers about symptoms and what to do if you thought you'd come into contact with someone exposed to the virus. They also had pictures of the guys even though everyone knew them already. Cindy said they were just a couple of town drunks who closed down the bars every night."

"So did she have a clue about how they'd gotten exposed?"

"That's the interesting tidbit. She said the government guys poked around about whether you knew what their activities had been or who they'd been with, whether you'd noticed anyone around town who looked like they were from the Middle East."

"In Salida? What?" I laughed out loud at the thought.

"No kidding. The questions made you think the government thought they were part of some terrorist cell."

"Right. The town drunks."

"That's exactly what Cindy said. Give either one of these guys a couple of beers and they'd tell you anything you wanted to know, but mostly stuff you couldn't care less about. Big talkers. Big bullshitters. But terrorists? She said it was the town joke."

"I never did hear. Did they survive?"

"Apparently not. So…" he paused.

I finished his sentence. "They can't defend themselves."

"Nope."

"Did anyone else end up with smallpox in town?"

"That's the good part. From what I remember from the CDC site—and Cindy confirmed this—you're only contagious in the few days before the pustules start showing and then while you have the pustules. These guys went bow hunting for a week. I guess while they were out, they both began to get really sick. Couldn't even get back to town. One of them used his cell phone to call some drinking buddy to come get them. The guy he called happened to be an EMT and knew something was way off-kilter by what these two guys were describing. He alerted the CDC of all things, and they came in and took care of it."

"Pretty smart for a small town EMT."

"If he was well trained, he should have been able to spot what was out of the ordinary. I think they're schooled pretty well in what to do if they bump up against something like this. Plus, keep in mind that with those two guys up the road in the federal pen, he probably had a heightened awareness."

"But he didn't get smallpox himself?"

"Nope. And nobody else did, either. Cindy said they came in and vaccinated the whole town just in case. They were told that if you get vaccinated within four days of exposure, the vaccine usually works. Once people got vaccinated, they weren't quarantined any more."

"Well there's some incentive for you."

"Git along, little doggies."

I laughed. "I think sheep is the better metaphor."

"Either way. No resistance."

"Well, it's not like I would have resisted either. How long could I be quarantined and keep my job?"

"True. You and a couple hundred million more people. Life would stop. Commerce would stop."

"Except for you Internet geeks."

"Gotta love the Internet."

"Mostly I just love one of the geeks."

Chapter
05

OVER THE NEXT WEEK, Eddy kept sending me links to articles about the Salida smallpox scare. Here was the funny thing: the same reporter could have written them all— the facts were that consistent. The reporter, however, definitely wasn't Cindy Marshall. Her story had a totally different ending, as well as ample discrepancies along the way. But whom do you believe? *The New York Times* and *Washington Post*, or Cindy Marshall, the old friend you run into at Costco?

The Times' version said nothing about the bow hunting, lots about the door-to-door canvassing by the CDC and FBI, and only sketchy details about another dozen who'd been infected and were now being treated in isolation at some undisclosed location. Cindy and *The Times* at least agreed that everyone in town had been vaccinated, which was why the quarantine had been lifted so quickly.

National smallpox anxiety ballooned again. It even began to consume the Baja Breeze crowd, although they were fifteen hundred miles away from the outbreak. Signs went up on doorways, bathroom stalls, and in the cafeteria. Whoever designed the signs used an exclamation mark machine gun and revealed a love for shouting with capital letters. I come from the less-is-more school of writing, so I had a hard time not rolling my eyes:

The Virus

SMALLPOX SYMPTOMS!!!!!
Smallpox is an AIRBORNE VIRUS!!
Be ALERT to anyone COUGHING or SNEEZING!!
If you begin to run a FEVER,
<u>IMMEDIATELY</u> contact the BAJA BREEZE
Company Health Care Workers!!
DO NOT TOUCH anyone or anything!!!
As VACCINATION information becomes available, we
will ALERT you as to WHEN, WHERE, and HOW to get <u>your</u>
VACCINATION!!

As people began to remember I commuted from Colorado, they dropped by my cubicle to get whatever gossipy particulars I might have by virtue of living in the same state as the outbreak. Maybe if the Baja Breeze people hadn't been so far behind with their data conversions—and every other task in the project—I might have felt chattier. But I didn't want them to drag me down with them. And since the work I didn't finish in California by Friday would be work I'd be doing in Colorado on Saturday and Sunday, I avoided bringing up Cindy Marshall's details.

I made an exception for Michael de Leon, though. We grabbed some Mexican fast food on Thursday and exchanged low points from the week. True to the realities of our jobs, Michael's low points were much lower than mine. After all, if the project didn't come in on time and on budget, it was his neck that would get chopped. Given the Baja Breeze skill set and work ethic, Michael fully expected to be without a neck—or a job—when this project finally finished, even though he was one of the company's most competent project managers.

"And now with all those smallpox posters up, people are starting to call in sick with fevers."

I laughed, but probably shouldn't have. "You're kidding."

Michael just shook his head and looked a little pale himself.

"They're staying home because they think they've got smallpox?"

"Apparently so, but I'm guessing they're not so conscientious about their fevers that they're not out shoe shopping."

"As long as no one coughs on them."

Michael rolled his eyes.

Someone at the next table rolled through a deep and raspy series of coughs.

I flinched, then caught Michael's eye. He'd flinched, too. We laughed nervously.

"Smoker's hack," I said and Michael nodded, but I know both of us were silently thinking, *I hope.*

"I hate all this media hype. It's the scare of the week. I mean, what are the odds? You live in Colorado. Are you afraid you're going to get smallpox?"

I shook my head. "Not very. I probably spend more of my anxiety vouchers on flying. Takeoffs, landings, crashing into other planes in the air—you know, all the irrational stuff."

He nodded even though he lived within driving distance of Baja Breeze. "And now you have to worry about ambient air."

"My theory is that I'm now immune to everything because I've been exposed to it all. Kind of like a kindergarten teacher."

"So what are people saying in Colorado?"

"If I were ever home, I could tell you. All I get is what Eddy sends me, and he's paranoid about everything."

Michael smiled. "Too much time to surf the Internet." I'd told him about Eddy's job hazard.

"Here's the funny thing, though. Eddy ran into an old friend of ours who's been living in Salida, where the outbreak was. She said no one else got exposed. These guys were just a couple of town drunks, and they weren't even in town during the contagious stage of the disease."

"But the papers are saying at least a dozen others are being treated."

I shrugged my shoulders. "Not according to Cindy."

"Couldn't it be, though? That they would whisk people out of town so they didn't spread the disease. Or the panic."

I shook my head. "It's a small mountain town that's twenty or thirty miles away from the next town of any size. People talk. They'd know someone who knew someone. You can't get a DUI in that town without everyone hearing about it. You don't think this would be big gossip?"

"So who are these other victims?"

I shrugged my shoulders again. "You tell me."

"It's all just kind of weird, isn't it?"

That was my word, but because I liked Michael, I let him use it. For the moment, there wasn't a better one.

Unfortunately, for my flight from San Francisco to Denver, I didn't need Ixquick or even Google. The posters at Baja Breeze had shouted about coughing and sneezing. Wouldn't you know it? My entire plane seemed to be carrying coughing and sneezing people from the West Coast to Colorado. The young man next to me suffered from a particularly wet hack. Even though he covered his mouth and nose with a well-traveled handkerchief, I could still see little sneeze droplets spray out into the sunlight and onto the seat in front of him. Somewhere over Utah, he started lightly snoring. I'm embarrassed to admit that I used his naptime to look for red blotches on his face. I assumed that's how the pustules began. Sure enough, he had five red bumps emerging on his cheeks and neck. The rational side of me said he was young enough to simply have a bad complexion. But the newly fearful side of me said it was more and this was the future. After all, who wouldn't long to go home to die if they thought they had a terminal illness even if the trip was the ultimate selfish act?

I started up my computer, initially to distract myself with some leftover work. Instead I couldn't help myself and read some of the CDC bulletins that Eddy had so kindly forwarded to me. The CDC information didn't encourage me. "The period of contagion begins with a two-to-four day nonspecific prodrome of fever and myalgias before rash onset." I had no idea what prodrome or myalgias meant, but I certainly understood fever. It was all I could do not to reach over and check my seatmate's forehead. He didn't *look* flushed or sweaty. He only *sounded* like he had walking pneumonia.

When we landed in Denver, I stopped in the restroom and scoured my face and hands and wiped down my leather jacket. None of the other women stared at me, which tells you something about the national mood.

Eddy tossed my bag into the back seat and greeted me with a wet kiss on the lips.

"Good kiss," I said as we pulled away from the curb. "Now we can both suffer through the ravages of smallpox together."

"I can't think of anyone I'd rather get ravaged with." He was in a good mood for having been by himself all week.

I leaned over and kissed him on the cheek, sorry that the decades and Detroit had put a console between our seats. I fell in love with him because of his loose black curls and blue, blue eyes, and I stayed in love with him because of his wit and intelligence. I missed him.

"I'm half serious. I sat next to a guy who sneezed and coughed the whole way from San Francisco to Denver. Even if it wasn't smallpox, whatever he had is going to be disgusting after the incubation period."

"I thought you were immune to every communicable virus in the continental United States."

"Or so I thought." I stared out the window, glad that I'd gotten home while there was still a trace of red on the mountains. "It's funny how your head changes with all of this."

Eddy nodded but didn't say anything.

"I'm not a fearful person. I'm careful and not stupid. I didn't worry about SARS or H1N1. I never worry about the flu. A window opened in my head this week, though."

"So you'll get vaccinated if it becomes available?"

I knew the answer to this already because I'd thought of nothing else since I'd buckled my seatbelt on the San Francisco flight.

"That was the worst flight I've ever been on." I watched his profile.

Eddy raised an eyebrow at me. "Worse than the lightening strike coming into Chicago last summer? Or the aborted landing in Wichita before that?" He had no trace of cynicism in his voice, which he would have had a right to have. I'd sworn off flying forever with both of those flights, even though I was back on a plane the following week.

"This was a different kind of fear. Those were sudden and dramatic. But they were also flukes. How many hundreds of thousands of miles have I flown, and I've never experienced either of those before or since? This is different," I said again, more to process why than because it was a new thought. "There was never a moment of sheer panic. In fact, my heart rate probably never even bumped up. But this is a very tangible fear. If I'm vaccinated, I can control the outcome. I don't have to pay attention to it anymore. I can spend my energy steeling myself against the more mundane communicable viruses or even E. coli."

"So you'll get vaccinated if it becomes available?"

I looked out the window again at the tangle of mountains fading into evening shadows. And then I looked at him again. "I don't want to be afraid."

Chapter
06

The best thing about Nebraska Beef Packing Corporation, my client in Timber, Nebraska, was that it wasn't Baja Breeze. I didn't see any navels. The visible cleavages fell more into the plentiful bosom category than the sexy breast one. And the only facial metal showed up in the smiles of the children that marched in frames across the desks of everyone who owned a desk.

The worst thing about Nebraska Beef Packing was that Timber was two hours from Lincoln, the closest airport. The second worst thing was that NBP was, at the end of the day, a meat packing company. Although I can long for a juicy steak, I'd just as soon pretend there's no connection between what comes wrapped in cellophane from my grocery store and what was hanging, bloody and heavy, on a hook just a few doors down from the conference room where I worked. A scent of something—maybe sour, maybe sharp—always hung in the air. I'd learned to bring a scented candle along and light it several times a day.

Plenty of people at NBP had worked at the company for longer than most of the Baja Breeze people had been alive, which was mostly a good thing. At least it was one of the reasons they were two weeks ahead in cleaning up their data to convert into the new system. But any strength overdone becomes a weakness, and if you need a good example, just take a look at what happens when someone works for the same company for thirty years, especially if you're trying to move someone from a pencil and Big Chief tablet to a computer. Still, aging meat odor and all, I would gladly have traded a Baja Breeze for two NBPs.

For all their differences, NBP and Baja Breeze did have one thing in common: fear of smallpox. There, in the middle of cow and corn country, the panic not only surfaced, but thrived. I figured this out without any help from bathroom stall posters the day I went to lunch with Scott Leinbach, the NBP project manager.

Scott was a fourth-generation Nebraskan, and a third-generation NBP employee. His paunchy middle and prematurely graying hair aged him an easy ten years, but he still had a handsome face in an earthy sort of way. We sat at a table in the NBP cafeteria, which except for the amazing beef stew, reminded me way too much of a grade school cafeteria, canned vegetable odor and all. Our conversation started the way all my conversations seemed to start with clients.

"How's the project going? Are you on schedule? Any ugly surprises we need to anticipate?"

Scott shrugged his shoulders and stirred a couple of packets of sugar into his tea. Maybe it was because he'd spent so many decades around cows, but he was one of the calmest people I'd ever met, certainly the most easy going project manager. "We're doing good. The shipping application is giving us fits, though."

Where had I heard that before?

"We can't get it to sync with FindIt."

"FindIt?"

"The RFID software."

"RFID?" I hadn't heard the Zaan team talk about this acronym before.

"Radio Frequency Identification. It's the way we track our packages. But everything else seems to be falling into place. We're not a complicated business. We buy cows; we kill and cut up cows;

we sell and ship the byproducts." He bit into his hamburger.

I probably winced. I know I momentarily bypassed a chunk of stew meat and went for some carrots.

"We're ahead on data conversion. Not as far ahead as I'd hoped, but ahead."

I'd *never* heard that before.

"We'll be ready." He stirred the iced tea some more. "It'll be good to get this done and get back to our real jobs. Timing's right. I think we're headed for an uptick in business."

"Really? What makes you say that?"

He shrugged his shoulders again, although he knew exactly what he meant. I think it was a Nebraska thing; I'd seen variations of the shrug all over town. "This smallpox outbreak. If it's anything like after 9/11, people will cocoon. They'll stay home more and eat out less. They'll splurge on the little things for themselves like a good steak from Osco."

I must have looked skeptical.

"Think about it," he said. "If you didn't have to get on a plane right now, would you?"

"No. But that has *nothing* to do with smallpox."

"Point taken." Clients, because they're usually fairly intelligent, can never figure out why Zaan consultants are willing to be gone from home Monday through Friday week after week. "So would you go sit in a crowded movie theater and cringe every time someone coughs a row behind you? Do you want to send your kids to school, knowing a place like that's already a Petri dish for every ugly communicable disease out there?"

I shook my head. "But won't people worry that someone's coughing all over their meat while they're butchering it?"

He shrugged his shoulders again. "We've done surveys. Most people have this picture in their head that the whole process is so automated that a live cow goes in the door over here and a box of packaged meat comes out over there, all untouched by human hands. So even though it's not true at all, it gives them one less thing to worry about."

"Perception is more powerful than reality." It was a stock phrase I used on every implementation. My job was eighty-five percent pattern recognition. It made me look smart when I only really had to be alert.

"Ain't it the truth? This time it actually works in our favor, unlike people's *E. coli* fears."

"So you're worried too?"

"Worried? Me? Hell yes. Aren't you?"

How did I answer that? Especially since on my flight to Lincoln, I'd done something that never would have occurred to me a month earlier: I brought some sterile hand wipes along and wiped the armrest and headrest on my airplane seat before I sat down. One person actually wore a disposable surgical mask on the plane, something I hadn't seen since I'd been in Korea several years earlier.

"Sure. I'm worried. I wouldn't be telling the truth if I didn't say I wasn't." I did my increasingly common ten-second mental sort of my life priorities to remember why I stuck with this job. These days "paycheck" topped the short list. "But I'm here this week."

He kind of laughed and shrugged the Nebraska shrug. "Well, if I lived in Colorado, I'd rather be in Nebraska these days, too. Even if it *is* Timber. I'll tell you one thing. We've vacationed in Colorado every summer since I was a kid and most winters for skiing, but this year, we're not going. Who knows what's out there."

"I've been telling myself that it's all contained. I mean, surely, if there's some terrorist cell trying to start an epidemic, wouldn't there be more cases popping up all over?"

"Really? You think it's been contained." It was a statement, not a question.

I thought about the contrast in The New York Times report and Cindy Marshall's story. "Hard to say." Scott was a nice guy. I had no reason not to trust him, but Eddy and I had talked in circles about it all weekend. We never came to a rational conclusion. I weighed the risk of sounding nutty with a client and came out on the careful side. "I think it's contained, but it's not the last we'll see of it." It seemed like a safe, yet honest, answer.

His eyes narrowed slightly and he slowly nodded his head. "That's an interesting suspicion."

I shrugged my shoulders and scraped out the last spoonful of stew. "What do you think? Is it contained?"

His eyes flickered around the room and he stirred his tea some more. Finally, he said, "Not a chance."

Chapter
07

On Friday, the end of the world began. Or so it seemed.

Eddy, of course, gave me a heads-up. A message from him pulsed blue at the bottom of my screen while I finished talking with the NBP Human Resources manager about company turnover and her latest grandchild. I tried my best to ignore the message, but I missed him and longed for even a five-minute cyberspace interlude with him.

EddytheWebMan: *hey*

MRiderZaan: Hey you.

EddytheWebMan: *see the news?*

MRiderZaan: Me? How likely is that?

EddytheWebMan: *how well i know … so glad you'll always need _me_*

MRiderZaan: Forever and ever Eddio…So what's happened?

EddytheWebMan: *More smallpox victims.*

MRiderZaan: Yeah? In Colorado?

EddytheWebMan: *detroit and some suburbs. maybe 18-20 people? they closed the entire detroit school system down, though. Pure panic.*

MRiderZaan: Ooooh … not good. Not good at all.

EddytheWebMan: *… yeah. lots of fallout. if you can believe the reports, of course.*

MRiderZaan: Hummmm ... and what does Detroit have to do with the terrorist cells in Colorado?

EddytheWebMan: *well isn't that a good q.*

The question had to hang for fifteen minutes with another interruption from the HR manager and pictures of not just the newest grandbaby, but of all her grandchildren. Twelve. She was from the Midwest. By the time I got back to Eddy, he must have been off someplace because he didn't respond to my gtalk. I had to pack up and leave for the airport before he returned.

Lincoln Airport is a long way from Detroit, but it didn't seem to matter. A scary time is a scary time, particularly for the exhausted traveling business crowd, which is what Fridays are full of. This particular Friday, we were probably all more skittish than exhausted. The new questions the TSA agents had started asking each passenger as they went through security didn't help: "Have you or anyone you've been in physical contact with run a fever in the last twenty-four hours?"

"No."

We were all sheep. If we had to tell them our underwear size or the last time we'd taken a shower, we'd do it just to be able to board our planes and go home. Would people be any more honest about this than the question they finally stopped asking us about carrying packages for total strangers?

"Have you or anyone you've been in physical contact with developed a cough in the last twenty-four hours?"

I shook my head again.

"I need a 'yes' or 'no,' Ma'am."

"No." I tried to not say it through gritted teeth. TSA agents are notorious for pulling rude people aside for a pat-down security check, the thinking being, I guess, that if you're impatient, you're probably also hiding a box cutter in your bra.

I only wanted to cocoon in the plane with my noise-canceling headphones. My seatmate, who turned out to be the Midwest territory manager for a ramen noodle company, only wanted to talk. He pulled off his own headphones.

"So did you hear about the new outbreak?" He was a balding, round-faced man with a red, bulbous nose. He could have been earning twice my salary or half. Business travelers are an oddly paid bunch.

I nodded. My headphones were on, but he knew I could hear him even with them on.

"Creepy, isn't it?"

I nodded again and smiled, then closed my eyes like I was going to sleep. He was breaking all the unspoken traveling rules. Business travelers *never* talk to other travelers unless the plane has sat on the tarmac for at least two hours. Even then, the rule is to begin with other travel horror stories. He must have felt desperate to talk.

"You from Colorado?"

I lifted an earphone. I could hear enough through the headphones, but if I talked with them on, it felt like I was in a cave. "Colorado Springs."

He nodded nervously. "Detroit's my territory. So's Cincinnati. I go into all those neighborhoods with my reps. Gotta keep all those customers happy."

"Cincinnati?" What did that have to do with anything?

"Yeah." He looked at me like I'd been wearing the headphones too long. "You didn't hear? Twenty to thirty people showed up with smallpox in Detroit. At least that many in Cincinnati and a half dozen in New Jersey. Some more in Jackson, Mississippi, and some small town in Idaho. Never heard of the place, but they're sick too." He shifted his eyes nervously around the plane. "I'm not traveling again until I can get vaccinated. I don't need this shit. It's tough enough being on the road every week."

Amen to that.

When I got off the plane in Denver, I made my usual stop in the restroom, but this time I threw up, too.

It was 9/11 redux. I received special dispensation from my Zaan manager not to travel the next week. He made it clear that I could travel if I wanted to, but there wouldn't be any repercussions if I chose to work from home. I thought it was kind of the big Z not to threaten firing us all for joining in the national panic. Most likely, though, they were just trying to ward off a mass exodus. It happened in 2001.

In my previous week's absence, Eddy had redecorated our office into Early Elementary School. He'd hung an enormous bulletin board on the wall over my desk. Across the bottom, he'd tacked individual calendar pages with handwritten notes on various days. A colorful map of the United States took up most of the rest of the corkboard. Red, black, yellow, and silver pinheads dotted the map: one red, one black, and one silver south of Colorado Springs; two black and twelve yellow in Salida, Colorado; bunches of yellow in Detroit, Cincinnati, New Jersey, Northern Idaho, and Jackson, Mississippi.

"Black is for people who have died from it, right?" Even my travel-dead brain could figure that one out.

Eddy nodded. He'd swiveled his office chair around so he could put his feet up on my desk. He was wearing a plain white T-shirt and faded blue sweatpants. His curly black hair still glistened wet from his shower. Any other Saturday morning we would have been talking about what came in the mail during the week and debating between Thai and Indian food for dinner.

"What's the silver for?"

"Silver is for a confirmed link to a terrorist cell."

Tired as I was, I knew it seemed off. "Seems like there should be more, especially with the new outbreaks."

"Yes. Curious, isn't it? One would think the government would be frantically chasing that crowd."

"Curious. That's a kind word for it." I nodded at the other pins. "So why red for the federal prison? Why yellow for all the others?

"Red is for an outbreak where people contracted smallpox, but didn't die."

"Why don't you have red in any of the other locations?"

"Yellow represents unconfirmed reports." He paused and let me think through what that meant. "They gave us a name for the three dead in Colorado and the prison survivor. For all the others, all we have up until now is the news reports that there are other victims. Without a name, it's just a rumor."

"Maybe they're protecting their privacy," I said.

"Maybe," he said.

"Maybe we'll never know," I said.

"Could be," he said.

"Does that make it any less of a threat?" Part of me felt frustrated that we were even having this discussion. Eddy stayed isolated all week long in his office, not having even to make eye contact with a real person if he didn't feel like going out. It gave him the luxury of feeding his paranoia and numbed him to my reality even though the truth was that anything I got exposed to Monday through Friday could become his problem as soon we kissed hello at the airport.

Eddy put his feet back on the floor and leaned toward me. He rested his arms on his knees and clasped his hands—his jock-on-the-basketball-bench position. I'd fallen in love with it decades ago. "No. It doesn't make it any less of a threat. But it certainly makes it a different kind of threat, doesn't it?"

"Maybe."

I stared at the calendar pages and map some more. I hadn't had the timeline in my head until I saw Eddy's notes. "You know what's weird is that there was one outbreak followed within a week by a second one. Nothing happened for three weeks, now we have outbreaks in five more locations. And they all get reported on the same day."

Eddy nodded. "Almost at the same time."

"Odd coincidence and odd timing." I had a fuzzy image of some poor contagious business traveler slogging from city to city over the course of a few days, unknowingly exposing innocents everywhere. My knees couldn't hold me anymore. I dropped in a chair. It could have been me. I could have been the source. I could have been a victim.

Eddy nodded some more. He was watching me think. "The outbreaks seem too plotted out."

"But why wait for three weeks between the second and third strike?"

"You tell me."

It didn't make sense. "What are they saying on the news about the potential link to terrorists?" Earlier that morning, I'd gathered up—Easter egg hunt-style—the Eddy articles from around the house. I'd even skimmed them, but I didn't remember seeing anything that would make you think this was coming.

"Just the usual. They're tracking down leads. They think this is linked to that missing smallpox vial from last summer. Now it's just a matter of dragging a couple of suspects in front of the TV cameras—if they can find them."

"You think about how quickly they named names and had

photos after 9/11 or after the Boston Marathon bombing. Why haven't the Feds been able to make faster traction on this?"

"Unless it isn't terrorists who are doing it." Eddy took my hand in his two hands and squeezed it.

"What do you mean? How did this all get started? What are you reading?"

"Nothing in the papers." He glanced at the floor. "Maybe a little on some Internet sites."

The confession.

"Eddio, you have way too much time on your hands."

He sounded a little sheepish. "People send me stuff. What can I do?"

"Delete? Ignore the blog sites?"

"And miss all the good conspiracy theories?"

I sighed. It was a pointless discussion.

"Here's what I think, Mz M."

"What you think or what your friends who are visited by aliens every full moon think?"

"Not *every* full moon. Just the months with the letter *r.*"

"We should all be so lucky to get our summers off."

"Exactly. We're well back into the *R* months again, so I'm on my own on this one."

"Yes you are, Eddio. Okay. Tell me what you think."

"I think the timing is odd because whoever is infecting these people expected more exposures and more hysteria after the Salida outbreak. Nothing happened, but it took a while to realize that those two drunks hadn't infected anyone else. But I've been noodling around about why they didn't hit a place like Detroit or New York. Why target a small town?"

I thought about that awhile. "It's too strange. Maybe the original goal was about scaring and containment. That would be a lot harder to do in a city."

"Right. Except they must have expected a ton of panic. So

they—whoever 'they' might be—had to regroup and figure out how to create some panic."

"I think they hit the jackpot. We're there now."

"The other thing I think is that we might never learn the names of the victims. It's not going to be 9/11 where we read the obits for years afterwards."

"Because you don't think those pins represent real victims." I knew his pattern.

"Cindy Marshall would probably say the same thing."

He had me there.

"So now what?"

"Now we wait and see. Some terrorist group claims responsibility or the guys in white shirts don't do anything but get the outbreaks contained? That tells us one thing."

"And if that's not what happens?"

"Then we see what the next big move is and who makes it."

Who could tell what the next big move was? Nothing happened the next week except that Eddy added more yellow pins to his map: in Montpelier, Vermont; a Dallas suburb; Socorro, New Mexico; New York City; and Los Angeles.

Every added pin mirrored the ratcheting up in national panic. People cleared the grocery store shelves and the malls were empty as tombs. The national and even the local stations carried a repeating scroll of what early symptoms looked like and what to do if you thought you were exposed.

The economy did a nose-dive that the White House insisted wasn't actually happening. They explained the plunge in the stock market as a momentary self-correcting blip. They also announced they were closer to getting sufficient immunizations but were still at least a month away, if not two or three, for enough vaccinations for everyone who wanted one—which included everyone in the country except Eddy and a few of his friends, *r* month or not. In the meantime, the vaccines they did have had to go to people in the infected areas.

Triage became the new word of the year: take care of the most vulnerable first.

The press rumbled about the incompetence of the White House. The White House grumbled off the record about the FDA obstacle course to getting a vaccine out fast. The press growled about the White House making excuses while putting the nation at risk. The White house attacked back with detailed press releases about all the regulatory handcuffs Congress had put on the FDA, which quadrupled the time it took to create enough doses and to ensure every dose was safe and effective. No one wanted the flu vaccine debacle of 2004-2005 with something as serious as smallpox. It didn't matter that only the FDA and the CDC remembered that mess.

The Senate announced hearings to get at the bottom of why the FBI hadn't tracked down the terrorist cell that started the whole epidemic.

And the airlines, hotel industry, rental car companies, and anyone else remotely associated with travel or tourism grew nervous about a domino of bankruptcies.

Yes, I know it was incredibly selfish, but me? I didn't care if it took them a year. I could stay home forever and ever and have my groceries delivered, fresh-packed meat and coughing butchers momentarily submerged far enough into my subconscious that I didn't lose my appetite.

I walked around the house all week, dizzy with the eigh-teen-hour windfall from no traveling that the week gave me and the luxury of crawling into bed every night with Eddy, which was where some of those extra twenty hours got whiled away. And since I wasn't distracted by the client or my Zaan colleagues, I truly got a third again as much done in two-thirds the time. Everyone won except Zaan since the company couldn't bill me out for the usual forty hours at the ridiculously high hourly fee they charged for me. Maybe they'd have to lay me off and give me a severance package.

By Thursday afternoon, the White House still hadn't come up with enough vaccines to put me on a plane on Sunday. It made me believe in the power of prayer. And I was beginning to re-think my vote in the next general election. There was a lot to be said for incompetence if it meant I got to sleep in my own bed every night.

Chapter
09

Usually, Sunday night is the worst night of the week for me since most Mondays find me on a plane. The only exception to this is when I have to fly out on Sunday, in which case, the worst night of the week is too close to call because a Sunday flight is the same as no weekend at all. To have two weeks in a row at home almost seemed worth the national crisis, although I hated to make that very public, seeing as it sounded so insensitive.
I really needed a different job.

Nevertheless, the second week without travel was as precious as the first. I don't know what a third week would have been like because on Wednesday I got an email from my manager.

> Team,
>   Zaan has arranged for priority on the smallpox vaccine list for people in the company who travel.
>   Please follow the instructions at: https://smallpox_vaccines@Zaan.com/benefits/sp to get vaccinated. Plan to resume your travel schedule as of Monday, Tuesday at the latest. If you're unable to obtain the vaccination as sched-uled, please contact me no later than Friday afternoon. Ken

The internal gtalk flew.

dbenningZaan: *Hi Maggie.*

MRiderZaan: Hey Denise.

dbenningZaan: *You depressed as I am?*

MRiderZaan: About going back on the road?

dbenningZaan: *What else?*

MRiderZaan: They shouldn't have let us remember what it's like to wake up in your own bed for a week straight.

dbenningZaan: *No kidding. They're better off keeping us mindless drones. Here's one for you. I just found out they changed my trash day from Tuesday to Monday <u>last January!</u> I cleaned out my refrigerator and freezer Monday night, put it out early on Tuesday, and cleaned up the mess all morning Wednesday ... YUCK! Now I've got to figure out what to do with my rapidly ripening garbage so the raccoons don't get into before next Wednesday.*

MRiderZaan: LOL! You never had smelly trash before now?

dbenningZaan: *Hell no. I don't think I've even had trash before except for frozen dinner containers and junk mail. And I always rinsed the containers out so the neighbors wouldn't swear at me while they cleaned up the raccoon leftovers.*

MRiderZaan: You know your neighbors? I wouldn't recognize mine if we arm-wrestled over the newspaper.

dbenningZaan: *You get a newspaper????? You do have a complicated life.*

MRiderZaan: Eddy gets the newspaper. He even reads it. And ripped out those articles that, come to think of it, were piling up again.

dbenningZaan: *Get your vaccine scheduled yet?*

MRiderZaan: Ugh. No. Have you?

dbenningZaan: *Yes ma'am. Tomorrow ... Unless I find another job without travel first.*

MRiderZaan: Call me if you get hired. Find out if they need someone to answer the phones and make coffee.

dbenningZaan: *You kidding? That's the job I'm interviewing for.*

MRiderZaan: So how did the big Z get bumped to the top of the vaccination list? Seem a little goofy to you that software implementations are suddenly critical to homeland security?

Denise always knew something the rest of us didn't. For her, the arrival of Google Talk had been a gift from God.

MRiderZaan: Must be the dividend of the Z's political contributions, no? Don't they own the Senate or something?

dbenningZaan: *I think the mega database contract Z got with the CDC was the dividend. Getting bumped to the top of the vaccine list falls more into the payola arena.*

MRiderZaan: Payola???? You gotta be kidding.

dbenningZaan: *LOL! Of course I'm kidding. But not about the database contract. You knew about that, right?*

MRiderZaan: Maybe I read something about that. CDC, huh?

dbenningZaan: *Yup. We're the show behind the show. Megabucks. Mega.*

MRiderZaan: Database? No applications?

dbenningZaan: *DB and something else we built for them. Something around keeping track of the spread of disease. A one-off, but there must be enough money in it that Z thought it was worth doing.*

While Denise and I gtalked, two or three more people sent me instant messages, including Michael de Leon, who wanted to know if I'd be back in the land of Baja Breeze the next week. Denise must have been getting pinged a bunch, too, because there were occasional long pauses while we conversed.

My own long pauses included checking out the Zaan internal website vaccination directions. It left me miserable. I had to print off a "Priority 1" vaccination document, drive an hour and a half to the University of Colorado in Boulder, plan on at least a two-hour wait, and allow at least forty-eight hours before traveling. It was a terrible, albeit not unexpected, price to pay for my two weeks at home.

The whole thing also triggered an unhappy evening.

"Why are you getting this vaccine?" Eddy asked over dinner on Thursday evening. He'd made a pot roast—comfort food— and bought some fresh Inca lilies and a dozen new candles for the table. We'd already split a bottle of wine, and I wasn't done drinking. Misery drives you to things like that.

"Look at your map with all the pinheads. What are there? A couple hundred?"

"And you believe those are all real?"

The map clearly meant something different to each of us.

"I don't have the luxury of not believing. Besides, if I don't, I lose my job. Ready for that?"

"It wouldn't happen right away," he said.

"It would happen soon enough. You ready to support both of us?" I'd touched on a sensitive subject.

"I could do it."

I shouldn't have had the wine if we were going to talk about this now. I knew going into it that somewhere I'd start crying. "Eddy, we've had this discussion before. You want to have it again? Here we go: Maggie—six-figure income base; amazing bonuses; Eddy—Up and down income, sometimes zip; Maggie—Benefits; Eddy—No benefits; Maggie—401K; Eddy—Piggy bank. You want me to keep going?"

"Not fair."

"Maybe not. But it's true. Do you really want to sell the Porsche? Give up the Caribbean dives? The first-class trips any- where in the world? Start draining our nest egg?"

"We could change our lifestyle. Step out for a while."

"Eddy, get real. No more Australian Outback? No more Ital- ian Riviera? No more ski weekends in Aspen?"

"Maggie, we make choices in life all the time. I'd be willing to make those choices if you just don't get the vaccine." It was the most romantic thing he'd said to me in ages and I totally missed it.

"I don't have a choice. It really is the vaccine and my job or no vaccine and no job."

"This is a job you want to quit anyway."

"But now? What do I do for a job?"

"You mean what do you do to define yourself?"

"Who's not being fair?"

"It's true. For too many years you've been 'Maggie the Wonder Woman who jets around the world saving CEOs from themselves but doesn't know where the dry cleaners are to pick up last week's silk suit.'"

"You're jealous. That's what this is about. If I don't get the vaccine then I stay stuck at home like you." I'd gone one step too far.

"*Like* me? Or *with* me?"

Now the tears came. "You know that's not it. Not it at all."

"How would I know? This is the longest stretch we've spent together at home since you started with Zaan."

"What were those three weeks about last summer in Greece?"

"Well, for starters, they were in Greece," he said.

"Do you think for a minute I don't love you?" His sigh was too long. I got up to get the box of Kleenexes off the refrigerator. "Is this really about the vaccine, or is it about us?"

He repeated the sigh. "Maggie. This is absolutely about the vaccine, but it's also just as absolutely about us, just not the way you're interpreting it." He pulled out a tissue and blew his nose, his only hint that the wine and conversation had taken him to the edge, as well. "I'm as tired as you are of your traveling. You think I truly like living like a monk five days a week? I miss you. I miss us. I miss going to lunch with you on a random day or taking an early morning hike up the canyon or even just sharing a bowl of popcorn and watching some mindless TV like we used to do."

I missed him too, week after week after week. I thought he knew that, but I couldn't even say it now because I couldn't get it out through my tears and past the growing pile of wadded up tissues. Years after Linda McCartney died of cancer, I read that she and Paul had never spent a night apart from each other. For months afterwards, I couldn't listen to his music because I was so jealous. I told Eddy about it and he just laughed at me, but I noticed he put his Beatles CDs to the back of his stack for a while.

"But if I quit, what will I do? I can't go live in a cubicle again or survive rush-hour traffic."

"Even if it means you'll be home every night? You'll find something," he said and took my hand across the table and squeezed it. The tender moment brought another flood of tears. "But even if you don't, we'll figure out how to live less extravagantly. People live happily on a whole lot less than either one of us make. The bottom line is that I think it's a really bad idea for you to get vaccinated. There's something very off about the whole thing."

"I don't see how the vaccine itself is bad. No matter how or who is spreading the virus, I'm tired of worrying about getting smallpox from some idiot on a plane."

"But that's just it. We don't know the how or who. So you have to be suspicious of the solution, too."

"Why do you look under every rock for a monster with an ulterior motive?"

"Why do you take everything at face value?"

"Because sometimes a vaccine is nothing more than a vaccine."

"And sometimes it's more. You can't ignore the weird pattern of exposure. We hear about all these exposures, but no names. It's been almost two weeks and there haven't been any more deaths because deaths would surface names. And now the vaccine is available months ahead of schedule."

"Eddy, I'm tired of being afraid."

He studied me. Shadows danced all around us from the dozen flickering candles. "Fear's a powerful tool," he finally said. "Look what it's gotten you to do."

Chapter
10

THE NUMBER 972 WAS A GOOD NUMBER, if for no other reason than it came before the number one thousand, which apparently was the number of vaccines the State of Colorado had for their daily allotment. If you showed up as number one thousand one, you were out of luck. It didn't matter if you'd driven six hours to get there. It didn't matter if you had a "Priority 1" card. It didn't matter if you had taken your last vacation day to make the trip. One through one thousand were magic numbers; one thousand one and beyond weren't.

Zaan had somehow missed this factoid on their website instructions. So it was sheer good fortune that I filled up with gas the night before instead of that morning. The extra seven minutes would have put me over the top and I would have had to make the drive again on Saturday—which carried a magic number of five hundred since the makeshift clinic would only be open till noon—or Monday, assuming my manager with the friendly font attitude would have forgiven another day not on the road and billable.

All the chitchat drifting down toward us latecomers—although prior to this, I'd never considered seven forty-five late—said that some people had arrived as early as 4:00 a.m. to stake out a place in line. Being first in line when the clinic opened was their bonus. But in the end, everyone had at least a four-hour wait. I just didn't have to bring a sleeping bag for mine.

From what I gathered out of the line gossip, the other people getting vaccinated were mostly doctors, nurses, emergency medical technicians, firefighters and police officers. But there were plenty of people like me who traveled and could easily and unknowingly carry the virus across the country.

Accustomed as I was to waiting in line—ticket, security, baggage, taxi, hotel—this nearly took me over the edge. The day started out efficiently enough. We were each given a ticket with our number on it and a packet of papers to fill out that asked for everything but our underwear size:

Citizenship
Social security number
Date of birth
Location of birth
Medical history
Current address
Phone numbers—work, home, cell
Email addresses—work and personal
Next of kin names—parents, spouse, children
Employer

Within the first fifteen minutes, they pulled ten groups of twenty-five people each out of the auditorium. It gave me hope that number 972 would get called before lunch, but when they didn't pull the next ten groups until after ten o'clock, I realized it wasn't going to happen. The instructions said we could leave and return later in the day, but I had no place to go except to find an outlet for my laptop, which I managed to do in a gathering area inside the building. I would have been totally out of luck with the outlet except that I always carry a multi-plug adapter with me so I can talk someone into letting me share his or her outlet.

I could spot the other business traveler types because they were all hunched over their computers and grumbling into their cell phones about the inefficient day. The firefighters and police officers, who were more adept in the art of waiting, lounged in our area, too, They were having a good time just shooting the breeze and making occasional doughnut, sandwich, coffee, pizza, or any-kind-of-food runs. I could have kicked myself for not bringing my noise-canceling headphones because the firefighter/police crowd kept growing and getting louder. I don't know where the medical people were hanging out. Maybe they somehow got special dispensation to cut the line and be in the first group to be vaccinated.

By lunchtime, the firefighter/police crowd had ballooned sufficiently that there was no possible way I could concentrate enough to work. I pulled out my Kindle and tried to read, but that clearly didn't have a chance of happening either with all the noise.

Somehow a pizza box and a six-pack of icy Cokes ended up on my table and for the price of the space to share, the invading firefighters let me join them and their conversation.

"How'd you get so lucky to be a Priority One?" a beefy balding guy named Carl asked me.

I shrugged my shoulders. I'd spent enough time in Nebraska to do it right. "I travel. I guess the theory is that I can unknowingly be exposed to the virus in San Francisco and end up exposing everyone on the plane who then expose people on other planes, airports, and cities."

Carl nodded his head, maybe a little skeptically. "It could happen."

"Is your job on the line if you don't get the vaccine?" someone else asked.

"Not in so many words. But I refuse to travel without getting vaccinated, and if I can't travel, I'm less likely to be billable. If

I'm not billable, I'm flotsam." I took a piece of pizza. No surprise that it was meat lovers. "What about you? Are you required to be vaccinated?"

"Required, but no one is objecting," Carl said. He seemed to be the spokesman for the group. "I'd get vaccines for everything on God's green earth if it were available. You wouldn't believe the crud we're exposed to."

Several others nodded.

Some guy with honest-to-goodness naturally orange hair disagreed. "I don't mind the vaccine. I get flu shots every year. What I don't like is all the stuff they're getting out of us to get the vaccine."

The others shuffled. They seemed uncomfortable, but I wasn't sure.

"You mean the information sheet you have to fill out?"

Orange hair guy casually waved me off. "That stuff is nothing. They haven't asked for any information that isn't in a dozen other places already. It's the other stuff. The fingerprinting, the saliva samples stuff."

"Huh?" This was the first I'd heard of this. Eddy would've immediately bolted.

I caught glances from the other firefighters.

"You didn't know?"

I shook my head.

"They fingerprint you and scrape a few cells out of your mouth."

"But why? What does that have to do with getting a vaccine?"

Orange hair guy did his own Nebraska shrug. "They take it back to 9/11. They say if they'd had DNA they would have been able to identify at least another five hundred people from the remains they uncovered. That still leaves over five hundred unidentified, but I guess they think it's worth it."

I know I stiffened. The others had stopped making eye contact. "So they'll have my fingerprints and DNA in exchange for the vaccine."

Orange hair guy nodded.

"You can't refuse?"

Orange hair guy shook his head. "You don't get the vaccine if you do."

"Really?"

"Really."

By the time they called my number, I'd invested too much time and wasn't willing to deal with the consequences. A woman at the computer took my form and started entering information.

"They're asking for a lot of stuff that doesn't seem related to smallpox or an epidemic."

"Uhhum." The woman was young, thin, and without noticeable body piercings. I took her for a straight shooter. She'd obviously been hired for her word-processing skills because she rapidly clicked away.

"What are they going to do with all the information?"

She shrugged her shoulders. Maybe she'd grown up in Nebraska.

"Why do they need to know where I was born?"

Another shoulder shrug. Definitely Nebraska-born. Why did she move to Denver?

When she came to the spot on my form that said I worked for Zaan, though, she perked up and finally got chatty. "We're using Zaan software for this."

I waited for the other shoe to drop, but it didn't. It dropped all the time with my clients because it was so hard for them to change from their old software to Zaan, regardless of which was better or easier to use. Change is change. The only kind of change most people like is the kind they get from a vending machine.

"It's really user-friendly."

"That's good to hear." I leaned over the computer screen and saw the familiar blue and green Zaan-style web form.

"We have to scan the forms in to get the signatures. It'll pick up the rest of the information, too, if we don't want to key it in. But most people have terrible handwriting. I spend as much time looking for errors to fix as I do just entering it myself." She studied the screen one more time, then clicked her mouse on the "OK" button. "Down the road, the plan is to have all these computer and scanning stations and have people enter their own information. The trouble is, it's a huge investment in computers if they're going to have enough for the initial big rush of people, and then they'll only need a fraction of them to maintain."

"The initial big rush?"

"Sure. There'll be enough vaccines to do the whole country within the next couple of months. Don't you think there'll be a huge demand?"

I thought about my own eagerness to get vaccinated and Eddy's reluctance. Once he knew how much information he'd have to give up, the reluctance would turn into refusal. Still, how many people were like me and how many were like Eddy?

She seemed to miss that I hadn't responded. "Do you know how many people we turned away today? At least a couple of thousand, maybe more. I hear it got ugly yesterday. Good thing so many of these guys are cops." She pointed me to a taped X on the carpet and took my picture. I wished I had worn a different shirt.

There was a pause and then the machine spit out a plastic card that looked like a credit card. She swiped it in another machine and studied a small screen readout. Satisfied, she handed the card to me. "Here's your health card. You'll need to carry this with you."

I looked at the picture. Definitely better than the driver's license I had to carry for the next eight years.

"Why do I need to carry it with me?"

"Proof of vaccination."

"Why do I need proof?"

She shrugged her shoulders and smiled, but her eyes were focused beyond me. She did a small stretch at her computer and looked back at me. "Almost done for the day. I'm bushed."

From the data-entry clerk on, the rest was an assembly line. First, someone fingerprinted me on a computer pad and then swiped my health card. Next, an attendant put my card into a reader and entered some information into a computer; then he took a quick scrape of the inside of my cheek. It was painless, but I was glad the firefighters had warned me, or I would have thought that was somehow the vaccine. Next, someone prepped my arm with a sterile alcohol swab and asked if I was allergic to anything.

"Would it make a difference?"

"People with egg allergies seem to have trouble." She looked at me. "Are you allergic to eggs?"

I shook my head.

"Sorry, I need a verbal yes or no."

"No."

At the next stop, someone poked my arm with a local anesthetic. I waited about five minutes and then moved to the next station where the person had a very strange-looking gizmo that made a tiny slice on my left upper arm, inserted a nub of something, and stitched twice. He ran my health card through a card scanner, punched in some numbers and studied the screen a minute, then pressed "OK."

"I thought it would be a series of needle pricks like the old smallpox vaccine," I said.

It was the end of the day. The attendant had no sense of humor or history. "This is the new one," was all he said.

"But why the fingerprinting and the saliva sample?"

He rolled his eyes. He had one more immunization after me. "Ask your congressman."

At the final station, where I got a dressing for the incision, I finally met someone chatty. Maybe that explained the seven-and-a-half hour wait.

"This has really been a long day," I said.

"No kidding. I feel sorry for all of you having to wait like this." She had a sweet, matronly look. She could easily have had grandkids.

"If it took this long to vaccinate a thousand people, how will they ever do the rest of the city, let alone the rest of the state?" I asked.

"Good question." She swabbed my arm one more time and applied an elaborate Band-Aid that didn't actually rest on the incision but was raised at least a quarter inch above the skin. "I think they're using all you Priority One people as a dry run. The plan is to train more people to do what we're doing and then hold immunization clinics throughout the state in schools. Kinda like the old polio vaccination clinics. Remember those?" She looked at me, maybe for the first time. "No. Of course you don't. You're too young." She glanced to see if she had anyone waiting and then turned back to me. "There were designated days and places to go get the vaccine. I remember going to the grade school after church one Sunday. We lined up and got these sugar cubes coated in something pink. That was the vaccine. No needles, no nothing. I don't remember much about it except that my mother cried because she was so relieved we'd all been vaccinated."

"I don't understand why they need all this other stuff, the fingerprints, the saliva sample. Why can't they just give us the vaccine and be done with it?"

"Oh, honey, I know." Her voice was low and soothing. She could have just as easily been telling me not to worry about my bad day at school. "It does seem like a lot of unnecessary extra stuff, doesn't it?" Her eyes darted around the room behind me as she talked. "But they just told us they need the statistical information."

"They need fingerprints for statistics?"

She gave a very tiny shrug of her shoulders and her eyes darted some more. She handed me a packet of information. "Don't let the incision get wet. The sheet gives several ways to protect your arm from getting wet in the shower. The incision will be sore for the next few days. If the soreness doesn't go away within forty-eight hours, call this number." She pointed to the phone number at the top of the page. "You may develop a slight fever in the next twenty-four hours. Again, if it's not gone in forty-eight hours, call the number. Don't worry about the stitches. They'll dissolve within the next seven days. You'll have a tiny scar, but nothing like those old smallpox vaccine scars. It won't hurt your modeling career."

We both laughed even though she'd probably given the same line a hundred times that day already.

She read through several additional instructions and finished with one final caution: "In about .02 percent of vaccinations, the capsule doesn't dissolve properly and festers its way out of the skin, like a splinter would. If that happens, it's important that you call the number on the sheet immediately."

She sent me off with a grandmotherly pat. I half expected her to surprise me with a small bag of homemade cookies, but it didn't happen.

Not including the hideous wait time, from start to finish the vaccination process took about twenty minutes. Including traveling and waiting, I'd given up over twelve hours of my day. Of course, at the time, I couldn't begin to realize just how much I'd truly given up.

Chapter
II

Eddy had been agitated on Thursday. By Friday night, he was livid.

I talked to myself the whole way home from Denver about how much of the day I should tell him. But I'm no good with secrets, especially with Eddy, so in the end, I told him—saliva sample, finger printing, and all. Maybe it was a mistake, but it was a lesser mistake than not telling him.

"Why didn't you just walk out of there?" He was opening a bottle of wine as he talked, but I didn't think it was going to do much to mellow either of us. He'd already set out a basket with some sesame flatbread and a dish of his homemade garlic hummus.

"Because if I had, I'd be writing my letter of resignation right now."

"Who cares?" He was nearly shouting. In fifteen years of marriage, I'd *never* seen him so upset with me. "Who gives a damn? So instead, you give up the last shred of privacy you could ever have. And for what? A job that's sucking the lifeblood out of you and you want to quit anyway?"

I felt jittery on the inside but tried not to show it. "If it hadn't been a vaccination for this job, it'd be one for the next job. They're gearing up for the whole country to get immunized."

Eddy poured a couple of glasses of wine and handed one to me. "You still think this is about a vaccination, don't you?" He shook his head. "Maggie, Maggie, Maggie."

I hated the subtle condescension in his voice. I wasn't stupid. "It's definitely about a vaccination," I said, although I was far less sure than I sounded.

"You just said you spent twelve hours for a procedure that by itself, didn't take more than twenty minutes. And oh, by the way, they now have your fingerprints and DNA samples, along with every piece of personal information you have except your credit card information." He looked at me and groaned. "You didn't pay for the vaccine with your credit card, did you?"

He painted such a sticky web of conspiracy that I felt guilty that I'd laid down such an information trail. I couldn't look him in the eye.

He sighed. "It doesn't matter if you did. That information is the easiest information to get. It's just tied together more neatly now."

"I at least used my corporate American Express, not our personal Visa."

He just shook his head and stared at the floor.

"Look, it's not like most of that information isn't out there already. True, they don't have my DNA, but when I was on the Social Security project I had to pass a background check that included my fingerprints. So now they have one more piece of information. Big deal."

"Maggie, it *is* a big deal. I've been thinking about this a lot." He added more wine to his glass. I'd barely taken a sip from mine. "What's the biggest showstopper your Baja Breeze has for moving to Zaan software?"

"That the project manager has more cleavage than brain cells."

He smiled and took a slow sip of wine. "Okay. I'll give you that one. So what's their second biggest showstopper?"

It felt like a trick question, but it didn't matter. I only had one answer: "Data conversion."

"Exactly." He scooped a little hummus onto some flatbread and took a bite. "And the problem with data conversion isn't that the data doesn't exist. The problem is that it exists in multiple places and has lots of variations and errors. But to start over entering all the information from scratch is way too labor intensive. So the idea is to clean up the data in all the different systems and then bring it over into the new system, right?"

I nodded. It was easy to see where he was going with this.

"Now let's say you're the US government, and you want all of your information about people in a single place. Not some of it in the IRS system, some in the FBI and CIA systems, some of it in Social Security. You want one-stop shopping. But to get there, you're going to spend a gazillion dollars paying for government types or temps to key in all the information, complete with their own typos. And how do you hide that in a federal budget?"

He munched a little more on the flatbread. "I can see it now: 'Ten billion dollars for software and database technology and the clerks to type all of our citizens' personal information into a single system that's named, uh, Big Brother.' Wouldn't it be easier just to start from scratch and have you provide your most current information into the system? And along the way, you also get fingerprints and DNA samples. And the bonus is that you can still build interfaces between the new database and all the other databases so you can bring up Margaret M. Rider in the smallpox database and dive into what she paid to the IRS last year or whether she has an FBI file. One-click shopping."

"That last bit might be a stretch. Interfaces are tricky and expensive with dated systems."

"Okay. So maybe that's a future phase. But think about it. What's the one thing the National Security Agency can't do now with all their information about our phone calls and emails?"

I cringed and thought of our many conversations about what the NSA might be tracking with Eddy and his less than politically correct wanderings through the World Wide Web. "I give up. They already can do anything they want."

Eddy shook his head. "They can find the needle in the haystack right now. What they can't find is the guy who left the needle."

"And now they can."

"Which may be more important than the actual needle. After all, if they're so intent on tracking us all, do you think they'd be very worried about whether we're really guilty of something?"

I shook my head, weary of where this was all leading.

"What if they just happen not to like a guy's politics? Or religion. Or color of his skin."

"Or whatever website he's created."

"Touché." He touched his glass to mine.

"The drones are already out there. In use. We know that."

"Exactly." Eddy leaned onto the table and rubbed the back of his neck. "The money part wouldn't even be much of a showstopper. If you can spend eighty million a day to fight a war in some desert, you can surely scrape together ten or twenty days' worth of funds to build the ultimate database. It costs twice as much to do it this way, but it gets buried in the Homeland Security budget under the guise of protecting the nation from a smallpox epidemic that seems very real."

I felt slightly nauseous, but maybe that was one of the symptoms of the vaccination. "And everyone volunteers for it to boot," I said.

"You just did, and you're very smart."

"But feeling dumber by the minute."

"You were afraid. You said it yourself—and for good reason. Look at all the cases that have popped up around the country. And because the cases are so random geographically, it only increases the fear because you can't logically explain it away. The victims are in urban and rural areas. Maybe they're linked to terrorists, maybe not. All you know is that it could happen to you."

Something happened to me all right, and it wasn't smallpox. "I'm an idiot."

Eddy set down his wine glass and put his arms around me. "And I still love you."

Chapter
12

Worse? I'd volunteered—no, that's too charitable—I'd begged for it to happen. I'd made the drive, waited the day, and flung open the door to every critical identifier I had.

The very worst, though, was now I knew I'd been violated. Where Monday morning should have been lighter on my mind, I sank into a nasty funk knowing that I now traveled the country, for all practical purposes, naked.

I had one final insult that Monday. I was doing my inevitable dash with my carryon and computer bags from gate B89 to B22 in the Denver airport (a mile high and a mile long) and happened to glance at a new series of ads on a wall:

What do you need to know?

Who else needs to know it?

What will you be able to do when you know it?

Zaan: Now you can know it.

The universe tilted slightly and my heart stopped. I nearly got run over by the man behind me. He swooped around me at the last second and left a nasty glance in my direction in his wake.

I made it to my flight with less than five minutes to spare, but the pounding of my heart wasn't from the sprint. For the next two hours, I only wanted to sleep and read and sleep some more. Instead, the last question kept rolling through my head: What will you be able to do when you know it? I kept thinking of all those draft dodgers from the Vietnam War and how they burned their draft cards. Their selective service information stayed locked up inside the Pentagon fort, so the card burning didn't stop the machine. It only woke up a nation.

This new war had produced a new card: my health card ticked away like a tiny bomb inside my wallet. I wanted to shred it and mail the pieces somewhere, but I didn't know where to send it. It wouldn't have made any difference anyway since the card itself wasn't the evil thing but a symbol of it. Still, I pictured myself on the corner of Tejon Street and Pikes Peak Avenue in Colorado Springs' tiny downtown, taking scissors to my card or maybe swiping a magnet across the strip to wipe the information clean. Where was drama in that though?

I'd been missed at Baja Breeze. I'm always missed when there's a mess.

Since nearly all of the Zaan consultants except me were local, the project had kept on marching, marching, marching toward a go-live that was now at least a month behind, if not two. Michael de Leon needed help documenting what had gone wrong on the client side, most of which had to do with their project manager's inability to push her team on cleaning up the data and every other deadline. This took up the rest of my Monday, except for the hour the CEO had blocked out on my calendar to sort through how to communicate the, uh, shift in the schedule. That conversation was less productive since neither of us could openly talk about the mistake he'd made when he let himself get distracted by cleavage and long loose ebony hair.

I did the best I could with Michael and the CEO, but the whole time I kept thinking, "Am I selling a national health card to these people?"

I wasn't. I was selling them on the benefits of being able to compare apples to apples—actually Gala apples to Gala apples—in their accounting, as opposed to their current system, which more or less compared apples to bicycles. Still, it hung with me that I'd been purchased by the Evil Database Empire, and that's what I'd been selling to client after client.

I needed to become Catholic so I could go to confession and do penance. And I needed a couple of Advil.

By the time I got to the hotel, I was a wreck.

I ordered room service and two glasses of wine. Not a good beginning to a week, but it was the only beginning I could deal with. I called Eddy, and didn't get an answer, which left me with too much time on my computer. More specifically, it left me too much time to surf the Internet. That disease is contagious, too. I did an Ixquick search on "smallpox" and came up with over two million results. I poked around on the first twenty sites.

One, smallpoxscare.com, had a load of information about the virus, much of which I'd already seen on the CDC site, but still very informative because it organized the information better. It had a very accurate and complete description of the invasiveness of the vaccination process, which I hadn't seen anywhere else. If only Eddy had seen the post on Thursday, I could have made a more rational decision, but it hadn't been posted until that morning. The site also included links to articles from all over the place and a chat room that listed toward conspiracy theories. Again, the list and the chat were surprisingly familiar. It wasn't until I clicked on the map feature that I realized why I'd been experiencing a little déjà vu. The map and corresponding dots matched the one in our office, right down to the color-coding.

Eddy had been a busy boy.

I waited patiently to see if he'd pop up on gtalk or if he'd call first. Gtalk won.

MRiderZaan: Hey Eddio.
EddytheWebMan: *hey u*
MRiderZaan: Found a great website. _www.smallpoxscare. com_. Thought you'd find it interesting.
There was a longer pause than I would have liked, but it wasn't like I was surprised.
EddytheWebMan: *nailed me*
MRiderZaan: Sure did. You've been busy.
EddytheWebMan: *someone had to do it*
MRiderZaan: Call me.
EddytheWebMan: *xoxo*
MRiderZaan: u2
The phone rang a minute later.
"You mad?" he asked before I could say, "Hello."
"How could I be mad? You've been right all along."
"She finally admits it. Fifteen years of marriage and she finally admits what I've been telling her for years. I'm right. I've always been right."
"About the smallpox thing," I said.
"Oh. Oh yeah," he said
"And maybe about how I parallel park," I said.
"Oh yeah. Definitely about how you parallel park," he said.
"So how long has the site been up?"
"I finished it on Friday while you were in Denver. I was going to surprise you with it, but your details about getting the vaccination totally bummed me out. I didn't want to even think about it."
"So how long have you been working on it?"
"A while. I was going to tell you about it when I first started, but I was afraid it would make you mad that I was working on that and not something billable. You think I'm such a paranoid anyway."
"You are," I said.
"I am," he said.

"It's a great site. It has tons of good stuff." I clicked around while we talked. "Have you gotten a lot of hits?"

"Take a guess."

"I don't know." A thousand hits would be nothing at all, but still pretty good for a first weekend. Yet I'd found it on Ixquick and checked it out first because it had a crisp and catchy description. "Maybe ten thousand?" As soon as I said it, I regretted it. I didn't want to discourage him.

Eddy laughed softly on the other end. "You're not going to believe this. As of this moment, it's gotten 97,244 hits."

"What? Almost a hundred thousand hits in three days? Eddy, that's incredible. Absolutely incredible! You're not off by a decimal point are you?"

"You mean did I get 972,440 hits? Nope, but we'll see the day. Soon."

"What an irony. You get paid to do all these websites and the one you do on your own gets the hits."

"I know, I've been thinking all day about how to turn these hits into some money, but I don't want to cheapen it with advertisements."

"Hey, if *The New York Times* can do it, why can't you?"

"Because I'm Eddy the Web Man. It just looks like I'm cashing in on a tragedy. I'm not going to do that."

His nobility touched me. Paranoia and all, he was a good man.

"Do you love me, Eddy?" It just popped out. I knew the answer, but I had to hear it from him again. My Monday had been a train wreck. I couldn't do the job anymore. I couldn't turn chicken shit into chicken salad one more day.

"More than life itself." There was no pause. "More than a dog loves to scratch. More than a penguin loves to swim."

"I love you, too."

"More than a hawk loves to fly."

There was a long silence. I knew he was waiting for me

to get teary but probably didn't have a real clue why it would happen now.

"Eddy?"

"Yeah, Mz M?"

"I figured out the most important question."

"What is it?"

"Why do they need all this information?"

"We have to know who needs it and what they're going to do with it, too."

"True. But if we figure out the why, we'll know everything else."

"You're right. Again."

A FUNNY THING HAPPENED ON THE WAY TO FRIDAY. All along I'd survived my job because I found the work fun and intriguing. It was the travel that did me in. By Tuesday, I preferred the travel to the work. By Thursday, I was ready to be an insurgent.

Thank goodness there was only one more day in the workweek or I would have been arrested. Monday morning in the Denver airport, the scales had fallen off my eyes, and I caught a glimmer of the forest instead of just the trees. I was working for a company that brought information together like never before. Now I knew that wasn't always a good thing.

I no longer liked my work.

I slogged away, though, using half as many brain cells as usual, but in the distracted world of Baja Breeze, who could tell? I took honest-to-goodness lunches away from my desk and left at five, the normal leaving hour for most Americans except for the Zaan consultants, who left around seven or eight most nights, and the Baja Breeze crowd, who left at four unless they had to leave at three or three-thirty to pick up babies or go watch soccer games or just get out of there because they were going crazy.

I pretty much had the front door to myself when I left.

No one noticed except Michael de Leon, who wanted to go to lunch on Thursday. We walked the couple of blocks to a little shopping strip and indulged in Thai food. The Tiger Lily wasn't the best place to have a conversation because the tables overflowed with people, but Michael had an anonymous crush on a waitress there.

"How's the data conversion going?" I asked him even though I knew the answer. Clean data consumed most of my thinking that week.

He looked at the ceiling and shook his head. "Oh my God, you won't believe this. I had to sit Keri down this morning and explain to her once again what they had to do to clean up their data and why it was so important not to bring over bad data."

"You're talking about Carry, that ditz on the HR team, not Keri, the project manager, right?"

He rubbed his neck and shook his head again. For an odd second, he looked like Eddy—dark hair, soft smile, and tired gaze. "Keri the project manager."

"So apparently, she hasn't been reading any of those emails I've written for her to send out under her name."

"Oh, I think she's reading them. There just aren't any brain cells between her left ear and right ear to trap any of the information."

Kai, the unknowing object of Michael's unrequited love, came and took our order. Before she even left the table, Michael, who apparently had no flirting skills, started in again. "My ten-year-old niece can explain what data conversion is better than Keri."

Kai rolled her eyes. "Garbage in, garbage out."

We both looked at her and laughed.

"Hey," she said. "It's Silicon Valley." She jerked her head toward the kitchen. "Even the dishwasher can tell you how important it is to have clean data." She left the table but muttered back to us, "Of course, he's a computer science major at Stanford."

"Trolling for tips," I said.

"It works. It works," Michael said. "Course, she has great legs, too."

"So what are you going to do?"

"About Kai?" He sounded slightly eager. When you put in twelve-hour days, you don't have much of a social life. A waitress with great legs had to fuel him for weeks.

I laughed. "Yeah, about Kai, but also about Baja Breeze. If they don't clean up their data, they simply can't go live. What are you going to do?"

"Work twice as hard. Cover my backside with a pile of documentation." He fiddled with his glass of ice tea. "Or do what you're doing."

I'm sure I flushed. "What's that?"

"Check out?" He looked at me. "I'm not sure. Is that what you're doing?"

I should have had some kind of denial, but for all my thinking that week, I'd forgotten to think up an excuse. "What do you mean?"

"I mean, you show up at eight, you leave for lunch, you leave at five. While you're there, you get the work done, but there's something missing."

"I have to put in ten hours of overtime to prove my worth? My work's not good enough this week?"

"Maggie, your work is fabulous. On your worst day, your work is better than any ten people at Baja Breeze. But this week, it's all just been more mechanical somehow. No chicken shit, but no chicken salad." We'd talked about the chicken byproducts of my job lots of times.

"Has someone else noticed? Has anyone complained?" I was uncomfortable. I measured myself by what others thought. Michael mattered.

"No, no, no. Nothing like that. You can do this job in your sleep. I'm just trying to figure out what's going on." He fiddled with his straw and looked at me sideways. "Are you and Eddy on the outs?"

I shook my head. This was the third project Michael and I had been on together, but how well did I know him? He was smart, skilled, hardworking, generous, kind, and sometimes funny. But could I trust him?

"Then what is it?"

"It's complicated," I said. The understatement of the week.

Kai showed up then with steaming plates of curry. I savored the delicate blend of coriander, cumin, ginger, and lemon grass. Michael savored his view of Kai's legs.

"I confirmed with the dishwasher," she said. "Garbage in. Garbage out." I think she winked at Michael. He must have thought so, too, because he blushed and giggled a little uncomfortably.

When she left, I said, "Ask her out." I was glad to have a distraction.

"I was that obvious?"

"Ohhhh yeah."

"I don't have time for a relationship."

"Then make time."

"You're taking us off the subject."

"We had a subject?" I ladled several spoonfuls of curry over my rice. "This is why I prefer California projects. You know what I eat in Nebraska?"

"Beef."

"It's what's for dinner. That and iceberg lettuce and canned green beans."

"So what's going on?"

I couldn't believe his persistence. I guess that tenaciousness was what made him such a great project manager. Maybe it was a mistake—or maybe it was the curry—but I finally asked, "Did you get your smallpox vaccine yet?" Sometimes you just have to trust your instincts.

He shook his head. "What does that have to do with anything?"

"Everything." I laid out my vaccine day. He slowed his eating a little but didn't say anything.

"It's a lot of information to ask for, don't you think?"

He didn't really pause before he nodded.

"What do you think they need all that information for?" I asked.

Michael shrugged his shoulders slightly and shook his head.

"Put your project manager hat on," I said. "If you could get Baja Breeze's customers and vendors to eagerly enter their own information and, oh by the way, give you even more information than what they've given Baja Breeze to date, would that solve your data-conversion problems?"

He set his chopsticks down.

"Would that be a project manager's dream?"

He tilted his head in agreement.

"Now here's the kicker. Maybe the two are unrelated, but the mood I was in on Monday told me they're one and the same." I ticked off the mini billboards at the Denver airport: "What do you need to know? Who else needs to know it? What will you be able to do when you know it? Zaan: Now you can know it."

"Our new ad campaign." He sighed.

"You know we delivered the database technology and built the software for the CDC to track the spread of diseases."

"Not only do I know it, I know the Zaan project manager for that one. We were on a complicated project together a couple years ago. He's smart. Really smart."

"So what do you think his take on all this would be?"

"It'll be easy enough to find out. He's local."

SANJEEV SRIVASTAVA, THE ZAAN CDC PROJECT MANAGER, actually happened to be in town and agreed to meet us for dinner at an Indian restaurant. Sanjeev ordered for us. He could have been a cousin to the waiter. They both had the same rounded noses and deep-set black eyes, the same lean, wiry bodies. They conversed in a lilting, rolling speech. It was English, but I didn't understand them.

Now that we were here, it was too awkward. I was glad that Michael and Sanjeev were at least good friends. They talked about this and that, and we all complained about how wearing it was to work for Zaan. Sanjeev and I compared point status on airlines and hotels. I couldn't believe it, but he had even more than I did, so we had a bonding of sorts. The waiter began bringing course after course, all vegetarian. Michael and I split a bottle of wine. Sanjeev had hot tea.

Eventually, Michael edged toward the subject. "So you finally rolled off the CDC project?"

Sanjeev's eyes narrowed very, very slightly. "We finished it in August."

"What a grind," I said. "San Francisco to Atlanta. No wonder you have more miles. The time zone differences are a beast. West Coast to East Coast—that's the full stretch."

"It's grueling," he said. "I ended up spending some of my weekends there."

"So what did the CDC implement?" Michael asked.

Sanjeev didn't even pause. "Most of it was database stuff. We built some one-off software to enter the data."

"No kidding? New apps? Must have been a huge project."

"The Zaan portion was less than a hundred and twenty million. The entire project, though, was well over a billion."

"Whoa! What did they spend the other nine hundred million on?" Michael asked. We were all prima donnas. To think of the Zaan portion being only a fraction of the whole was humbling for all three of us.

Still, Sanjeev swaggered a little as he talked. "A lot of it was hardware. They had a whole staffing plan, too, and some training."

"But a billion? For the CDC? What in the world were they doing? Building a new atomic bomb?" I asked.

Sanjeev momentarily stopped eating and leaned back into his chair. "Like I said, we were a drop in the bucket. The reason we were even there was the power of our database. They needed information. We gave them a way to store it and organize it."

"That's a lot of money to spend on a database. I don't care how sophisticated it is," Michael said.

Sanjeev didn't bite. The three of us ate in awkward silence.

Finally, I asked, "What kind of an application did they build?"

Sanjeev tore off a piece of poori and sopped up some vegetables. He seemed intent on what he was doing. I couldn't tell if the silence was deliberate or accidental.

Michael asked again, "What kind of an app would the CDC need that we didn't already have?"

Sanjeev was an artist in silence. He just kept on eating.

I would have stopped asking, but Michael was on a mission. "Sanjeev." He waited until Sanjeev looked at him. "What kind of application did they build? What was worth a hundred and twenty million to the CDC?"

I could have sworn he looked at my upper left arm, the one

that had a slowly healing small, crusty red bump. "It was a simple one. They only needed to be able to store, organize, and retrieve information. Tracking the information was important, too," he said. He shifted his eyes around the room.

"But about what?" Michael asked.

"The epidemic du jour."

"You mean smallpox?" I asked.

He lowered his voice. "That would seem to be the one."

Chapter
15

"HE NEVER ACTUALLY GOT RUDE," I told Eddy on the way home from the airport. "He just clammed up. Said he signed a nondisclosure agreement with the CDC."

"Is that unusual?"

I thought for a minute back through my projects. "On one level, it's not unusual at all. Every time a company issues me a temporary contractor badge, I have to sign a statement like that. But it never kept anyone from talking about their projects or using those projects as examples to inject a come-to-Jesus moment into the next project."

"But isn't that kind of thing usually about disclosing financial information or trade secrets? "

"Yeah. That's exactly what it's about. Sanjeev wouldn't talk about the project itself, but he went into some detail about why he couldn't talk about it. He said the CDC had lawyers sit with each consultant individually and explain what they could talk about and what they couldn't."

"Maybe that was his message."

"Maybe so." I thought about that for a while. "Michael says Sanjeev is a good guy, which is why he thought it would be worth our while to talk to him. Sanjeev also said they did this intense background check on everyone. It sounded pretty much like what I went through to get vaccinated."

"You mean they did the fingerprinting and the saliva sample?" Eddy raised an eyebrow in my direction. "Just to work on some software and a database? That's a little intense, isn't it?"

I nodded. "Here's the funny thing, though. I asked him if he'd gotten his vaccination yet."

"And?"

We'd pulled into our drive, but neither of us made a move to get out of the car.

"He didn't say anything for a long time, and I thought maybe he hadn't heard me. So I asked him again."

"Did he answer you?"

I gently rubbed the tender red spot on my arm. "He said it was the last thing they did before they wrapped up the project."

Eddy carried my suitcase into the house. That was our division of labor: I dragged my bags through every airport in the world, but when it reached our property line, he took over. I took a quick shower and found something that didn't smell like a suitcase to change into while Eddy heated up some chicken tortilla soup and threw together a green salad.

"So when did they finish the project?" Eddy asked when we sat down to eat.

"August."

"August?" Eddy tilted his head.

"August."

"But the first—"

"Yes. I know. The first smallpox death was reported in September. He refused to say anything else at that point and made it clear that Michael and I should just drop the subject. Not just for the evening, but drop it period. That we really didn't want to go there."

"He threatened you?" Eddy had hardly touched his soup.

"No, no, no. Not personally." What had he done? Had he said

something specifically or was it just the cumulative effect of the evening? It was hard to put my finger on anything tangible. "He seemed really agitated. He kept fiddling with his silverware and napkin. Even after we stopped talking about the CDC project, he kept looking around the restaurant. He wouldn't talk at all when the waiter came around."

"So why did all that make you feel threatened?"

"When we left the restaurant that night, the three of us stood outside the restaurant and chatted a couple of minutes. Just before he walked off, he said something to the effect that what you know *can* hurt you, that this was one of those things to stay below the radar on. And then he left."

Eddy scratched his head. He still hadn't touched his soup. "So what do you think he meant?"

I finally told Eddy what I'd been thinking about non-stop for the last twenty-four hours. "I think building a website about smallpox isn't under the radar. What do you think?"

He just shook his head and finally started eating his soup.

I SHOULD HAVE CALLED IN SICK, but in all the years I'd worked for Zaan, I'd never missed a day of travel or work and, frankly, wasn't all that sure what excuse I would need to stay home. If my man-ager told me to rest up and fly out on Tuesday, then it wasn't worth the effort of ditching on Monday.

The only positive thing about traveling was that with every-one's high anxiety about smallpox, far fewer people were flying, so the lines were shorter and the planes only half full. Of course, I don't think any of the airlines thought that was a positive thing. And their response was only logical: they started cutting flights, which meant that instead of a door-to-door trip to Ne-braska Beef Products of seven and half hours, my new schedule stretched out to nine hours. Already the airlines—those that had survived the 9/11 economic catastrophe and the 2008 economic collapse—were making noises about needing government sub-sidies if the US was going to keep the big players (and the big employers) around.

In fact, this smallpox epidemic was taking its toll on just about everyone except NBP, which had seen a bump in numbers, particularly the higher end cuts, just as Scott Leinbach, the NBP project manager, had predicted. As he pointed out, if people can't afford to go on vacation because they're worried about losing their jobs, they indulge in a pricier steak to comfort themselves.

National crisis or not, NBP was in a celebratory mood. The project was going very well, revenue was up, and Nebraska had only twelve newly reported cases of smallpox in a corner not close to Timber. As a thank-you to the project team for successfully completing the third out of four rounds of software testing, the CEO invited the entire team to his house for a late afternoon barbecue. Ordinarily, a cookout in November in Nebraska doesn't fit my definition of a good time, but the NBP people promised the CEO had a house big enough for all of us, and Bob Litten wasn't CEO of a beef packing plant for nothing.

By Colorado standards, Bob Litten's house was dated but palatial. The sprawling fifties brick rancher set on five acres of lawn and landscaped gardens put me in a short photo-snapping frenzy. Never mind that the guest bathroom was pink ceramic, circa 1956 (I couldn't help myself and checked the stamped date on the inside of the toilet lid), and the kitchen hadn't been updated since the almond years of the eighties—when I stepped out onto the deck, I realized why they hadn't remembered to remodel: the view of green, rolling hills that swept into a fireball sunset made up for anything manmade on the other side of the sliding glass doors. People rave about Colorado's beauty. And it's true, our mountains are amazing. But who in Nebraska can feel shortchanged when they can see five miles into a dusk like that?

The evening temperature was a gift from the gods. It lingered no lower than an unseasonably mild mid-sixties, which would be a pleasant June evening in Colorado. We caught the last of the sunset and toasted it and the project's success with a local microbrew.

Nebraska Beef Packing Company may have been exporting beef to the entire world, but I discovered a secret that night: they kept the best for themselves. I had never, *in my entire life*, had a steak so tender and flavorful. Who needed a knife? Or even a fork. It nearly fell into luscious, edible pieces with just a glance.

I forgave the iceberg lettuce salad and canned corn. Who cared?

The amazing steak, the heart-stopping sunset, the unpretentiousness of a house built and decorated decades ago—and, okay, more microbrews than I drink in a week—left me careless in my talk. I should have planned better.

As the last of the sunset faded into purples and blacks, Marcia Wells, the sweet, matronly purchasing lead, and I found ourselves out on the deck sometime after the cheesecake but before the cognac.

Those Nebraskans had a knack for drinking.

Craig, her husband, who was losing his battle with a creeping middle-age paunch, joined us while we were still comparing project war stories. I remembered meeting him earlier at some other celebratory dinner and liking his straightforward style. Craig had brought Marcia's jacket out although the evening still held enough of the day's heat that none of us wanted one yet. He waited patiently until it seemed as though we didn't need to talk about data validation or test scripts one more time before he steered us in another direction.

"Maggie, so how are things in Colorado?"

There were a hundred ways to answer that question, but I went with the least complicated. "Good. I miss being there."

"Pretty place, huh?"

"It is. A different pretty than this, but still beautiful." Most Coloradoans can be so egotistical about the state. I wanted them to know I understood every land had its splendor. "I've lived there forever. Have you been to Colorado?"

Craig Wells nodded his head. "Mostly up in the Summit County area to ski. Isn't Colorado Springs close to where that first smallpox outbreak was?"

Ah, the crux of the conversation. We'd arrived quickly.

I nodded. There wasn't anything else to say.

Craig waited, too. Marcia had less patience. "Didn't all that make you nervous?"

If she only knew.

"It did," I said. I realized I shouldn't have had that last beer, or perhaps even the one before it. My filters were gone, and we were headed into dangerous territory.

"Have you been vaccinated?" Craig asked.

I nodded again. I'd forgotten about it for the last three hours or so. The mention of it made my arm tingle slightly. "Have you?"

Craig shook his head. He rested his muscular arms on the deck rail. Maybe twenty years earlier when the three of us had been in high school, he would have been a handsome boy, a football star. "I've got a client right now who refused the vaccine. He's a doctor, so it complicates things."

I'd forgotten he was an attorney. I perked up and my head cleared a tiny bit. "So what's happening with him?"

"We're still in the middle of it, so I can't say much, but it's been interesting to see who's coming out of the woodwork on the case. The Feds swooped in from the beginning."

"What?"

He raised his eyebrows and tilted his head. "Small town doctor? Rural Nebraska? Not a likely terrorist for five hundred miles. Someone needs to prove a point." He took a long swallow of beer.

My head swirled with the information. I wondered if he'd surfed Eddy's site. Give it twenty-four hours, and he'd see a reference to this case on it.

"The vaccine is a real invasion of privacy, isn't it?"

I nodded. "It is. Without question."

"But you went ahead with it anyway?"

"I did," I said. "I don't know if you can comprehend the panic I felt before then. At the time, it seemed like a good solution."

"Funny how easy it is to lead sheep to the slaughter."

"Craig!" Marcia sounded mortified that he'd insulted me, but it's only an insult if it's not true.

"It's okay, Marcia. I've been sorry ever since."

The stars flickered into the night sky. Even with only the quarter moon, I think I could have read a book by the light. We all stayed quiet while the night came on. It impressed me that fourteen thousand nights of emerging stars hadn't jaded Marcia and Craig. Maybe I could live in Nebraska someday.

"What's at stake for your client?"

Craig paused before answering. Maybe he was double-checking his own beer intake and downed filters. But he finally answered, "Could be a lot. Worst-case scenario he could lose his license. Believe it or not, they're hinting at prison time."

"For not getting a vaccine?" Even given every conversation I'd had with Eddy, I could hardly believe this one.

"I know. When I first took on the case, I thought it would be pretty simple. But he's a healthcare worker and has the potential to infect others. You can't send your kindergartner off without a measles shot. Turns out you can't practice medicine without a smallpox vaccination, even if you don't think this is a real epidemic." He casually glanced around at the crowd on the deck and then looked back at me. "Or even if you don't think the vaccine is really a vaccine."

"Craig." Marcia's voice was a mix of embarrassment and wistfulness.

I sighed. "It's okay, Marcia. I guess I have my questions, too." My moment of understatement. "You clearly have doubts. What's your research telling you?"

Craig finally said, "It's a ruse. The whole epidemic isn't real."

"Really?" My own heart pounded in my ears. "Then what do you think these smallpox reports really are? What's the purpose?"

"It's to get us to do something. That's what this kind of stuff is always about."

Marcia sighed softly. It looked like she was trying to catch Craig's eye. She gave a tiny headshake. But we were in too deep.

Craig was looking at me, not her, so he missed it. Maybe he'd seen enough tiny headshakes over the years that he no longer paid any attention.

"This kind of stuff?"

"Remember the scare in the late eighties about the FDA finding cyanide in the grapes from Chile? You know about that one?"

I did. This was a favorite conspiracy theory of Eddy's. "They made grocery stores dump all their Chilean grapes and stopped imports. All because someone had called the US embassy in Santiago and claimed they'd pricked a couple of grapes with cyanide."

"Exactly. The US government stopped imports on thousands of tons of grapes. Two grapes out of three thousand tons? You think that was truly about consumer safety?"

I shook my head. Even without Eddy's paranoia tendencies, I had that one figured out. "It was political. The US wanted Chile to do something and flexed its muscle just to make sure Chile did it."

"No kidding. The mad cow scare is the same thing. You think because they 'find' one cow with mad cow disease that people are going to stop eating beef? They could stop the imports from Canada, which probably isn't as straightforward as it looks either. They certainly couldn't shut down the domestic beef industry. But if the media hypes it enough, you can get them to eat a whole lot less. You think that single cow or even a thousand sick cows would kill as many people as the air pollution the government allows companies to spew out every single day?" Craig snorted softly and shook his head. "The government wanted to send a message to the meat industry."

Eddy loved that conspiracy theory, too, so I knew it well. "So what was the government's message?" That was the missing part to Eddy's theory.

Marcia and Craig looked at each other. She'd stayed silent up till now, although her misery was clearly growing. She couldn't have held her arms tighter across her chest. Craig nudged her with his elbow. "Marsh, tell her what came out of that. It's not like it's any kind of a secret around town."

She looked around the deck at the other pockets of people. Most of them had beers in hand and were growing more boisterous in the still-warm evening. We, on the other hand, had moved in closer and dropped our voices. Marcia was shaking ever so slightly, but it wasn't from the temperature. She still had the jacket draped over her shoulders that Craig had brought her.

"Tell her what the concessions were, Marsh. The local paper reported heavily on it, but somehow it never got onto the national news radar."

Marcia sighed again. "The meat industry agreed to incorporate tracking devices into every meat package within two years."

"You mean like bar coding?" I didn't get it. For all the drama, it didn't sound all that ominous. "Don't companies already track products by lot, date, regions, and all that?"

"Sure. And we think that's sufficient. If, God forbid, *E. coli* shows up in a hamburger, the package will tell us where the hamburger was ground, what cow it came out of, and where the other hamburger shipments went to. The consumer checks to see that their hamburger matches or doesn't match that description. If it does, they bring it back and the store gives them a new one or a refund, which we pay for. Or the consumer can just cook the hamburger till it's well done and not worry about it at all."

"But the government wanted more for some reason," Craig said. She wasn't telling the story fast enough.

Marcia nodded. Her eyes were all over the deck but not on us. "They want us to truly track by individual package."

"But how is that any better?" I still didn't get it.

"How old is your refrigerator?" Craig asked.

It was a non sequitur. My face must have showed it, but I answered anyway. "I don't know. We've lived in our house for twelve years, and we bought it new then. So I guess twelve years old."

"Hang onto it. Get it fixed if the compressor goes out. All the new ones now have receivers for radio frequency identification, or RFID. You know what that is?"

I nodded. I remembered my conversation with Scott Leinbach.

"Well, get this. If you put a package of meat into your refrigerator that has an RFID—the thing the government wants the meat processors to use—your refrigerator collects that information and stores it."

"But then what? I mean beyond the discomfort of one more loss in my sense of privacy. I guess I'm not clear on why it's a big deal. Is it the cost?"

Marcia waved her hand like the cost was nothing. "The price of the ink as long as the antenna is printed in copper. It adds fractions of a cent, but that's not the problem." She looked at Craig.

"Here's where this is headed. You have high cholesterol. Your doctor says to cut out fats. You end up with a heart attack, so your insurance company subpoenas your refrigerator's RFID receiver. They see that you purchase, on average, five pounds of red meat every week, go through a pound of butter every two weeks, and use a dozen eggs every two weeks. They say they don't have to pay your health care costs because you didn't follow your doctor's orders." Craig tilted his empty beer bottle at me. "An alcoholic. He stores beer in his refrigerator." He left that one hanging. "Now do you see where this is headed?"

"This isn't science fiction? The ability to track to that level?"

"Not at all," Craig said. "The technology is all here today. Some companies are using it, some aren't yet. Gillette's doing it. Coke, Proctor & Gamble. Walmart tracks aggressively. They can tie the information right back to your charge card or those shopper cards that Osco and the other grocery chains are already using to track your every purchase."

"But the meat industry doesn't have a choice. We were bought during the mad cow scare," Marcia said.

"It all comes down to dollars," Craig said. "The government can shut down the beef industry overnight if it wants to. That mad cow business was just an opening volley to let us know what the consequences were if we didn't cooperate."

"But why would the government want to shut down the meat industry?" This seemed a stretch.

Craig shrugged his shoulder. "Call me the cynical attorney, but it doesn't really matter. If there's no reason today, there will be tomorrow."

"The military is doing it," Marcia said.

Craig shook his head at the sky. "The military is *huge* into this. I've read that they embedded RFIDs into every soldier in the Iraq War. They said it would reduce friendly fire because they could track who was an enemy and who was an ally."

Marcia shrugged her shoulders. "I've heard that's not true. That's just conspiracy talk."

Craig looked at her as though they'd had this discussion a hundred times already. "You know, I don't even care if it's true or not. The capability is there right now. If they're not doing it today, they'll be doing it tomorrow. And not just to military personnel. They'll be embedding it in everyone."

I shivered even though the temperature hadn't dropped.

"So what do you think of that vaccination now?"

Chapter
17

For the first time ever, I was the one to unnerve Eddy.

I called him on my cell as soon as I got to my hotel room. We hung up and a minute later, he called me on the hotel phone. For once, his paranoia of cell phones made perfect sense. Timber Holiday Inn was just another speed-dial number on his phone.

"Did you have a good evening?"

"Well I had an interesting evening," I said. "Are you online?"

"Did the sun come up this morning?"

"Do an Ixquick search on RFID."

"F as in Frank?"

"Yup."

The pause on the other end lasted no more than five seconds. "Got it. Over five hundred thousand results. Big topic."

"There's your evening of reading."

"Give me a few minutes. I'll call you back."

I got ready for bed while my laptop booted up, then crawled under the covers and connected to the Holiday Inn's wireless. Eddy always told me to avoid the Wi-Fi systems because it was so easy to get hijacked, but I trusted Zaan's firewall. Maybe more than I should have. I did a quick search for Craig's legal case and found links to the local paper that were pretty light on information, but I sent them to Eddy anyway. He only needed a breadcrumb. Then I searched for RFID and started surfing while I waited for Eddy to call back. One site in particular, www.spychips.com, was loaded with all kinds of articles, pictures of RFID styles, and information.

The phone rang and I picked it up.

"One word," he said.

"Chilling," I said.

Fifteen years of marriage. Same skin.

"You think that's what the vaccines are about?"

"I know that's what they're about. It didn't register when Michael and I had dinner with Sanjeev, but when I talked to the NBP people tonight, it suddenly all made sense. Sanjeev said that Zaan built a simple application for the database. He said the CDC only needed to be able to store, organize, and retrieve information. It's the most basic kind of software. Then he added that tracking was important, too. When he said it, I was thinking about tracking basic information, which to me is the same as organizing and retrieving information—"

"—but he meant tracking as in tracking people," Eddy finished my sentence.

"That's what he meant. I'm sure."

"Unbelievable."

"And here's another one for you. I just sent you a link for an 'RFID Overview.' Tell me when you get it."

I heard Eddy's Outlook email tone. "Got it." There was a pause. "Looks like a good big picture of—" He stopped mid sentence.

"Do you see what I see?" I knew he did. It had taken my breath away, too.

"Zaan is a huge player."

"It only makes sense. If you're going to suddenly be overloaded with information, a good database is your best friend."

"You gotta quit working for that company."

"I do."

But I didn't. Quit working for Zaan, that is.

Instead, I finished my week at NBP and returned to that messy land of Baja Breeze the following week, then continued the flip-flop between Nebraska and California all over again. What a contrast.

Evenings, I job hunted, but no one seemed to be hiring, especially for someone with such nebulous skills as mine. At least, no one listed "corporate therapist" as a job description. So I checked with all my contacts from over the years, polished my resume some more, and shopped it with headhunters, who promised me I'd be easy to place. They were wrong. The economy had ground to an ugly halt. The few jobs that offered the most promise meant a significant paycut, a serious move, just as much time on the road—or worse, a grueling daily commute to Denver.

I prayed for the inevitable layoffs and the severance packages they'd bring to start and to start with me. But my phone didn't ring.

Weekends, Eddy and I sorted through our finances. His website now had well over a million hits, and he was getting daily inquiries about advertising. He could have paid our bills in a heartbeat with the offers, but he refused to compromise the site. So he kept on updating and maintaining the site—now with links to RFID sites and Craig's case in Nebraska—out of the goodness of his heart and our checkbook. It wasn't a battle I wanted to pick with him, although I really didn't think *The Wall Street Journal* and CNN advertising was all that much of a compromise.

We decided to try to hang on till spring when we could put our house on the market, our lovely old log-and-stone heat-guzzling monster that had been built in the late 1800s. It made us sad, but downsizing would give us a dozen options, including me not working at all for a while. Eddy would have liked to do it at that exact moment—have me quit—but I couldn't imagine the huge and sudden pay cut.

He finally agreed, but only if it meant I wouldn't have to start taking drugs to get me up in the morning to face the day.

That became our benchmark then.

"Do you need any drugs?" he would ask.

"Not yet. Not today. Maybe tomorrow," I would respond.

In early December, I was in Nebraska. NBP was in their final round of testing before go-live. I was hacking away at the last-minute messages to send out, which were made all the easier because all the software worked, including the shipping. Who would have believed it?

Eddy pinged me.

EddytheWebMan: *Hey. u there?*

MRiderZaan: Eddio... Whassup?

EddytheWebMan: *did you see the news this a.m.?*

MRiderZaan: Nope.

Some things never change.

EddytheWebMan: *our favorite president just announced that there are finally sufficient vaccines available for the whole US of A.*

MRiderZaan: Not just priority 1 & 2.

EddytheWebMan: *everyone*

MRiderZaan: So the riots will stop?

EddytheWebMan: *guess so*

MRiderZaan: Guess you'd better get yours scheduled.

EddytheWebMan: *LOL*

MRiderZaan: Yeah. Laughing out loud, too.

Maybe now the economy would start bouncing back.

I checked the CDC site for details. It gave a link to all the local vaccination places. Colorado Springs listed at least three dozen locations for inoculations. People could also go to their family doctors, but it would cost a hundred dollars plus office visit fees instead of twenty dollars per person.

Convenience cost.

Most NBP people, like the rest of the country, were ready to go under the knife, Marcia Wells being the exception rather than the rule. Our only other conversation she and I had about smallpox vaccination had been the day after the barbecue, and it was a little like the proverbial morning-after conversation. Too much beer, too much loose conversation, too many revealed nutty ideas will do that to you. Still, I think we both felt connected to the other one.

I took a chance and sent her the link to the CDC vaccination site along with a note: "I'm sure you and Craig will be lining up for yours right after my husband. ;) "

She responded two minutes later: "We may be the last three people in the country to get vaccinated."

I replied: "Then why would you need one? Everyone else will be inoculated. You'll be perfectly safe."

She responded, "At least from smallpox. Can't say the same for the government goons."

I left it at that. It could have deteriorated, and at the end of the day, both of us were susceptible to our corporate big brothers checking our email conversations. I was more vulnerable than she was. I was pretty sure Zaan had a whole department that only read emails that passed through cyberspace.

The more you're afraid, the more you have to do to protect yourself.

Chapter
18

On December fifteenth, the government announced one last carrot: after January eighteenth, all air travel within the fifty states would require proof of smallpox vaccination. Now that we had the means to get protected, no one had the excuse not to do it.

It was kind of them to at least wait until after the holidays.

Eddy and I spent Christmas at home. We should have traveled to see his sister Karen in Virginia, but I just couldn't bear getting on a plane the one week I didn't have to. We invited Karen and her family to come see us using our air miles, but they waited too long to make up their minds until there weren't any free seats left. Eddy finally agreed to schedule a trip to Virginia after the first of the year. It would be the last time he could fly domestically since he would never get the vaccination. Someday, maybe the two of us would make a road trip there.

We called Karen on Christmas Day, toasted our long-gone parents and our childhoods, and invited other Colorado orphans to dinner on the twenty-fifth.

I was lucky to still have friends since my social life had totally dried up over the years from all my time on the road. They were lucky that Eddy roasted the goose. During all those traveling years, I'd lost whatever knack I had for cooking things. As Eddy had pointed out to me multiple times, how much culinary finesse did it take to dial room service? I could still make a salad—unless I had to toast the nuts. And I could still manage desserts—as long as the packaging wasn't too complicated.

Eddy did let me make the stuffing for the goose, only because mine used to be prizewinning and he was in charge of the oven. I had a little trouble with it this time because to get the taste and texture right, I had to keep adding more ingredients.

Eddy teased me that it was soup-kitchen size by the time I got it just right. I suggested we invite more people for dinner, and he could cook a second goose so it wouldn't be so obvious. He pointed out it was that kind of thinking that got me in trouble with the stuffing in the first place.

Before we were even through the appetizers, the conversation turned to the new travel requirement for smallpox vaccinations. Myra and Rick Daley had already gotten themselves and their twin seven-year-olds vaccinated. The unofficial word at the local grade school was that schools in Colorado Springs would start requiring the vaccination by February or March anyway, so it made sense to get it done.

"Didn't all the requirements bother you?" Tina Bastante asked. Our longtime friend Pete Kawalski had married her the summer before, so I didn't know her very well. Her question was interesting, though, because she was a doctor, a family practitioner.

"Well, sure," Myra said. "But what are you going to do? We have a spring break trip planned for Hawaii, so we'd need it for that anyway."

"You have questions about it?" Rick asked. He poked Myra with his elbow as if to say, "See, I'm not the only one."

Myra, who was a striking bottle-blond against her husband's beak-nosed, stoop-shouldered profile, just rolled her eyes and gave Rick a look. "I'm not having this discussion again. We're not going to stop traveling, and our kids will need it anyway for school before the end of the semester. What options do we have? Besides, I don't actually *mind* being protected from a smallpox epidemic."

Rick ignored his wife. We'd seen plenty of sniping between them over the years. This was a reminder, once again, that they were a lot more fun individually than they were as a couple.

"Did you get vaccinated?" Rick tilted his wine glass at Tina.

She sighed. "I did. I had to. All health care workers were a Priority One. That included hospital housekeeping and dietary workers, not just doctors and nurses." I had a flash of Craig Wells' client and wondered how his case was proceeding. Eddy hadn't found any updates that told us anything new.

Pete rubbed his wife's neck. It was a sweet gesture. "Tina really struggled over it. Said it was highly invasive for what it was supposed to do. But what was she going to do? Quit medicine?"

Tina shook her head. She was a fine-featured, dark-haired beauty, at least ten years younger than the rest of us, including Pete. "If I'd had a choice, I wouldn't have. Or I would have at least waited until some outrage surfaced about all the fingerprinting and stuff."

A kindred spirit.

"But she loves her job," Pete said.

Well, maybe not totally kindred. Travel aside, I did have to endure the team at Baja Breeze.

I glanced at Eddy, who'd been uncharacteristically quiet. He returned my look but busied himself with basting the goose.

Rick picked up another mini quiche, the delicate, flaky Eddy kind, not the Costco-frozen, stick-it-in-the-oven, even-Maggie-could-do-it (most of the time) kind. "So why hasn't there been some outrage out there? I keep waiting to see protests or editorials or something. But people just keep lining up and volunteering."

Like sheep to the slaughter.

"There's some protest out there," Eddy said. He knew. He'd

posted everything he could find on his website. "But you're right. It's very low-key and kind of fringe. A few columnists in the major papers like *The New York Times* and the *San Francisco Chronicle*. Some stuff in smaller papers that never hits the national media. The protest doesn't seem to have legs."

"Why do you think that is?" Pete asked.

"Fear," I finally said. "People think they don't have options."

"That's right," Myra said. "You understand that, Maggie, because you were a Priority One, too, weren't you?"

I nodded. Tina looked at me.

Rick said, "My theory is that we've all been psychologically beaten into submission by 9/11 and all that homeland security shit. Scare people enough, and they'll volunteer—no, they'll beg you—to let them get the vaccine. We're a nation with battered-wife syndrome. Not only do we not know how to get out of the mess, we keep returning to get beat up some more." It was the kind of comment you'd expect from the clinical psychologist in the group, but I agreed with it.

Pete poured a little more wine into Tina's glass, then topped off Rick's and Eddy's. I shook my head at more. I had to pace myself. I only got goose once a year and I intended to fully taste it. Pete talked while he poured. "No kidding. Talk about irony, Tina's cousin is a firefighter in Chicago. He said the day he got his vaccination there was a crowd of at least a couple thousand people who weren't Priority One. They got really ugly, tried to force their way into the building. The police inside the building who were waiting to get vaccinated managed to calm the crowd."

"I think that's happened a bunch of places," I said and repeated the same kind of story I'd heard from the data entry clerk when I got my vaccination.

"There were reports like that early on. They got some press," Eddy confirmed. "There haven't been as many reports about people who refused to get fingerprinted or their cells scraped.

But I've found a few first-hand accounts by bloggers. A couple of them were arrested for refusing. One claims he was roughed up by the police and ended up in the hospital. While he was there, they vaccinated him."

"Talk about irony," Tina said.

"Yeah, but bloggers," Myra said. "Can you trust that? I mean you can write anything you want, say it happened, and put it out on the Internet. Then it's the gospel and everybody quotes it like it came from CNN."

The others looked at Eddy to see if the hair was standing up on the back of his neck, but I knew he wasn't offended at all. He'd said the same thing every time he read a blog he disagreed with. "You're absolutely right, Myra. Here's a paradox, though. Just because it's on CNN or Fox News, though, doesn't make it true either."

"Well I know which source I'm more likely to believe."

"Maybe. Tell me this, then, Myra."

I studied my wine glass. I knew where he was headed.

"How many confirmed reports are there of people who have died from smallpox?"

She shook her head. "I don't know. A thousand or more?"

Eddy shook his head. "Three. The prisoner in Florence and the two guys in Salida."

"Not true. They announce every night on the national news what the new death toll is. It's growing all the time."

Eddy shook his head again. "Do they ever give a name? Do they ever interview a family member or hospital personnel or anyone who might have a personal connection to the victim?"

"What does that have to do with whether there really are victims out there?"

"They only interview CDC personnel and people in the administration and then announce where there were more outbreaks."

"That's your proof?" Myra asked. "Look, if I died of smallpox, you think Rick would want his face on the evening news about it? You're a pariah if you've had any contact with smallpox. Why would you want everyone to know it?"

"Myra," Pete said. "If you contracted smallpox and died from it, don't you think we'd all know about it already? Too many people want their fifteen minutes of fame. And while Rick would certainly be way too private to go on national television and cry and grieve, there's plenty of others who would be glad for the chance to have a little camera time." He helped himself to a scoop of crab dip. "You know, Eddy, that actually makes sense. I hadn't put it together, but that explains why I've had this uneasiness."

Eddy nodded. "So maybe there aren't any real deaths. How many real people do you think have contracted smallpox?" He opened the oven and basted the goose again before continuing.

"The media would have us believe several thousand," Rick said.

"Again, how many confirmed reports?"

"In addition to the three that have died: one," Tina said.

Myra shook her head. "I just don't buy it. I don't believe this whole thing has been cooked up. Drive down to Salida. They had at least a dozen people there who came down with it."

Eddy looked at me, but it was Tina who spoke. "Actually, we've had a number of discussions at work about this. Glen, my nurse practitioner, is from Salida. He says the two guys who died from it didn't expose anyone else. They were up in the mountains for a week of bow hunting during their contagious period. No one in town knows of anyone else who got it."

Eddy could have prepped her, but I could tell from the look on his face that he hadn't. He was clearly pleased that she'd confirmed everything he'd heard from our friend Cindy Marshall.

"Salida's small," Pete said.

Tina nodded. "Glen said the town really buzzed when the news came out in the paper. But no one knew of a single person who'd gotten sick. Not one. A town that small, *somebody* had to know at least one person."

"So *The New York Times* is wrong." Myrna said and huffed just a little. She looked like she didn't believe Tina. "Why would the news report that people are sick and dying if it's not true?"

Tina shrugged her shoulders. "You tell me." Tina sighed and then lowered her voice even though it was just the six of us and the cooking goose in the kitchen. "He said the CDC guys made everyone nervous."

"About what?" I asked. "That the vaccine doesn't really work?"

Tina shook her head. "Creepier than that. More along the lines that it could happen again. People getting exposed that is. Only maybe next time it won't be smallpox." She paused and took a bite of crab dip. We all waited. "It'll be something there's no vaccine for. Maybe it'll be something in the city water supply. Or the veggies at Walmart will get sprayed with something."

"So who did the CDC guys say were going to do this? The terrorists? I don't get why they would poison the water supply if people talked about whether there were smallpox victims or not in Salida." Myrna clearly wasn't buying the direction of this conversation.

Tina looked at Pete who looked at Eddy who looked at me.

Eddy finally said, "Myrna, I don't think the threat came from the terrorists."

"What are you talking about? That sounds so paranoid," Myrna said. "You guys and your conspiracy theories." She looked at the rest of us for some support, but no one made eye contact.

"Maybe," Tina said. "All I know is that Glen was pretty freaked out by the whole thing." She paused again. "I guess I'm with Eddy on this." She tilted her wine glass toward him. "What you see isn't what we've got."

The goose, of course, was the expected hit. As a nice bonus, everyone, even Myra and Rick's twins, graciously complimented the stuffing, as well. Eddy fixed up bags of all the leftovers for everyone and then fixed additional bags of stuffing to send for their neighbors and relatives. That would leave us enough till New Year's, as long as we had some every day for every meal. Including breakfast.

I knew Eddy would think twice about putting me in charge of the stuffing ever again.

On Monday after New Year's, we both headed to the airport, Eddy to see his sister, me to NBP for the last time to tie up loose ends. They'd gone live on Zaan without a hitch, just as everyone expected. I was convinced Zaan should use the NBP project team as Zaan contractors for future projects. I'd never seen a company knock out an implementation as cleanly as they had.

Eddy dropped me off with his driver's license at the United door. While he parked the car, I scanned us both into the self-service check in and then went to wait in the security line. We knew it would be brutal after the holidays even with the slow down in air travel, but we never expected the incredibly long line that snaked back to the escalators and wound back toward the ticketing desks, at least a hundred and fifty feet of bodies. In all my years of Monday travel out of the Springs, I'd never seen anything like it. Even then it seemed like we had plenty of time, given that I have a high level of gate anxiety and always try to be at the airport at least an hour ahead. On Mondays that usually means I'm sitting at the gate fifty-five minutes before departure.

Eddy joined me after about fifteen minutes. My gate anxiety was creeping up. We were just past the escalators, which meant that if we kept on track, we might make it to the gate at departure time minus five minutes. We were going to miss our flight.

"Holy Pazolies," Eddy said. "No wonder you hate to fly. How can you stand lines like this?"

"I've never seen it like this. And it's moving like sludge on a cold day. I don't know if we're going to make it."

"Uh oh. If the optimist says that, I need to start seriously worrying. I may be in over my head on this one."

I pressed the United 1K speed dial number on my cell phone and worked my way through the number choices until I reached a real person.

"Hi. I'm standing in the security line in Colorado Springs and it's like stopped. If I miss my flight, when's the next one I can catch to get to Lincoln, Nebraska, today?"

Okay, I admit it. Gate anxiety drives bad behavior or, as Eddy sometimes points out, "me" behavior.

I gave her my information and Eddy's, too. With my United status, the customer service rep on the other end didn't dare ask me why I hadn't gotten to the airport two hours ahead, which was the official stance. Like I needed an hour and fifty-five minutes at the departure gate every Monday morning.

She gave me some options, which were better for Eddy than me, but we'd still make it to Lincoln and Dulles by the end of the day.

I tried to relax. I'd never missed a flight because of something I did, but there's a first for everything. Fortunately, I didn't think my manager, who was rumored to have missed multiple flights over the years due to, uh, food poisoning, wouldn't even send me a nasty gram, making it the one stupid sin I could commit myself and not get fired.

We inched closer till we at least got to the point of showing our IDs and boarding passes. The humorless—and I know she was humorless from the forty-five or more Monday mornings I'd smiled at her without a response—TSA agent said, "Your health cards, please."

Eddy and I looked at each other. I pulled out my wallet, glad for the first time that I hadn't shredded it on the corner of Tejon and Pikes Peak like I'd fantasized, and handed it to her.

The TSA agent took my card and swiped it in a card reader, compared the information on the screen to my ticket and driver's license, and handed it back. She pointed off to the left line. "Over there," she said and held her hand out for Eddy's card.

"I don't have one," Eddy said.

"We thought the proof of vaccination requirement didn't begin until January eighteenth," I said.

"It doesn't," the TSA agent said mechanically and for the first time it occurred to me she was humorless because she was actually a robot. "But you won't be able to get on your return flight without it, so we're not letting people take off unless they have proof they can get on their return flight."

Clever Eddy didn't bite. "So when am I returning?" he asked her.

"How would I know?" the TSA agent responded a little huffily.

"Exactly," Eddy said.

I stiffened because I knew it only took a wave of the TSA's hand, and he would be banished to the far right, the line of thorough and completely humiliating searches that would keep us from getting on a flight for two hours by the looks of it this morning.

But then Eddy smiled at the TSA agent. Luckily for him, there wasn't a woman on either side of twenty that didn't melt a little, okay—a lot, from that smile. "Tell you what," he paused and looked at her badge, "Jasmine. Now that's a pretty name. Jasmine. Very exotic. Matches your eyes." He smiled again.

And she actually smiled back. The first time in a year. Holy Pazolies is right. I needed to travel with this man more often.

"Jasmine, I give you my word that I'll be returning by the twelfth. If I miss that flight, I can come back on the thirteenth. And if I miss that one, I'll return on the fourteenth. You get the picture, Jasmine."

She nodded, no doubt in defiance of all her training.

"And if the gods go crazy and I can't return on one of those days and get stuck there till the eighteenth, I swear I'll return by train." And then—this is the truth—he actually winked at her. It was all I could do not to laugh out loud.

Jasmine shook her head and tried to hide another smile. "Okay, Mr. Rider, you get a free pass today. Just so you know, though, you'll need your health card for the train, too." She waved her hand off to the left. "Go ahead and get in the TSA pre-check line."

Eddy smiled back at Jasmine and said, "Thanks," while he politely steered me to the left before I could swear at the government. Out loud.

The TSA pre-check line moved at its normal pace, and we reached the metal detector within ten minutes. Once again, a TSA agent asked for my boarding pass and my health card. I glanced at Eddy and handed my card to the agent, who swiped it in a card reader and matched it against my boarding pass. Who knows what could have changed between the first TSA agent and the second one, but they weren't going to be taking any chances this morning, I guess. Satisfied that Maggie Rider matched Maggie Rider, he motioned me on.

Eddy put his hands up like he was under arrest. "I don't have my health card because I didn't think I'd need it since I'm returning before the eighteenth."

"Then I need to see some more ID."

Eddy pulled out his wallet and showed his driver's license, which the TSA agent matched against his ticket. He waved Eddy on but said, "Don't try to fly after the eighteenth without it. You'll be stuck at the airport and won't get a refund on your ticket. It's not the airline's fault if you can't meet the government's deadline."

"Yes, sir," Eddy said. Fortunately, the agent didn't recognize Eddy's "you're an idiot" tone and let him pass.

We reached the gate as the plane for Denver was boarding, my gate anxiety pattern forever ratcheted up to gate angst. I felt slightly nauseous as I thought about how much longer my travel days had just become.

We settled into our seats. I grabbed one of the three remaining blankets on the plane, stowed my computer bag under the seat, put my noise-canceling headphones on, took out my Kindle to read, and started sinking into my zone, forgetting for the moment that Eddy was in the seat beside me.

He picked up my hand and kissed it. I looked at him and took off my headphones.

He smiled. "You have the drill down, don't you?"

"It's how I survive."

He nodded. He leaned in closer to me and talked, not exactly in a whisper, but low enough that the people in front and behind couldn't hear him. It's the distinguisher between business travelers and tourists. I was proud of him that he knew it instinctively. "So how are you going to survive security from now on?"

"I don't know. That was quite the ordeal. Maybe it was just because too many people didn't have health cards yet and they're pointlessly grilling them."

"Ya' think?"

I sighed and shook my head. "No."

"If they're that tough before the regulation goes into effect, what will they do afterwards?"

"Did you see all those people in the extra security line? All but two or three were there because they didn't have your charm."

"Really?" He really did sound surprised.

"I know it. There are three people max standing in that line on any Monday, and that assumes the other lines are as full as they were today. That little show was nothing but sheer retribution. Jasmine didn't like someone? She waved them to the right. It didn't matter if the person deserved to be a little righteously indignant. They said a cross word to her, they were banished to an extra-thorough search and would miss their plane. It's the ultimate power trip: control by fear and back it up with punishment."

"And that's being multiplied times ten thousand at all the airports across America this morning."

"And the lesson is?"

"Get your health card, ma'am, and we'll make your life easy."

FINALLY THE NATION TALKED BACK. It was one thing to ask so much invasive information for the vaccination, require the vaccination for domestic travel by a certain date, and even to start checking health cards to make sure the new system would work. It was another thing entirely for the TSA to respond to legitimate frustration by banishing people to more thorough security. Nearly twenty thousand people had missed their flights that Monday morning, an unheard-of number, although the White House claimed it was closer to two thousand people and poked at the media for blowing it all out of proportion. The airlines, which got totally snarled from trying to rebook all the angry people—whether it was two thousand or ten times that—even timidly protested.

It led the news reports and dominated talk radio, which I tuned into for a change on my drive from Lincoln to NBP. As the day wore on, the discussion veered closer and closer to a common theme: why is the government collecting so much information about us?

The White House responded late Tuesday when the administration apparently finally figured out this wasn't going to just blow over. The president's press secretary read a statement but wouldn't take any questions.

CNN kept running snippets of the footage and then summarizing, although in my opinion, "summarizing" a five-minute statement changes the meaning of the word. In short, the White House blamed an over-zealous Transportation Security Administration directive that instructed TSA agents to begin careful scrutiny of health cards as a dry run for January eighteenth. The administration regretted the inconvenience to all the people who were delayed and would look into where the directive might have been misinterpreted. Disciplinary action would be taken if necessary.

In other words, since this administration only saw actual responsibility in the trenches where the message played out, down the road we could expect someone to get fired over their rude mishandling of so many travelers. But the guy at the top would be ignored since it couldn't be his fault if his directive got twisted as it traveled down through the ranks.

It was another annoying moment in American history. That explanation seemed to settle people down and the mini insurrection disappeared before the first person could stand on a downtown Colorado Springs street corner and publicly shred her health card.

Of course, there were those lonely souls on the Internet wilderness that kept raising dissenting voices. The mainstream media ignored them though. After all, anyone can build a website or post a blog and say it's the truth.

I stopped by Scott Leinbach's office on Thursday to say goodbye and once again compliment him on his flawless execution of the project.

He modestly blushed and shrugged his shoulders. "I keep telling you, it really wasn't that tough. I had a good team of people who were willing to work hard. Our biggest headache the whole time was with the shipping. Once Zaan figured out that the shipping problem wasn't because of what NBP was trying to do but was a bug in the interface between Zaan and FindIt, it got resolved within a week."

"FindIt?" Hello. "The tracking software."

"Yeah. Our supplier for the RFID. Zaan ended up changing some of the coding in the software, and that fixed everything."

The hair on the back of my neck stood up. "I guess your tracking system is pretty critical."

Scott nodded. "It means we can track everything—pallets, boxes of meat, even individual packages. It's pretty cool, really." He opened a bottom desk drawer and rummaged around until he found a manila envelope that contained a square Styrofoam meat packaging tray and some labels. I was glad his attention was somewhere else for the moment. I truly worried I might faint from all the blood rushing to my head.

"Take a look at this." He handed the Styrofoam tray to me. "See anything?"

"It's just a square plate like the ones my meat comes on at the grocery store." I sat on the corner of his desk. It was far more personal than I ever get with clients, but the two other chairs in the room had stacks of loose papers on them. I had to sit.

"Exactly. Now hold it up to the light."

I did. I knew what I was looking for.

"See anything?"

"The little spot at the center where the mold release dot is. Looks like there's a dot with thin lines coming out of the center on both sides."

"You've got good eyes."

Or a sufficient imagination—I wasn't sure myself.

"That's the RFID. Every single one is different, so we can track right down to the individual package if we want. Here's another example." He handed me three labels. "Can you find it on these?"

Two labels had RFIDs that jumped out at me because they were the size of a dime, and I knew to look for something with tendrils, even if the tendrils wound around the center in a pattern. I couldn't find it on the third one.

"You won't see it on that one. It's embedded within the ink on the label, even the copper antenna."

"Amazing." The word had more meaning than Scott could ever know.

"It is, isn't it? It's the coolest new tool for business. You start putting these IDs into your packaging, and poof, you can track losses right down to the individual package. We can tell if our employees are helping themselves to a package of sirloins a couple times a week or which route a carrier is having so much loss on. Stores love it because some day soon it'll stop shoplifting entirely."

"Really?"

"The technology is there already, they just have to install it. You know how the big box stores like Sam's and Costco have someone who looks at your receipt and your cart before you walk out the door? Eventually, they'll have a receipt reader and an RFID reader at the door. You feed in your receipt, and the RFID reader will scan the contents of the cart. If they match up, the doors open and you're on your way. They don't match up, the RFID reader lists what hasn't been paid for and adds that on to your bill."

"What if I'm wearing a sweater I bought there yesterday? Do I get charged for it a second time?"

"Details, details." Scott laughed and waved his hand. "It should show up that you bought it the day before."

"But if I'm wearing a shoplifted sweater that's identical to the one I bought, the reader would catch it."

"Exactly. Because it's not showing up as paid for in the database. Every single item has a different ID. If you're trying to track losses, it's a pretty effortless way to do that."

"Isn't that a little creepy, too?" I asked.

The question seemed to take him by surprise. "In what way?" He furrowed his heavy brows. "Maybe. I guess if you're the shoplifter. I don't see how it would be intrusive otherwise."

I had no intention of picking a fight with Scott. He was about as nice of a client as I'd ever worked with, but it was all I could do not to pull up my shirt sleeve and ask him if he thought it was okay to track people like NBP tracked a package of meat.

He clearly loved the RFID concept because he kept right on talking. "It's an amazing way for a store to track inventory. They run a report every night—hell, every hour if that's what they want. It tells them exactly what's been sold in a day, what items are or aren't turning over, what items are dated and need to be pulled, and then it all hits their purchasing system and triggers the purchasing process in the suppliers' systems. Walmart's already pretty sophisticated with this kind of purchasing process. It just takes it to the next level and requires even fewer people to do it."

"And what happens when people get their purchases home? What happens to the RFID?"

Scott shrugged his shoulders and waved his hand casually again. "Who cares? I suppose down the road there'll be technology to tap into that, too. New refrigerators have RFID readers in them. Someday soon your refrigerator will tell you everything you have in it, that your ketchup is outdated, how close your milk is to the expiration date." He brightened and laughed. "Maybe we can get your refrigerator to signal that you're out of filet mignons and the local store is having a sale on them."

I smiled, but I'm not sure it looked very sincere.

PETE AND TINA INVITED US FOR DINNER on the following Friday. The chance to have a real social life made me a little giddy all week. I double-checked with Eddy to see if they wanted us to bring stuffing, but he said he was pretty sure it was just the two of us and not four hundred others.

I shouldn't have been surprised about the dinner invite. After all, we were good enough friends to eat Christmas dinner together. It's just that they, like Eddy and me, lived frantically busy lives. They juggled a complicated childcare schedule from Pete's first marriage and intense jobs—Tina had a busy family practice and Pete owned an auto body shop with high maintenance employees. Where weekends were merely sacred to us, they were nearly nonexistent for Pete and Tina.

So I knew this was about more than having a social evening.

Eddy and Pete had been friends ever since my first fender-bender with the Porsche, so we knew his ex-wife Barb, who was a shrew and a half. Tina, even though she had to have plenty of Type A in her, was bright, funny, and sweet.

Tina met us at the door, leaving Pete to unpack dinner from a local gourmet deli. The four of us small-talked through some wine and munchies, which was pleasant but not dynamic enough for me to figure out why we were together again only three weeks after Christmas. Unfortunately, that was probably more a reflection on *my* Type A personality: I needed a purpose, an agenda, and action items or the evening should get written up on someone's performance review.

A grip on reality is really what I needed.

Failing that, I let Eddy pour me a second glass of wine while he launched into a funny story about how the TSA only hires people whose names start with *J*, like Jasmine and Jimmy, and then trains them to make life miserable for people who have names that start with other letters, like *E*.

It was even funny to me, and I hadn't laughed at all the day we traveled together.

"So does that mean you're going to get your smallpox vaccination and health card so you can travel more easily?" Pete asked. He said it to Eddy but glanced at Tina, who glanced at me. I was watching Eddy. Now we'd gotten to the agenda.

"Well, probably not." Eddy looked at me, then back at his friend. "Are you going to get one, Pete?"

"Nope," he said and shook his head. "Not now. Not ever."

"What about for your boys?" I asked.

Tina studied the bottom of her wine glass.

"I say absolutely not. But Barb says we gotta do it if they're going to stay in school. After Christmas, they came home with a paper saying if they didn't have the vaccine by February first, they wouldn't be allowed back."

"So what do you say, Tina?" I thought I knew based on what she said at Christmas, but I wanted to know what she knew now.

Pete chewed on his lower lip but waited for her to answer. She swirled the last of the wine in her glass. Finally, Pete stroked her upper arm with the back of his fingers. "Show 'em what you did, Tina."

She slipped her cardigan off her left arm and carefully pulled up the sleeve of her shirt underneath. Her smallpox vaccination had a bandage over it.

I wasn't exactly sure what we were seeing, but Eddy nodded his head. "You removed it."

"Removed the vaccine?" I asked.

"I removed the capsule," she said. "I'm not sure there was ever a vaccine."

"The capsule." I looked at Eddy, who nodded very slightly at me. "What do you mean, you're not sure there was ever a vaccine?"

Tina got up and went to her purse. She took out two small envelopes, the size that's sometimes used for one or two pills. She opened one and dropped the contents into her hand for us to see. All I could see in her palm was an opaque soft plastic bead, about the size of a small flat pinto bean.

"That's the vaccine?"

She nodded.

"How do you know it's not some kind of time release?"

"Could be, but I'm pretty sure it's not. Take a look at this." She dumped the contents from the other envelope into her hand. In contrast, it looked like it, too, had once been an opaque plastic bead, but it had been cut open. The cut had mangled the insides somewhat, but I still recognized the tiny mass and copper tendrils that wound neatly around the center.

"You know what you have there." It wasn't a question.

Tina nodded. "An RFID. I finally figured it out from Eddy's website." She tilted her head toward him. He toasted her with his wine glass.

"The whole thing just seemed off-kilter somehow," she said. "All the questions, the fingerprinting, the DNA samples—that's not something we'd ever do for any reason, and certainly not for a vaccine. The whole idea of a vaccine is to get the patient in and get him out so you can get the next patient in. The information inquisition was just too weird. I mean, who cares what your citizenship is?"

Eddy leaned back in his chair, his fingers entwined behind his head. "Well, now. Isn't that an interesting question?"

I felt grim. "You're right. I hadn't thought about it from that angle yet, but I'm sure it's coming." I looked at Tina, "But that's a whole other discussion. Tell us how you ended up with that capsule cut open like that."

"Those of us who were trained to do the inoculations were given an entire day of training—you'd have thought this was some kind of brain surgery the way they talked to us. But a lot of it wasn't even about how to insert the capsule. It was about all the other stuff like how important it was to fill out the forms, what to do if we had people with needle phobias or got anxious—that was their word: 'anxious'—and how to handle the capsules, especially if they spontaneously festered out."

She'd sat down while talking and now she poured herself another glass of wine; her hands had a tiny tremor. "They spent almost as long on how to handle the rejected capsule as they did on how to insert it, even though they claimed the rejection rate was supposed to be somewhere around two in ten thousand vaccinations. We were supposed to put it in special packaging and FedEx it to the CDC. Before the patient left, we were supposed to insert a new capsule some other place on the body, preferably the same arm, but if not, then insert it on the other arm or a hip and then re-enter the number of the new capsule into the health cards. Under no circumstances were we to touch the capsule after it had been rejected. They emphasized that we would be putting ourselves at risk with the exposure."

Tina made a little harrumphing noise. "We're doctors, for God's sake. We deal with high-risk health situations all the time. We can't wear plastic gloves and a mask and hold the thing with a tweezers?"

"Or wear plastic gloves and a mask and hold the thing with a tweezers while you cut it open and find out what the big mystery is," Pete said. He raised his eyebrows slightly and shook his head, like he couldn't believe what his wife had done.

"That's right. That's exactly what I did, too. Last week this guy came in to the office with his inoculation oozing with pus, and my first thought was that the vaccine had triggered the virus. So we isolated him and I got all garbed up before I got a good look at it and realized it was just an ordinary infection from a guy who didn't have very good hygiene and hadn't taken care of the incision very well." She huffed a little about that. "You can bet that's going to start happening more and more. This isn't just a shot. You have to keep the incisions clean just like any other minor surgery." She rolled her eyes.

"Anyway, I removed the old capsule and inserted a new one into his other arm. Then the receptionist updated the card with the new capsule number. After he left, I cleaned up the capsule and was actually going to put it in the canister and send it like we were instructed to do when it struck me that this thing hadn't dissolved one iota. It didn't look anything like the pictures they'd shown us during training."

"So the good doctor did what any good doctor would do. She examined it," Pete said.

"I did. I cut it open and then was clueless about what it was. I knew Eddy had some kind of a website because we'd talked about it at Christmas. So I did my research." She smiled a little shyly.

"And you figured out that it was an RFID," I said.

She nodded. "Forget the health risks of walking around with that thing transmitting from inside your body, I was just plain offended that the government did that and called it in my best interest. I'd bet our house that there's nothing at all in that capsule that prevents smallpox."

Pete nodded, "That's the ultimate insult. We're still not protected if there's a true terrorist outbreak."

"So you removed your own capsule?" Eddy asked. "How did you do that?"

I know he was picturing what I was picturing—empty bottle of whiskey, bullet with teeth marks, hunting knife with lots of blood on it.

"My sister's in medical school at CU. She came down last weekend and I talked her through it."

Eddy and I both blanched anyway.

"She'll make a good doctor."

"What did you do with the one you removed from that guy? Don't you have to send it back and document everything?" Eddy asked.

"I do. I just haven't quite figured out what my story is yet. But I will by Monday."

By the time we left Pete and Tina's, I'd gathered my resolve to have my "vaccination" removed. I didn't say anything to Eddy, though, until we were nestled like two spoons in bed, Eddy's arm draped over me.

"I'm going to have it removed," I said.

Same skin. He knew what I meant.

"Don't do it for me," he said.

"I'm not. It's for me. It's for my own integrity."

He pulled me a little tighter. Eddy, ever the pessimist, said, "Maybe you should wait to see what happens to Tina."

I, ever the optimist, said, "Nothing's happened so far. I need to do it now."

Or I'd lose my nerve.

"We'll figure it out." He kissed the back of my head. "I love you."

"You too, Eddio. Forever and ever."

I called Tina on Saturday morning. She sounded sleepy but said she'd been up for a while. She agreed to meet me at her office and told me what to do, say, and wear. Saturdays were for emergencies. Although she wasn't scheduled to work, it wouldn't be unusual for her to be around the office. Tina hadn't told anyone about removing her own capsule and didn't think it would be good to get the word started around town that she was in the business of doing it. She would remove mine because she knew she could trust me since Pete and Eddy were good friends and Eddy was so active in his dissent over the whole thing.

It had snowed overnight while the temperature hovered between just above freezing and just below, so the roads were shiny and slick. I crept through the empty streets, wondering, debating whether this was smart or stupid.

I mentally followed the twisting paths for all the possibilities. I had my health card and had made it through security uneventfully multiple times with it. Maybe down the road, there would be some kind of passive or—God forbid—active receiver that would require I had the RFID implant to, I don't know, use my charge card or get approved for a job or file my income taxes or—

But why would I want to live in that kind of a world?

That's what I always came back to.

Why would I choose to live in a country that required me to be tracked?

I asked for Tina at the reception desk and told them I was an old friend of hers and just in town. Her husband, Pete, said I'd find her here.

Tina showed up at the front desk a minute later. She acted sufficiently surprised to see me and I acted sufficiently pleased to see her. Neither of us could have majored in theater, but we passed the test. She motioned me back to her office, shut the door, and sat me down. After all, this was a medical consultation.

"Are you sure you want to do this, Maggie?"

"Is there a reason not to?"

Tina shrugged her shoulder and shook her head slightly. "I don't know what the ramifications might be. From a medical perspective, I'm not convinced it'll change your level of immunity. These aren't time-release inoculations. If they have any power to immunize you, it's in the coating itself. But the two that I've seen haven't changed color or texture, so that tells me that there's probably nothing there."

"Are you sorry you removed yours?"

She lowered her voice to a whisper, even though it was just the two of us. "What I'm sorry about is that I implanted so many of them."

"No apparent repercussions, though?"

"None that I know of. You're the traveler, though. Maybe you'll bump up against something."

I shook my head. "The only thing they've done so far is checked the information on my health card."

"The only thing you're aware of," Tina corrected me.

I conceded that.

She set to work swabbing the skin, giving me a local anesthetic, and locating the alien bump in my arm. As she worked, she talked.

"I got an email this morning saying that we should begin implanting the capsules in the hip. I think it's because it'll be easier to bury it deeper and so it'll be harder to do exactly what we're doing."

"You think they're doing that because people are already removing them?"

She stopped what she was doing and looked at me funny. "Don't you read all the stuff on Eddy's site?"

"I haven't been on it for a while. I guess I never read it thoroughly. I figure he tells me the earth-shattering things." Had Eddy set me up for this?

Tina didn't say anything except, "You might not want to watch for the next minute or so."

She was absolutely right. I didn't.

Where was a good bottle of whiskey and a bullet when you needed one?

"What did you do with the capsule?" Eddy asked the minute I stepped in the door.

"I brought it home with me. I thought I'd check your website to see what you're advising."

He blushed, but just barely.

"Did you set the whole thing up with Pete and Tina?"

"No. I found out when you did on Friday night that she'd had her capsule removed."

"But you knew that people were starting to remove them."

He paused, then nodded. "There are a few accounts. But very few."

"If I hadn't decided to remove mine, what would you have done to get me to?"

He chewed on his lower lip and lightly tapped his pen on his desk. "Don't know," he finally said.

"But you would have done something, right?"

He shook his head. "We would have figured something out. Eventually."

You don't stay married for fifteen years unless you get progressively smarter about which battles to pick. Eddy wasn't ever a manipulator, so I gave him the benefit of the doubt on this one. After all, it's not like it surprised me that he wanted me to remove the vaccine capsule. He hadn't wanted me to get it in the first place. Still, I let myself be a little cool all day, which I regretted later.

Chapter
23

Depressed as I was about all the time I spent in airports, giving up yet another thirty minutes made me teary all Sunday evening. But with Monday being Martin Luther King, Jr's, birthday and the last day to fly before the health card enforcement, I knew the security line would be the stuff of business traveler legends. I considered flying out Sunday evening, but the only thing I would have gained would have been the expectation that I'd be at Baja Breeze at nine o'clock on Monday morning instead of noon. And I'd lose Sunday evening on top of it.

So I got up at three and headed to the airport at four for a six thirty flight. There was something very wrong with this picture.

Usually, I'd take a cab for a flight that early, but Eddy insisted the night before that he wanted to take me, so I let him. He pulled up to the United door, hopped out, and unloaded my suitcase. He kissed me firmly on the lips and patted my rear as if to say, "Go get 'em, Tiger." I never felt like a tiger, and never, ever at four thirty in the morning.

True to my worries, the security line had already grown beyond the escalator. I did the self-service check-in and then began my wait in line. I had a good book going on my Kindle, so I kind of read, but reading, tending a suitcase and computer bag, and shuffling a foot or two every couple of minutes didn't lend itself to retention, so I finally put my Kindle away and concentrated on how miserable my life had become. It was much easier.

I people-watched, too. It was simple to spot the business travelers. In this line, they were the ones who had to be multi-tasking, even at that early hour. I wondered how many cell phone batteries would die just from the minutes in the security line, although I couldn't figure out whom they'd be calling at that hour. Probably other colleagues they knew were traveling. I certainly hoped not relatives. There was something slightly repulsive about watching them carry on, business as usual. These had been my silent, anonymous colleagues. We understood each other's looks as the casual travelers slowed down our routines. We shared the common code of people who knew too much detail about which hotels in which hotel chains had the best shampoo, coffee, and pillows. To see them stand in line so passively, absorbing yet one more layer of inconvenience and privacy intrusion all to chase some business made me feel empty.

I watched; I shuffled forward. I watched some more; I shuffled forward some more. Jasmine, who was at her usual spot, seemed as unhappy to be there as most of the travelers. I tried to see if she had some kind of a pattern to who got banished to where. Maybe the ones to the right were truly a little ruder. They were certainly more animated. Another lesson: stay docile. I watched the clock in security, which was set five minutes fast and had been as long as I'd been a regular traveler, in spite of daylight savings changes twice a year. It always seemed a little mean to me. As if standing in line wasn't stressful enough, the clock pretended to take five precious extra minutes away. If the airport personnel could co-ordinate nearly a million passengers a year, couldn't they set the right time on the clock?

I inched closer to Jasmine. Even as slowly as the line moved, I was pretty sure I'd make it to my gate before they started boarding. That was good. But it was bad to have to block out even more travel time from this day forward. I could see they had all of the metal detectors going and a full staff, so even if it took me longer than other mornings to get to Jasmine, the TSA pre-check line looked like it was going at normal speed.

I finally reached Jasmine. We did our ritual. She swiped, checked, rechecked, compared, and released me. I stayed friendly, yet passive, careful not to appear obsequious in case she had already grown tired of people who pretended to be friends with her. I thought about all the ways my life was good and why I could endure this. The first was easy, the second continued to grow harder and harder.

Surprisingly, the line slowed now. I kept checking my pace against the other lines. We were still moving faster, so I was definitely in the correct line, but my math wasn't working like it usually did. I kept looking at the clock and subtracting five minutes. I could still probably get to the gate before boarding, even if this took me another twenty minutes.

A man two people ahead of me kept making phone calls. It was close to eight o'clock on the East Coast, so there'd be no stopping him now. He kept grumbling to the people on the other end about the "Godawful TSA hicks" delaying everything. He'd already missed his flight and rearranged a new one—that call was now thirty minutes old. I preferred to stay invisible, but his voice kept drawing looks from the other lines. He had a phone, a computer bag, and manicured nails. And he clearly had the TSA pre-check clearance. What was it that he didn't understand about staying below the radar?

By the time he made it to the table with the tubs, he was a marked man. The security people let him go through the metal detector and then immediately escorted him off away from the main security area. Even then, he was too loud and honest. What an idiot. I knew for a fact he had at least two extra hours to wait for his next flight.

The TSA agent asked for my boarding pass and health card. He swiped the card, compared it to my boarding pass, and waved me through the metal detector. The TSA on the other side watched the reader at the top of the detector, and then he glanced at my face. He was new.

"Ma'am, please go through again."

"Me?" I said, although it was a stupid question. Obviously, there wasn't anyone behind me yet. But I had no metal on me, not even a bra with an underwire. Surely the machine wasn't picking up on the fillings in my teeth, which, come to think of it, were porcelain anyway.

He nodded and motioned with his hands.

I stepped on the other side, waited for his nod, and walked through again. His eyes stayed on the top of the detector.

"May I see your health card, please?"

Oh shit.

"My health card?" But not my boarding pass. My heart pounded and my palms immediately felt damp.

He nodded.

I handed it to him, and he gestured for another TSA agent. He handed her my card and told me to follow her. I didn't want to think about what this meant, but the only thing different this week compared to last week was that I had a new bandage and small stitches on my arm. And no RFID.

I had to think very fast, but I wasn't used to this kind of fast thinking. I never had to improvise to get myself out of trouble. Why hadn't I at least thought about this possibility? Where would I start to lie? What had to be the truth?

The TSA agent positioned me in the security stance to do her wanding—arms out, feet spread on the footprints on the mat. She waved the handheld metal detector up and down and around my body. I relaxed a very tiny bit. Maybe this was still about metal and it was just a momentarily malfunctioning machine. If it wasn't—well, I tried to concentrate and think about what kinds of questions they'd ask me, and what I would say. She carefully patted me down, using her palms where it was okay to touch, the back of her hands where I might be offended. Did she feel my heart pounding when she patted down my chest?

I finally thought clearly enough to ask, "What could have set the metal detector off? I've learned to be very good on travel days. I never wear anything metal." I smiled at her, but she didn't respond. Maybe I'd asked the question too late.

I was sweating now. Could she smell it?

"Please point to the things that are yours in security."

Not good. They would search these, too. I would miss my flight for sure now, but I felt strangely calm about that for the first time in all my travel years. I identified my suitcase, laptop, laptop case, shoes, and leather jacket.

The TSA agent escorted me out of the main security area and into what had been an airline gate turned into a series of not-so-temporary looking clear glass booths. I couldn't kid myself. This wasn't about metal at all. "I'm afraid I'm going to miss my plane," I said. I knew it wouldn't make any difference, but couldn't think of anything else to say. I should have asked what this was all about. I should have sounded far more surprised and far less edgy.

The first TSA agent got help from a second one and carried all my things to a table outside the booth where I could see my stuff while they went through it piece by piece.

I sat in the booth alone and waited, for what? I wasn't sure, but I knew it couldn't be good.

The cranky, loud talker, who had been ahead of me in line, sat in the booth next to me. There were two people in there with him. The three were talking, and the traveler was very agitated, but I couldn't hear what they said. The booths were more sound-proof than I'd realized. Even though I couldn't hear, I could see that the businessman was being too clear about the whole matter. He kept shaking a finger at the other two and his mouth and eyes worked animatedly in tandem. He could have used some coaching in playing his cards closer to his chest, but it was too late now.

I shouldn't have even been watching him. Not at all. I had my own story to think about, and I hadn't made up a good one yet. My stomach gurgled a warning. I'd gotten up too early to be in a natural rhythm for anything. If things didn't get resolved quickly, I'd be sick quickly.

Satisfied that I hadn't hidden any box cutters, bombs, or broken down shotguns in my luggage, the TSAs zipped everything up again, slapped a sticker on it that I'd never seen before and brought my stuff into the cubicle with me.

"May I go now?" I asked, thinking there might be a one in a hundred chance.

"No."

I sighed and tried my best to look like the agitated traveler I could have been.

"May I at least get my cell phone out so I can reschedule the flight you made me miss?" I cringed inwardly as soon as I said "you." The first rule in negotiating is to not intentionally antagonize the other person. Now I was the idiot.

"No."

"How much longer will this take? Why am I in here?"

But the TSA agent walked out of the booth and closed the door behind her.

I knew every step was deliberate—the pat-down, the thorough luggage examination, the lack of explanation, the solitude in the clear booth. It was meant to rattle me, and it did. But I think it was also supposed to give me enough time and a bad enough case of nerves that whatever story I'd concocted prior to this morning would start to fray and unravel as I had time to think about it. But since I had to have an explanation in the first place before it could start to come undone, my story was still together by the time the TSA agent came in to question me. After all, I only needed three lies: why I didn't have an RFID anymore; who took it out; and why didn't the person replace it with a new one?

The first one was easy and probably not quickly proven false. I'd had an infection and my arm was really sore and tender, so I had it removed. That made the third lie logical—I was skittish about having another one inserted. It wasn't legal, but it was what I'd have to go with. The second lie was the hardest of all. How could I not know who removed it?

If Zaan had taught me anything, it was confidence in myself. I'd stood up to tough CEOs and cantankerous unions. I might not have all the right answers, but I also wasn't easily intimidated.

Strategy was everything.

ABOUT SIX THIRTY, TWO TSA AGENTS ESCORTED my neighbor, the foolishly visible businessman, out of his booth. His face was an angry red but he wasn't talking. I saw him gather his things and head out of the security area. I couldn't tell if they were escorting him to his gate or back out of the airport. He certainly wasn't happy, but you don't have to get arrested to be upset in an airport.

A few minutes later, a slight and balding man finally made it to my booth and introduced himself. "You're Margaret Rider?" He had good, blue eyes and an earnest expression. He was at the top of his career, which should have depressed him immensely.

"I am."

"I'm Mr. Greggen, the TSA manager for the Colorado Springs airport." He looked like he'd slept in his clothes. Maybe he had. What could they be paying the TSA manager at an airport with twelve gates? Fewer if you consider the one co-opted by the TSA.

"What seems to be the problem here?" I started out with my pleasant and no-nonsense tone. No anger, but no sweetness either. This was business. "No one is telling me why you're detaining me. I've missed my flight, and I'm not even allowed to use my cell phone to call and arrange for another flight or to let my client know that I'll be late." My insides jiggled quietly, but I didn't think I sounded nervous or angry, even though I was unquestionably both.

"Well, Margaret, we seem to have a problem with your health card."

"Excuse me, I didn't catch your name." He had my first name. I didn't have his. I did my best to keep him off guard. That would be my only chance.

"I'm Mr. Greggen," he said again. This immediately made the rules clearer.

"Certainly," I said. His was a small game, but I wasn't going to let him play it. "Please call me Mrs. Rider." I smiled in a friendly way. I've been told I have a very disarming smile.

He nodded, but didn't return the smile.

I may have been making things worse for myself, but I wanted him to understand that I was more street-smart than he first thought. People often do that to me because I'm told I look at least ten years younger than I am. I think it's the money, which buys good hair color, silk suits, and a knack for makeup. Eddy says I turn heads, but I've never noticed. Still, if I've learned anything from Eddy it's that men tend to be driven by the tiny brain below their belts rather than the real one above. I took advantage of that now.

"Now help me understand why you've been holding me for over thirty minutes." I smiled again.

"Well, as I said, there seems to be some problem with your health card."

"And what is that?"

"It would appear that your health card shows that you've been vaccinated."

"I was."

"But you no longer have the vaccination." He stated it like it was a fact.

"My understanding is that the government isn't requiring a vaccination until the eighteenth." No answer, no lie required. One down, two to go.

"Are you currently vaccinated?" It would have been a good time for him to use my name, but he didn't. He clearly didn't want to call me Mrs. Rider.

"I don't understand why we're having this conversation. The requirement doesn't go into effect until tomorrow."

No response from Mr. Greggen.

"Is that correct? Or do I have my dates wrong?"

He didn't need to know my stomach was upside down.

"You have your dates correct."

"Then why am I sitting here and why are you asking these questions?" I stayed pleasant but persistent. I'd had lots of practice at this. He had no idea who he was up against.

"Who removed it, Mrs. Rider?"

"Did we establish that I *did* have it removed? Or was that purely conjecture on your part? I forget." More smile. More dazzling white teeth.

Mr. Greggen didn't respond immediately. His eyes darted sideways like he was hoping for some insight to redeem him. "Why does your health card show you have a vaccination, but you don't actually have it?"

"Mr. Greggen, frankly I'm troubled that you keep asking whether I have the vaccination when it's not even required yet. I'm very bothered that you are accusing me of this when I don't understand how you could know whether I have it or not."

Good. His eyes darted around the tiny room and he kept swallowing, like that would save him.

Me? I was perilously close to throwing up.

"You've kept me isolated long enough that I've missed my flight," I continued. "You've cost me a great deal of money, and you haven't had any justification for this."

He reddened. His forehead beaded up with small dots of sweat. "Your health card is a problem," he said. I don't think the conversation was going at all the way he'd expected.

"If you insist on holding me without a reason, then I'll need to call my attorney, as well as my friend, Chris Edahart. You know Chris, I'm sure, since you're quoted from time to time in *The Gazette*." Chris Edahart was not my friend and had, in fact, never heard of me. But Mr. Greggen—the man with no first name—didn't need to know the level of my intimacy with the managing editor of the Colorado Springs *Gazette*.

Mr. Greggen didn't say anything. It didn't take a rocket scientist—or a consultant—to realize he had found himself stuck in a corner.

"You know, it's funny. Chris and his wife, Ellen, were over for dinner just last week." I should have stopped while I was ahead. I had no idea what Chris Edahart wife's name was. I didn't even know if he was married. I couldn't help myself, though. Mr. Greggen looked queasy. "Anyway, we were having this off-the-wall conversation about civil liberties. You know the discussion: when is it okay to sacrifice personal liberty for the greater good, and when do you need to take a stand? Of course, Chris, being the kind of thinker he is, came out far more liberal than I did. But—" I smiled a broad, white smile, "I'm certainly becoming a believer in more personal responsibility and less, shall we say, Big Brother, even as we speak." I kept eye contact. I had nothing to lose.

The man, however, hadn't reached his level in the new organization just by surviving. Finally, he said, "Look, I don't know who you know or what you're doing. But you need to have a vaccination. Your card says you have it. The receiver—" he'd said the word without realizing it "—says you don't. Today, you're right, that's legal." He leaned in and whispered. "You realize that tomorrow, this would be a felony."

Got it. Where was the restroom?

"A felony?" Some other voice was coming out of some other body.

"A felony," he repeated.

"To fly without a vaccination?"

"To have a discrepancy between what your card says and what is reality."

"And how would I know that?"

"Read the amendment to the Homeland Security Act."

"I'll be sure to do that on my flight to San Francisco." I smiled again. No doubt, it was a sicker-looking smile. "May I go now so I can rearrange my day?"

"Sure," Mr. Greggen said. He was a little weasel of a man. "Have a nice day."

I grabbed my things and then headed straight to the restroom so I could throw up. If they had cameras there, well, so be it. It was either the restroom or the concourse. I thought the restroom was more discreet.

Afterwards, I brushed my teeth with the emergency travel toothbrush I carried in my computer bag, although up till now, that hadn't been the emergency I'd saved it for. Mostly, though, I held myself against the sink and tried not to shake. The interrogation had told me multiple things:

1.   They clearly had RFID receivers to determine if the vaccination matched the health card.
2.   I had just barely escaped a felony. Is that what Martha Stewart had been accused of? Unlike her, I would have no mansion to return to.
3.   I was in deep, perhaps unredeemable, shit.

I collected myself and called Zaan corporate travel to rearrange my travel only to find out that my original flight had been delayed and I could still catch it if I raced to the gate.

It wasn't until we were in the air that it registered what a colossal mistake I'd just made. All that game-playing adrenaline made me stupid, stupid, stupid. I should have caught a cab and gone home. Things might have turned out significantly different if I had.

At the very least, I should have called Eddy before I called Zaan travel. He would have been a beacon of common sense. But he'd so persistently ingrained in me that if you were going to use a cell phone, you might just as well walk over to all your neighbors—well, and the NSA—and give them a typewritten copy of what you expected to say in your telephone conversation. This would also be the appropriate time to give them all your charge card, checking account, and social security numbers.

So instead, I sat on my flight—patient on the outside, hysterical on the inside. I was too nervous to think, too upset to even read. Mostly, I just sat with my face in my hands and tried not to think about what I was going to do.

FRANK ZAPPA ONCE SAID, "There is more stupidity than hydrogen in the universe, and it has a longer shelf life."

And he said it without ever having met me.

Mr. Greggen had rattled me so much that I could only think about getting on the plane and not, stupidly, about getting home again. What kind of a machine had I turned into? I dropped my load off at my desk at Baja Breeze and headed for a conference room for a private space to call Eddy on a landline.

"Eddy," I said as soon as he said hello. And then I started to sob. I'd held it in all morning and I couldn't anymore.

"Maggie, what's wrong? What happened?"

I couldn't stop crying and hearing his soothing voice on the other end made it worse, not better. Things would never be the same again. I finally set the receiver down for a minute while I hunted down a handful of Kleenexes out of some stranger's cubicle.

When I came back, I was only slightly more collected. But gradually I managed to get the story out in a trickle of bits and pieces.

When he'd finally put together enough of my story, he said, "So the bottom line is they knew you'd removed the capsule."

"Yes."

"But they didn't say how?"

"They knew it as soon as I walked through the metal detector."

"Damn. That should have been so obvious to us. In the larger scheme of things, the easiest part would be to add a receiver to the security process."

"It's an interesting dual system. You have to have the health card, but they're surreptitiously checking the accuracy of the health card with what's embedded in your arm."

"And the numbers have to match," he said.

"According to Tina," I said.

"Tina!" We both said it at the same time. I hadn't even thought of her since I sat in that glass booth purgatory.

"I'll call her as soon as we get off the phone."

"Tell her that I didn't ever tell them about her."

"But they asked about who removed it?"

"They did. I steered them back to whether in fact it had been removed."

"But the next person might not be so adept."

"The next person will be questioned after the eighteenth. It'll be a felony. They'll give up all the information they have as a bargaining chip." I started shaking again and the tears started welling up. It would have been me. What would I have said to escape a prison sentence?

We were both quiet for a moment. I'm sure Eddy was thinking through his own version of what might have been. He was the first to talk. "So now we have to figure out how to get you home."

I sniffled. It was the only response I could get out. Finally, I said, "Maybe you can FedEx my capsule to me at Baja Breeze. I can tape it on my arm or carry it in my pocket. Surely that would get me past the RFID receiver. It's not like the receiver could pick up that it's not embedded in my body, could it?"

"No. I don't want you to take the risk."

"It'll still match my health card. I think it could work," I said. Maggie the optimist.

"But we didn't anticipate this fiasco. Maggie, I just don't know if I can bear the idea of your going through security again." Eddy the pessimist.

"Just mail it. We can make a final decision after you've sent it. In the meantime, you can do some Googling. If you spot a red flag, we'll know before we try it."

I felt a tiny bit calmer.

It wasn't till after we hung up and I mentally sorted through the day one more time that I realized we had a tiny glitch: Mr. Greggen had kept my health card.

I immediately dialed Eddy back, but the line was busy. He must have picked up the phone to call Tina. I left a voicemail for him, scrambling to find the number for the phone I was calling from. I waited fifteen long minutes and tried calling again. This time the line wasn't busy, but no one answered. I wondered if he was already on his way to FedEx.

I went back to my desk and booted up my computer. While I waited for it to finish, I checked my cell phone and saw I had a message from Eddy. He'd tried calling the number back, but it rang into some other office. I tried calling him again from the phone in my cubicle, but he didn't answer.

I opened up email and tried to work, but it just wasn't going to happen. There wasn't a single thing that looked remotely important enough to even read, let alone think about and respond to, so I shut everything down again. I'd ended up with a whole day I couldn't bill a minute for, but that was the least of my problems. I packed up my computer and headed out the door to the hotel. Michael's cube was empty when I passed it. It was just as well. I wasn't ready to have any kind of a conversation with him until I talked more to Eddy.

When I got to my hotel room, I called Eddy and told him to call me as soon as he got in. And then I waited less than patiently for the phone to ring. I got online to see if he was on gtalk, but he wasn't. So I went to the concierge's lounge and got a glass of wine and some veggies and dip. There was no flashing light on my phone when I got back to my room. I drank the wine and looked at the veggies. I had no appetite. I turned on the TV and tried to find something familiar, so I wouldn't have to concentrate. I caught the last of *Jeopardy* and then found a station hosting a *Friends* marathon. It was a double win: familiar and mindless. I turned the sound down on the TV and surfed the Internet.

Around eight, I went back to the lounge, got a refill of wine, and returned to my room. Still no flashing light. I called home and the answering machine picked up again. This wasn't like him to leave in the evening, so the only logical conclusion I could come up with was that I should be worried. Given how my morning started, I decided I should be really worried.

I finally turned off my computer and the TV. I crawled into bed to try to sleep, but my nerves continued to jangle, so I lay with my eyes shut, my mind wide awake.

Finally, at about eleven fifteen my time—twelve fifteen in Colorado—the phone rang.

"Eddy?" I said before he could say hello. "What's going on? Are you okay?"

"I'm fine." He sounded tired. "But Tina's not."

"What?"

"I didn't get to her in time."

"What do you mean? What happened?"

"As soon as we got off the phone this afternoon, I called to her office. The receptionist was really vague but said Tina wasn't in the office. So I called her at home, thinking maybe she was off today. There was no answer there, and I just got the answering machine at Pete's body shop. So I called back to Tina's office and said I was a close friend of Tina's. I had a family emergency and needed to reach her. The receptionist wouldn't tell me anything except that she didn't expect Tina in for the rest of the week. So that's when I took off to try to track them down. It just didn't sound right."

"So what happened to her?" Wild possibilities tumbled through my head. At least Eddy was okay.

"I'm getting there. I drove over to Pete's shop because I thought they'd be more likely to tell me something. I caught Freddy, that ponytailed guy. He said Pete was at the police station because the Feds had come in and arrested Tina."

"Arrested her?" Oh my God. "For what? For what she did to me?"

"They've got a list of things, apparently, and yeah, that's one of them, although Pete says they don't have any names, just accusations. But the whole list they're charging her with is all homeland security violations."

"So they'll be felonies."

"Looks like it."

"You found Pete, then?"

"I did, finally. He was at the downtown police station, trying to track down what had happened to Tina. No one would tell him. They just kept giving him a runaround. At first they denied she was there or had even been brought in, but then he got some clerk to admit that there were all kinds of Feds taking over some of the interrogation rooms."

"Did Pete get a good attorney?"

"He found one, but it's too early to tell if he's good. They finally gave him a list of the charges, but he wasn't able to even talk to Tina yet."

"What? Why not?"

"They'd already taken her some place else."

"You mean like Florence?" The federal penitentiary, the one where the first person died of smallpox while being held without bond waiting for trial—it meant the rules had changed.

"They won't say."

"But they can't just whisk her away. They have to give her access to her attorney, don't they?"

Eddy sighed. "Apparently not under the Homeland Security Act. If they say she's a threat to national security, all legal protection disappears."

"Eddy—"

"I know."

Neither of us talked for a minute, too overwhelmed with possibilities.

"Pete must be beyond crazy."

"He is."

I started crying softly. I didn't want Eddy to hear me. The day had started all about me, and now something even worse had happened.

"I'm going to write up some stuff for the website. I'll post as much detail as I can and then try to summarize the rest."

"Don't. Please."

"Maggie, I don't have a choice."

"No. Look at what could happen to you. You have to stay under the radar." He could hear my tears, I'm sure.

"That's exactly why I have to do it. As long as people stay under the radar, this can continue to grow."

I could barely breathe through my tears, but I managed to whisper. "I love you, Eddio."

"You, too, Mz M. More than you'll ever know."

I hung up the phone before it registered that we hadn't talked about my missing health card or how I would ever get home again. The small things.

I lay back in bed, expecting to never sleep again. But I'd been in an adrenaline-fueled free-fall since six that morning; exhaustion finally won. I slept like a drugged woman until the alarm buzzed me awake at six thirty.

Chapter
27

DON'T ASK ME WHY I EVEN WENT INTO WORK on Tuesday. It's not like I could put three interesting words together or that I would even have a job by the end of the week. I went in, I guess, because I was like a terminally ill patient straightening out my life details in anticipation of my impending death. In fact, that was closer to the truth than I cared to admit. My life as I knew it was over.

As I was logging on, Michael stopped by my cubicle.

"You okay?"

"No," I said. "Not remotely." I didn't dare even try to say more because that would only guarantee I'd start crying instead.

"What's going on?"

I shook my head. It was too complicated to explain.

"You want to go to lunch today?" he asked.

"Sure."

He smiled. "Thai okay? I'm always up for Thai."

I at least had the presence of mind to write out Eddy's website on a sticky note for Michael. I knew there'd be something about yesterday there already. It was his style. "Memorize it and then shred it." I smiled grimly.

Michael laughed.

"I'm not kidding, Michael."

I spent the rest of the morning cobbling together a PowerPoint presentation for Michael to present to the project executive steering committee and ghostwriting an email for the CEO to thank the Baja Breeze team for the long hours they were investing to make this a successful project. It was all I could do not to embed an eye-rolling icon in the email signature. Regardless, as I reviewed the email, I realized I was teetering ever closer to the chicken shit side of the equation.

During a late-morning conference call with the Zaan training consultant and the Baja Breeze training staff and their manager who was working from home because the traffic report was bad —I swear that's what she told me—I brought up Eddy's site. I only needed to half-listen on the call or, more accurately, I could have skipped the call altogether, but that would have required someone such as the traffic-phobic training manager to summarize the call in an email and give me a few simple details to put in future communications about upcoming Zaan training.

Eddy hadn't shown up on gtalk yet, and by looking at the site it was easy to tell why. He'd pulled an all-nighter, no doubt a victim of his own adrenaline free-fall. Next to the now-permanent box that listed things people had been detained or arrested for, the home page held two unattributed "news briefs." The knowing eye—mine—could easily see that the news stories didn't come from any official source but were created by Eddy. He and I had had lots of discussions about whether this was ethical. I came down on the side that said a spade should announce itself a spade. Let people make up their own minds whether the substance and the source had credibility. He always argued that he only played the game that everyone, especially the government, played in releasing propaganda under the guise of news. Let the buyer beware.

Tina's story was first and then mine, as it should have been. I had been terrified, yes, but mostly I faced inconvenience. God only knew what Tina faced. In spite of my phone calls to Eddy, he also had a lot more details about Tina since he spent half the night with Pete trying to track down where she was. Both news blurbs linked to more detailed accounts, although mine was sketchy and avoided giving my name or even telling whether in fact I still had my vaccination. Basically, it informed the reader of the Gestapo tactics, confirmed airport security checked the vaccination against the health card, and warned about the threat of a felony if the health card didn't match the vaccination.

The ensuing information about Tina included the list of charges against her. Under the Homeland Security Act, Eddy noted, every item on the list was a felony. My stomach softly flipped over and over as I read them:

- Aiding and abetting terrorist activity
- Deliberately contributing to spreading the smallpox virus
- Destroying government property
- Illegally withholding information
- Falsifying information
- Contributing to the criminal behavior in others
- Performing subversive activities
- Organizing a terrorist cell (Eddy clarified this bullet: under Homeland Security, any group of two or more who discussed subversive activities could be convicted of this.)

How could Tina defend herself against those kinds of charges? Especially if the government could deny her access to legal council.

"You got that, Maggie?" Geanna, the Zaan training consultant, asked.

"I think I got most of it." Not true at all. There wasn't a single thing I could repeat from the call except that the traffic report looked bad. I'd be backpedaling with Geanna to cover my butt on this one. Or maybe I just wouldn't do it since I'd be gone soon. It was the most comforting thought I'd had in thirty-six hours.

We ended the call, but I couldn't tear myself away from Eddy's work. I wished he would get on gtalk so I could find out if he knew anything more. I tried calling home, but the answering machine picked up. He might have had the ringer turned down to sleep, or maybe he was in the shower. Or maybe he was out on his white horse riding the streets of Colorado Springs, poking around in ways that could only take him bad places. I hoped it wasn't the last. Mixed metaphor or not, there wasn't a white horse rider alive who knew how to stay under the radar.

"DID YOU HAVE A CHANCE TO LOOK AT THE SITE?" I asked Michael as soon as we were out of earshot of the smokers who congregated outside the Baja Breeze building. We walked briskly in the direction of the restaurant. Everything Zaan consultants did, we did briskly.

He nodded. Unfortunately, he had the same sick look on his face that I know I had.

"And?"

He shook his head. "It's all so unbelievable."

"All is a pretty broad word."

"All. Every bit of it." He ended with a hedge. "If it's true, that is."

"It's true."

He ran his fingers through his hair. "The RFID stuff, the charade the government is running, the Homeland Security stuff."

"Did you read the two news briefs on the first page?"

"Yeah. I skimmed them."

"That second one? The one about the woman nearly getting arrested at the airport? That was me."

Abruptly, he stopped walking and stared at me. "I should have guessed." He sighed and started walking again. "What are you going to do?"

"I don't know. Here's another one for you. Eddy avoided

pointing out that the doctor, the one in the first news brief, was the one who removed my vaccination capsule."

"Are the two connected? Do you think you were detained because they knew about her?"

I shook my head. "I don't think so. I think they detected that I didn't have the vaccination anymore."

"But now they'll connect the dots. You'll be tainted, too."

"If she gives them my name."

"Will she?"

Selfishly, I'd thought about this possibility at least ten or fifteen times every minute since my alarm had sounded. "How can she not? If they'd carted me down to the federal penitentiary and did God knows what to me, would I have been able to maintain my integrity and not implicate her?"

"You didn't though."

"Michael, I was held at the airport for an hour. If that little TSA Nazi had been only a little better skilled, who knows what I would have told him to get out of there."

"You're selling yourself short."

"I wish." I knew I wasn't, though. "I think I'm just human, which is why they can get away with this crime in the first place."

We reached the Tiger Lily and found a table in long-legged Kai's station. Michael wouldn't even need actual food to be happy with lunch.

"How are you going to get home this weekend?" he asked as soon as we were seated.

I shook my head and shrugged my shoulders. Any more, and I'd get teary eyed.

"Are you going to get re-vaccinated?"

"Are you kidding? That's the last thing I'll do. Have you gotten vaccinated?"

He shook his head. "I'm passing on this one. And after looking at Eddy's site, I know I made the right choice."

Kai arrived at that moment to confirm my curry choice for the day. She flirted with Michael and somewhere in there confirmed that he wanted his usual.

"Your usual? How often do you eat here?" I asked when Kai left.

Michael blushed. "Maybe once or twice a week." His eyes darted to the left. "Sometimes three times."

Thai food three times a week seemed a little much even for a man in love. Unless you were Thai, of course.

"But you still haven't asked her out."

"I will some day."

I rolled my eyes, but I was glad to be distracted from my own problems for two minutes.

"What if she says no?" He sounded genuinely worried.

"What's the worst that could happen? You'd have to start eating more pizza." We passed two pizzerias to get to the Tiger Lily. "Or you might actually have to eat in the Baja Breeze cafeteria."

Kai set down our drinks and our lunches, mine a spicy yellow curry and Michael's a delicately scented basil chicken. The place hadn't filled up yet, and she didn't seem to be in a hurry to move on. "So what's the go-live date du jour?"

Right. Once or twice a week.

Michael smiled shyly at her. "They're still saying March first, come hell or high water."

Kai rolled her eyes.

"Unless, of course, someone gets a hangnail," he added.

Kai laughed. "I don't know how you can stand it."

"Well, a good close Thai restaurant seems to be helping him a lot." I smiled at her and winked at Michael.

Michael giggled softly and turned red.

Kai patted Michael's hand and laughed. "And I'm doing whatever I can to help."

"Are you?" I asked her.

"Anything for my best tipper." She smiled broadly.

"Are you doing anything on Saturday night?"

Michael's eyes widened, and he looked like he wanted to just slide under the table.

Kai looked a little taken aback. "Uh. No. Do you need someone to build code or something?" She said it like she actually could but truly regretted making the offer.

I waved my hand. "No, nothing like that. Michael's not doing anything on Saturday night either. But he'd love to go dancing. I'll bet you're a great dancer, Kai."

Her eyes brightened and she threw her head to the side and laughed. Her perfectly straight jet-black hair swung easily with the move. "I'd *love* to go dancing. It's so nice of you to ask." She winked at me. "What time are you going to pick me up?"

The exchange had clearly rattled Michael. He looked at his watch as if that would tell him the time for Saturday night.

"I think eight," I said. "What do you think, Michael?"

Kai wagged her finger. "Let's make it seven. I'll cook you dinner before we go dancing." She smiled at him. "I know what you like."

Poor Michael just shook his head. He needed all the coaching he could get.

I said, "Michael, now it's your turn to say, 'Okay. See you at seven.'"

"Okay. Okay. Seven."

Kai laughed and scooted off to take the orders for another table.

"How do you know that I don't already have plans for Saturday?" he whispered across the table.

I rolled my eyes. "Right. And if you did, what would it have to be that you wouldn't cancel to go out with Kai?" I spooned some curry over my rice. "Maybe if your sister were getting married you'd cancel." It was his family joke. He had an exotically beautiful sister in her mid-thirties; his mother had been lighting candles for her for fifteen years to no avail.

He thought for a moment. "No. I'd probably ask my sister to move her wedding date." He clicked his chopsticks together a couple times and grabbed a piece of chicken. "She can get married any time. How many first dates does a guy get with someone like Kai?"

"Good. So you're not mad at me." I smiled.

He smiled, too.

"You owe me one, now. You know that." I smiled again.

We ate in silence for a few minutes. The distraction of the matchmaking took some of the edge off my own bad situation.

"So what do you think I should do?" I finally asked.

Apparently, the matchmaking had distracted Michael even more. He gave me a blank look.

"About traveling," I said.

He nodded. I wasn't sure if he was truly back in the conversation, but I gave him the benefit of the doubt.

"I can't do the commute between here and Colorado Springs anymore. When I leave this time, I won't be coming back."

Michael groaned and leaned back in his chair. "Surely we can figure out something." He tapped his chopsticks against his plate.

"Michael, we both know my heart hasn't been in this for months. Yesterday was just the last straw. I'm not going to get re-vaccinated."

"Maybe you can get an apartment out here. You wouldn't have to commute as often."

I actually laughed, probably the first time in two days. "You must be kidding. I can hardly tolerate the travel as it is. You think I'd give up even more time with Eddy just to keep working for this ... this ... " I didn't have a word for Zaan that I could say out loud.

"This deranged company?" Michael said it for me.

"That's too kind." I ate a few spoonfuls of curry and rice. "You know we're a major player behind all the RFID stuff."

Michael shrugged his shoulders. "If it wouldn't be us, it'd be somebody else. That's not a reason to leave."

"Are you kidding me?"

He looked a little startled.

"Where's the integrity in that? I don't care if somebody else might do it if Zaan didn't. Zaan is making all this possible. I don't want to be here anymore. Travel or no."

He leaned toward me across the table. "So what are you going to do? Quit?"

I rubbed my forehead. If I knew the answer to that, I'd already be out of here. "I don't know. Probably." I looked back at him, and it came to me. "Or maybe call in my chit. You owe me one." I smiled and tilted my head towards Kai, who was chatting with customers a couple of tables over, her eyes a little more animated than usual. "A big one."

He sighed. It fell somewhere between blissful and painful. "So what's the favor?"

"I want to meet with Sanjeev again."

"No," Michael said immediately. "He'll never meet with you—with us—again. He made it clear we were sticking our noses where they didn't belong."

"But he's our best source."

"Ours? How did this get to be my problem?"

"Michael." I probably sounded huffier than I should have. "Are you living in this country? Aren't you totally freaked out by all of this?"

He didn't answer.

"You think just because you haven't been detained this past week or because you don't have to travel this month that this isn't your problem. Can't you see where this is headed? Once most people have the vaccination, the sky is the limit." I lowered my voiced to a near whisper. "Where will the government stop?"

I glanced around the room. No one seemed to be paying any attention to us. "Tonight you spend a little time exploring some of the links Eddy has on his website about RFIDs. Take a look at all the possibilities. Europe is testing RFIDs in their Euros. The excuse is that they'll be able to track bank robbers and counterfeiters. But, oh by the way, they'll also be able to track what you do with the cash you withdraw from your ATM."

"Does it matter?" Michael asked but not very convincingly.

"I don't know? Does it? Isn't that the whole excuse the government gives about every Big Brother move? If you don't have anything to hide, why should it matter?"

"Look, I know it's creepy, but again, why would I care? I leave the airport, go to the hotel, go back to the airport, and go back home. They can pull up my credit card receipts and find out pretty much the same thing."

"Michael, that's just it. We're like that tired old cliché of the frog in boiling water. The frog swims around in a pot of water. You gradually turn up the heat on the pot. The water temperature creeps up, up, up until the frog literally boils alive because it never sensed when it was too hot. That's us. If you'd told us thirty years ago that the government would track every phone call we make and every email we write and then embed little radio tags in everyone's arm, the whole country would have freaked out and stormed the White House to throw the bum out. Instead, we've become so accustomed to losing our privacy and identity that we can live with just about anything because 'we're not doing anything wrong, so why should we care?'"

"You know what I mean."

"Unfortunately, I do. Until it somehow infringes on my activities, it's not worth getting into a frenzy over. Well here's the deal. The government decided it didn't like the fact that my friend Tina Bastante wasn't following the rules to a T. So now she's sitting in a federal penitentiary—no lawyer, no trial, no rights. Is that really the kind of country you want to live in?"

I didn't know how irritated he was at me by now, but I didn't care, either. "The most horrific violation of our civil rights just brings a shrug and an 'oh well, at least we're safe from terrorists.' What's next? A brand on the forehead so people can see at once if we're terrorists—make that potential terrorists?"

"It's wrong. I know it's wrong. But there's nothing we can do about it."

"I don't believe that."

His eyes shifted around the room. He lowered his voice. "Look, I know you can't begin to identify with me on this, but even though I'm a naturalized citizen, if I do something or get involved in something, the government can put me on the next plane back to the Philippines. No trial, no lawyer, no suitcase even. They just call me an undesirable, and I can never come back." Michael waved his chopsticks at me like a father lecturing a child. "Your friend Tina and her lost constitutional rights? That applies to everyone who wasn't born on this soil."

"What are you talking about? You're here legally. How can they ship you off?"

"Sanjeev's probably even more vulnerable than I am. He's probably just here on a green card. He can't even get many unpaid parking tickets, or they'll send him packing. It's the homeland security stuff. It's been growing ever since 9/11."

"You really believe they'd deport you?"

"I *know* they'd do that to me. My dad knows this guy from Penang who's been here for twenty years. He has a kid who's twenty-two, maybe twenty-three. The kid got caught with an ounce of marijuana and they sent *him* back to Malaysia."

"They sent him back to a country he left when he was two-years old? That's absurd." It wasn't that I didn't believe Michael, but it truly was, for want of a better word, absurd.

"No kidding. Not only that, the guy's attorney said that he could have been born here and they could have sent him back to Malaysia. It doesn't happen very often, but it *has* happened."

"And it only has to happen once and you make lots of believers."

"Word like that flies through immigrant communities. You think there's a Malaysian in California who doesn't know that story? I'll guarantee you that there wasn't a Malaysian in the state who smoked dope for a month following that." He actually laughed a little. "Or a Filipino."

"So you're saying that Sanjeev will refuse to help no matter what."

"Think about it. He's married, has a couple of kids, a house. Half his family and in-laws are living here now. What's he willing to risk?" He drummed his fingers lightly on the table. "What would you be willing to risk?"

I didn't answer.

"Where's your friend Tina from originally?" He said it kindly, in case it hadn't already occurred to me what he meant.

"El Salvador. Her family escaped the war down there." Tina had been five at the time. Only a few gruesome bits and pieces of her story had bubbled out into conversation in the two years we'd known her, all of them eased to the surface only after a couple glasses of wine.

"Illegals?"

"At the time. They got their citizenship during one of those amnesty times. They're legal now."

"She took a huge risk doing what she did," Michael said softly. "Maybe they're holding her in a federal penitentiary. Maybe she's already back in El Salvador."

I shook my head, not sure what would be the better of the two. "If she'd been deported, surely they would have let her contact her husband."

Michael glanced around the room, then looked me in the eye. "If she were in a situation to call him."

"What do you mean?" My heart rate picked up a couple beats.

He shook his head. "You Americans are so naïve."

"What do you mean, 'you Americans'? You're an American, too."

He shifted his eyes slightly. "Here we've just been having

this conversation about what the government does under the guise of a vaccination, and you still want to believe they play fair in everything else they do. You know all the stuff that came out about Guantanamo Bay. The US would never get its hands dirty by torturing. Oh no. That's barbaric. But they don't have any trouble doing 'enhanced interrogation' or putting those poor detainees on a plane to Afghanistan or Iraq or one of those places where they don't have any scruples about it. Some place where the US probably trained them in the latest technique of squeezing the last shred of information out of a brain before their pulse finally stops. Same end, just easier press conferences."

My throat felt thick. I couldn't think about Tina. Pretty, smart, vivacious Tina.

"Even the military feels sheepish about how many 'heart attacks' detainees have died from." He looked grim.

"Look." My voice caught. I paused and tried to push back the fear. "All I know is that the one person who can help us is Sanjeev. He knows what Zaan did there. He knows who did the software development. He knows the Achilles heel."

"What if there isn't an Achilles heel?"

"Michael," I laughed. "It's software. Some of it's nothing but heels. It'll have one. We just have to get to the right person."

"Sanjeev won't help."

"Try anyway."

Kai arrived at that moment with our ticket and her address and phone number. She'd circled "Saturday at 7:00" in red. "You looked a little distracted, so I wrote everything down." She smiled, no doubt distracting him further.

"I wouldn't miss it for anything."

Chapter
29

WHEN I GOT BACK TO MY COMPUTER, I saw I had a message—which turned out to be four instant messages—flashing from Eddy. I knew without looking that at least one of the messages would be a little (well-deserved) kick in the shins for leaving my computer running unattended for an hour. Habits die hard when inconvenience is the price for changing.

EddytheWebMan: *hey mz m.*

EddytheWebMan: *u there?*

EddytheWebMan: *ping me when you get back*

And sure enough, the little kick in the shins:

EddytheWebMan: *and a plague on your project for leaving your computer unattended this long.*

MRiderZaan: Hey.

EddytheWebMan: *where were you and why didnt you sign off?*

MRiderZaan: Stepped away for 5 minutes and it turned into lunch with Michael. My bad.

And not exactly true, either.

MRiderZaan: What's the latest on Tina?

EddytheWebMan: *not a whole lot more than what we knew last night ... pete's ready to buy a gun*

My fingers fumbled on the keyboard just thinking about where Tina could be at the moment. And what could be happening to her. This wasn't the moment to tell Eddy.

MRiderZaan: So he hasn't been able to even see her yet?

EddytheWebMan: *no contact at all ... still not even sure where she's being held ... all he knows is what he managed to drag out of the clerk at the police station last night ... and that little chick with the loose lips is probably looking for a job today*

MRiderZaan: So what's Pete doing to get some answers?

EddytheWebMan: *calling in all his cards ... he's been the car man for too long in this town ... knows too many fender bender stories and protected some serious butt over the years*

MRiderZaan: Lucky for him he has some leverage.

EddytheWebMan: *here's the other thing ...*

MRiderZaan: Yeah?

EddytheWebMan: *i'm getting megahits to the website these days.*

MRiderZaan: Even more than usual???? What were you up to? 14M?

EddytheWebMan: *14.8m ... but who's counting? the two stories on the front page are getting big attention ... the today show, good morning America, fox ... even cnn finally woke up.*

MRiderZaan: And???

EddytheWebMan: *they want interviews ... i be the man*

MRiderZaan: Whoohoo!!! You <u>are</u> the man! That's ble!lHtredi-

MRiderZaan: Except for that nasty little staying under the radar business.

EddytheWebMan: *i know i know ... thought of that too ... but hey i'm hardly under it now either*

MRiderZaan: ... and it is a_cool, cool opportunity.

EddytheWebMan: *it gives huge visibility to tina's situation too... maybe it's worth it*

MRiderZaan: Promise you'll think about it more before leaping.

EddytheWebMan: *will do*

MRiderZaan: When's this happening?

EddytheWebMan: *tomorrow for gma or today show ... both want an exclusive first ... fox will pick up the crumbs tomorrow pm or thursday*

MRiderZaan: uh ... not much time to think ... Maybe you can put a plug in for my plight, too. I still don't know how I'm getting home.

EddytheWebMan: *i know mz m. i haven't forgotten that or u ... tina's trip to the big house just seemed to trump everything.*

MRiderZaan: As it should.

EddytheWebMan: *gotta run.*

MRiderZaan: Me too.

EddytheWebMan: *xoxo*

MRiderZaan: u2

Chapter
30

EDDY NEEDED AN AGENT or at least someone who could give some sage advice about what to negotiate for, what to expect, and what to avoid. Barring that, he could have at least used twenty-four hours to think about a TV interview instead of twelve. In the end, he went with Good Morning America.

His segment ran in the first hour, and then they repeated clips of it in the second hour news segments, so they must have snagged some mega response with the first showing.

I'd assumed the segment would be just a straight interview with Eddy about his website and the attention it was garnering with this latest report about Tina Bastante. Instead, GMA had lined up a spokesman for the CDC who joined Eddy in a split screen for a point counterpoint sparring. Of course Eddy won. Even if I weren't eternally and totally devoted to him, I would believe that. The CDC sent in the B-team, no doubt because they foolishly assumed Eddy would either be a fringe conspiracy fanatic or a twenty-something funky web designer that would start every sentence with "Dude." They were completely wrong on both counts.

The CDC spokesman, Paul Wilder, was ten years Eddy's senior and slightly overweight. He looked like someone found him a tie at the last minute and someone who had never met the first someone found him a jacket right after that. In contrast,

Eddy had dressed all by himself. Whether it was intentional or not, Eddy went for more of an Ozzie and Harriet look—crisp, cream shirt unbuttoned at the top with the rust colored cashmere cardigan I'd given him for Christmas. That combined with his blue eyes, innocent smile, and the crinkles around his eyes when he laughed gave him a deceptively simple, everyday-Joe look. That part was pretty much true. He also looked relaxed, which I knew he wasn't.

The CDC guy made the mistake of trying to rattle Eddy by belittling him for not only having these far-fetched conspiracy theories, but posting them to his website so everyone could see them. Eddy looked surprised and puzzled from the get go. "Conspiracy theory?" he asked in response to Paul Wilder's first volley. "What part of smallpoxscare.com isn't grounded in fact?"

Here's where the CDC man should have done his homework. Nowhere on Eddy's website was there something that wasn't factual. There was no link to a Conspiracy Theories page. He didn't even actually refer to the government unless the department played a role somewhere. So he had posted lots of CDC's own press releases right beside tiny but contradictory, questioning news items from *The New York Times* or the *Washington Post* that had been buried back on section B, page 32, right next to the ad for Bali bras. Even the accounts of Tina's and my Monday in hell were written as straight news rather than editorial tirades.

I have a thing for men with restraint.

The cumulative effect, however, pulsed with a more sinister undertone. After all, at least a month before he knew for sure they were connected, he *had* raised the specter of radio frequency identification tags. So the CDC man may have been on the right track, but technically, he didn't have a single specific example to use. In the few seconds of fumbling that followed, Eddy took the offensive.

"Perhaps you'd be willing to explain what happened to Dr. Bastante," Eddy began. "She was handcuffed and led out of her office. Her office searched as though she were a criminal. Yet she hasn't been able to contact a lawyer or even her husband. He has no idea where she's being held or why. Is this the new future for law-abiding citizens?"

"If she were law-abiding, I'm sure this wouldn't have happened to her."

"So what's she been charged with, Mr. Wilder?" He knew full well what she'd been charged with. He'd posted it to the website himself.

"I'm not aware of the particulars of her case. That would be under the authority of the Department of Homeland Security, not the CDC." He smirked slightly. A mistake.

Eddy looked surprised and he turned to talk to someone off camera. "Isn't this why you invited me to be on the show this morning? To talk about the attention smallpoxscare.com has been generating because of the information about Dr. Tina Bastante?" He paused a moment, then turned back to the camera. "Perhaps, Mr. Wilder, you weren't given the same information I was. What were you invited to talk about?"

Mr. Wilder cleared his throat and lined up the ends of his tie—a nervous gesture that was all the more obvious because his girth caused the too-short tie to end a couple shirt buttons too soon. "I was told we'd be talking about the foolishness you have posted on your website. The stuff that's making people second-guess the wisdom of getting the smallpox vaccination. Your foolishness—" Uh oh. A CDC man with a small-vocabulary. "—is putting the nation at risk. We're already in a crisis. Over fifteen hundred people have died from the disease and nearly sixty-five hundred have symptoms. You and this foolish—" three times in three sentences; this man needed coaching "—website will drive those numbers significantly higher if people are afraid to get vaccinated."

"I see, and what on smallpoxscare.com is making people do that?"

I laughed out loud. He couldn't have asked a more dangerous question.

Paul Wilder didn't laugh, though. "How dare you scare people away from getting the vaccine? Is that what you want on your shoulders? The knowledge that you single-handedly let this horrific epidemic—"

"Mr. Wilder," Eddy held up his hands as though stopping the tirade, but he didn't try to talk over him. "Mr. Wilder. Excuse me." He gave a shrug to the camera.

Robin Roberts interrupted, "Mr. Wilder, I think Mr. Rider has a good question. "What is it on his website that's making people afraid to get the vaccination?"

The CDC man poked his finger repeatedly toward the camera, I guess because that was the closest he could get to poking at Eddy's shirt. "How many more people have to die from this gruesome disease? How many? Before this man takes down his website?"

Robin Roberts said, "Mr. Wilder, we have thirty seconds. What last comment do you have for our listeners?"

Poor Mr. Wilder's face glistened red, "This man and his website will end up killing more people than all those al Qaeda terrorists combined. He needs to be stopped! He's so worried about one doctor who—" Paul Wilder's mike went dead.

"And Mr. Rider? Any last comments?"

"Thanks. I'm not sure if Mr. Wilder's comment is a threat, but it's suddenly very clear to me that the last thing the government wants is for people to go to smallpoxscare.com. Maybe they're afraid people will discover something they don't want them to know. However, I believe Ambrose Redmoon said it best: 'Courage is not the absence of fear, but rather the judgment that something else is more important than fear.' Whatever is happening to this country is more important than fear. I hope people will have the courage to check out smallpoxscare.com for more information about what's really happening." He smiled.

Mr. Wilder grimaced.

They really should have sent in the A-team.

FOUR TIMES IN FOUR MINUTES. Eddy couldn't have asked for better publicity for his website. I couldn't believe the CDC had been so stupid that they let him put in so many plugs for the very thing they were trying to get people not to go look at.

But things aren't always what they seem to be, as I was once again reminded as soon as I logged in at Baja Breeze. Eddy pinged me before I could even download my email.

EddytheWebMan: *u there?*

MRiderZaan: I am ... Eddio ... you were fabulous ... you knocked 'em dead!

EddytheWebMan: *yeah ... well*

MRiderZaan: I couldn't believe how that CDC idiot kept handing you great openings to pumping your web site.

EddytheWebMan: *yeah ... well ...*

MRiderZaan: So are you checking the hits? You have to have a gazillion more.

EddytheWebMan: *i do. here's the other thing i have.*

MRiderZaan: What?

EddytheWebMan: *i have your health card.*

MRiderZaan: What??? Did that sleazeball CDC guy give it to you?

EddytheWebMan: *no*

MRiderZaan: ???

EddytheWebMan: *it was sitting on my computer keyboard when i got home this a.m.*

Oh Lord. My fingers froze on the keyboard.

EddytheWebMan: *u there?*

MRiderZaan: Yes. But I'm not breathing.

EddytheWebMan: *i know*

MRiderZaan: So someone was in our house while you were gone.

EddytheWebMan: *yes. not good.*

MRiderZaan: No. Not good at all. Any other sign?

EddytheWebMan: *who needs a second sign? i understand the first one perfectly: doesn't matter what's happening in public ... they'll do any damn thing they want in private because who can stop them?*

MRiderZaan: I think I'm going to be sick.

EddytheWebMan: *nothing would make them happier.*

MRiderZaan: I know.

EddytheWebMan: *mz m?*

MRiderZaan: Yeah?

EddytheWebMan: *stay put this weekend. now more than ever we have to have a plan.*

MRiderZaan: You have one?

EddytheWebMan: *nope ... but i'll think of something ... eventually*

MRiderZaan: I'm counting on you Eddio ... What about Tina? Any news?

EddytheWebMan: *nothing. nada. zip. pete's on the verge of needing hospital time.*

MRiderZaan: I would be too. Think she's been deported?

I couldn't help myself. It just slipped out.

EddytheWebMan: *huh? that's a heart stopper ... think it's possible?*

MRiderZaan: Could be. Had an interesting conversation with Michael about it yesterday ...

EddytheWebMan: *tell me about it later. don't think i'll raise the possibility with pete … he really would kill someone … or lots of someones …*

MRiderZaan: No doubt.

EddytheWebMan: *gotta run … xoxo*

MRiderZaan: u2

I X'd out of Eddy's gtalk and then pinged him again.

MRiderZaan: Eddio … u there? What time are you headed out for the Fox interview?

EddytheWebMan: *Signed off at 8:47 a.m. PST.*

I tried to work through my email. For at least four minutes plus the forty-five-minute afterglow, I thought there was a chance we'd turned the corner. Naiveté will do that to you. Now my day had turned heavy. I knew I'd be there until sometime the next week or maybe forever. I had to figure out what to do but nothing came to me.

Late morning, I stopped by Michael's cubicle.

"Did you see Eddy on *Good Morning America* this morning?"

Michael nodded. "Very impressive. Even if the CDC guy hadn't been so inarticulate, Eddy was good."

"Did you hear back from Sanjeev?"

Michael sighed. "I didn't even try. He'll say no. I already know that."

I glanced over my shoulder and then rose to my tiptoes to scout who might be within earshot. Unfortunately, the closest ears—the ones belonging to the people in the adjacent cubicles—weren't visible to me unless I climbed up on Michael's desk. I tilted my head toward the elevator. "Walk me down to get some coffee?" I knew he was busy, but I really needed to talk to someone about my health card reappearing.

He grimaced slightly. "Can it wait till lunch? I'm buried."

"Please?"

He sighed but got up and followed me.

As soon as we were clear of the cubicles, I said, "We've had an interesting little complication."

"In what way?"

"My health card showed up again."

"You found it then? The TSA didn't take it after all?" He perked up slightly.

"I didn't find it. It showed up. Big difference." I glanced around again to see if anyone was close. "It was on Eddy's computer when he got back from his interview this morning."

Michael's eyes widened. He backed up against the wall like he needed the support.

"We have to talk to Sanjeev again, Michael. He's the only starting point we have."

The elevator dinged, and a moment later the doors opened. A Baja Breeze VP got off and headed toward the executive suite without a smile or a hello in our direction. I'd learned long ago that consultants were either gods or invisible, depending on the state of the implementation. No question what state we were in at the moment.

Michael shook his head while he waited for the VP to disappear. "I'm not arguing with you, Maggie. But we've been through this already. He won't take the risk. I know he won't."

"So he saves his own skin. What does he lose for everyone else in the process?"

Michael sighed.

"We have to talk him into it."

I didn't trust Michael to follow through, so I took matters into my own hands.

"Do you have his home address?"

Michael shook his head. "Just his email, cell phone number, and gtalk name."

"Give me what you have."

I grabbed a salad to go downstairs in the company cafeteria and spent the rest of my lunch hour at my desk. Usually, when I do that, I'm knocking out some major project. Today, I surfed the Net. I felt guilty about it, which really irritated me.

First, I set Sanjeev up as a buddy in my Google Talk. He was on gtalk at the moment, for what that was worth. Then I started digging for information on him. I began with the Zaan corporate employee website. Like the rest of us, Sanjeev didn't have an actual office. Instead, when he wasn't at a client site, he worked out of his house. Even though he worked from home, he gave the address for corporate headquarters as his work address. It meant nothing in this situation. I used the Denver Zaan office for my work address, even though I hadn't been there for over a year.

My next hope was that he would still have a landline, but that was a slim possibility. After all the belt tightening in the economic downturn after 9/11 and again in 2008, most people had given up their office phones and only had their cell phones, which wouldn't be traceable. Sure enough, I did a reverse search on the phone number and it came up without any information. Still, I at least had his area code. Since it was different than the area code for headquarters, I had hope that it might be for where he lived. I felt lucky to at least have that since some employees lived in areas that didn't get good cell plans. They got their phone plans using Zaan headquarters as their home address.

Then I did an Ixquick search for Sanjeev Srivastava in California: sixteen Sanjeev Srivastavas popped up. Apparently, it was the John Brown of Indian names. I doubted there were two Margaret Riders in Colorado. I felt lily-white and very egocentric. By eliminating the ones that had a different area code than Sanjeev's Zaan number, I was down to three.

Three was better than sixteen, but it was still two too many.

I scratched my head and thought for a few minutes. My ill-formed plan required the right address. I could have tried calling, but surprise gave me a better hand of cards to play.

Finally, I went to find Michael. I needed more clues. "Do you know Sanjeev's wife's name?"

He chewed his lower lip for a minute. "P something. I think."

It was worth a try. I went back and searched "P Srivastava." A list of eighty-six P Srivastavas popped up. I skimmed for the 408 area code that Sanjeev had, which narrowed the list to six. I wrote down the P Srivastava names and took the list back to quiz Michael with. I wasn't altogether sure which ones were male and which ones were female names.

"Praveen, Priyanka, Padma—"

"Padma," he said before I could get the rest of the names out.

"Good." I went back and did a reverse search on the phone number that was listed for Padma Srivastava. The name that popped up? Sanjeev and Padma Srivastava.

I'd hit gold. At least I was pretty sure.

Once I had that, I went to Mapquest and first plugged in Sanjeev's address. I knew already that he was in the San Jose area, which Mapquest confirmed. Then I mapped the distance between his address and my hotel. He was less than an hour away.

I'd had a project in San Jose a couple of years earlier, so I knew the area a little. Mostly, I just went to work and then went to the hotel and ordered room service. I could still remember a funky little vegetarian restaurant that I stopped by at least once a week to get my quota—and at least two other people's quota—of piña colada smoothies. As I recall, that was also the project I had to go out and buy a whole new wardrobe of slacks, size eight.

Damn smoothies.

I searched for vegetarian restaurants in San Jose and then for anything within a radius of two miles of the Sheraton I'd lived in, and I finally stumbled over it: Greens & Beans.

My homework done, I printed off two pages from Eddy's

website: the page with RFID information and the first page, which now included an updated link to his *Good Morning America* interview. The accounts of Tina's and my experiences were pretty much unchanged from the first posting. I noticed that Eddy hadn't updated my account with the news that my health card had reappeared. But then I realized, he'd never added that tidbit to begin with.

At the bottom of the page, I wrote in red ink: Greens & Beans 7:30 p.m., Thursday. I found an envelope with a Baja Breeze return address, tucked the letter inside, and sealed it. Even without my name anywhere on the envelope, Sanjeev would know the letter was from me—assuming I could deliver it without some federal type swooping in on Sanjeev or me. Although in the long run, I'm sure I was inadvertently leaving enough breadcrumbs at every step that the Feds would be able to saunter in, rather than swoop. By the time the envelope made its way back to Baja Breeze and some federal type made the connection, I'd probably already be locked up some place because of all the other breadcrumbs I was inadvertently leaving. That, or I'd be on a plane back to England, the land of some long-gone ancestor.

Is that how it would be for me?

Chapter
32

Eddy didn't call or ping me the rest of the day. I could only assume he'd been running late for his interview with Fox News and ran out of time, but it still irritated me a little. Well, to tell you the truth, the irritation hovered on worry. If he were willing to carry a cell phone, even one with minimal minutes, he could at least call me while he drove. But he hated the things even more than he distrusted them. Now, more than ever, he would never give in.

I cut out of Baja Breeze early—early being just after six—and headed south to San Jose. Traffic still clogged 101. I should have waited thirty minutes and I would have ended up in San Jose about the same time, but at the moment, I truly preferred sitting in traffic to sitting in a cubicle, grim though they both were. While I drove, I scanned for a radio station that had something in a language I could understand, finally settling on some local radio personality who roared on and on with some caller about these ingrates who land on American soil and then flout the laws and *then*—more roaring—want some kind of immunity. I reached to scan for a new station—Chinese was preferable to this garbage—just as the caller said, "You'd think a doctor of all people would appreciate her life here."

A doctor. Her life. My sinuses cleared. They were ranting about Tina. Eddy's five minutes of fame on *Good Morning* America had kicked a soft spot somewhere. I turned the volume up.

172

"You'd think a doctor, of all people, would understand this horrific epidemic," the man who only roared said.

Horrific epidemic? The CDC man's words from Eddy's interview this morning.

The caller sneered. "Exactly. I say give *her* a dose of smallpox and see how she feels about digging out those vaccinations."

I gasped and reached for the scan button but didn't press it. I couldn't listen, yet I couldn't turn it off. I was frozen in that in between state of revulsion and fascination. What kind of horrible people would say something like that? The two voices traded nasty, empty ideas for several more minutes until they cut to a commercial.

The next caller began a tirade about something else that was probably the same as this because it was hateful and mean. It just had a different name and description. The radio guy roared about that, too. I guess it was his job.

I wiped the palms of my hands on my slacks and tried to stay focused on the road.

Sanjeev had to help.

When I got to San Jose, I found a Target and pulled into the parking lot. I had one chance at my plan. If I screwed this up, I didn't have another idea. My hands shook and the back of my neck ached. It was only seven fifteen, but it felt like midnight to my body. The short harangue on the radio had left me on the verge of tears. I needed to talk to Eddy, but when I tried the home phone, he didn't answer. I thought his Fox interview had been four-ish, so he should have been back home by now. I wondered if he was at Pete's, shoring him up for whatever discontent Tina's situation had become a lightning rod for. It was the right place for him to be, but I was sorry he wasn't at home for me.

Finally, I ran my fingers through my hair and put on some lipstick and headed into the store. I only needed to pick up a few things, but I took a cart anyway, as much for a crutch as for what it needed to carry. I didn't trust my knees.

Back in the car, I checked my Mapquest directions and found the Pizza Hut closest to Sanjeev's. I ordered a medium vegetarian pizza to go and then sat and waited for it. I should have been starving, and in fact, I probably was, but I'd lost touch with all those physical signals. I could only feel the throbbing of my heart, the pounding behind my eyes, the tightness in my throat. When the pizza was finally ready, I got back in the car, tied my auburn curls up in a ponytail, and pulled on the Giants baseball cap and T-shirt I'd just bought. I loaded up my eyes with eye makeup and swiped another layer of lipstick on. If someone was looking for me specifically, they'd still be able to figure out it was me, but in the dusky evening light, I hoped I could pass for just one more teenager delivering pizza.

My last step was to put the Baja Breeze envelop in a plastic bag and put it inside the pizza box. And then I headed over to Sanjeev Srivastava's house.

He lived in one of those modest California neighborhoods that probably started in the six-hundred-thousand range, even in San Jose. The houses, all one level, sort of Spanish stucco ranchers built sometime in the eighties, were a dizzying repetition of each other, distinguished only by a wildly blooming bougainvillea here, a carefully tamed pfitzer there. My heart verged on exploding in my ears by the time I pulled up to Sanjeev's house. A few cars were scattered along the street, but they looked empty. If someone was watching the address, I couldn't tell.

The place looked dark except for a light in a room at the back of the house, which cast a yellow shadow through the front window and onto the lawn. There were no cars in the drive, but the garage door was down, so that didn't tell me anything. Sanjeev could be home or not.

I took a couple of deep breaths, gathering in every molecule of courage in my bones. What was the worst that could happen? Sanjeev himself could answer the door and slam it back in my face, right?

Well, no. If he were being watched, I would be seen, which could put his family and him on the next plane to Bangalore. And I would have been the one to leave the trail as surely as if I'd painted a bright red arrow up his sidewalk. There were a lot worse things that could happen than getting a door slammed in my face. But the longer I sat, the more suspicious I looked, so I forced myself to get out of the car and walk like a pizza delivery person, which I thought would be fast and direct. Gotta get those pizzas delivered.

I rang the bell and waited. This is the truth. A fire engine could have raced up the street behind me and I wouldn't have heard the siren because of all the blood rushing through my head. I counted to ten and then counted to ten again before I pressed the doorbell again. The door opened at that moment. And there he stood, looking more tired and somehow smaller than he had when we'd met just a week earlier.

For some dumb reason, I had expected Sanjeev's wife or mother or kids to answer. It didn't occur to me that he'd actually be home, even though it was closing in on eight. Too much Zaan conditioning, I guess. What kind of a project manager would be home before his kids went to bed?

"Vegetarian pizza?" I said and looked him in the eye.

He ignored me and looked at the pizza box in my hand. He shook his head but still didn't make eye contact. "Pizza? We didn't order a pizza. You must have the wrong address."

"I have an order for Sanjeev Srivastava." I held the box out to him.

At the sound of his name, his eyes finally connected with mine and widened. He suddenly put his hand against the doorjamb, like he was going to pass out, but he didn't. His eyes narrowed and his mouth shaped around the word "What—" but no sound came out.

From behind him, dishes rattled in the kitchen. They'd had curry for dinner and something with garlic. A chirrupy child's voice rattled off a question; an older, mellower voice answered. Sanjeev glanced back to the noise, then turned toward me again. He took the pizza box and shuffled awkwardly on his feet. I could have sworn he no longer was looking at me but past me. Then he gave a very, very small shake of his head and closed the door.

I didn't let myself think until I'd driven out of the neighborhood and back to a street with a strip of fast food places. I pulled into Baja Fresh, more to calm myself than because I thought I could keep a taco down.

It was real. The fear was there. It wasn't just my imagination. I wiped my palms again and closed my eyes. I hadn't seen anything specific—no cameras, no people peeking out the window from a neighboring house. Yet Sanjeev had the look of a caged animal, a watched caged animal. I had to talk to Eddy, cell phone or not. But the phone rang and then switched to the answering machine. Maybe he was with Pete or out celebrating his interviews from today. But a little voice inside me softly snorted. I tried not to think about where else he could be.

When my nerves had finally settled down and my blood pressure dropped out of stroke range, I pulled out of the parking lot and headed back north to my hotel. Less than an hour later, I arrived in one piece, but I couldn't have told you a thing about the drive except that I was pretty sure I hadn't hit another car.

I ordered soup from room service and called home. It was nearly ten o'clock in Colorado, but the answering machine picked up. I wanted to pour out my whole evening to him. I desperately needed him to tell me I'd done the right thing. Instead, I left as cheery a message as I could for him to call me, then began mentally drumming my fingers.

While I waited for room service, I turned on my computer and got online. As I waited for systems to load, I flipped through the TV channels until I found Fox News. It would have been nice to know when they expected to run the segment with Eddy or if they even planned to run it that same day. Maybe I'd already missed it, but I knew they could film the interview and not run it for several days or not run it at all if they decided it wasn't shrill enough. Eddy still hadn't called or logged in to gtalk by the time I finished eating, so I called home again. This time I didn't leave a message. He knew I'd be an arm's reach from the phone all night. He'd call. He always did.

I surfed the Internet for a while, looking for any news about Tina, but very little popped up. What did pointed me back to Eddy's site. Disheartened that his *Good Morning America* interview hadn't generated more visibility for her, I turned off the computer, packed it away, and got ready for bed.

By Letterman time, I finally decided Fox wouldn't be running his segment, so I switched over to CBS. I tried to stay annoyed with—rather than anxious about—Eddy not calling. I'd pumped enough adrenaline through my body for a week with my trip to Sanjeev, and now this worry about Eddy not calling etched away at the little remaining energy I had. The next thing I knew, Letterman had turned into an old James Bond movie, and the clock read 2:00 a.m. I turned off the TV and lay there, debating whether to call Eddy and wake him or wait till morning.

Nerves trumped common sense, and I dialed. The phone rang four times, then switched to the answering machine.

Now I was awake.

I dialed again, but the line was busy. Some day we'd get voicemail service and call waiting and caller ID—all that helpful telephone stuff that our friends had had for twenty years. Tonight

I'd suffer from the inconvenience of waiting until the answering machine finished before I could dial again.

I got up and drank a glass of water, then dialed again. Once more, the phone rang four times before it went to the answering machine.

He wasn't home.

I waited five more minutes and dialed one final time. One final, painful time, the machine kicked in.

It was one of the most selfish moments of my life: I prayed he wasn't home because of Tina and not because something had happened to him.

I DON'T KNOW WHEN I FELL ASLEEP AGAIN. I wouldn't have even been sure I'd slept except for a hideous dream in which Eddy and I floated on a crimson sea. Chameleons scuttled all around us in a boat that kept changing sizes. A pox-covered Sanjeev was with us and then he wasn't. The only constant in the dream was a tsunami that hovered in the air above us. I woke with a start at 5:50 and called home—again three times. Once more, only the answering machine kicked in.

My stomach swirled.

I fought down the panic. I could taste it, felt its pulsing sensation as it tightened around my head and chest. Surely, this couldn't have anything to do with my trip to Sanjeev's house. Nothing could happen that fast, could it? I lay in bed drifting through all the horrible possibilities and fighting back the tears that came anyway. I sorted backwards through the day before, trying to remember the last I'd talked to him. I'd tried calling him a bunch, but that early morning gtalk conversation was the last contact I'd had with him, the one just after his *Good Morning America* interview when he'd come home and found my health card. I picked through my memory of that gtalk. He'd told me to stay put for the weekend until he could figure out a plan—which may have been the most logical plan at the moment, but it was the least logical plan if he'd been arrested.

It was closing in on twenty-four hours, long enough for any-thing—*anything*—to happen.

At least when they came to get Tina, she had an office full of witnesses to call Pete. Eddy had no one, not even me, because I was thirteen hundred miles from home. Stranded. Helpless. My only hope was that this still had something to do with Tina.

Calling Pete would either confirm my best hope or my scariest nightmare. I lay there, sorting through which was worse: not knowing and worrying about the worst—but also clinging to the fragile possibility that Eddy's sudden disappearance had a logical explanation—or knowing the worst.

Finally, I turned on the light. Eddy, my rock, had tumbled away in the night. I needed to know. Knowing is always better than not knowing.

I scrolled through the numbers on my cell phone even though I knew I didn't have Pete's number programmed in. I booted up my computer and got online to do a search for Pete's phone num-ber. His auto body shop number popped up, but there was no home number. I remembered him complaining about having an unlisted number and discovering that his number still popped up if you did a search on the Internet. Eddy had told him how to fix it, where to send a request and get it removed.

Apparently, the process worked.

I got up and showered, trying to move forward with my day. But I couldn't even move out of the shower. For forty minutes I leaned against the wall, soaking in the steamy stream of water and letting my own tears flow. His wit, his constancy, his gentle nature—I couldn't think about life without him, but a dark shield had dropped between this moment and the future. Life without him was all I could think about. He'd been my best friend for decades. We shared the same skin.

In between jags of sobbing, I kept telling myself that I didn't know something had happened to him. He could be with Pete, helping Tina. Surely, though, sometime during the night, he could have found a phone and called. I was glad for the momentary flashes of anger at him for *not* calling since they brought me back from some abyss I didn't want to discover. Anger is better than total emptiness.

I finally dragged myself out of the shower and called him again, hanging up at the click that signaled the machine had started. It was now eight o'clock in Colorado. I called Pete's shop and got some man, maybe the ponytailed guy Eddy had talked to a lifetime ago. Pete had already been in and was on a doughnut run at the moment. He'd be back, but probably not for long the guy said. He didn't elaborate.

I debated whether to tell him who I was and what I needed. Would Pete's business phone be tapped these days? How could it not be?

"Any more news about Tina?" I asked. It was the wrong way to start.

There was no sound on the other end of the phone line.

"My husband is Eddy Rider. The guy who's been helping Pete."

"Sorry. You could tell me you're Mother Teresa. I can't give out information to people I don't know."

I bit my tongue. If I'd told him I was Mother Teresa, he'd have to figure out if I sounded like a sainted dead woman. "Please just tell me if Pete is with Eddy."

"If you don't know, I'm sure as hell not telling you over the phone."

The phone clicked off.

"Wait—" My reflexes two seconds too slow.

I pressed redial, but it went to voicemail. Had he taken the phone off the hook or did he immediately call Pete? I left a message to have Pete call me on my cell phone and gave the number. I didn't think the information would complicate my life more. Actually, I didn't care. I was desperate to hear anything.

I carried the phone with me for the next thirty minutes while I got ready, not daring to risk missing the phone ring over the noise of the hair blower or even my battery powered toothbrush. But nothing happened. I kept sorting through what Pete's employee had said for every potential meaning. But it was just too rich with all possibilities—too many of them ugly. If it was possible to know less after a phone call, I did. Through it all, I kept putting on my mascara and eyeliner, wiping it off after my tears smeared it yet once more, and putting it on again. Finally, I gave up. The puffy redness would have to be my eye makeup this morning. No one would notice at Baja Breeze anyway. It wasn't about them.

Just before I walked out the door, I tried Pete's shop again. The phone rang and then went to voicemail. It could have been that they didn't hear it over the shop noise, but I suspected caller ID. Icy fingers of panic kept marching up and down my spine.

The drive to Baja Breeze took me up 101 and through a jungle of overpasses and concrete ribbons of highways. I always spent the ten-minute drive concentrating on earthquake detection. Random, senseless death at my tender age was one thing. Getting squashed between layers of highway while selling my soul to the evil Zaan Empire was another thing entirely. I had a couple minutes—more if traffic was bad—where I had no alternative plan, even if I could see the highway rolling down on me from a mile away. This morning, I'm sad to say, I let it distract me once again. I paid a heavy price. This time, it made me miss Pete's return call.

He left a simple voice message that told me what I didn't want to hear. "Hi Maggie. I'm returning your call. Nothing new to report about Tina." Anguished exhaustion etched his voice. I'd lived with the whisper of the worst for the last few hours; he'd carried it on his back for nearly a week. I felt bad for not calling him earlier, but I felt even more miserable because he confirmed my worst fears: Eddy's disappearance had nothing to do with Tina's situation.

I pulled into the Baja Breeze parking lot and sat trying to sort out my sorely limited options. Any other time, I'd fly home even though the flight would have come out of my pocket. Zaan allowed only rare emergencies, preferably the kind where someone ended up dead and the someone was your spouse or a blood relative no more than a generation removed. In-law and grandparent deaths resulted in snippy comments up the chain.

It was all a moot point, though. I couldn't fly—which only made me sicker. Plus, I now had risked everything to meet with Sanjeev. I didn't even know if he would show, but if I missed our meeting, he'd never risk it again. I knew that.

This moment was like that nightmare time between sleep and waking where you're frozen, completely unable to move or make a sound, but you need to run or scream. The tears started building again, this time as much from abject helplessness as from fear of what had happened to Eddy. Even if I threw away my meeting with Sanjeev, if I pulled out of the parking lot that very moment, it would take me two days to drive home. But I could only help him from home. If he'd been arrested, the longer I waited to get home, the colder the trail would be. He could disappear into the Homeland Security rat hole and never surface again.

I was already probably twelve hours too late, maybe nearly twenty-four. My choices were lousy and getting worse.

I tried calling Pete's shop again, but I only got voicemail. I pressed stop on my phone before the message ended. How could Pete have anything left in him to track through the labyrinth to find Eddy? Every cell in him would be devoted to Tina's plight. I wouldn't—couldn't—be any different.

I ached. My heart told me to go home, my head told me to stay in California. My stomach told me to go back to the hotel and stay close to the bathroom for the day.

But the heart trumps everything. I had to go. Calm settled over me the moment I made the decision. I headed into Baja Breeze to tell Michael I was leaving, probably for good. I laughed out loud at the strangeness of the moment. The worst possible event had finally snapped the golden Zaan handcuffs, and it felt good. If I would only have believed that two months ago, I'd be in Colorado Springs and I'd know exactly where Eddy was. If I'd only listened to my heart earlier.

I stopped at the ATM in the cafeteria to get cash for the trip. Two days on the road, even without using a charge card trail, shouldn't cost more than five hundred. I pressed the numbers on the screen and waited impatiently for the machine to spit out my money. Instead, the screen flashed, "Insufficient Funds." Annoyed, I rolled my eyes and walked away. How could a bank machine not have five hundred on a Thursday morning? I'd just have to make a stop somewhere else. A few steps away, I had a "Duh" moment: I was the one with insufficient funds, not the machine. It made no sense because we'd had over three thousand in our account the last time I'd withdrawn money, which had been Sunday night. Eddy often moved money around between accounts, but he always left enough in for emergencies and for automatic withdrawals. I went back to the machine and worked through the menu until the machine spit out a paper with my bank balance: $214.43.

I stared at the screen, a new knot forming in my stomach as I tried to figure out where three thousand could have gone in four long days. Unless it went some place with Eddy. "Yes!" I said out loud and laughed. The brain fog I'd been living with cleared slightly.

The gtalk conversation: "Stay put this weekend." He'd been telling me something.

There was no guarantee that the Feds hadn't stepped into the middle of his plans, but the chance that he'd exited on his own crept up. My hoped-for meeting with Sanjeev tipped the balance in the head and heart debate. I would stay.

No doubt, my stomach would have to figure out what to do with that information.

Chapter
34

I LOGGED IN. Fifty unread emails popped up, a third of them about some data loader issue that looked like Greek to me. I scrolled through them fast, deleting as quickly as I read the first few lines. Of the half-dozen that required my attention, none was critical.

I didn't know what I was doing there. But I was billable. Hooray.

The day dragged. I had three meetings to endure, one with the CEO. I didn't think I could suffer one more conversation about how to communicate a slip in the go-live date. They took two-hour lunches; they hadn't done their homework; they had an incompetent woman running the show who spent more time on her hair than managing her team; and the CEO thought with his penis. Those were the reasons, and I was tired of finessing the story any more.

Somehow, I muddled through the day. I called home every hour, on the hour. When the answering machine clicked on, I hung up. I tried Pete again just before lunch and left a message to call and give me an update on Eddy. If he knew something had happened, I desperately hoped he'd call back and give me clues. If Eddy had, in fact, left town, I prayed Pete would call, curious about the cryptic message. He didn't call.

I didn't have a scenario for that.

The Virus

By five, I couldn't take it anymore. I packed up my stuff and stopped by Michael's cubicle to try one more time to talk him into going to meet Sanjeev with me. Although not actually short with me, he'd bordered on it the other three times I'd asked him. No, he wouldn't go with me, and yes, I was a fool for contacting Sanjeev again. He wasn't at his desk, which was just as well. I didn't want to be talked out of this trip. I left, hitting the thick of rush-hour traffic as I headed to San Jose. I didn't care at all, even when we came to a five-minute dead stop around the San Mateo Bridge.

I got to San Jose a few minutes after six thirty, intentionally parking the car a couple blocks away and walking to Greens & Beans. I didn't think I'd been followed, but if I had been, they'd have to get a little exercise. From time to time, I stopped to window shop, using the pause to see what other people around me did. Nothing looked out of the ordinary, but what did I know? I was a communication consultant, not a private detective.

Maybe it was the walk, or maybe I'd used up all my nervousness the night before, but tonight I felt surprisingly calm, although "empty" might have been a better description. Last night's pounding heart had slowed to a soft throb.

When I got to the restaurant, I ordered a piña colada smoothie and a veggie pita since I didn't truly expect Sanjeev to join me for a real dinner. The place looked like I remembered it. The walls were painted like luscious lettuce leaves and the brightly painted tables like beans. About half of the tables were full, but I found one with a well-thumbed newspaper in a quiet corner where I could watch the place without anyone accusing me of staring. I hadn't really remembered the clientele from before, but somehow tonight it looked a little more cleaned up, like a real suits crowd. Most of them dined alone and were reading books. I'm not sure what that told me about vegetarians, but I was pretty sure it told me something.

187

I paid special attention to those who followed me into the restaurant. Most of them ordered carry-out and didn't so much as glance in my direction. Only an older, frizzy-looking hippie type stayed and ate. But she didn't have anything to read and was gone within twenty minutes, well before Sanjeev was supposed to show up. Others drifted in and out, but no one paid any attention to me and no one hung out.

No Indians showed up, either.

The clock ticked slowly. I nibbled on my pita and savored the smoothie, trying to drag both of them out long enough that no one would chase me off my table. The newspaper was already a day old and a local paper at that. I didn't really care much about the mess the local school board was in or the new billion-dollar hospital complex that was nearing completion, but I was glad for the chance to look distracted. My head was anything but. I knew all along it was a long shot for him to show up, but I had to believe he would. Otherwise, I didn't have a clue what to do next.

By seven forty-five, Sanjeev still hadn't arrived. I tried not to think about what that meant, but I was pretty sure I knew any-way. The waitress came and cleared off the table and I pretended to ponder the dessert options. Again. The place had cleared considerably, so with the light inside and the dark outside, those of us inside were as obvious as if someone had been watching TV. Still, I stuck it out. I'd spent my own day in hell wondering about Eddy. Surely, Sanjeev could give me ten minutes.

I ordered a coffee.

At eight thirty I knew he wasn't coming. Actually, I'd known it since the night before, but I finally knew I couldn't pretend anymore. The waitress came over one last time to see if I needed anything. I shook my head and said, "I was waiting for a friend, but I guess he couldn't make it."

She pulled a loose strand of wildly curly hair back and gave me a half-smile. "An Indian guy? Tired eyes, on the short side?"

"Yes," I said, probably too eagerly.

She nodded casually. "He was in here earlier this afternoon. Left something for you. He said he couldn't make it tonight but we should give it to you, only he never said who to give it to. I guess he figured we'd know when we saw you."

"And you did." I smiled. It was all I could do not to throw my arms around her and sob in relief.

She brought me the bill and a small, sealed envelope. "Sorry I didn't know it was you, or I would have given it to you when you ordered."

"No problem. Thanks." I slipped the envelope in my purse. "Can you point me to the restroom?"

She tilted her head towards the kitchen. "First door on your left."

I left a twenty, which was nearly double my bill. I didn't know if that would buy her silence or trigger her memory of my face in case anyone asked about me, but I bet on the former. After all, it was a vegetarian restaurant. If vegetarians couldn't be discreet, whom could you count on?

I slipped out of my chair and headed to the restroom, but instead of stopping, I proceeded through the kitchen and out the back door, waving as I invaded their space. They only smiled and waved back, so we must have been friends. I wished I'd known that earlier, too.

The back side of the restaurant had a small, low-watt bulb by the door, which illuminated a pile of neatly stacked garbage bags. Once I made it beyond that dim circle of light, I was in the dark. I cut over a street and then zigzagged a couple of blocks until I found my car, my footsteps echoing in the empty evening. As far as I could tell, no one followed me.

Now my heart pounded. I fumbled with the key, then locked the door as soon as I closed it. I slit open the envelope with my key and pulled out a single sheet of typing paper. Tight cursive words filled the page, but the writing was too small to make out in the dim streetlight. As a final insult to the evening, I'd have to go buy reading glasses or find better lighting. At least he wrote something, I kept telling myself as I circled a few blocks looking for a gas station. My fingers trembling, I pulled out the paper for the second time.

> *Please, please, please do not contact me again. I tried to tell you the first time to leave this alone, but since you didn't, I'll make it clearer for you. I am being watched constantly. My phone is tapped. My children are followed to school and to their friends' homes. Why? Because they want to make sure that I do not tell any-one the details of what Zaan did at CDC. As far as the company is concerned, we weren't there. Everything has been expunged from Zaan records. If you don't believe me, check for yourself. If you still do not believe you should stop nosing around, then maybe this will convince you. There were 3 lead software developers on the project designing the new software. In the past month, one was killed in a traffic accident, another died from a heart attack, and the third one is in intensive care with smallpox. They do not think he will live. I saw him with my own eyes. It is a terrible, terrible disease. They all should have obeyed the rules. They were warned. I am very sorry about this doctor who has been arrested, but I cannot risk my family or my future.*
>
> *If you try to contact me again, I will have to tell the Homeland Security people. They will come after you, but I will do it to keep them from coming after me. I am sorry. I really am.*

It was worse, far worse than I'd thought. I read the note again, mostly in disbelief. I'd not only reached a dead end, but for good measure, the road back had been napalmed, as well. If the Feds killed the developers to keep them from talking, how much more desperate must they be to arrest Eddy? My throat thickened—I just couldn't go there without totally melting down. If Eddy had disappeared on his own, he had to stay disappeared. Forever.

I began sobbing.

I don't know how I made it back to my hotel. Exhaustion and tears blinded me. I crept along in the right lane, fearful of every car that didn't pass me, fearful of the ones that raced around me. Back in my room, I crumbled on my bed and reread the note. Just before I fell asleep, I tried our home phone again, mostly just to hear Eddy's voice on the machine. It might be the only way I'd ever hear his voice again.

IN THE MORNING, THE WORLD WAS STILL THE SAME. Only worse because the little sleep I got came in restless waves of dreams.

Still, I went in to work.

All I can say is that this "gotta be billable" mentality was a Zaan disease. On 9/11, I was working at a client site in Maryland with another Zaan consultant. When the first plane hit the World Trade Center, someone poked his head into the office where we were working and told us what had happened. We stopped for a few minutes and stepped into another office to watch the morning news and footage of the plane hitting the tower over and over and over. Then we went back to work. It was a freaky accident, nothing more.

When the second plane hit, the same guy stuck his head in our office and said, "You're not going to believe this." Once again, we went to watch. Coincidences being what they are, we knew this wasn't one of them. We knew it was a terrorist attack. But my colleague, who was the classic manufacturing curmudgeon complete with a gravelly voice, pulled me away from the TV and said, "We're billable. We need to be working."

Our world had just turned upside down. Perhaps there would be no tomorrow. Who cared whether we billed five hours or a hundred hours that week? Our life as we knew it had ended. But what did I do? I went back to my spreadsheet and tried to concentrate—in spite of the sad reality that I still planned to fly home that afternoon.

Even now as I thought about it, I couldn't believe I was such a robot. It was only after the third plane hit the Pentagon, less than fifteen miles away from where we sat, that I told my colleague I was done for the day. I drove back to my hotel and spent the evening in a haze, hypnotized by the scenes repeating on TV: strike, explosion, collapse; strike, explosion, collapse.

Every consultant I knew identified with the people in the plane. It could have been us.

It could have been me.

Without realizing it, I'd just repeated that mindless behavior. In the face of a crisis, I'd kept right on working. The show must go on. The client must be billed. Zaan must make the Wall Street analysts happy.

I wasn't even late to work.

I logged in and checked email to see if someone from Baja Breeze had dumped a mini crisis on me to solve, quickly punching my way through the several dozen emails that popped up. The only thing pressing that surfaced was an email from the CEO, who wanted my help with a couple of PowerPoint slides for a meeting he had at one o'clock.

I hesitated about how to respond to him, trying my best to come up with a professional response. In that minute, a gtalk flashed at me from the bottom of my screen. My heart stopped: EddytheWebMan was pinging me.

I laughed out loud and opened his gtalk. Life could go on again.
EddytheWebMan: *Hi, Maggie.*

Hi, Maggie? What happened to mz m? And what was up with the capital letters and punctuation?

MRiderZaan: Eddio!! What happened????

EddytheWebMan: *What do you mean?*

I paused. The back of my neck tingled. I wasn't talking to

Eddy. That knife blade I'd been carrying around in my stomach for thirty-six hours? It suddenly twisted.

MRiderZaan: Where were you yesterday? I tried calling.

It was all I could do to keep my fingers steady on the keyboard. Who was this in our house on Eddy's computer?

EddytheWebMan: *Did you? I must have turned the ringer off. Sorry, Sweetheart.*

Sweetheart?

MRiderZaan: No problem.

It was the understatement of the century. My head was exploding. How did this person hack into Eddy's computer? The man had a gazillion passwords to get through.

EddytheWebMan: *Call me, okay?*

MRiderZaan: Sure. Give me a minute.

This was too bizarre. Where was this headed? Why would this pretender want me to call? To track me by my cell phone position? That would be simple enough to get without my having to make a phone call. I hesitated another minute, then hit the speed dial on my cell phone. The phone rang and rang and rang. The answering machine didn't pick up.

This was quite a game we were playing.

MRiderZaan: What's going on? I called but you didn't answer and the answering machine didn't come on.

EddytheWebMan: *That's what I was afraid of. I don't know what the deal is. The phone must not be working. Call me on my cell phone.*

Ahhh. My light bulb moment. The pretender wanted Eddy's cell phone number; from there Eddy could be tracked as easily as if he carried a tracking signal in his pocket.

MRiderZaan: Sure... Only one problem.

EddytheWebMan: *What's that?*

MRiderZaan: You don't own a cell phone.

I didn't even wait for a response.

MRiderZaan: Who are you? What are you doing in my house? How did you hack into Eddy's computer?
EddytheWebMan: *Signed off at 8:33 a.m. PST.*

Chapter
36

Phone the police. Tell them to fly to my house and catch the intruder while he still had his sticky fingers on Eddy's keyboard. Oh, and by the way, find out where Eddy disappeared to.

The only flaw? I wasn't normal anymore. Even if I'd maintained a thin veneer of normalcy in my past life, at 6:00 a.m. Monday morning, Mr. Greggen, the TSA Nazi, shattered it. By midnight Monday, the news of Tina's arrest crushed the remaining slivers of trust that might have survived.

No police would be invited to my home. I didn't know how far the cancer had spread its mutated cells throughout the government. I'm sure there were still very honest cops out there—most of them probably were, in fact. But it only took a single bad one in the right place to be cooperating with the Homeland Security people.

I felt violated, desecrated. Worse, there was nothing I would do to stop the intrusion. Whoever it was could be there for hours, days if he wanted. It was creepy, sitting thirteen hundred miles away from my home and knowing that someone was in my house, rifling through files, pawing through drawers and closets, digging through boxes to find—what? What would they find? The only slightly anarchistic aspect in our lives was Eddy's website, and they could see that from any computer in the world.

What could they be looking for?

Maybe they were like me. Maybe they were looking for Eddy.

My head buzzed and my skin tingled. I was caught between the sickening knowledge that some stranger—or more likely a group of strangers—had an unobstructed day to examine the things in my life in minutia and the flush of relief that confirmed Eddy wasn't trapped in some Homeland Security federal penitentiary nightmare.

The day dragged. For the moment, I lived in a tar pit. My feet couldn't move. My hands fumbled. My head traveled in a fog. Somehow I knocked out the PowerPoint slides for the CEO and began working on the intro for the project monthly newsletter. Truthfully, instead of writing something new and fresh for Baja Breeze, I searched through all the newsletters I'd done for other companies and plagiarized. Who would know? Who would care? I looked productive, but a fifth grader could have done it while watching MTV.

At noon, I made a to-go salad in the cafeteria and realized I'd miss the Baja Breeze potato salad more than anything else when I rolled off the project. What does that tell you about the people I was working with? I returned to my cubicle to keep hacking away at the newsletter, translating the techno talk into English—as if anyone would care. This was a company of shoppers, not readers. I was sorry Zaan wasn't billing a higher hourly rate for my time.

Among my friends, I'm known as the comma queen—which is certainly better than being known as the colon queen. Anyway, what requires enormous concentration from the average person is more of a reflex for me. Half my brain added and deleted punctuation while the other half kept thinking about Eddy, Eddy, Eddy. Early afternoon, someone knocked tentatively on my cubicle frame. I turned around to see a slightly heavyset Tom Hanks look-alike standing just outside the invisible entrance to my space.

"Hi. Are you Maggie Rider?"

I nodded.

He reached out his hand as he introduced himself. "I'm Mario Seneca."

The name didn't register. But I met new Baja Breeze people nearly every day. He looked older and tidier than most. He must have been a new hire.

"Do you have a minute?" He smiled.

I had but I wasn't inclined to give him details. I nodded.

"Mind if we step into a conference room?" He motioned with an open hand.

I should have thought through that one a minute, but the Baja Breeze folks were always looking over their shoulders. They seemed to think they had important secrets to tell me. Usually it involved someone else on the project team. Besides, there was that tar-pit-brain-fog thing going on. I had no common sense left.

I followed him around the corner and into a vacant conference room.

"How can I help you?" I asked.

"Well, for starters, we need to get in touch with Eddy."

I jerked back. "You're not with Baja Breeze?"

He looked puzzled.

Yeah, right. What kind of an idiot would assume that?

"Who are you? How did you get to my cubicle without being escorted by a Baja Breeze employee?"

He smiled a genuine Tom Hanks smile. I wanted to shoot him for looking so harmless. "I'm with the DHS, CDC Division, the Center for Disease Control." He pulled out his wallet and flipped it open. Before he could shut it, I grabbed it and studied it. It looked as genuine as anything, but how could I tell? I'd never seen a real CDC badge before.

The DHS stumped me for a moment before I realized it stood for Department of Homeland Security.

"Why do you need Eddy?" My stomach tightened. I should have never let myself zone out on commas on a day like today.

"We need to get in touch with him."

My brain fog cleared ever so slightly. "Then why are you here in California? Eddy is in Colorado."

"Is he?" He gave me his Tom Hanks smile again. I would never be able to watch another one of his movies. He leaned across the table and folded his hands. He looked kindly, even gentle. "He seems to have disappeared."

"He's in Colorado. He and I had an instant message conversation this morning. I'm sure you know that." I smiled, but I'm sure it looked like I was chewing glass.

"No. I didn't know that."

How much did I tip my hand? I said nothing.

"Maggie, you can make this easy or you can make this hard."

"Really?" I put my hands under the table and squeezed them between my legs. It was the only way to keep them from shaking. "Is that some kind of a threat?"

He shook his head. "It's no threat. I don't know where you get the idea that we're the bad guy."

"Maybe from the radio frequency identification tags you're passing off as vaccines? Maybe from—" I stopped myself before I could mention the deaths of the developers. I couldn't believe I'd come so close to that stupid move.

Mario sighed. "I don't know where your friend Dr. Bastante came up with that. But you and I know it's ludicrous." He laughed lightly. "The government has its hands plenty full just trying to stop this epidemic. Why would it want to track people on top of everything else?"

His voice was dangerously soothing. For a flash of a second, I wanted to believe him, or maybe I was afraid he was right and this whole thing had been some kind of horrible nightmare that Eddy and his paranoia had accidentally created. I didn't trust my voice or what would come out of my mouth, so I only said, "I don't believe you." My heart pounded. I hated that it sounded like a child's response.

"Why not?"

The question was a trap for someone or something. If I said I'd seen the RFID that Tina had showed me, it would be material evidence against her. I tried to remember what Eddy had on his website. Was she already compromised? I didn't think so. He would never have done something to put her at risk.

Did I dare point out my own nightmare Monday morning as I went through security? I opted for safe even though he surely had to know. "There's too much evidence out there already."

"And most of it's on Eddy's site, which is why we need to talk to him."

"Like you're talking to Tina?"

His eyes narrowed slightly, but the smile stayed.

"Where is Tina? What have you done with her?"

He ignored my question. "Maggie, we're worried that because of Eddy's website, a lot of people are not going to get their vaccination and will be dangerously exposed. Or worse," he nodded slightly at me, "they'll get it removed and have just enough exposure to smallpox from the vaccine that they'll actually end up getting sick from the vaccine and won't have the immunity to stop it."

He knew, of course. How could he not? I couldn't stop the red flush from rising on my neck and face.

"We've had at least a dozen of those cases." He paused and then casually added, "The incubation period is seven to seventeen days. You should know something in the next week or two."

I had a single moment of clarity, probably the only one in the entire conversation. "Really? Give me the names of the victims. I'd like to talk to them about the circumstances."

"Ah, the little come-on. If we don't give you names, the

people don't exist." He shook his head. The smile never left his face. "Maggie, you understand confidentiality issues. You know we can't do that."

"You can give them my name and phone number, then. They can certainly call me."

He paused and chewed his lip slightly. "I'd like to do that. I really would, but none of them have survived the disease." He folded his arms and leaned on the table.

I thought about the developer Sanjeev wrote about. Had he died?

Mario Seneca seemed to study the table's wood grain a moment, then looked me in the eye. "It's a horrific death. You know that, don't you? You should see the last anguished days of these people. Their bodies are totally covered in pustules, even their throats and eyes. They're silenced and blinded. Then the blisters rip away from the underlying skin. It's extraordinarily painful. Extraordinarily. But they stay alert to the end." He dropped his voice, but his eyes stayed steady on mine. "It's not something you ever want to go through or see someone you love go through."

"Surely, *that's* a threat?" I could no longer stop shaking. How could he not hear my heart pounding?

"I guess you could call it that." He took a business card out of his pocket and placed it in front of me. "Have Eddy call me. Today. We'll make sure neither of you get sick."

And then he left.

I stared at the business card, nearly touching it and then not. Finally, I went to the restroom and got a couple of wet and dry paper towels. I scooped the business card into the trashcan and wiped down the table where it had been. It was probably a stupid reaction, but I couldn't help myself.

Fear is a funny thing. It has a taste, a rhythm, as it pulses through your body, its powerful current distorting time and truth. I'd seen with my own eyes the cut-open vaccination capsule with its spidery copper antenna. I'd been stopped at airport security because I no longer had my vaccination—something they could only know if the capsule contained an RFID. And now I had Sanjeev's handwritten note in my pocket.

Yet fear had a voice, too. It whispered that those bits of information meant nothing. Smallpox produced a hideous death. How could we know for sure there weren't honest-to-God victims out there? How could we know there wasn't an epidemic raging through the country that the government was frantically trying to stop?

What if we were wrong?

Chapter
37

NEEDLESS TO SAY, MY DAY WAS PRETTY WELL SHOT. I couldn't think, couldn't write, couldn't even face a comma.

I returned to my desk, determined to close down my computer and leave. I'd go back to the hotel, but there would be no graphic news clips to stare at, no frantic reports of the day's events to hear over and over. Whatever was happening moved like a cloud settling slowly down until it became a fog, obscuring reality and stifling reason.

Leaving early wasn't a solution, and I knew it. I still wouldn't know where Eddy was. I still wouldn't know how I would get home. I still would carry Mario Seneca's not-so-subtle threat on my shoulder as it whispered the future in my ear.

My brain and part of my heart had shut down, though, so I disconnected from the Internet and closed my open files and programs. When I closed down Outlook, an odd message popped up: *"There are still e-mail messages in your Outbox. Do you want to exit anyway? Exiting in 15 seconds."*

I watched the seconds count down to eight before the message registered in my fried brain, which was thinking more about smallpox symptoms than one more computer message, however unusual. I clicked on "No." Then I closed down Outlook again to see if the message had said what I thought it said.

It did. I clicked on "No" again.

There could be only one explanation: Mr. Seneca from the CDC apparently had an associate who had a task, one a bit more devious. Evidently, our federal friends didn't want to depend on mere threats to reel Eddy in.

I fumbled around, looking for the Outbox in the program. I always opened Outlook and worked offline because I used its calendar and task functions. I never used it for email, though, since we were mandated to use the Zaan email system, so I didn't know the Outlook email function very well. Finally I found the Outbox. There was a single message showing. From me to Eddy. Of course. Who else would it be from and to? The subject line said, "Emergency!! Call me on my cell ASAP!!!

I opened the message to see what I'd been frantically trying to reach Eddy about.

Eddy,

Your sister and her family have been in a horrible accident. Josh was killed and Karen's in a coma and may be brain dead. Both kids are in critical condition. We have to make some tough decisions. CALL ME!!!

I mentally kicked myself. How stupid could I be to ignore Eddy's number one rule? I left my computer running with my email open and nearly paid a price. Fortunately, Mr. Seneca's cohort must have been email-illiterate to think I'd have an empty Outlook inbox. He also must not have checked to make sure the message had been sent. At least that's what it looked like. I double-checked my Zaan email Sent and Trash folders to make sure he hadn't sent a similar message from there. Nothing showed up.

I suppose he could have been clever enough to send a message in both systems, delete the message from my Zaan Sent and Trash email folders, but I didn't see the point in alerting me with the unsent Outlook message. This didn't seem to have the same value as leaving my health card for Eddy.

After slowly examining the possibilities from twenty different angles, I decided the email sender was simply incompetent.

Finally. A point for the good guys. That would make the score about one to ninety-nine. Or maybe two to ninety-nine: they didn't have Eddy.

I did one final check, searching for all activity for the day and then sorting the list by type. Just because my intruder was an email incompetent didn't mean he wasn't a whiz at installing new spyware software.

Sure enough, Mr. Seneca's buddy had left—in Eddy's vernacular—a chestnut. I found a Spectorsoft.exe file, an executable that looked vaguely familiar and had arrived on my computer at 1:28, a point in time that my friend from the DHS was turning me inside out. I gently drummed my fingers on the keyboard, trying to decide what to do next. I resisted the temptation to log back on to the network and did an Ixquick search for more information, which would confirm that I should extract this leech before it could wrap its bloodsucking tentacles around every particle of information I had. They'd turned even my machine against me since every email, every gtalk, every keystroke could now be captured whenever I was online. I held on to a fragile thread of privacy only if I worked offline. Forever.

I don't know when the knot in my stomach had begun to grow, maybe with the announcement of the first reported smallpox case. Now that knot surged to all my extremities, weighing my body down as surely as if lead flowed in my veins. I couldn't take it any more. I missed Eddy. I needed him. We were so tangled together that I didn't know where my thoughts started and his stopped. And now, if the Feds got to him first—I couldn't think about it. I wouldn't think about it.

It was all I could think about.

I closed out the search window and finished shutting down the computer. On the drive back to the hotel I anxiously studied the corner the Feds had trapped me—us—in. I could pack my bags and leave California that night. My job could only last another week or two at the most anyway. What difference would it make if I just walked off the project with no more than an email apology to Michael.

But where would I go?

Maybe Eddy was holing up in Pete's basement only a few miles from our house, but I didn't think so since he surely would have tried to contact me one way or another. Which left me with zero ideas. We had no favorite mountain hideout. Our closest relatives were a thousand miles in the opposite direction. Even old college friends weren't on the path between Colorado and California, and I couldn't imagine him heading any other direction.

It made no sense to stay. It made no sense to leave.

Here's an irony that nearly sent me into the back end of a Hummer when I thought of it: we should have paid more attention to all those Homeland Security alerts that recommended making plans for where to meet up with your family again in the event of a terrorist attack. But then, we'd never even bought duct tape.

I could wait for Eddy to contact me, but what if the Feds got to him first?

I nearly rear-ended the Hummer again.

Around dinnertime, I reluctantly roused out of my depressed stupor. I had few options, but if I didn't choose one, I'd have even fewer. Whatever I did on my own computer was a poison of sorts, but somehow I needed to get in touch with Eddy.

In all my years of travel, I'd never used a business center in a hotel, but it seemed like the logical place to start. Even if they had the same spyware software, I didn't think they could track it to one Maggie Rider. Or this Maggie Rider, which was all that mattered at the end of the day.

The place was empty, no doubt because the few business travelers who actually used hotel business centers had finally gone home, and the weekend crowd would only use it if there were a death in the family. I logged onto a computer and then stared at the screen, not sure how to become invisible. I mentally juggled whether to email Eddy directly or go through his website. And then I juggled some more since I was pretty sure Mr. Seneca's cohort could track all my email regardless of whether it originated on my computer or my inbox.

"Can I help you with something?"

I looked up at the business center receptionist, who was all of seventeen. He might not have even been mature enough to shave yet. At least his voice had changed. I must have given him a stupid look.

"I mean you've been sitting there for a long time and haven't done anything. Can I help you with something?"

I shook my head. "I'm just really tired. Sorry."

"If there's anything I can do, just let me know."

I nodded and smiled. When he left, I opened up Internet Explorer and typed in Eddy's website URL. The familiar graphics popped up, and I rapidly clicked through the links to see if he'd been on the site since Wednesday morning. A single entry had been added as of this afternoon, something I'd totally missed because I hadn't turned on the TV or radio. Eddy had posted a press release from the White House noting that as of February first, all people entering the US from any port—by air, rail, land, or sea—would need proof of a vaccination. It didn't matter if it was a Mexican trucker entering the US for two hours to deliver a load of fruit, a carload of Canadians coming across the border to shop for the day, or the Pope himself. Every single person of any nationality had to be vaccinated to set foot on American soil.

No doubt someone somewhere was happy that the illegal immigration problem would be solved once and for all.

It was a bittersweet moment since it confirmed Eddy was still somewhere. Sadly, the noose tightened a tiny bit more for every other person on the planet.

I couldn't dare send an email directly to Eddy, so I clicked on "Contact Us," but I immediately closed the email form that popped up. I couldn't send something from maggie.rider@Zaan.com. Too many eyes spied in too many unknown places.

I opened up Gmail and created a new identity, then returned to Eddy's site and clicked on "Contact Us." An email message popped up, and I typed in my information:

```
To: smallpoxscare@webmaster.com
From: MZM@gmail.com
Subject: EddytheWebMan
Message:
Thanks for gtalking on Thursday morning.
I have a chestnut to tell you about.
xoxo, Mz M.
```

I thought about the xoxo a minute and then deleted it. It would be highly unlikely that someone emailing him would seal it with kisses and hugs. I changed the Mz M to MZM, too. He'd recognize it.

I sent it with a prayer, hoping I hadn't inadvertently used a word that would get snagged by the Homeland Security filters for a closer inspection. Even if Eddy were sleeping, he had to spot the signature on the email. Paranoid that he was, he'd catch both my clues—that someone had been on his computer and that one or both of us was being tracked. Lighter, I headed back to my room to order room service and catch CNN for the first time that week. Surely there'd be explosive responses from all the countries insulted by this new restriction. At the very least, wouldn't the Queen of England be offended?

Maybe someone forgot to tell the Queen, as well as the rest of the world. There was barely a news buzz on CNN or Fox, which meant that *if* it even made the network evening news, at most it would have gotten thirty seconds, and that would have been buried well into the half hour. Finally, around nine, CNN had a couple of senators, one Republican and one Democrat, debating the new requirements. They could have both been press secretaries for the president for all the heat they generated. I couldn't figure out why there wasn't any outrage. None. Instead they pattered on about the worry of all the potential terrorists flowing across the borders. At one point, the moderator asked about whether non-US citizens would see the information requirements as being invasive.

One of them, I couldn't remember which one since they sounded like blood brothers, actually appeared startled. He looked at the other senator as though no one had raised privacy as an issue with this topic. "Maybe my esteemed colleague has another perspective, but I would think all those folks would be glad to have the opportunity to get vaccinated. After all, this virus doesn't recognize borders."

His esteemed colleague nodded in agreement. "I know there's been some fuss about people having to give their social security numbers up one more time, but frankly, I don't get it. Why would people care about that when we're fighting a gruesome epidemic here?"

"I couldn't agree more," the first senator said. "I mean, if my wife ended up with smallpox just because she didn't like the idea of giving her social security number to the government," he paused and then, almost as a punch line, added, "again." Everyone chuckled. "And then she put our family and everyone she came into contact with at risk, well, what kind of selfish behavior is that?"

The other senator shook his head and shrugged his shoulders. "You know, Tim," he said to the moderator, "if you'd told people fifty years ago that they'd be putting up with the traffic we have today or twenty years ago you'd told people they'd be glued to their cell phones and computers they would have revolted. They would have refused the benefits of easy transportation and instant communication because they couldn't imagine what they'd be gaining for what—at the time—they thought they'd be losing. Give people a few years and they'll look back on this moment and roll their eyes. They'll be glad to give up an insignificant amount of information for the enormous good they'll be gaining."

"So what will people be gaining, Senator Epson?" the moderator obligingly asked.

Senator Epson smiled. "Well, for starters—and this is by far the most important thing—they'll be gaining peace of mind because they won't have to worry about this horrific epidemic."

Horrific epidemic. That made three times in three days. Someone had passed out a script.

"Second, we're using the data we're collecting to give us the ability to track terrorists who attempt to come into the country. As a side benefit, we'll also be able to identify illegal aliens and those who overstay their visas. Tim, I believe most Americans would agree that's easily worth giving up a little personal information for."

The other senator nodded his best senatorial nod. "Ten years ago, if people had realized there'd be a surveillance camera in every 7-Eleven or street corner, what would they have thought? But if you walk the streets of central London for a day, you'll be photographed literally thousands of times. But do people stop going to London? Absolutely not. It's busier than it ever was. And the payoff? The worst crime you have to worry about in London is getting your pockets picked. People seem to understand the value of giving up a little information for a lot of safety."

I turned the sound down and watched the talking heads. They looked serious and sincere with their starched white shirts and crisply knotted ties. They knitted their eyebrows and nodded solemnly. It didn't matter what they were saying. No one in America was listening anyway. They were all watching some finale to a Survivor show, eyes glued to the TV, arms extended and sleeves rolled up while the government pricked and prodded and stripped them of the last iota of privacy they had.

My fingers itched to get on a keyboard and check my new Gmail account, but the business center would never be open at this hour and I didn't dare log in on my own computer. I'd have to wait. I fell into a restless sleep and dreamed of Londoners goose-stepping after pickpockets.

What had we become?

Chapter
38

Somewhere in our wedding vows Eddy and I had promised to love, cherish, and savor lazy Saturday mornings of champagne and Belgian waffles. We had a few of those where we barely made it to the first matinee because we'd slept so late. Within months of getting married, though, we grew up and discovered that Saturday was the day to get things done.

Welcome to adulthood.

It was also the day to spend together. Even counting the years I'd worked for Zaan, I hadn't missed a Saturday at home unless I was on an overseas project. This was an absolute first, to be stuck in a hotel in Burlingame, California. No champagne. No waffles. No Eddy. Just all the worry I could carry.

I woke at six and tried to go back to sleep. The business center wouldn't be open for hours. I had nothing to do but check my new Gmail account. Even then, I wasn't sure I'd have anything to do. I lay in bed trying to figure out what to do with these two days I didn't want. I had too much time on my hands to think—to think about Eddy, developers who died, and corporations that compromised their country for a buck. And about vaccinations gone awry. How empty was Mario Seneca's threat? Seven to seventeen days after exposure. Ten days to go before I would know for sure.

I shoved the covers off and got out of bed, as if movement could knock the anxiety away. I refused to let myself be consumed with fear since that would sap the energy I needed to figure out how to get out of this whole mess. Which, I'm sure, was exactly what Mario Seneca wanted: no extra brain cells for me.

I showered and dressed and continued to try to shake off my fears, which were now deliriously happy at the chance to eat away my stomach lining. Finally, at seven thirty, I headed downstairs to the business center, only to discover that without business travelers on a Saturday, the hotel had no reason to open its business center before noon.

Maybe I was crying. I certainly felt like it even though my cheeks were dry. Tony, my friendly night manager, noticed anyway even though he was across the room.

"Something I can help you with Mrs. Rider?"

"Tony." I sighed and tried not to sound emotional. You'd think with all the practice I'd had, I'd be pretty good at it, but I wasn't. Grief is grief. "I was hoping to get into the business center. I'm, uh, having trouble with my computer and I have to get on email." I'm a lousy liar, so I surprised even myself.

"I can let you in." He disappeared out a door behind the reception counter and reappeared on the lobby side. "I wouldn't ordinarily do this, but you're such a good customer, I know I can trust you in there. Don't worry about logging the time. It'll be on us this time."

"Thank you. I really appreciate your bending the rules." And if I'd known, I would have been downstairs at 6:05.

"Don't mention it." He unlocked the door and flicked the lights on. "Hey, did you have a good anniversary?"

"Anniversary?" My anniversary was on the other side of the year.

"On Thursday? When your husband surprised you and showed up here?"

"Huh?" The words were all in English, but in the order he delivered them, none of them made sense. Eddy? Thursday? Here?

Tony missed my confusion. "Yeah, he was all excited about surprising you. He said he drove in from Colorado."

I shook my head. Could Eddy have arrived and I missed the signal to contact him? My heart beat faster. "My husband showed up on Thursday?"

Tony flushed and stuttered a little. "Yeah, I'm sure it was Thursday. Dark curly hair, nice looking. A little stocky."

A little stocky? "Looks a little like Tom Hanks?"

"That's him." Tony laughed awkwardly, glad I guess because he thought he would still have a job after this conversation.

I tried to control my breathing. "That's not my husband." I fumbled around for my wallet and pulled out the only picture I had of Eddy, a cheery post-hiking shot that blazed with color.

Tony flushed and he jingled his keys. He shook his head. "Not the guy."

"So let me get this straight." I tried to keep my voice even. "You gave someone a key to my room because he said he was my husband?"

"He showed me his driver's license." Tony looked every bit as miserable as I felt. "It never occurred to me that it wasn't real." His eyes widened. "Why would someone go to all that trouble?"

I brushed off the question. Thursday night I'd sat waiting for hours for Sanjeev to show. Had my man Mario waited for me in my room? Had he just spent the time searching it? What did he expect to find?

"So he still has my key?"

Tony nodded weakly. "Who was it? Why would someone pretend to be your husband?"

I still didn't answer his question. "Then I need to move to a different room." I looked at him. "Now." My heart sank since it would delay checking my Gmail account for another few minutes.

He nodded.

He put me in the honeymoon suite, which was pointless. I packed up my things, checking for anything that looked different or disturbed. But everything seemed to be where I'd left it.

Mr. Seneca seemed to have a purpose-filled life, though. Maybe he hadn't been trying to find something. Maybe he'd left something. A bug, a video camera. What were the possibilities?

I pulled the door shut behind me and immediately felt lighter. Whatever Mr. Seneca left in my room, the folks at Homeland Security would be playing big brother to someone else.

Chapter
39

 and I started my day over.

When my MZM Gmail started to load, I had to swivel my chair around and study a rack of tourist brochures. Thirty seconds can be a lifetime.

It did me no good. MZM@gmail.com was empty. Nothing. No Eddy message, not even a pornographic come-on or an enticement to lower interest rates. It was oddly reassuring that Gmail hadn't sold my email address in the fifteen hours the account had been open.

That left me with Jola Pavelkavich, my one friend who lived on the dark side as a Zaan software developer. Three years earlier, we'd discovered each other serendipitously on a Boston/San Francisco flight when I booted up my computer and the Zaan wallpaper appeared. The six hours made us, if not fast friends, at least commiserating co-workers. When I had the rare reason to visit Zaan headquarters, we always met for lunch.

It was time to cash in my single remaining chit. And Jola Pavelkavich was, at the very least, an easy Internet search.

Within fifteen minutes I was in my car, started plugging in the address into the Hertz Neverlost navigation system. As I waited for the GPS to load street names, I jolted awake and shut the car off again. What was Neverlost if it wasn't the ultimate tracking device? I wiped my palms on my pants and tried to stop shaking. I'd nearly left a Hertz breadcrumb trail to Jola's. Then a worse thought hit: I'd driven this same car to Sanjeev's house on Wednesday, Neverlost directions and all.

Oh Lord. What had I done?

I was too shaky to drive, too shaky even to trust my legs for a head-clearing walk. I was in way over my head. I sat, catatonic with indecision. Hours, or maybe only minutes, later, a tapping at my window startled me. Tony watched me from the other side of the glass.

"You okay, Mrs. Rider?"

I nodded, then shook my head, turned on the car, and rolled down the window. "I need to go into the city, but I don't want to drive." I handed the paper with Jola's address to him. "How much would a cab cost?"

He studied it a moment. "Do you know what the major cross streets are?"

I scratched my head, trying to retrieve the general vicinity. "Maybe Lombard and Grant?"

"You could probably do that for forty or fifty dollars. But it'd be a lot cheaper to take BART into the city and then grab a cab. It's probably faster, too, even on a Saturday." He chewed on his lip a second or two. "Look, I'm on my way home. Why don't I just give you a lift to the nearest BART station?"

Jola lived in a slim lavender house on a sloped street filled with other shoulder-to-shoulder painted houses. Only in San Francisco could a lavender house look understated. Pink January flowers filled window boxes and a porch pot. I rang the bell and crossed my fingers that she had no weekend life.

"Maggie?" She wore a thick terry robe that covered all but her bare ankles and feet. I'd gotten her out of bed.

"Jola."

"What ... what are you doing here?" Her almond Slavic eyes widened. Her short bleached white hair spiked without a pattern. Together, they gave her a triangle face.

"I'm so sorry to surprise you like this. I hope I'm not interrupting anything."

Jola shook her head and smiled graciously. She opened the door wider, inviting me in.

"I'm sorry to bother you on a Saturday like this, but I'm hoping you can help me."

"What's going on?" She still had that giveaway Polish lilt in her speech.

"It's complicated, and you're the only person I could think of who might know what to do."

I'd thought her to be spare and lean in all that she did. Her tiny house confirmed it. The living room and kitchen combined into a long open space and looked like it had been lifted straight from an Ikea store. She put on hot water for tea and found some dark, grain-laden bread, butter, and raspberry jam. Then she sat at the simple maple table with me. It wasn't till then that I noticed she didn't just have a morning tired look; she'd been crying.

"I think I've come at a bad time, Jola. I should have called. I'm sorry."

"It's okay, really." She propped her elbow on the table and rubbed her neck "We've just had a bad run of things at work. A good friend of mine died Thursday." She patted her pocket but burst into tears before she could find a tissue. "This smallpox thing is terrible, isn't it?"

"Your friend died of smallpox?" The words tumbled out in an anxious rush, but Jola didn't seem to notice through her tears. I'd come hoping for a contact, someone who could direct me to the right software development group at Zaan. Instead, I'd hit the jackpot.

She held up three fingers. "It's the third developer to die at Zaan in the last month. We all feel ... what's the word? Ginced?"

All her words were softer somehow, remnants of a childhood filled with few vowels and an abundance of *S's, Z's,* and *C's.*

"Jinxed?" For the first time in a week, I felt the opposite.

She nodded. "Jinxed. That's the word everyone keeps using."

The teakettle shrilled and she got up to get some mugs and tea bags. The tears didn't stop during all the tea fixing, so we sat quietly, each with our own thoughts until Jola reached a tearless interlude.

"There were less than a hundred in our development group. What are the odds?"

"So you knew all three of them well?"

Her eyes shifted away from me and she started rubbing her forehead, but it didn't do any good. The tears spilled over anyway. "Daniel better than the others. He was the one who died from smallpox. We started at Zaan within a week of each other and survived six massive layoffs over the years. You know how it is. All that trouble, it bonds you." She tried to laugh but it caught in her throat and came out as a sob.

"Jola—" I reached across the table and squeezed her forearm. "I'm so sorry—" There was nothing I could say to fill the void, yet it was all I could do not to sprint through all I wanted to say. I counted to ten in my head. "It must be very painful for you."

She nodded. "He was kind, the kindest man you'd ever want to meet."

"And now you must be worried that you've been exposed."

She shook her head. "That's probably the only good thing. He'd taken a sudden leave of absence to take care of his mother back in Russia who'd had a stroke. The next thing we heard was that he was in an isolation unit at UCSF Medical Center, and that he was dying from smallpox." The words produced more fumbling for a tissue.

"So he died in San Francisco and not Russia?"

"I know. We thought that was odd, too."

"Did they have any idea how he was exposed? Have others around him gotten smallpox, too?"

She shook her head again. "In Development, we're all past the incubation period. Just to be safe, though, the CDC came in and vaccinated everyone who wasn't already vaccinated."

Why wasn't I surprised?

"Jola." I hesitated. This seemed like such a lousy time to talk about anything but losing her friend. "Jola, the other two that died? One died in a traffic accident, and one from a heart attack. Is that right?"

She paused and tilted her head slightly. For the moment, her eyes didn't brim with tears. "You heard about them, then?"

"Thirdhand. I don't even know their names. All I know is that those two and your friend Daniel had one thing in common." I paused, waited and watched. "Do you know what that is?"

Jola nodded her head ever so slightly, and even though it was just the two of us in her house, she lowered her voice to a whisper. "The CDC project. There's a rumor floating through the group that their deaths are connected to that."

"What do you think?"

The tears had pretty much stopped, and now another emotion crept over her face. I knew what it was because I'd seen it in my own mirror a hundred times in the last few weeks.

"But why? Why would they end up dead because of that project?"

"What were they doing there? Do you know?" I asked her, even though I already knew.

"It wasn't that complicated. They were building some one-off software to enter data and run reports. They were building some interfaces, too, between Zaan and some other systems. This one started with our core human resources application and then they customized it to pieces. I picked up that the report running had to be pretty sophisticated and very powerful since it needed to do more than report. It needed to be able to also flag items in real time."

"Did any of them ever talk about the project with the rest of you?"

She blew her nose and shook her head. "The company more or less sequestered them in their own space. Lots of the rest of us helped with some of the routine stuff, but we didn't have regular meetings like we often do when we're building new software."

"Is that common?"

"Every project is different." She shrugged her shoulders. "We didn't think about it at the time."

"Are there any rumors at work about how the software is tied into this massive smallpox vaccination campaign?"

Jola didn't respond right away. Instead, she lightly drummed her fingers against the raspberry jam jar. Her eyes shifted down, then up, down again and up. Finally, she nodded. "There're rumors that the vaccination isn't a vaccination at all. It's a tracking device. A people-tracking device."

"And we built the software to make it happen."

She nodded.

I told her what I knew about RFIDs and finished with getting detained at the airport. "I had mine removed, and they somehow knew it when I went through security. They almost didn't let me fly even though I didn't have to have proof of it until the next day. Here's what's creepy: my health card had all the right information, but somehow they were able to detect that the vaccination itself was no longer in my arm."

Subconsciously, she rubbed her upper left arm, the vaccination arm. "It fits, doesn't it?"

"So that brings me here. To your house." I studied her eyes, but she didn't cringe or look away. "That ability to track people is the core of what they're doing. If we can change the software, maybe we can inch back from the precipice."

Jola closed her eyes. "There's also talk that the rumors are what ... what led to their deaths."

It wasn't a non sequitur.

She sighed heavily. "They weren't supposed to say a word about what they were working on. Nothing. But people always talk. Some of us started asking questions, too, more so once the project finished."

"So who do you think didn't like it that they were talking? Who do you think we have to be afraid of?"

More pauses. More finger drumming. More eye shifting. "Talk at the office is that we don't think Zaan would be behind it. What would be in it for them?" She looked me in the eye. "But you never know. We've both worked for the company long enough to know it's highly dysfunctional. If they thought Wall Street analysts would prefer dead employees to laid-off employees, they'd oblige." She snorted softly. "Anything for an extra penny of profit per share."

"So you don't think Zaan's behind it."

"Not directly. They might be cooperating by giving access to information, but until Wall Street dictates otherwise, I don't think so."

"Then who?" I wanted her to say it.

"Homeland Security. The Center for Disease Control. I don't know. Somebody in the federal government. Who do you think it is?"

"I think you're right."

We let the silence take its time.

Finally, I said, "So the stakes are very high."

"And their resources are infinite if they want to stop us."

"Which they will." Eddy's story tumbled out, from website to disappearance to Mario Seneca's visits. Jola unearthed another box of Kleenexes while I added in the awful details about Tina Bastante.

When I finished, I said once again, "So that brings me here. To your house. You're the only hope we have for stopping this disaster."

She ran her fingers through her short hair and whispered something Polish.

"Can you change the software?" I asked her again.

She rested her chin on her folded hands. Her answer wasn't immediate, but when she gave it, it sounded firm and final. "No. I don't know how I can do that. I helped, but it's like building a shelf in a garage in a new house and then being asked to change the plumbing. Just because you help doesn't mean you understand the framework, the architecture."

I took another tissue and blew my nose. "So what are our options?"

"We don't have any."

I LEFT WITH A HANDFUL OF KLEENEXES, directions to the local branch library, and plans for how to stay in touch. I worried that of the three, only the tissues had concrete value. The library was less than a mile away, easily walkable in most of Colorado Springs, less so on the hills of San Francisco on a cool, mist-shrouded day. Still, it gave me time to think and to walk off a little of my discouragement.

The library branch smelled like a library should, of dust and ideas. They'd tucked the computer room in the far back behind a glass wall, deftly separating the old—the sturdy oak desks with green-shaded lamps and rows of book stacks—from the new. I chose a computer toward the back that let me face the entrance to the room. I didn't think anyone had followed me, but I also didn't trust my ability to spot someone. Once again, I regretted not honing my paranoid side all those years I had Eddy to coach me. Even though I'd left Jola's computer not more than thirty minutes earlier, I began with a quick look at my MZM Gmail account. There'd been no message from Eddy then, and there was none now.

I did a quick check to see if there was an obituary for Sanjeev Srivastava, a morbid activity that I tried to stay intellectual about. If I'd found one, I wouldn't have been able to sleep from the guilt of having flagged him as a risk to the Homeland Security goons and drones. But when nothing surfaced, I still didn't know anything. He could have been deported or worse, detained and exposed.

If they found Eddy first, there'd be no option of deportation. If.

Something let go inside me and my fingers trembled on the keyboard.

Eddy's website had some new links about the White House press release regarding the vaccination requirements for anyone entering the US, but they were mostly to foreign media. The global outrage warmed my heart and confirmed that common sense still survived, somewhere. Eddy had included links to the *The New York Times* and the *The Wall Street Journal*, but those articles focused on the short notification time and only gave a quick nod to the international ire that had surfaced.

"Ire" was an interesting word choice, particularly since that's how both papers referred to it. "Horrific epidemic" showed up in both articles, too. The script was expanding.

In a new twist, Eddy had made his site counter visible. He'd always been cynical about webmasters who did that, his argument being that they were just cocky showoffs. Of course, he'd never built a site that hit a million visitors in a year. Except for smallpoxscare.com. The site had reached thirty million hits. No doubt Eddy was feeling a little cocky himself.

Jola had given me the names of the developers, which gave me something more to explore between checking my MZM Gmail account every five minutes. I didn't understand why Eddy would post new items to his website but not respond to my email, so the entire afternoon I floated through waves of emotion: fear that something had happened to him, anger at him for not contacting me, anxiety that this was only the beginning.

Without any other clues to chase, I searched the names of the three Zaan developers who had died. An eclectic assortment of trivia surfaced. The obituaries were exceptionally vague. Only one tidbit helped: in addition to grieving family members, Daniel Pogodov left a fiancé, Anna Denisov, another Russian. I followed the Ixquick trail on her and came up with an address, phone number, and—thank you Lord Jesus—the name of the restaurant she owned in Palo Alto. With that sweet success, I dug deeper and searched the names of everyone listed in the obituaries, sorting and cross-referencing addresses and phone numbers that seemed likely. I weighed the value of what I might learn against the risk of using my credit card to do a more detailed search and finally came down on the side of starting with what I had already. Better to stay under the radar until I'd exhausted every lead. As a finale, I sent another email to Eddy at smallpoxscare@webmaster.com. In it, I included links to the three obituaries and a brief note that they were the three Zaan software developers for the CDC project. I closed with my usual xoxo, which seemed inane given how desperate I was to see him again. And then, hard as it was to do, I erased it. No point in leaving even more breadcrumbs.

I cleared my Internet cache, fruitlessly checked my Gmail account one last time, and then headed to the closest BART station, a mile or so away. I zipped my leather jacket and wished for some gloves since the mist had turned into a chilly drizzle. It also had cleared the sidewalks of pedestrians, which made it easier for me to check periodically behind me for anyone on foot. Never mind that, logically, no one should have been able to find me at the library in the first place. But after discovering Mario Seneca's trespass, I didn't dare trust logic anymore.

As I got closer to the BART station, fingers of fog reached up the street, pulling in the space around me and creating soft echoes of my own footsteps. At first, I thought surely someone was behind me, but I couldn't see more than half a block in any direction. The second time I heard the echoes, I slipped into a doorway and waited for at least ten minutes. Nothing passed in front of me. My heart beat faster. I tried to shake off the sense that someone was out there, someone who was waiting for me. My strides grew longer and faster until I saw the sign for the BART station. A worn-looking man in jeans and a Giants sweatshirt leaned against the brick wall just beyond the door. It didn't make sense for someone to be standing in the rain when they could be dry on the other side of the door. I debated whether to keep on walking and see what he would do, but I had no idea where I would go next. Just then, I caught a whiff of cigarette smoke and realized he was there because he couldn't smoke inside the building.

I needed more faith and less imagination.

He looked at me and gave a nod of acknowledgement as I passed him. I didn't think strangers did that to strangers in a city, so then I had to start my worrying all over again. He didn't follow me down the steps to the tracks, though. The platform was empty except for a young family and an elderly couple, hardly the sort to feed suspicions. We were the only ones to get on the subway when it arrived.

What if going forward, every day was like today?

I rode BART all the way out to the airport and caught the shuttle back to the hotel. Tonight I would eat Russian food in Palo Alto.

The way I saw it, I had three options. One, I could take a cab everywhere and either drain my cash or risk using a charge card. Two, I could rent a second car, one without a GPS system but with another credit card flag. Or three, I could keep on using the car I had but not use the Neverlost system.

I had no idea how visible I was with the Neverlost system turned off, but the more I thought about it, the more it seemed a safe bet (except, of course, for the inevitable hours I'd spend being lost). After all, if you have your computer disconnected from the Internet, can hackers still get into your computer? Coming up with that analogy gave me pause since I knew highly sophisticated hackers could still hack into a computer that was turned off but had a WAN line connected.

Still, the reality was that nobody needed a GPS system to follow me. I was in a car and a total novice about where I was going.

I voted to stick with my current car sans the Neverlost and with downloaded directions from the computer in the business center.

Fortunately, I actually had a clue how to get around Palo Alto without Neverlost since the Silicon Valley apex was also the headquarters for Zaan. I loved the sedate, lush town. If I'd had the chance—and an extra two or three million dollars—I would have moved there in a heartbeat.

As I drove, I tried to figure out why I was even going to see Daniel Pogodov's fiancé. It wasn't like he would have whispered sweet programming nothings into her ear just before he died. Maybe, though, he told her something, anything that would be another breadcrumb in this lost cause. Even the likelihood that Anna would be working so soon after Daniel's gruesome death was a long shot. It was hopeless. If I quit kidding myself, I'd admit the real reason I went was because I couldn't face the helplessness of sitting in a hotel room by myself on a Saturday night. As long as I moved my feet, I could give myself a little hope.

I cruised down California Avenue, where Anna's restaurant was, but decided it was safer to park at the Zaan campus and walk the few blocks. Even though it was early Saturday evening, at least a hundred other cars scattered the Zaan parking lot. I couldn't believe they were all using the parking lot as a decoy for sleuthing, so it gave me one more reason to mutter under my breath at my employer.

I recognized the location of Anya's Place, Anna's resta-urant, because it was a reincarnation of an American bistro where I'd eaten a couple of times with a co-worker who rated ambiance higher than palatability. The bistro had deserved a premature death.

It was early for dinner, but already the place, which had retained its predecessor's charm, was half full. While I waited for a hostess to spot me, I watched ruby-cheeked waitresses in black skirts, white dress shirts, and black bow ties bustle through the maze of tables, artfully balancing trays piled with plates of appetizers, shot glasses and a disproportionate number of vodka bottles. It was, for sure, a Russian restaurant.

"One for dinner?" The hostess, who was decidedly new to the language, picked up a single menu. Her puffy red eyes detracted from an otherwise striking profile.

I smiled as friendly as I could. "Actually, I was hoping to see Anna. I know it's a terrible time because of Daniel's death, but I was hoping I could catch her and give her my condolences in person." Everything was a stretch, but I banked on a little advantage because of her simple comprehension level and my familiarity with the situation.

"Is so terrible," she whispered. I was afraid tears would follow, but maybe she was cried out. "We all luffed him. A good man. He was good."

"It must be so difficult for Anna."

"She cry all the time." And it looked for the moment that the hostess was going to follow suit.

I nodded and fumbled in my purse for my own stash of tissues. Daniel, Eddy, true love—it all wrapped up into the same depressing package. My tears—genuine ones—started up again. "Is Anna here by any chance?" The most I could hope for was a willingness to divulge a home address, but the hostess turned and motioned me to follow her. We wound through the kitchen, where I unfortunately remembered I hadn't eaten since the bread at Jola's, and up a narrow staircase. The hostess knocked on the door. Russian spilled out on both sides of the door and then it opened.

Anna, at least I assumed that's who it was, opened the door to a cozy office filled with lots of ferns and geraniums and two cats. She gave me a puzzled look. "I'm sorry. Do I know you?" Although not nearly as pronounced, her accent still clearly marked her for a new arrival.

"I work at Zaan. I'm a good friend of Jola Pavelkavich." I wasn't even sure if Anna had ever heard of Jola, but it sounded better than just making the Zaan connection.

Whether she was weakened by grief or I'd said the right combination, I didn't know, but she let me in and sweetly dismissed the hostess. The two exchanged cheek kisses and then the hostess clattered down the stairs, sniffling as she went. I tried not to think about the agonizingly good smells wafting up from the kitchen.

"I'm so very sorry about Daniel."

Anna nodded and blew her nose into a honest-to-goodness handkerchief. I hadn't seen one of those since my grandmother died in 1988. She gently lifted a calico cat off an overstuffed chair and invited me to sit. She sat in a second overstuffed chair, feet tucked under her, and absently stroked the cat.

"I spent the morning with Jola. I didn't know Daniel myself—" I thought I'd better be straight with her, "—but I wanted to tell you what I know about his death."

Her eyes, which already seemed to fill half her face, widened.

I took my risk. "I believe he was murdered."

"Murdered?" She shook her head and watched me very carefully. "I thought you knew." She dabbed at her eyes, which had never stopped overflowing, and whispered, "He died of smallpox."

"I know he died of smallpox. What I have come to believe is that Homeland Security exposed him to the virus." I watched her. She didn't seem startled by my comment. "They didn't want him to be able to talk about his work on the Center for Disease Control project."

She kept on petting the cat. A second one, a thinner, younger version of the first, lightly jumped into her lap and nestled under her other hand. Finally, she said, "Why you think this? Why you think they expose him?"

"There are so many reasons, not the least of which is that he was the final lead software developer to die on that project in a month's time. That's not coincidence."

She shook her head, but I wasn't sure if it was in agreement or in resignation.

"Anna. We're sisters. I'm afraid I'm going to lose the man I love, too." I dug out another Kleenex from my purse and blew my nose. "My husband has put together a website that questions whether this is a real epidemic or whether it's been created to scare people into getting vaccinated." I watched her eyes. They didn't blink. "Homeland Security is looking for him. They've threatened me that he could be infected with smallpox if he doesn't shut down his website. They would do this to protect what they've put in place. I believe it."

She looked out the sole window into the colorless evening. A minute passed. The cats purred in her arms. She finally looked back at me. "I believe you."

"Has anyone from Homeland Security come to visit you? Or from the Center for Disease Control?"

Her tears had slowed. She blew her nose. "Yes. But they only say dangerous things. They didn't sound sorry at all that he died. They say—but not say ..." she fumbled for the word.

"They implied?" I offered.

She nodded. "Yes. They don't say it, but I know what they mean. If anyone ask about his work, I have to tell them, or I get myself sick with smallpox too."

"Will you tell them?" I already knew the answer.

She snorted softly. "I am Russian. You think I help the people who kill the man I love? What is fear when you have lost love?"

It was true. I understood exactly what she meant.

"I remember when the wall fell. I am only seven, but it is fearful and joyful time. Both. We did not know what happens, but we think the best will come." She tilted her mouth up into a half smile. "But it doesn't. Instead, the worst comes. We have chaos. My mother is very sad. She keep telling me about this 'freedom' thing. She say before the wall fell, Soviets had freedom and Americans had freedom. But here is difference. Americans have individual freedom. They work or live wherever they want. They say whatever they want. But they can't walk their streets at night. Is dangerous. They worry about crime, about rapes and murders. The Soviets, though, has corporate freedom. We have to be careful about what we say or do. We cannot live just anywhere or go to just any school or get just any job. But we have no fear of crime. We can walk anywhere in Moscow at one in the morning and not worry about getting mugged." She paused and stroked the cats. "Here is the ... I think irony. At the end of the day, we do not get either kind of freedom. We lose our corporate freedom and do not gain individual freedom."

"And now in the US, we're losing both."

She nodded. "Humans. We are interesting beasts."

"It's all about control." I'd already come to that conclusion.

She nodded again. "Is all about control."

Whether she heard my growling stomach or had a kind heart, I don't know. But she ordered up a bottle of vodka and a sturdy assortment of appetizers. Without negotiating, we came up with an acceptable division of responsibilities: she managed the vodka, and I the caviar, salmon and cucumber canapés, and the pickled mushrooms. She was a determined woman, though, because a bottle of fruity dry wine for me arrived with the next course, a beet borscht that sang, and garlic-saturated rolls. Still later, another bottle of wine accompanied the trip up the stairs to complement plates of moist, fork-tender chicken Kiev, lumpy mashed potatoes, and a vinegary cucumber salad. By then, she was fast friends with me and was far beyond caring that I lagged indecently behind her in all the toasts—every single one, by the way, to unfairly lost love, which could have taken us all the way back to junior high.

Throughout the evening, Anna cycled multiple times through tears, confidential whispers, and giggles. By the time a lavish chocolate torte arrived, she had cycled back to whispers. At the moment, we were suffering from the alcohol's compounding impact on Anna's deteriorating vocabulary and accent and my ability to decipher. So when she leaned into her forkful of chocolate layers and told me she had the secret ingredient, I was pretty sure that meant vodka laced even the dessert.

Those Russians.

"No, no, no, no, no, Maggie."

"No vodka in the torte?"

She unleashed a spasm of giggles and wagged her finger at me. "No, no, no. I haf secret ingredient for the security." She snapped her fingers repeatedly as if trying to summon the word out of the air. "For the homeland security."

"The secret ingredient?"

She nodded and rose. Either she tilted slightly, or the room listed. It could have been both. Gingerly, she navigated around our chairs to a cluttered desk behind me, hanging on to anything firmly planted along the way and muttering in soft, buzzy Russian sounds. She reached the desk without a 9-1-1 incident and then fumbled with a loaded key chain to unlock a lower drawer. That accomplished, she pulled out a locked metal box, and again, the keys jangled in her hands until she found the right one. Whatever the secret ingredient was, she'd kept it under lock and key, lock and key. It wouldn't have stopped Homeland Security, but all the noise the keys made would have kept an intrusion from staying covert.

"Six weeks. Six weeks! And now I give up." She pulled out a pack of cigarettes and offered it in my direction. I shook my head. It didn't seem like much of a secret ingredient.

"Och, you Americans." She knocked one out of the pack and struck a shiny gold lighter, eventually connecting the flame with the end of the cigarette. "You have give up all the good vices." She sucked in heavily and closed her eyes. I was afraid she'd topple over, but she stayed standing.

Nervously, I eyed the lit end of her cigarette as she groped her way back to her chair. We both sighed as she sat. She took another long, loving drag on her cigarette.

"This is your secret ingredient?"

She tilted her head slightly, no doubt translating through the multiple languages of vodka, cigarette smoke, and English. "Och!" She slapped her forehead and waved her cigarette. "Desperation make me forget."

Actually, I was pretty sure it was the vodka.

She picked up her phone receiver and had a short conspiratorial conversation. A few minutes later, the hostess appeared with a restaurant menu.

I don't think it was just the vodka and wine, but I needed hope, not even more food.

The hostess handed Anna the menu and then, even though I understood zero Russian, clearly chastised her for the smoking. Anna let her pick the cigarette out of her hand, getting a soft kiss on her forehead as a reward. And then we were alone again. Anna opened the menu and pulled out a business envelope that had been tucked behind the sheet of entrees.

"The ingredient secret." She handed me the envelope.

For nearly a week, I'd been chasing something without knowing what it could be. Even now, I didn't know what I held in my hands, but I understood the moment. Reverently, I removed the handwritten pages, the first in Russian, the rest, although not exactly in English, very familiar to anyone who recognized JavaScript, the programming language of Zaan.

Anna's eyes brimmed with tears. "He call it a 'back door.' He say it will take you inside the software to fix the problem."

The problem. Such a benign way to describe life as we'd come to know it.

We toasted each other one last time and kissed cheeks in a Russian farewell. I tucked my copy of the gold inside my purse and left out the restaurant's back door, stumbling slightly through the alleys until I found my car again.

Thank goodness I had a panic button on the key chain.

I ADMIT IT: I WAS BAD. I drove myself back to the hotel instead of taking a cab. I did a pretty good job of staying between the mostly stationary lines and hit my exit (not literally, of course, although I could have since I've done that more than once when I was stone-cold sober) the first time. So, all in all, I was quite pleased with myself.

Even better, I had a starting point. I had a way for someone to hack into the software and do something. What, I didn't know. But it was a significantly better point than I'd been at even six hours earlier. The entire drive, I desperately wanted to call someone—Eddy, mostly—but I would have gladly settled for Jola or Michael or even Sanjeev if I wouldn't have gotten him deported. I knew better, though. I might as well have called Mario Seneca.

The week's emotional roller coaster of fear, anger, and euphoria—and now alcohol—had sapped my last brain cell. The combination could have been lethal. By the time I reached the top floor at the hotel, it was all I could do to stay vertical.

The elevator doors opened into an intimate lounge where the hotel hosted their nightly happy hour and morning continental breakfast for their most frequent guests. At one in the morning, it should have been empty. Instead, a slightly disheveled man dozed uncomfortably on the leather sofa. He had that traveling look, like he'd just crossed the country and couldn't even make it to his room without flopping on the first couch he saw for a nap. Maybe he, too, had a vodka story to tell.

I should have been wary.

As I stepped out of the elevator, he jerked awake and was on his feet almost at the same moment. His blue eyes, frazzled from the sudden waking, connected with mine. "Maggie Rider?" he said.

My heart stopped. I'm sure I glanced at my purse—a dead give-away that I had something valuable to protect. I froze in my spot, which was the only thing I could think of given my own alcohol fog. The elevator door closed behind me, cutting off a fast escape.

"You're Maggie Rider. I know you are." The tall, sinewy man looked to be in his early fifties, but it was hard to tell with the gray stubble on his face and his thinning hair. He had a fine, aristocratic nose, and a cleft in his chin. With a shave and a good night's rest, he would have been handsome.

Finally, a few brain cells shook loose from their stupor. "Who are you?" I kept my eyes on his face so I wouldn't look at my purse again.

"I'm Phil Generett. I'm with—I *was* with the Department of Homeland Security." He edged a step closer and raised his hands slightly toward me, palms out, as if trying to approach a wild animal for capture.

My heart started beating again, faster and heavier. I hastily glanced around the sitting room for an escape route, knowing in advance that I only had two ways to go: the hallway on the other side of this man and the closed elevator behind me. "What do you want? Why are you here?" I wished I'd sounded meaner. I hated these people.

"I need to talk to you." His voice stayed soft and he took another step towards me.

"Don't come a step closer, or I'll scream loud enough to wake people three floors below." This was assuming, of course, that I didn't burst into tears first, but I didn't tell him that part.

"I need to talk to your husband, to Eddy."

"Never. Never in a thousand years. Why would I lead you to him? So you can give him smallpox like you gave Daniel Pogodov? So you can take him away like you did Tina Bastante?"

He didn't move except to motion a little with his open hands to quiet me. "I know you've been through a terrible ordeal. I've seen your file. That's why I'm here. I've been through my own horrible, horrible—" he stopped as his voice caught. I swear he was on the verge of crying, but he halted a moment before.

"Leave me alone. Just leave me alone," I said. "I don't know how you found me or what you want or what you think you can get from me, but I'll never take you to Eddy."

He took a deep, slow breath and started again. "I've been through my own horrendous time, which is why I've come so far to talk to you."

"There's nothing I have to say to Homeland Security. I won't talk to you. I won't talk to anyone from there. Now leave me alone."

"No, no, no. I'm not with the DHS anymore. That's why I came looking for you."

I snorted. "Why should I believe you? I've heard it all from your Mario Seneca."

"Mario." He shook his head.

I couldn't read what he meant.

"Look. I just have to show you something so you'll believe me." He lifted his wallet out of his back pocket and pulled out a worn, folded newspaper clipping. "Here. If you read this, maybe you'll believe me." He handed the clipping to me, but I refused to take it. It was a trick and I wasn't going to be stupid enough to fall for it.

His hand shook slightly. His eyes begged me. But I still didn't touch it.

Finally, he opened it and held it out for me. It was an obituary from the *Washington Post*, dated three days earlier. The striking young woman had the same fine nose and cleft chin as the man in front of me. I took the clipping from his hand and read the saga of this brilliant, engaging young woman whose list of early achievements filled half the column. Her unexpected exposure to smallpox and subsequent agonizing death occurred in her junior year at Columbia, just after she left for a semester of study in Paris. Her mother, grandparents, and an infant brother had preceded her in death. Survivors included only her father.

Phil wearily sat down on the couch. When he spoke again, his voice was hoarse with defeat. He spoke so softly I could hardly hear him. "My job at the DHS was to chase the terrorists who started this grisly epidemic. My job became difficult when I realized it was us—the DHS—that I was chasing. I made the mistake of telling my supervisor that I was going to the press to expose the whole sordid mess." He laughed a dry, humorless laugh. "They said I wouldn't want to do that since I might be surprised about who else would get exposed. I didn't get it. I thought they meant it would go up the chain and this mess would taint the DHS director or even the president, which was exactly what I wanted. Instead, they meant the real kind of exposure. The kind that kills the one you love most." He buried his face in his hands and sobbed broken, jagged fistfuls of air.

It was déjà vu. First Anna, and now this man, the latter's story a shadow of the other's. If he was acting, if this was a DHS trick, it was an unmatched performance. He could have moved a stone to tears. Being more of the dripping sponge sort myself, I let go, too. Since I was already too spent before I even began, in a moment, I'd collapsed into the chair across from him, digging for tissues in my purse and vaguely wondering how I'd fallen so far from grace in such a short time.

I gritted my teeth while I tried to stop my tears. He was still the enemy, no matter what story he invented.

"She never got on the plane for Paris. Instead, they held her at security in the airport and then transported her to a holding area outside DC. That's how it's done. They don't want to accidentally start a *real* epidemic." He choked on a laugh. "What an irony." He stopped to blow his nose and wipe his eyes. "They told me that if I talked to anyone, ever, about my suspicions, they'd expose her."

"What were they going to do? Hold her forever?"

He sighed. "I made the mistake of asking the same thing."

"And they said?"

"They said they would if they had to." His voice caught again. "You don't have children—" His eyes drooped, and he twisted his hands together in a strangely apologetic look. "I'm sorry. I've seen your file."

I was too weary to even be offended, much less surprised.

"You don't have children," he began again, "but it sounds like you and Eddy are still passionate about each other after all these years, so maybe you can understand what it feels like to have lost the only thing you ever truly cared about in life."

I could. I did. Every minute of the past week.

"It made me crazy. I promised everything and signed my name in blood. I even turned over the document that I was writing up for the *The Washington Post* reporter. That was my mistake. They saw how serious I was—that I'd already written something. And they realized I understood players and details." He ran his fingers through his thinning hair and looked at me. "So they went ahead and exposed her." He said something else, but it was so garbled from his tears that I could only guess. His body shook in silent sobs.

I waited, my own tears slower and softer.

"I didn't even get a chance to say goodbye. Once they took her, that was it." He took a series of slow, deep breaths before he could finish. "Is there anything more cruel?"

Neither of us spoke. It was the ultimate rhetorical question.

Finally, when his emotions had seemed to settle back below the surface again, he blew his nose one more time. "They've been watching me. Ever since they told me she'd been exposed, they watched to see what I'd do. But here's another irony for you. I've spent all my time chasing down terrorists. I've learned a few tricks of my own." The humorless laugh returned. "The funeral is on Monday, but I left town. No one expected that. I bought a cheap car and drove west. I had your file. I knew Eddy had disappeared, but I knew where I could find you. I want him to post my story on his website. I don't even trust the press anymore."

I believed him. I really did. But I couldn't let go of my mistrust that easily. Besides, it was a moot point since I didn't know where Eddy was. "Phil, even if I knew where he was, I wouldn't take you to him. You have to understand that."

He nodded and twisted his hands again. "I do. But I don't have any other place to go. Eddy's website is the one everyone in DHS is most afraid of. If he posts my story, it'll get the national attention we need to stop this thing in its tracks."

"Do you really believe that?"

"You have any other ideas for stopping this?"

It was a dangerous question, one I wasn't going to answer.

He reached under the couch and pulled out a thin manila envelope. "Take it. Read it. If you believe me, I'll give you the rest of what I have. Leave a message for me at the Starbucks on Powell Street. Tell them the message is for Frank."

I took the envelope. Once again, my heart pounded.

"You should know, Maggie, that you don't have much longer to produce Eddy. Twenty-four hours? Two days max from when they first contacted you. They want him bad. If he doesn't surface, they'll use you as bait. Live or die, either way you lose."

It wasn't an idle threat. It was the truth. My head tightened: I was well past the twenty-four-hour mark. "They find him, though, and they'll kill him."

"Which is why you need to disappear. Don't wait."

I knew he was right. I was drained of everything, though.

"Why are they doing this, Phil? Why does the government want to be able to track everyone in the country?"

He grunted softly. "They have knowledge, they gain control. They get control, they have the ultimate power. No more political dissent. No more crime. No more street gangs. No more unwanted immigrants. No more whatever the hot issue du jour is. You jaywalk? They'll know. They'll take corrective action. You jaywalk again? They'll know. The second time, it won't be corrective action. It'll be a solution."

"All under the guise of stopping terrorism.

"Or a smallpox epidemic."

"Or a national propensity to jaywalk."

"You got it." He leaned toward me. "And the pièce de résistance? The folks running the country? They'll never lose power because they control everything. Including you."

He stood, finally ready to leave. "One more thing? Check the hems of your clothes. Ten to one says our friend Mario has slipped in a few RFIDs. The active kind. He'll find and follow you one way or another."

"Mr. Seneca is an artful sort of guy."

Phil Generett tilted his head slightly and nodded. And then he was out the emergency stair exit, his footsteps echoing on the metal stairs until the door closed firmly behind him.

An RFID tag. Duh.

I scrambled to check the hems and seams of each article of clothing: underwear, jackets, slacks, everything. If he added an RFID, he would have had a hard time camouflaging it unless he had a knack for sewing. Sure enough. The hem of the right leg on my khaki silk slacks had a couple of stitches missing. I carefully felt the fabric and thought I detected something stiff. I dug around in my makeup bag for my tweezers, then gingerly poked into the hem until I retrieved a spidery wafer the size of a dime.

Phil Generett had been right: I'd been tagged.

I felt every centimeter of every single item I owned and found three more devices, which I flushed down the toilet.

Track that, you bastards.

Even with those successes, I didn't know if I could trust that I'd caught all of the RFIDs. If he'd planted one—or several—in my suitcase, they could be too easily lost in the folds and stiff seams.

I stared at my possessions, a sad, sick feeling in my stomach. My computer first, and now my clothes and suitcase had become my enemy, betraying my moves as easily as my cell phone.

They were just things.

So I was mad at myself for crying about saying goodbye to my Hugo Boss suit and Santorelli tweed jacket, the sweet little Ann Taylor cashmere sweater, and even the nameless bargain rack black lace skirt that went on every trip since it was fun enough to fit every single occasion. Except work.

I kept my shoes and jewelry but not the cosmetics. He could have pried off a top and dropped an RFID into a lotion or conditioner. It was painful, but when I weighed the things versus life, I knew. I had to dump them. The few possessions that seemed clean went into a hotel laundry bag. The rest stayed in my suitcase. I'd take a short nap and risk that there'd be no midnight knock on my door. Then I'd leave my contaminated suitcase with the hotel night clerk for safekeeping. Some day I'd be back for it.

There are so many ways to delude oneself.

I finally crawled into bed at 3:00 a.m. in an RFID-free nightgown. Moments before I swirled away into a netherworld of pox-filled nightmares, I remembered Jola and Anna. Had I led the DHS to them?

And then I remembered the manila envelope.

A high-pitched, relentless pounding yanked me to the surface of my dreams.

They'd come for me in the night after all. In a panicked frenzy, I fumbled in the dark for my bag and stumbled to the door, then to the balcony, then to the phone to call for help, never quite grasping what I could do to save myself. I had no plan. I couldn't think.

The screeching sound rhythmically persisted for a full minute before all that adrenaline finally spread from my limbs into my brain and woke me up.

I turned off the alarm.

The angry noise stayed in my ears, though, as the blood kept right on rushing through my system until I could calm my heart. If I needed prodding to get out of there, I'd just gotten it. I quickly showered and dressed, sorting, sorting, sorting through my few options as I got ready. Whatever I did, I had to figure out how to give myself as much lead-time as possible.

I made a quick stop at the front desk. Lucky me, my friend Tony stood a sleepy guard over the early checkouts. I left my suitcase with him and asked for a late checkout, which he generously made for four o'clock. I also left my rental car keys with him and asked him to call Hertz late afternoon to come pick it up. The two things combined would make them think I was returning to my hotel room. It gave me more than a ten-hour lead. Never mind that I still didn't have any idea where I was going to go, especially at this hour of the morning.

If Tony thought I looked exceptionally frazzled, he politely ignored it.

The things they must teach them in hotel management.

I caught the shuttle to the airport so I could take BART some place. The bus station stuck in my mind, but I didn't know where I'd go or even where the bus station was. The ideas rattled around and around as I rode a nearly empty BART toward the city. The others in the car had that bed-head, bleary-eyed early morning flight look, so I was pretty sure no one had caught up with me. Just in case, though, I got off at the first station. No one else did.

A good sign. A very good sign.

I sat on a bench outside the station and watched the morning colors creep along the horizon and the tree silhouettes delineate into branches, leaves, and bark. The coffee out of the machine was surprisingly good: dark and complex. If I hadn't been on the run, it might have been a cozy morning. As it was, anyone who passed by could have mistaken me for a bag lady, maybe an upscale one since my bag was from the Sheraton, complete with a laptop. God knows why I didn't leave it since I couldn't use it without being tracked.

I sipped and thought. I didn't know where Eddy was. I had a limited amount of cash. I had the JavaScript from Daniel and the unread web exposé from Phil Generett. If I got on a bus, I would be heading away from anyone I knew who had the skills to use Daniel's silver bullet. Or I might be one step closer to Eddy posting Phil's revelation on smallpoxscare.com for millions to read, assuming—of course—that it was anything worth reading. I retrieved the manila envelope from my Sheraton bag and skimmed the dozen pages. The first several pages began with a methodical accounting of who had made what decisions in what meetings. Since I didn't recognize names, the bone-chilling decisions next to their names meant little to me. It would take a real Washington insider to determine the value of the information. I couldn't help but be disappointed. Where was the smoking gun?

The next few pages listed all events up to the president's announcement on Friday that everyone entering the country would need proof of vaccination. The existing timeline was helpful in that it provided more detail than Eddy had on his site. All of this information was out there already, just uncollected. Eddy would have called it a lot of freestanding trees. Collected, it became a forest.

The timeline also included anticipated DHS mandates through May first. If true, the list would ultimately incorporate every segment of society: all food handlers—from farm workers through McDonald's dishwashers—by February fifteenth; all newborns, preschoolers, school children, and college students by March first; all travelers, including bus, train, and intercity systems, by April first; anyone part of a public gathering—defined as loosely as shopping in a mall or attending a Little League baseball game—by May first. The projected timeline was certainly chilling but, without seeing the backup documentation, hardly the stuff to trigger holding a daughter hostage and then exposing her to smallpox. If Eddy posted this to his website, he could quickly be made to look like the ultimate nut, particularly since this administration seemed especially gifted in the art of changing the conversation by focusing on someone else's single misstep.

I began to worry that all this useless information meant Phil Generett's midnight visit was really something else. And then I reached the second-to-last page, which was an Excel spreadsheet, rows 3259-3284. A series of columns listed names, dates, triggers, status, locations, and notes. This particular page had been sorted by date, beginning on Monday of this past week. Phil had highlighted row 3272:

Name: Bastante, Dr. Tina.
Date: 17-JAN
Trigger: Removed vaccinations without authorization
Status: Detained
Location: La Vista Correctional Facility, Pueblo, CO
Notes: Decision to deport or expose: 22-JAN

Yesterday. They were going to decide her fate yesterday. The papers shook in my hands. Somehow, Tina—detainee number 3,272—had bought a few extra days. My stomach tightened and my eyes blurred as I thought about the horror of her past week. I pressed my back against the wall behind me and squeezed my eyes shut as I tried to maintain my balance. This casual row in a list of thousands was my friend, a real person, identified only by a date, a trigger, a status, a location, and a detached notation.

The names above and below her hadn't all been allowed a grace period. A few still had the status of "Detained, undetermined," but the rest were listed as either exposed or deported. The notes themselves revealed little. Cryptic comments, void of judgment, followed each name: Deported to Syria, Refused to cooperate, Guantanamo, Brother to Aaron Swartzendruber, Member of Philadelphia Center for Peace and Justice.

If I understood the list, over three thousand people had been detained, deported, or deliberately exposed to smallpox. If this list was real, it was more than a smoking gun. It was a napalm bomb.

And what an irony. There were, in fact, real victims. Just not the kind the government wanted us to know about.

My heart weighed so much I nearly forgot to look at the final page. The truth? I'm sorry I did. It detailed the lives of Edward and Margaret Rider, as well as their crimes against humanity. Eddy had taunted the myth. I had dared to be married to him.

I don't truly think it was wasted time, but I sat there for at least another fifteen minutes separating out my choices. At one point, I rummaged around in my purse for change to call Jola from the pay phone at the station. Instead of finding a wayward quarter, though, I felt an odd bump under the fabric lining. Even though the device was nearly paper thin, it could still only mean one thing. A blue moment later, my fingers found the gap in a seam of the lining and worked the RFID to the surface. It looked different from the ones in my clothes, but it still had distinctive, coppery tendrils wound in a tight, large spiral. I dumped the rest of my purse contents onto a newspaper and sorted through it piece by piece. Nothing else surfaced, but that didn't tell me whether I could trust my fingers and eyes.

I only had the number for Anna's restaurant. No one would be there at this hour anyway, so I couldn't call her to warn her. I finally scrounged up enough change to call Jola. It was a mistake: in spite of the ungodly early hour, the phone only rang and rang and rang. I added it to my list of things to obsess about. Worry and guilt are a bad mix.

I was frozen to the spot, tired of being the rodent in this dangerous cat and mouse game. Yet I knew I had to do something. I didn't know how quickly they could track me to this spot, but I knew I'd better assume minutes, not hours.

"Excuse me, Miss."

I looked up, half expecting to see a DHS badge flipped open. Instead, a gray, slightly shrunken woman paused in front of me. "Yes?"

"Do you have any change for a twenty? I thought I had another five, but I can't find it." The purse slung over her arm looked warehouse size. If it had been full, she would have listed from the weight. It was a beautiful thing to see. She'd never spot the added fraction of an ounce from the RFID.

I dug around in my own wallet and unearthed a bill. "I don't have change, but I do have a five." As I handed her the money, I casually dropped the tracking device into her gaping bag.

"Oh, you don't have to give me the money, dear."

"No, no. Really, it's fine." I'd just bought a cheap and wonderful ticket for my RFID to hitch a ride into the city. She owed me much more than I owed her. I just hoped I wasn't leading DHS straight to her Iranian son-in-law. I'd have to bury that guilt before I let it grow.

BART arrived and I helped the woman into a car, thankful that this small diversion could help.

Slightly less weighed-down, I called Michael, even though he'd abandoned me when I needed to connect with Sanjeev. I knew his cell phone number by heart, and in spite of everything, I trusted him.

A drowsy voice answered. "Hello?"

"Michael?"

There was a very long pause. "Maggie?"

"I know it's early, but I need your help."

Another long pause. "Did the sun wake you, Maggie?"

"I'm sorry. Really I am. But I'm desperate."

"Well. It's, uh, not terribly convenient right now."

"Can I come stay at your place for a few days?"

The pause grew longer. Maybe I'd made a terrible mistake. "You want to stay at my place? You do know it's seven in the morning on a Sunday?"

"I know. I'm really sorry. I'll sleep on the couch. I'll sleep in a closet. I just have to get out of my hotel. This whole thing has gotten way out of hand."

He didn't talk for a minute, but I could hear him sighing, not just breathing, on the other end.

"So here's the, uh, deal." Another pause with more sighing. "I'm not exactly at my place."

"What do you mean?"

"Well, the thing with Kai? The dinner, the dancing, it, uh, turned into ... uh, more."

More. How discreet.

I blushed. How stupid of me to forget the date I'd set up for him. Life had gone marching on. "Right. Sorry. I'm really sorry."

We had an awkward pause. I heard some distant conversation on his end. "But you could come to Kai's place. She says she'll fix breakfast."

"No. No, no. I don't want to intrude." I'll just hang on by my fingernails another fifteen minutes. Don't worry about me.

More distant conversation. Then, "No problem, really. We'll figure out something."

He gave me the address, a ten-dollar cab ride away.

I did my sighing after we hung up. Mostly they were ones of temporary relief.

KAI LIVED ON A WINDING, bougainvillea-lined hill within walking distance of the Tiger Lily. Her third-floor apartment faced in the direction of the bay, and by standing on tiptoes on her balcony, you could actually glimpse a tiny sliver of blue water through the forest of other apartments.

Everyone loves a water view.

By the time I got there, Kai already had coffee made and had Michael chopping vegetables for omelets while she threw stuff together for some kind of coffeecake. He looked sleepy and in a little disarray, but otherwise happy. Maybe I shouldn't have since I knew as much about Kai as she could see of the bay, but I poured out my story anyway, at least the part about Sanjeev's threat and the DHS hit list. I even pulled out the page with the detainees listed and the final page that marked Eddy and me.

Michael didn't interrupt, but he kept shaking his head while he chopped.

Kai was more wide-eyed. "So what will you do?" she asked.

"I don't know." I shook my head. "I don't even know where Eddy is. But I have to find him before they do."

"And at the same time, you have to stay hidden." Kai threw some of the vegetables into sizzling oil. The pungent scent of garlic immediately filled the tiny space. She shook her head.

"I can't believe this is happening here. I can't believe it. This is why my family came to America, to escape government tyranny. And now—" She gave a quick stir to the vegetables. "—now, look at this. I just can't believe it." But even as she said it, it was clear she absolutely did believe it.

Michael groaned softly. He'd finished his chopping and now leaned against the counter, a cup of coffee in his hand. "I still don't know why you didn't just stay under the radar. After everything you knew, why did Eddy think he should keep that website up?"

I stared at him. "So you think we should have just saved our skins? That that's the first priority?"

"That's not what I'm saying." He ran his fingers through his wayward hair and looked to Kai for help, which she didn't look like she was going to give. You can only get so much from a fourteen-hour date.

"What I mean is that ... I mean, what can you do? You're tilting at windmills. You'll end up dying—or worse, and you won't have changed anything."

"So who will stop this mess?"

"She's right," Kai said impatiently. "Someone has to have courage here."

I liked her. I was still a little irritated with Michael, but our friendship would survive that. He had an honest heart even if he didn't have much nerve.

"But how do you fight Homeland Security?" he asked. "Not in the courts. They've proven that one over and over."

"Information. The more people know about what DHS is doing, the more vulnerable they are."

"I don't want to point out the obvious here, Maggie, but all of Eddy's information hasn't exactly been even a speed bump for DHS. They're all paranoid about it and want to put Eddy in front of a firing squad, but they're still able to scare people into getting vaccinated."

"Then you find the chink in their armor," Kai said. She

poured beaten eggs into a couple of omelet pans and swirled them around.

"How are you going to do that?" Michael asked. "They spent a hundred and twenty million on the Zaan share alone."

Kai waved her spatula at him. "What do you mean? It's just software. You guys wrote the code. How tough can that be?"

"Don't get me started." Michael rolled his eyes.

"Exactly," Kai said. "Look at how many bodies you've thrown at the shipping application to get it to *start* working. How tough can it be to get the software to *stop* working?"

"It *is* just software," I said. "People hack into systems all the time. They plant a little stick of dynamite, let the virus run its course, and never pause."

Michael shook his head. "It's one thing to hack into Microsoft. They're notorious for having so many vulnerable spots. Zaan is bulletproof, though. It's what we're known for in the industry."

"It's bulletproof unless—" I hesitated. I still didn't truly know Kai.

"Unless—?" Michael asked

"Unless you have a back door—"

"—into the software?" he finished my sentence

I nodded.

"Do you?" Kai asked.

I paused, then nodded. "I think I do. Daniel Pogodov, the Zaan developer who died from smallpox, sent some JavaScript to his girlfriend. He said it would get us into the software."

Michael and Kai looked at each other. I wasn't quite sure what passed between them.

"What do you have?" Michael finally said.

I picked up my Sheraton laundry bag and retrieved the pages Anna had given me. Michael spread them out on the counter and studied them.

"Does it look like Zaan programming?" I asked.

He shrugged his shoulders. "It could be. I don't truly know. I only see some of the programming stuff, but I never have to actually touch it." He studied the pages a little longer. "It's definitely written in Java."

In between pulling the coffeecake out of the oven and sliding a couple of giant omelets onto a serving platter, Kai looked over Michael's shoulder and did her own studying. "So what are you going to do with it?"

"I know someone in Zaan Development. I'm hoping she can take this information and find that chink in the armor."

Neither Michael nor Kai said anything while we took a moment to serve ourselves and another minute to savor what Kai had accomplished. Without question, waiting tables was a waste of her talents.

"Have you shown her this yet?" Michael asked. "Can she make sense of it?"

I shook my head. "I tried calling her this morning, but she didn't answer the phone."

Kai must have read my face. "Maybe she stayed with a friend last night." She glanced at Michael and kind of giggled. "It happens."

He blushed. "Or maybe she turned the ringer off on her phone." He glanced at Kai. "Like *I* should on a weekend."

"Maybe." I still had to live with the electronic breadcrumb trail I'd left.

"Here's an idea," Kai said. "This dishwasher at the restaurant who's working his way through Stanford? He's some kind of programming whiz, always coming in and bragging about hacking into this company or that system. Claims he never does anything, just goes in and looks around."

"Why would he do this? What's in it for him?" Michael asked.

I shrugged my shoulders. "Why does anyone hack into a system? For the fun of it. For the challenge."

Kai tilted her head slightly. "For him, maybe it's more. He's Russian." As if that said it all.

I twitched at the coincidence. "Russian?" I hadn't thought through how I was going to get Daniel's first page translated. This seemed peculiarly convenient. I tried to shake it off.

Kai nodded, missing my uneasiness. "He's older, somewhere in his late thirties. He lived under communism long enough that it shaped his view of the world. At heart, he's an anarchist."

A geeky anarchist. The world really needed one more of them.

"So you really think he'd do this, even with the risk?" Michael asked. "This isn't your ordinary jail time if he gets caught."

"For him? The risk would be the carrot. He'd do it in a heartbeat."

This conversation had leaped too far too fast. As thrilled as I was that Michael and now Kai, too, were willing to help me, I just wasn't ready to hand this over to a total stranger.

But Kai didn't notice. She swept the papers together in a stack and left the room. A minute later, she came back with the originals and copies. "The restaurant's closed tonight, so I know he's not working. I'll invite him over for a beer, and we'll see what he can do with this."

She finally must have realized how on edge I was because she patted my hand and smiled. "Relax, Maggie. We're going to make this work." Then she leaned over to Michael and kissed him on the cheek. "I'm so excited. I've always wanted to save the world."

They both laughed, but I didn't.

WHAT I REALLY NEEDED WAS A GOOD NIGHT'S SLEEP. But since it was closing in on noon, I settled for a fifteen-minute nap on the couch followed by a little Gmail time on Kai's computer. I shouldn't have wasted the nap time. There, in heartwarming black and white, was a short, sweet message from Easy. Easy Rider, my dad's nickname for the only one of my boyfriends he ever liked.

Mz M, Heard you were in town. How about dinner at your favorite SF restaurant ... date 1 time ... rez under my favorite movie star.

He was here, in California. Finally, all the worry that had sapped my energy and clarity came to a sharp end. I was weak. My childhood—or at least life from the last eighteen years—flooded through me, filling me with intense nostalgia. My skin had returned.

His code was simple enough: we would meet at Sam's Chowder Bowl, a hole in the wall seafood place down by the Embarcadero that had the best fish and chips on the planet. He wanted to meet at four o'clock, the hour of our first date ever. Back then, he'd been too broke to take me to dinner and a movie, so I gladly settled for a matinee and an Eddy-built picnic. The reservation name was a decoy. The takeout place only had six tables and took as many dinner reservations as your average Burger King.

But the decoy told me he didn't trust email even with the new addresses we each had.

Now I faced a dilemma: should I tell Michael and Kai I was going to meet Eddy? Or should I keep those cards close to my chest? They'd been generous and quick-thinking; Michael had been my friend for ages—at least in Zaan years. Somehow, though, the morning had left me uneasy, like figuring out a puzzle too quickly. Sometimes, the solution is for real. Sometimes, there has to be a hitch.

I went with my instincts and told them I was going to Jola's house to see if she could figure out anything with the JavaScript. Kai said to get her to come and meet Stepan the Dishwasher.

We should all have such a moniker.

Kai called a cab for me, which I took to the closest BART station. From there, I took BART for several stops, jumped out at the last possible moment, and waited for another train. I rode that to the end of the line, walked a few blocks, and hopped on a streetcar. I backtracked with a cab to within walking distance of Jola's. I hadn't seen a single person follow me yet. In fact, for all I knew no humans had to be on the ground because they could track me from the sky by way of some unfound RFID on me. Still, there was a whisper of something, an uneasiness that shadowed me. People looked vaguely familiar on streetcars and sidewalks. When they looked at me, I felt disquieted. When they quickly glanced away, I became anxious. The only thing I could be sure about was that the effort distracted me from thinking nonstop about Eddy and counting down the minutes till I saw him again.

A block from Jola's, I stopped at a corner coffee shop, not quite ready to knock on her door and know for sure she wasn't home. I could see her house from the coffee shop window, the lavender siding and pink flowers a lovely bookmark on the extravagantly painted row. I might not have even noticed the dark sedan parked a couple of houses up the hill except that two people sat in the car, not talking, not sightseeing, not even reading a map as far as I could tell. It wasn't a Sunday thing to do, and it made me nervous.

I watched them as I sipped my coffee. For five minutes, then ten minutes, they just sat. They were waiting for someone. Maybe Jola.

Maybe me.

I dialed Jola's number. The phone rang over and over. I hung up and told myself that the only thing *that* told me was that Jola wasn't home. Probably. I would have felt much better if I'd talked to her in person and she could have confirmed that there'd been no knock on the door in the middle of the night. I tried calling Anya's Place, Anna's restaurant in Palo Alto. After the first ring, a recording said that the restaurant was closed due to a death and that it would reopen on Tuesday as usual. A small worry poked at me. Why was the restaurant open on Saturday night but not Sunday? Why wasn't it just closed until after the funeral?

I was surprised at how easily I could suspect even the smallest event. I was beginning to think I had an unexpected gift for paranoia.

I returned to my table by the window and watched the two people in the dark car up the street. Something had woken them up. The passenger talked on a phone and the headlights came on. The car was running and they were ready to move.

The two of them suddenly looked animated, and the driver actually pointed down the street. Suddenly, the headlights flicked off and both people—one of them Mario Seneca, the other a black guy with a shaved head—stepped out of the car and started giant striding in the direction of the coffee shop.

In the direction of me.

"You have a back door?" I frantically asked the only woman behind the counter. "I need a back door, fast." She looked young and slightly worn already; she was my best chance. "My boy-friend's been beating on me, so I split. Now he sent some of his goon friends after me."

She shifted her eyes back and forth a moment. My ring finger suddenly weighed a thousand pounds.

I didn't have time for her to narrow her eyes and think about what might be true. "Please," I urged as softly as I could. "You can see them headed this way. The one guy is a government creep. He'll flash a badge at you. Just ignore him."

Maybe she'd had a brush with the law—after all, it was San Francisco—but that triggered something. She flipped open the half door next to her and waved me back toward a small hallway beyond. I took three steps and shoved open a metal door, finding myself in a dingy interior hall with a half-dozen doors opening into it. At the end of the hall, an exit sign pointed the way out to the left. I hoped and ran, bursting into the cool afternoon air a moment later.

The door emptied out onto the opposite street of the coffee shop. It gave me a half-block head start, as long as they didn't figure out what had happened and leap the counter after me. I sprinted across the street, wishing for more trees or cars to provide a tiny bit of cover. An alley miraculously opened up on my left, and I ducked in, praying that it didn't dead end in a heap of trashcans. In my last fleeting glance up the street, I saw Mario Seneca round the corner. He shouted something angry and dashed across the street. A car screeched to a halt just behind him. His weight was in my favor, but for all I knew, his partner could have been a marathon runner.

The worst happened: the alley dead-ended a hundred feet in front of me. A hammer pounded in my chest. I couldn't think fast enough. A fraction away from crazy, I scanned the sheer walls for something, a dangling fire escape, a dumpster, an open doorway. Anything to disappear into. But the place was clean of even a rain gutter. Then, at the last moment, the alley broke open to my right; daylight spilled in from the street ahead. I tried to listen for footsteps beating on the street ahead or the alley behind, but nothing was louder than my own adrenaline rushing through my head. Mario had to be closing in behind me, but I didn't dare look.

Ahead, the alley dumped out onto a quiet street lined with clean, colorful row houses.

Retail. That's what I needed. Where was a mall when I desperately needed one?

I glanced to the right, the direction someone would be running from. The street was empty. I headed left, then left again at the first corner. It was the least logical direction since it took me uphill and closer to, rather than further from, the corner coffee shop. The street, still residential, at least had cars crammed bumper to bumper against the curb. I squeezed between two and dropped on fours to see if I could see running feet. Thirty seconds later black pants raced into the street, did a small dance of uncertainty, and then took off downhill. Slower khaki pants followed twenty paces behind. Khaki pants did the same confused downhill-then-straight-ahead-then-downhill shuffle and disappeared in the same direction as black pants.

I was momentarily lost to them.

I stayed crouched between the cars for at least ten minutes that might have been ten days. I didn't see black or khaki pants return, so I peeked out between the cars on the sidewalk side. Again, nothing. I took a deep breath, stood, and scanned the empty street downhill from me, which was filled with a dozen shops and restaurants. Then as casually as I could, I did a Sunday stroll back towards and through the alley, back up the street, and flagged the first cab I saw. From a third floor window, someone could have seen the sweat on my forehead.

The cab took me to Sausalito on the other side of the Golden Gate Bridge. Mario and his friend would never think to look for me there, but just to be safe, I asked the cab driver for a bag and emptied my sunglasses, cash, credit cards, and some loose junk out of my purse, creating new nuances in the meaning of "bag lady." I made a lousy trade—my six-month old Coach bag for the cab fare—but I was thankful that I'd at least snagged one of the more sophisticated cabbies in San Francisco.

I was now stripped of nearly everything external that defined me.

Logic told me that the DHS had been staking out Jola's place because I'd led them there the day before. I was sick—really sick—about that, but I couldn't change it. On a gut level, though, I couldn't shake my fear that I still carried some RFID on me. Maybe I'd swallowed one at lunch. Maybe they had sprinkled RFID dust on me while I slept.

Maybe they'd finally gotten so clever that they simply knew.

I sat on the wharf, shaking and waiting for the ferry that would take me back across the Bay to Pier 39 in time to meet Eddy at four. For a chilly January Sunday, a surprising number of tourists strolled the walk by the sea. If they were looking for me, they didn't seem to spot me. Just before the ferry shoved off the pier, I hopped on.

I was the last passenger on. Even though the line between sea and sky was thick and wet, I rode on the deck and wished for a clearer head. Big-as-turkey seagulls floated beside the boat, but I didn't have any bread to throw them.

Four o'clock crept closer. My anxiety inched higher.

Once we docked, I headed toward the seafood dive, all the while glancing behind, ahead, and behind me again. Even though I was sure I'd given them the slip, I was so terrible at this game they might have been waiting for me at the next bench.

Tucked inside a small warren of tourist shops, Sam's Chowder Bowl was the perfect place to meet. The bell on the door jingled a welcome as I entered the warm, slightly steamy café. The tiny space was empty except for a powerfully attractive dark-haired man at a corner table. I didn't let myself make eye contact with

Eddy until I'd finished ordering and paying. If the clerk thought I was weird for getting a little weepy over a mid-afternoon lunch, he kept from rolling his eyes. I took my Coke and headed for Eddy's table. He stood up and casually kissed me, as though we were a comfortable couple separated for a few hours and not the nightmare week we'd just endured. My heart pounded. He squeezed my hand tight and pulled me into the seat next to him facing the door and counter.

"You're safe."

"Thank God you're here."

"I love you."

"I can't believe this is happening."

Our words softly tumbled over each other. He rubbed my neck and held my hand. I intertwined the fingers of the hand that was on top of mine. The details of the last couple of hours poured out in a nearly incoherent stream.

"But you don't think you were followed here?"

"I don't think so. I don't know."

His fingers squeezed mine tighter.

"I was so worried about you."

"I knew you would be, and I felt terrible about it, but after I found your health card on my computer, I knew I had to get out of there. I didn't trust your cell phone, and I was afraid your hotel or work phone might have been tapped. I didn't dare email you, either. I just threw some things in a suitcase, cleaned off everything I could from my desktop computer, and took my laptop. I split town before they could miss me for not showing up at the Fox interview."

"But they hacked into your computer on Friday and gtalked me."

"The idiots. Like they could pass for someone on gtalk. They weren't even smart enough to be suspicious about how easy it was to get into my computer."

"So you changed your passwords?"

"Removed them. I wanted to see if they'd come back, and what they'd do. The extra five minutes it took might give me some good fingerprints."

I knew he meant the computer tracking kind of fingerprints, not the FBI kind.

"*If* we ever go home again," he said softly.

"If we go home again." I knew he was right, but I hadn't put it into words until this moment.

He sighed. "I know. But there are a lot worse things to give up than our leather couch and loveseat." He lightly kissed my cheek. "I brought our photo albums and videos and the jewelry your mother left you. If I missed anything we can't live without, we can have Pete retrieve it and send it if he ever gets his head back on straight."

"Send it? To where?"

"I don't know yet. We'll figure it out later."

"So how did you get to California?"

"I drove. Here's the deal. On the way out of town, I sold Pete the Porsche for cash. He gave me some old Audi that he'd fixed up and the owners could never pay him for it. I got as far as Denver before I had second thoughts about racing across the country in an Audi, so I made some used-car lot guy a great trade for an old blue Taurus."

I laughed out loud. "A Taurus? The most generic car in the universe?"

"You want to disappear? How can you do it better than in a car that looks like every other car on the road?"

I picked up our orders at the counter and grabbed a handful of napkins. Eddy had been surprisingly brilliant about this whole escaping thing, but maybe that's what you get for always assuming the worst is going to happen. When it does, who could be better prepared?

We ate in silence for a few minutes. The fish was even better than I remembered—a crisp golden light batter on the outside, melt-in-your-mouth flaky on the inside. For that matter, I could have eaten just the tarter sauce with a spoon.

I reached for my second piece. "They're desperate to find you—to find both of us because they want me to lead them to you."

"I know. I know. I just don't know what to do."

"I have so much to tell you." I pulled the pages out of the manila envelope. "Maybe I've stumbled across some starting points." I leafed through it till I got to the page with Tina's information. "Take a look at this. There really are smallpox victims. But they're victims DHS has intentionally infected to punish or coerce or use as bait." I pointed to Tina's line. "Has Pete heard anything?"

Eddy shook his head and studied the page. "He's gone crazy. He keeps sending me emails that hardly make sense. If he saw this, he'd assault the penitentiary single-handedly."

"It's what I'd do."

"I know. I can't blame him." He sighed. "Where did you get this?"

"From the father of this woman." I gave him the obituary for Phil Generett's daughter. "They exposed her because he threatened to go to the media with what he knew."

"But he went anyway?"

I shook my head. "He promised not to, even gave them what he was going to turn over to the press. They were so freaked out by what he'd put together that they exposed her anyway and then watched to see what he would do. He found me and gave this stuff to me as a teaser. He wants you to post it all to your website." Even as I said it, the story sounded invented, with a hole at every turn.

He skimmed the pages, ignoring the bios of Edward and Margaret Rider and concentrating on the first few pages of the who, what, and when. "You know what this is?" he asked.

"At least a little."

"It's unbelievable." His hands shook slightly as he ate. "If it's true and if he has the paper trail to back it up, it's the smoking gun every federal prosecutor could ever dream of." He poked at the paper, leaving a tiny grease drop. "Look at these names and titles. Steven Wisenburg, Richard Champs—both are at the cabinet level. They meet with the president every day." He pointed to another name: Lester Goodencamp. "He's director of Homeland Security, one of the few who worked his way up the ranks and stayed."

"Not exactly household names."

"Which works in their favor. Everyone knows the president and VP. Fewer people know the visible congressmen. Hardly anyone can name a cabinet member unless we're in the middle of a war, and then only the Secretary of Defense or State." He wiped his hands on a napkin and studied the pages more closely. "These decisions—they're outrageous: 'Identify RFID supplier,' 'Determine order of vaccination rollout,' 'Approve marketing strategy.' Look at these dates. Some of them date back a couple of years. Every one of them is before last September, months before the first reported smallpox case. Unbelievable. Absolutely unbelievable."

"It's almost too neat and tidy, isn't it?"

Eddy paused and slowly nodded. "Does he have more documentation to back this up?"

"He said he did." I told Eddy how I was supposed to contact Phil again. "But maybe it's a trap."

"Maybe." He stared at the pages. "Maybe."

As he mulled over that one, I took Anna's papers out of the envelope and spread them out.

"Here's more."

"From the same guy?"

I shook my head. "It's something entirely different. It's the programming script to get us into the CDC software through the back door."

Eddy looked at me and gave a half laugh. "How the hell did you come up with this?"

I fumbled to explain that whole vodka-hazed, tear-drenched night.

"So you bonded and she trusted you." That was the sense Eddy made of it.

"I guess so."

"Do you think you could have been set up?"

I shifted my eyes a little. "I don't know. Could be." I thought some more. "Does it look like it?"

"I don't have any way of knowing. But if it's a setup, the trap will close on anyone who gets close."

Michael, Kai, Stepan the Dishwasher. Me. Eddy.

"Here's the problem, Mz M." He'd finished his fish and was picking up the final deep fried breading crumbs with his fingers with one hand and had returned to massaging my neck with his other. "I have an anonymous friend out there. Some-one's been feeding me stuff—obscure articles out of major newspapers, advance notice of presidential announcements, a couple insider emails that initially contradicted the official word from the White House only to be proven accurate a few days later."

"Your own cyber Deep Throat."

"Exactly. So far, everything has been one hundred percent on the money. Not a mislead yet."

"But now?"

"I got an email this morning that was very personal. It said the DHS had already approached you unsuccessfully. They'd backed off to give you a chance to bring me in, but as of noon today, it was time to 'change Maggie's status,' which now makes more sense to me."

Every cell in my body shifted. There were only three status choices: Detained, Deported, Exposed.

With the crumbs cleaned up, Eddy took my hand again and whispered. "So here's the other thing. My source says that the backup plan is to set us up. He says, in fact, the backup plan has been put into motion." Our eyes locked. "And we bit."

"So. We're toast."

"We're toast."

"Unless we can figure out how we've been set up."

"Unless."

Eddy and I didn't talk for minutes. Our fingers stayed entwined while we sorted through possibilities.

"Okay. Give me all the things that happened this week. Where do you think we could have gotten hooked?"

I started with Sanjeev and his warning note to me, which I had along. Nothing in it suggested a setup. We set it aside.

My next encounter with DHS was Friday with Mario Seneca and his unseen partner who installed the spyware software on my computer. He warned me, and then somewhere along the way, convinced the hotel to let him into my room, where he planted RFIDs in my clothes.

"It's possible they thought of the spyware and RFID plants as the backup plan."

"Maybe," I said. "But it's not like we 'bit.' It's just something we might not have discovered."

"Probably so."

That left my visit with Jola, my vodka evening with Anna, and my morning with Michael and Kai.

"Jola didn't give you anything, though, right?"

"Just the names of the lead developers."

"So she's probably clean."

"Except that the DHS was there today, outside her house." My heart thudded at the thought of the DHS finding Jola because of me. "Maybe they tracked me to her house and compromised her."

"It could be. But they were waiting for someone—either you or Jola, so it sounds more like they were waiting to catch someone, not that we'd already taken the bait."

I nodded.

"So then you went to Anna's."

"But first, I spent hours in the library researching. I found Anna's name in Daniel's obituary."

"Which could have been a plant."

I had to think about that a minute. "I guess it's possible, but if you'd seen her, you'd believe her."

"That or she was a world-class actress."

I agreed halfheartedly. I had to stay open to all possibilities.

"Maybe she's legit, but someone sent her the letter in Daniel's name."

"And handwriting?"

"It could have been forced. Daniel could have been threatened with Anna being exposed if he didn't cooperate."

I thought about that possible chain of events. "That's entirely possible. But all this assumes we would have uncovered Anna, made the connection, and she would have trusted us enough to hand over the Java instructions."

"Anything's possible." Eddy tilted his head back and forth a couple times. "They could be laying out multiple traps for us. That's the one we just happened to fall into."

"So the next-likely is Phil Generett."

"It was quite a story."

"But it came with an obituary."

"Surely, that sort of thing could be planted."

"But why would he warn me about the RFID implants? And tell me I had less than forty-eight hours grace before the DHS came after me?"

"To build credibility?"

"Like your cyber Deep Throat who's been right every time?"

Eddy gave a sober nod.

"The worst that could happen is that you'd upload all his information and be wrong. But who would know or care before the story spread?"

"Unless we contact him for the rest of the story, meet him to pick up the rest of the document, and get arrested by a swarm of DHS guys."

I mentally shuffled that information into various paradigms. "It could happen." I thought some more. "It's a risk, though, that you wouldn't upload the pages you already have. Besides, you should have seen him. Again, it was an award-winning performance."

"So that leaves us with Michael, Kai, and Stepan the Stanford student dishwasher," Eddy said.

"It was too easy, wasn't it?"

"Seems that way. Except that it could never have fallen into place without Jola giving the name of Anna, who gave you the JavaScript back door."

"And that's way too much of a coincidence."

Eddy tilted his head in agreement.

We sat quietly some more. I said, "Who has the most to gain from catching us?"

"Good question. For that matter, what do any of them have to gain from this?"

"Money? A promotion for Phil Generett?"

"Seems like there'd be easier ways to earn either one."

None of it seemed likely. But then, Kai thought Stepan would be happy to hack into the CDC just for the fun of it. There's no telling what people would do to entertain themselves.

"Of course, there's one final possibility," I said. "Your cyber Deep Throat planted the suspicion for suspicion sake. If he can get us to second-guess everything and everybody, then we won't follow through with whatever plan we're building."

Eddy didn't say anything for a very long time. Finally, he sighed. "It's a very real option."

"So that leaves us where?"

"With nothing."

"That's what I was afraid of."

By the time we parted, only a few dusky colors outlined the city's hills, leaving the buildings and trees in tints and shades of purple. A crisp breeze whipped in from the Bay, scattering leaves and scraps of paper along the nearly empty streets. My wallet was fat with cash again, so I hailed a passing cab and sunk into its back seat for the quiet ride to Kai's. For the first few minutes, I watched out the back to see if anyone followed us, but in the fading light, I couldn't distinguish one set of headlights from another.

Eddy and I hadn't come up with much at all except a good rendezvous plan. But at least I'd seen him, touched him, kissed him again. We'd meet again in twenty-four hours. In the mean time, I would get together with Stepan, our new best hacker friend, and send a message to Phil Generett for more of his document. The plan kept us from standing still, but it didn't do much to figure out where the trap lay.

Stepan the Dishwasher was already nursing a beer and munching on peanuts by the handful when I walked in the door at Kai's. He stood to shake my hand, wiping the salt off first on his pant leg. His eyes, a dazzling Caribbean blue, could have single-handedly made me fall in love with him. He had that Slavic broad forehead and patrician nose, thin pale lips, and close-cropped white-blond hair. His features—and his striking eyes—combined into a pleasing combination. He was tall, too. He would stand out in a crowd for multiple reasons.

The three of them—Kai, Michael, and Stepan—were crowded around Kai's small kitchen table, Daniel's papers in front of them.

"Stepan has been translating the Russian for us," Michael said. "It's quite a story."

"He was lead developer on project," Stepan began. His minor grammatical flaw heightened the jagged edges and determined *R*'s of his accent. "When he start the project, it seem easy and simple. But then he see more and more. He has to tie software into RFID tracking. So he leave a back door in the software. In case this is bad as he think, he can--" here he cleared his throat and laughed uncomfortably. "He can 'fix' software to work differently." He nodded at me, a check to see if I understood what he meant by fix.

I understood perfectly.

"That's this Java." Stepan held up Daniel's script. "He give to friend for safekeeping and say to hide it from government."

"So can you fix it? Can you hack in to the CDC site and make the changes?" I asked.

The three others exchanged looks. My suspicion radar pinged, but there wasn't anything I could do about it.

"Yes. Yes, of course." Stepan waved his hands a bit. I apparently had asked a stupid question. "I can get in with this. But you must understand. He set it up for more than just to get in and change code. Code they can fix. He set it up for virus."

"A software virus?"

Stepan's mouth spread into a weird, tobacco-stained grin. "He say he stop a make-believe virus with a real virus." He laughed sharply. "Very clever, this Russian. Don't you think?"

Kai and Michael looked at me. I nodded. They relaxed ever so slightly.

"You can make this virus happen?" I asked.

"Yes." He shrugged his shoulders as though this were child's play. "Daniel do this very smart. Here is what he design. You go through security with health card. They scan it. Every thirty minutes the data automatically get uploaded to central server. At midnight, server is backed up again. The virus has a time clock. It releases twenty-four hours after it enters the system."

"Perfect," Kai laughed. "An incubation period."

Stepan shrugged his shoulders. "Incubation? I don't know this word."

"The time between exposure to a virus and the symptoms appearing."

"Ah, yes. I understand this 'incubation.'" Stepan smiled. With no tobacco teeth showing, it was beautiful. "It is the same with this virus."

"And you can do this?" I asked. It sounded too clever to be true.

"Yes. Is difficult, but yes, I can do this. But to do this like he write it, I will need health card and vaccination capsules. You can get these?"

A trap or not, my heart sank. I wanted to believe Stepan was legit. Now, even if he turned out to be, we were at a dead end. How could we ever get health cards and vaccination capsules?

Stepan patted around in the pockets of his jacket he'd draped over his chair. He found his cigarettes and offered them around. We all declined, so he tapped one out for himself and then patted his pockets again for matches. Before he could light up, Kai discreetly rose and opened the patio doors to her balcony. "Perhaps you'd be more comfortable smoking out here. Even at night, the view is lovely."

He scrunched his nose and snorted lightly, but he got up from the table. "I smoke. You talk. We come up with something." He waved his unlit cigarette at us. "Look at this smart bunch. An American, Asian, Spanish, and Russian." No one corrected his mistake about Michael's nationality. "We are very crafty countries. We think of a way."

He left the patio door slightly ajar just in case we were lying about wanting a smoke.

"Do you believe him?" Kai asked softly. "I mean about being able to hack his way in."

"Well, he's certainly very arrogant about his abilities," Michael said.

Kai smiled almost shyly at Michael. "He'd make a lousy Filipino."

Michael winked at her and draped his arm over her shoulder. What a time to flirt.

"He can be arrogant," I said trying to pull them back. "He knows there's no way we can get health cards and vaccination capsules." I watched Stepan's silhouette leaning on the balcony railing, the orange dot of the cigarette butt glowing brighter and then fading.

"Don't you know anyone in medicine? Anyone who would have access to blank health cards?" Kai asked.

I chewed on my thumbnail, nervous about where this was leading. Michael watched me.

"What about your friend, the doctor who was arrested this week?" he asked.

I shook my head. "She's the last person who could help us. She still hasn't surfaced."

"But what about people in her office or her family? Would they still have access?"

My heart grew heavier with each question. I just couldn't believe that Michael would set me up. "Even if they could, they're halfway across the country. Too many things can go wrong."

Kai nodded. "I think we have to look closer. Surely someone we know and trust would have access to health cards."

Stepan took one last draw on his cigarette on the balcony rail and then flicked the still glowing butt. The small shooting star fell into the darkness below. "Any ideas?" he asked as he came through the door.

"Nothing," Kai said and shook her head.

"What about black market cards?" Michael asked.

"Too early," Stepan said confidently. "People don't need black market. They can get it easy enough the legal way. But with the new requirements for people crossing the borders, they'll be out there eventually."

"How many do you need?" I thought of my own card, although I was pretty sure Eddy hadn't bothered to bring it, and he certainly wouldn't have brought the vaccination capsule that matched it.

"Ten," Stepan said.

"Ten?" Kai repeated.

"Ten." He held up all ten fingers. "I need one for each terminal number. Zero to nine."

"What will that do?" I asked. Ten seemed a dangerously high number.

"But I still don't understand why you need all ten numbers," Michael said.

"Is because the virus will take terminal number and make all numbers that number. So all health cards ending in zero turn all numbers to zero. All cards ending in one turn all numbers to one. And so on."

"So if my number ends in a two," I asked, "all heath cards that end in a two become two-two-two, two--"

"Yes. All of them."

"So the database ends up with only ten numbers: zero through nine."

"And they're spread over the entire population?" Michael added.

"Every number in the database, no matter when it is last entered into the system."

I laughed out loud. If this was a setup, it was a glorious one. "And the database is destroyed."

"Yes. Exactly," Stepan said.

We all should have smoked a cigarette. It was like coming down off great sex.

"But what about … " Michael paused. We all looked at him. We didn't want to hear about any glitches. "What about the vaccination capsules? Aren't they the same number as the cards? Wouldn't they be able to read the capsule numbers and reconfigure the health card numbers?"

The bubble burst. It wasn't a "what if" we wanted to hear.

"Unless—" Kai began tentatively. "Unless you can find your husband." She looked at me. "And he can post something to his website to warn people. To tell them what is going on. We take advantage of the chaos before the government can reorganize enough."

It was just too neat and tidy.

Stepan shrugged a shoulder. "Perhaps. But first we have to get the health cards."

Michael nodded, "And then we have to find ten people willing to use them."

Well, maybe it wasn't as neat and tidy as we'd like.

Chapter
46

IT'S NOT A GOOD THING TO SUSPECT the only people who can help you. It makes for odd conversations and too many stolen glances. Even worse, it's miserable to be forced to trust nearly total strangers. Here I was, though, trusting Phil Generett, a man I'd met at midnight in a hotel far from home, who offered the silver bullet.

Stepan left Kai's around midnight. Michael, Kai, and I revived ourselves with a fresh pot of coffee and examined the possible angles that Phil Generett represented. If either Michael or Kai was the one setting Eddy and me up, they didn't betray themselves with unexpected questions or over-the-top pressure for me to produce Eddy. Kai couldn't quite believe that he and I hadn't had contact, but the heart of the disbelief was the scariness of bearing the unknown for so long, not that I wasn't trying hard enough to find him.

I didn't even hint at my meeting with Eddy. It was the one card I had to hold close.

Kai offered to carry the note to Starbucks to contact Phil. In it, we had very clear instructions about where to go and what to do. If he didn't show up, that told me something, but not much. If he agreed to follow the directions, it still didn't tell me much. The guillotine blade might be waiting for a better moment to drop.

The rendezvous plan was inspired. Of course, the inspiration might have been Kai's since this would be a perfect time to capture two birds with one net if they wanted to find Phil Generett anywhere close to as much as they wanted to find Eddy.

A Green Extreme convention had descended on San Francisco's Moscone Convention Center over the weekend. Day passes were cheap, and Kai knew the place well since she worked part-time for a caterer that often won convention contracts. Inside the convention center, a dozen kiosks sold the ubiquitous green shirts and caps that were synonymous with the giant tech company that sponsored the event. I slipped on a long-sleeved green T-shirt and pulled my ponytail through the gap in the green baseball cap.

Invigorated by my new invisibility, I took up watch. Kai had told me to hang out at the west end of the balcony of Moscone South. It would give me the clearest view of the escalator and Phil Generett if he showed. While the balcony view was easily the best position, I decided not to be so easy in case Kai had told someone else where I'd be standing. Instead, I found a corner just inside the main entrance where I could stay tucked away. I could see the escalator fairly well, and the bank of main doors really well. Frankly, my problem wasn't going to be that I couldn't see the escalator well enough. Rather, I didn't trust my ability to recognize even Mario Seneca in a crowd like this, let alone a new surveillance team. Even worse, the first and last time I'd met Phil, I'd been tired, distressed, and buzzed from vodka. I wasn't even sure if I'd recognize him again.

I studied the rivers of people and made an insightful note to myself: geeky wasn't as geeky as it used to be—or maybe I'd been surrounded by pocket-protector types for so long at Zaan that my yardstick had shrunk a couple of inches. I tried to look for patterns, to see if the same people meandered or, like me, stayed in an unobtrusive corner. No one stuck out. But the only thing that told me was that no one stuck out. Maybe I hadn't been followed. Maybe no one would follow Phil Generett. Maybe we'd be nabbed fifteen seconds after the two of us connected.

About nine forty-five, a full half hour before my note said to meet, my eye caught a lanky, balding man coming out of the exhibition hall. He looked like my man Phil. It was the height, the fine thin nose, the cleft in his chin. His eyes darted around the room. Even when he strolled over to a literature kiosk and picked up a brochure, his eyes weren't on the paper in his hand. They were everywhere else. It was Phil.

It wasn't our meeting point, but maybe it was better.

Casually, I made my way across the room, wishing I had eyes like a fly. I noticed he didn't have anything with him that could look like a ream of documentation. I tried not to worry, but lacked imagination. I picked up the same brochure he had, a glossy Fujitsu marketing piece.

"Think Fujitsu can pick up a larger share of the laptop market?" I asked him.

The green shirt and cap had done their trick. Only two feet away, he saw me as me for the first time. A tiny smile appeared.

"It's getting harder and harder to crack Apple's momentum." The brochure shook slightly in his hands and his forehead glistened, even though it was cool in the convention center.

I waited.

"Have you seen their display?" He tilted his head toward the exhibition hall.

"I hear the Sony booth is better." In the end, I still wanted to control where we met.

"Yeah? I'll check it out in a few minutes."

I smiled and put the brochure back in the rack and headed into the maze of the exhibition hall. I glanced back and saw him continue to peruse the kiosk although his eyes still weren't on the brochures. He could have been looking for his backups. He could have been watching to see if he'd been followed. I wouldn't know for the next few minutes.

According to the map, the Sony exhibition was to the far right, Fujitsu to the left. I went left, nonchalantly checking out the various displays and scanning the crowd for a familiar face that followed my erratic path. I picked up a black canvas bag and some pens from the Oracle booth. It used to be that exhibitors at these places couldn't throw goodies at you fast enough as you walked past. Now you were lucky to get a free keychain. I'd remember Oracle's generosity next time I wanted to update my business applications. I took what I could and signed up for some drawings. My luck, this would be the one time my card would get drawn out of the hat, but some untraceable woman named Jane Dille would win the free tablet.

I gave myself twenty minutes to make my way over to the Sony booth, which had a comfortable collection of techies milling around the innovative display. Phil Generett, his head a half head higher than anyone else's, stood in front of a sleek, flat screen monitor that seemed unattached to anything by even the thinnest wire.

He glanced at me, then angled off toward one of the elaborate hors d'oeuvre buffets. As I passed the booth, I realized why: a bank of nine monitors reflected every corner of the display. Even though the video probably wasn't fed beyond the Sony booth, there wasn't any reason to be captured on camera if we could help it. I studied the booth on the opposite side of the aisle as I walked past and slipped in line behind Phil for a plate of shrimp and tiny crab cakes.

"Where's Eddy?" he asked softly. He rattled some coins in his pants pocket and lightly tapped his foot. He still didn't have anything that looked like documentation. He carried no bag.

My own anxiety ratcheted up. "I don't know." It was the truth.

We didn't want to know where the other person stayed, only how to get in touch.

His eyes darted. I did not like this.

"That was the plan. I gave you a sample so you could see what I had. I trusted you. You've got to trust me."

I shook my head. "Not going to happen. It's way too risky for him." And this was way, way too risky for me. My own eyes darted.

He ran his fingers through his thinning hair. "This is my only chance. The funeral is in process right now." His voice caught and it took him a full minute before he could talk again. If this frazzled man in front of me was acting, it was the finest live performance I'd ever seen. "The funeral is happening right now," he repeated. "They know I'm not there, so they'll flip into panic mode. I don't have time for another meeting—I have to leave the country."

"I don't know why you can't give it to me." I really didn't. Eddy and I had that same skin in the business. "What do you think I'm going to do with it? Destroy it? Turn you in?"

The line inched forward. He looked ready to bolt.

"No, no. It's just that—" He paused.

Nervous as I already was, he was making me more nervous. If he could have just stood calmly in line, no one would have noticed us. But all his fidgeting made him a magnet.

"Look," I said carefully. "We—Eddy and I want to get the truth out as much as you. If you have documentation to back up what you gave me, we've got the smoking gun."

He laughed tensely. "Lady, if you think that's a smoking gun, wait'll you see the rest of it." He leaned toward me and whispered, "It'll bring this government down. Not just knock them out of office, it'll put them in prison."

"You have proof this was all deliberate?"

"I do." He glanced all around us. "So what do you think they'll do to try to stop it from happening?"

"What wouldn't they do?"

He cocked his finger and thumb into a gun and poked my arm. "Exactly."

"So will you trust me enough to give me the documentation?"

He took one final visual sweep of the chaotic hall and, I swear, whispered, "You already have it," before he slipped out of the line and disappeared into a swarm of passersby.

This hadn't gone at all like it was supposed to. The only thing worse that could have happened would have been for Mario Seneca to materialize and slap handcuffs on me.

How could I already have the documentation?

I ducked into the ladies' restroom and dropped my Oracle bag into the trash. The ratio of men to women at a techie convention is about the same as at a professional football game, so of the ten stalls, nine were vacant. I stepped into the first stall and halfway through relieving myself, I had an epiphany, which isn't the typical moment I usually have them. Two minutes later, I retrieved the Oracle bag out of the trash and dumped the contents on the faux marble counter. Pens, business cards, and key chains scattered out. In addition, one USB flash drive, smaller than a thin disposable cigarette lighter, tumbled out of the bag.

At least it looked like a flash drive. It could just as easily have been a homing device. I understood the government had a knack for that sort of thing.

I STARED AT IT. If it had been radioactive, I couldn't have been more miserable.

Of all the possible setups, this was the most elegant. Phil Generett, a total stranger forty-eight hours earlier, had tracked me down and handed me the silver bullet. How could I refuse it, even though the entire history of humanity is of greed—for money, power, lust, or control—triumphing common sense. My brain told me to dump it in the trashcan. My heart said take the risk.

So I compromised.

The W Hotel, a too-cool sister hotel to the Sheraton, was only a block from the convention center. Since the Sheraton and the W are both part of the Starwood hotel chain, my frequent stay status gave me an edge in asking favors, even if I didn't have a room there at the moment. I didn't feel the least bit embarrassed about asking for an envelope, flashing my Starwood Preferred Guest card, and asking if I could leave something in the hotel safe.

I'd entered on Mission Street, detoured to the third floor where I deposited the green shirt and hat in a housekeeping cart, and left by 3rd Street.

For the first time in days, I didn't worry about being followed. If the flash drive was a tracking device, I now had a head start. I caught a cab to Chinatown, where even on a damp Monday morning in January tourists roamed the streets. From there, I took a streetcar down to the Embarcadero and found the Blue Bottle Coffee Shop. Eddy already sat at a back corner table.

He kissed me lightly on the cheek and held my hand under the table.

"Did he meet you?"

"He did."

"And?"

"He only wanted to give it to you, but I must have convinced him. When he left, he dropped a flash drive in my bag."

Eddy's eyes widened slightly. "No hard copies?"

I shook my head.

"Do you have it with you?"

I shook my head again and told him about the W hotel safe. "I couldn't be sure it wasn't some kind of a tracking device."

"Good thinking."

I could feel his foot tapping next to mine.

"Or it could have a virus," he said a minute later.

I thought of our own virus plan. "Maybe even something time-release, so whoever downloads information from your website gets the virus."

"Or it could track cookies—who visits the website."

"So what do we do?"

Eddy sipped his coffee. Two elderly window shoppers stood three feet away from us on the other side of the glass and pointed to the flaky almond croissant on my plate. I glanced at Eddy and then around the room for a back door. The women moved on. I realized I hadn't been breathing. Nothing would ever seem benign to me again.

"The first thing we do is find out if it's a tracking device," he said.

"How do we do that?"

"Buy a cheap laptop and test it. If it works, we download everything to the laptop and leave the flash drive. If it doesn't work, we drop it in someone else's bag and run like the wind."

I laughed in spite of myself. "And then?"

"Then," he paused and thought for a minute. "Then we buy a high-speed printer and scanner. We print off the information and re-scan it back into my laptop. No virus can go from soft copy to hard copy."

"What if it's a thousand pages?"

"Then it'll take us all night. I'm ready to pull an all-nighter, aren't you?" He winked at me.

I squeezed his hand.

"How did the meeting go with that programmer? The Russian. Did the instructions make sense to him?"

"Stepan? He was very confident that he could hack his way into the system based on the information from Anna."

"I'd say that's terrific, except that I hear a 'but' coming."

"You do. Here's the deal. He says that Daniel left a back door into the software not just so he could go back in, but so he could go back in to plant a virus."

"That's perfect—"

"The idea, yes. The reality, no. He says to make it work, he needs ten health cards and the matching vaccination capsules. He'll program them to plant the virus in the DHS system so that twenty-four hours after they're scanned in, all the numbers in the database will default to the terminal number for each entry."

"So all the health cards ending in zero become all zeros in the database?"

"Exactly. And all cards ending in one become all ones and so on."

"So you end up with only ten numbers in the database for the entire population?"

I nodded.

Eddy laughed out loud. "I love it." He was quiet for a minute and I could almost hear his brain buzzing. "But what about the vaccination capsules? Couldn't they just rescan the vaccination capsules and reissue the cards?"

"Probably. Unless we time it with the release of Phil Generett's information and people are so outraged that they refuse."

He nodded slowly and smiled. "It's so simple it's beautiful."

"The pessimist says this? Don't confuse me," I said. "Again, the idea is simple, but how do we get the health cards and the vaccination capsules?"

Eddy chewed on his lower lip.

"And how do we know for sure that Phil Generett's information is true, that it's not a setup? And, for that matter, where do we come up with those ten people willing to risk going through security with a false health card that will plant the virus?"

"I don't know. All I know is that we don't have a choice."

Eddy and I power-shopped in one of the shoebox-size electronics stores near Pier 39. We could just as easily have been in Hong Kong since, except for us, everyone on both sides of the counter was Asian. Within twenty minutes Eddy had picked out a cheap, fast Toshiba and a backup hard drive.

"So who are you betting on?"

To anyone else, it was a non sequitur. I knew, though, the question was about who might be setting us up.

I shook my head. "I still don't know."

"I'm betting on Phil Generett."

"He's the most logical—unless you've seen him in person. He's crazy with grief."

"Like Pete."

My feet were killing me. "No doubt."

"Well then, what about Michael or his Thai friend?"

I shook my head. "I kept looking for signs, but again, they'd have to be amazing actors to pull it off. Kai, maybe, since I've never met her before this project, but Michael? Not a chance."

Eddy handed the clerk a wad of cash.

"Besides," I continued when we were outside. "I started that project before this whole smallpox thing began."

"True."

"You didn't put your website together until I'd been at Baja Breeze at least six months."

"They could have bribed her or threatened her to be part of the set up."

I nodded and thought about it for a minute. "Anything is possible. But I don't think that's one of the things."

We were back in the coffee shop and Eddy was working his magic on the computer, loading the software and setting preferences. I knew what was coming, and it made me nervous.

"Maybe Stepan? Is he the plant?"

"He could be. He's arrogant. He's been through tough times. You never know what a person will do for money. He talks, though, like he's doing this for the sheer challenge of it."

"Maybe he's doing it for both. Challenge and money."

"Maybe."

We split a humongous California-style sandwich loaded with veggies.

"So Stepan is our most likely setup?"

"Unless the instructions themselves are the setup."

"So we don't know anything more than we did twenty-four hours ago."

I shook my head. "If we just knew who had the most to gain."

We left our oasis, me by cab and Eddy on foot. He'd picked up two cheap disposable phones so we could call each other. Even though we were pretty sure the numbers were untraceable to us, Eddy was still very strict with instructions: we were to use code names, keep the messages short, and leave the phone on for no more than five minutes at a time. That was the magic number that it took to triangulate a cell phone signal and find the location of the person with the phone.

Sheesh. The things I had to do to get a cell phone into Eddy's hand.

Happy hour was rocking and rolling at the W hotel bar. Green Extreme convention-goers jammed the place, talking and laughing over the music enough to raise the decibel level to just above the equivalent of a jet engine. If they were waiting for me, I'd never spot them in the jumble of people. But then, they'd never be able to spirit me away because I could get help by wrapping myself around a few dozen legs on the way out. It was the perfect place to work.

I retrieved the flash drive from the front desk and managed to find the corner of a couch to sit on. Unfortunately, the corner happened to be next to some guy who had been at happy hour since the day before.

"Well, this is a nice shurprise." He patted my knee.

I gave him my best touch-my-knee-again-and-I'll-break-your-fingers look, which eventually seeped into his brain. He turned his back to me, wobbling a bit on the couch.

I've been to conventions before.

I booted up the computer, plugged in the flash drive, and held my breath. The computer found the device.

So far so good.

I opened the drive. Over a hundred files filled the screen. If the USB stick was a tracking device, it was in addition to what looked like an information bonanza. I clicked on a few files and opened them, skimming them for anything obvious. They were definitely about the smallpox epidemic, but I couldn't tell whether they were in anticipation of or a response to it. I sorted the files by type and found the Excel spreadsheet that I'd seen with Tina's information. Surely, this alone could bring down a government.

I finally breathed again.

I downloaded the files, removed the USB stick, and closed down the computer. I was tempted to drop the device in the pocket of the knee-toucher next to me, but I returned it to the hotel safe instead.

Back in a cab once again, I phoned Eddy. When his voicemail picked up, I simply said, "Done. It worked like it was supposed to."

The cab dropped me off six blocks away from the coffee shop, where I dropped the computer off for Eddy to pick up. To get back to Kai's, I took a cab and then BART. At the station closest to Kai's, I walked up the hill to her place. It took me nearly an hour, but it also cleared my brain. On the half hour, as planned, I turned on the phone. A single message showed. It could only be from Eddy.

"Got it. By the way, I also figured out how to get the items we need. I'll explain when I see you tomorrow."

MICHAEL AND KAI WERE HAVING A GLASS OF WINE and a plate of shrimp lettuce wraps on the balcony when I got there. I joined them, mesmerized by the city lights that sprinkled out around us to the edges of the world.

"You're home early," I said to Michael. I didn't ask if he'd moved in since that would be begging the obvious.

He squeezed the back of Kai's neck affectionately. "Software implementations aren't quite as exciting these days."

She smiled shyly at him, and they both giggled a little. If it had been anyone but Michael, I would have rolled my eyes.

"Did Phil Generett show up?" Kai asked.

"He did." I had my story ready since I still didn't want to tip my hand that Eddy was in town. Just in case.

"And?"

"And he had a flash drive with his files. We attached it to a computer at one of the booths and opened up the drive. It was loaded." It was only a small stretch of the story.

"Yes!" Kai shook her fists in the air and laughed. "Where is it? What did you do with it?"

"I left it at a place for safekeeping with instructions for what to do if I don't claim it."

"Still no word from Eddy?" Michael asked.

I was a terrible liar, but it was dark, so I had a better chance.

"Nothing. But I know in my heart he has to be okay." I took a sip of wine. "I just have to believe it."

Kai nodded. "You know these things."

"Did Stepan come to work today?" I asked.

"He did. I was just telling Michael about it when you got here."

"Was he able to make any headway?"

"He was up all night working on it. He got into the software and made his changes."

This didn't sound good. He was into the software way too early. "He's not worried about them finding the changes?"

Kai shrugged her shoulders. "That's what I asked him, but he said he only set up the trigger. He didn't change anything that would be a red flag."

Still, it made me edgy.

"He wanted to know if we came up with any ideas for how to get the health cards."

"I don't know. Maybe. I'm working on some angles." I sounded too hesitant. "When does he need them?"

"He's ready whenever we can get the cards to him."

"I'll know something tomorrow."

"And then we'll still need ten people to go through security with the cards," Michael said. "There are only three of us, four if Stepan will use a card, too."

"The two of you will do this? You'll risk getting caught and … and whatever might happen as a result?"

They looked at each other.

"We will. We've talked through the consequences, and we believe it's worth it," Michael said softly. "This isn't the America we thought we were coming to."

Michael and Kai slept with each other that night. I slept with guilt for even being suspicious about their motives and loyalty.

Every time I woke up, which was too often, I counted the people who might be willing to take this risk with the infected health cards. Michael, Kai, Eddy, and me. Stepan maybe. Anna possibly, if she hadn't been swallowed up by DHS after I led them to her.

The rock in my stomach grew larger.

Phil Generett surely would do it. If I could find him again.

That took me to seven. And too many of them were maybes, too many ifs.

Jola was another possibility. Another rock joined the first one in my stomach. This one was bigger. I should have checked my Gmail account to see if she'd tried to contact me. Another layer of guilt settled over me even though today of all days I'd had a good excuse for being distracted.

If we could contact Pete, I was sure he'd leap at the chance. The logistics would be complicated—would we send the card to him or would he leave Colorado and Tina's ghost to come to California?

Even if he did, we'd only be at nine.

We had to have ten.

Michael was long gone to Baja Breeze by the time Kai and I were up and having coffee on the balcony. Far away at the crease between earth and sky, the bay sparkled, a sapphire in a nest of trees and concrete.

"Are you worried about where this will lead?" I asked her.

She didn't answer at first but let the coffee steam swirl up against her cheeks. "Yes," she finally said. She looked at me. "How can we not be?"

"Can we do this any other way?"

"I don't know what it would be. Even if you can get the flash drive to Eddy to post the information, it's not enough. There's plenty of information out there already and not just on Eddy's site."

She wrapped her hands around her coffee mug and held it close to her face but didn't drink. "Ever since 9/11, people have been so afraid to stand up and point out the obvious. No. Not just afraid—they've been intimidated, threatened, and even punished for going against the official version. The media is worthless. Reporters don't investigate, and they never challenge because they're so worried about what might happen to them."

She got up and stretched. Her dark hair swung over her face, and for a moment, she looked like a cat. "I've got to get ready for work." She looked at me and sighed. "If we don't grab this chance now, Maggie, what will life be like in a week or a month?" She raised her eyebrows. "Think what it could be like in a year."

For Eddy and me? We'd never be able to run for a year. Forget any noble ideas about doing this for the country. We had to do this for us.

Once Kai left, I used her computer to check my Gmail account and then kicked myself for not checking it on Sunday. Jola had sent a message on Saturday evening that she had to leave town suddenly for an aunt's funeral. She'd return to San Francisco on Wednesday.

It might have been the same kind of sudden "emergency" that took Daniel Pogodov away. I had no way of knowing. Nevertheless, I sent her a new email and composed it as carefully as I could:

```
J,

Tag. You're it. Home will never be the
same again. Dinner soon?

mzm
```

Eddy would have understood it all. *If* Jola checked her email, I hoped she would at least be wary and respond before heading home.

I went into my account settings and changed the account name and email address to MariaZiewojackMagda@gmail.com, the signal we'd agreed on for bad news. If anyone tried to reply to the email, they'd get an error. Anyone with a little email sophistication could still trace the email back to MZM@gmail.com, but I hoped that if anyone was tracking Jola's Hotmail account, the false email would send them scrambling in a different direction for awhile.

It was Tuesday, so I met Eddy at the main library on Larkin Street in the 900 numbers, the travel section. He was casually paging through a Fodor's guide to Honduras, a country I'd never exactly thought of as a tourist destination. I hoped it didn't portend the future. Beside him was a paper shopping bag with handles.

"Hey," he whispered and furtively kissed me.

"Hey back."

He picked up the shopping bag and tilted his head for me to follow him. He headed to a back staircase where we went up several flights of stairs and ended up in the historical section. A scattering of maybe a dozen people sat at the heavy walnut tables that lined the center of the room. None of them looked up from what they were doing. Eddy wound his way through clumps of stacks to a small conference room. The single window in it had an easel and flipchart angled in front of it, which prevented anyone from seeing in the room but kept it also from looking like we were hiding.

"Lunch?" He smiled and unloaded a small deli feast, including a half bottle of champagne and two plastic champagne flutes. Some librarian would be wagging a finger if she could see us now.

"I take it Phil Generett's documents were the real thing."

"Actually, we're celebrating two things."

"It's about time. I can't remember the last time we celebrated *one* thing."

"A toast," he said and raised his champagne. "Unless Phil Generett et al have been frantically manufacturing emails and memos to set us up for this moment—"

"Which, we have to remember, is absolutely a possibility."

"A confusing possibility since I can't figure out what they'd gain given what I've seen, but yes, it's absolutely a possibility." He continued to hold his champagne up in a toast. "Unless we've been scammed," he began again, "this is not just the smoking gun. This is the gun itself being fired in slow motion. It's the fingerprints. It's the face of the triggermen."

I got goose bumps. "Who's behind it all?"

"It doesn't stop until you get to the very top."

"The president?"

"And all his men.

"And the proof is there?"

Eddy sighed sadly. "Unequivocally. Meeting minutes, decisions made, and at least three emails from the man himself approving plans."

We clinked, or rather clunked, plastic glasses together. For the record, no matter how sweet the moment, champagne should always be drunk out of glass flutes.

"What cocky bastards. They used email and didn't even worry about it being traced some day? Were they planning to stay in office forever?"

Eddy shrugged. "If no one stops them, in a matter of weeks it'll be a moot point. They'll be able to track everyone in the country, including their political enemies. Here's the really clever thing. They won't ever even need to require it. The strategy is to make it so you can't go anywhere in public unless you have the health card and vaccination. According to the timeline, for all practical purposes, you'll need a health card and vaccination if you step outside your house to water the lawn." He half smiled. "And the system they built for this? They simply type in a name and the health card number pops up. A few more keystrokes, and a GPS—a global positioning satellite—tells them where that person is to an accuracy of a few feet. Anywhere in the world."

"God help us."

"I couldn't have said it better myself." Eddy tilted his champagne glass and the last drop trickled out. "According to the memos, the system will be running by February first. A week from now."

"And the country volunteered for it."

Eddy smiled. "It's all about clean data. You were the one who told me that."

I downed my own champagne and wished for some of Anna's vodka. I finally understood why the Russians drank at nine in the morning.

"You said we were toasting two things."

"Ah yes. The second thing," Eddy said and poured another round. "We'll have ten health cards and ten vaccination capsules by ten o'clock tomorrow morning."

He clunked his flute against mine and tossed down the champagne again. My glass stayed frozen in midair.

"You're kidding! How in the world could you have pulled that off?"

"Don't ask. Don't tell."

"Don't tease me, Eddio. How did you do it?"

He lowered his voice to a whisper even though only a wiretap could have heard us. "I got hold of Pete."

"Tina's Pete?"

"We know another Pete?"

"But how could he get the cards?"

"From Tina's office. Tina had duplicate keys for everything, and he knew the alarm code. He was able to get them last night and overnight them to us this morning."

"Unbelievable." It truly was.

"I know. He sent them to Baja Breeze to your attention. They're guaranteed to be delivered no later than ten o'clock tomorrow morning."

"Absolutely unbelievable."

We devoured lunch, drained the last drop of champagne, and plotted out our next steps. Eddy updated me on what he'd accomplished in the hours we'd been apart. He'd managed to print off all the documentation and was slowly, very slowly, scanning it into his old laptop for posting it to his website.

"What are you going to post first?"

"I thought the Excel spreadsheet with the list of names of people who'd been arrested would raise the temperature out there."

"When are you going to post it?"

His eyes shifted back and forth. "Uh. It's out there already."

I took a quick breath. "Are you sure you shouldn't have waited? I mean even another twenty-four hours would give us a little more time to get organized."

"I thought about it." He studied the table for a long moment. "But if something happens to us—" Now he looked me in the eye. "If the worst happens, I wanted to set at least a piece of it in motion. This seemed like a good one to start with because it touches so many people personally and was so obvious to understand." He reached across the table and took my hands. "Do you really think they'll look any harder for us?"

One could only imagine.

As I discovered within fifteen minutes of leaving the library, we'd been lacking in imagination.

I'd taken a streetcar to the BART station where I was waiting for the next train. Compulsive reader that I am, I perused the information posted on the kiosk. You can find—and forget—a lot of useless information with that kind of reading. Today, it kept me from thinking about what the next twenty-four hours might bring. Unfortunately, the moment I saw Eddy's and my picture in the "SUSPECTED TERRORISTS" section behind the locked glass window, I realized I should have been more productive with my time.

I tried my hardest not to pass out since fainting in front of my own WANTED! poster would be too efficient for DHS. I stumbled up the stairs and back out onto the street to catch the streetcar someplace else. While I waited for the next streetcar, I put on my sunglasses and worried that those would draw attention on such a gloomy day. I left a message for Eddy. "You're famous. Now's the time for that surfer dude look you've always wanted." If he hadn't already seen the pictures, he would know.

I rode for ten minutes before I spotted a beauty shop. An hour and a half later, I emerged with chopped, perky blond spikes. I never knew I looked like Meg Ryan until I left all those loose auburn curls on the floor behind me.

It was just hair.

I told myself that twenty times as I rode BART to the end of the line where more Eddy and Maggie posters bloomed. I would not let myself think about how long it had taken me to grow my hair out, how it had become a signature of sorts, how it had turned heads.

From the BART station, I took a cab to Palo Alto to see if Anna's restaurant was permanently boarded up or if her answering machine message about being closed for a funeral was true. Fortunately, there's very little to read in a cab, so I thought about what I was doing. If the DHS were smart, I'd be walking into a perfect trap. I had the cab cruise past the restaurant first. Even though it was on the early side for happy hour, a few people sat at tables by the window. Anya's was open.

The cabbie dropped me off at the end of the street. My heart pounding, I doubled back through the alley until I got to the kitchen door, which was cracked open. A couple of chefs, their backs to the door, banged around with pans and bowls. I slipped in through the screen door and up the stairs to where I'd met Anna before. That door, too, stood open. Heavy Russian choral music marched out onto the landing.

Another reason they drank so much vodka.

Anna sat at her cluttered desk, reading glasses perched on her nose.

I tapped lightly on the door. Somehow, she heard the knock over the music and looked up. It took her a moment to recognize the new me. "Maggie?" She mouthed it rather than said it, or maybe I just couldn't hear her over the Russian choir. The look on her face, though, said it all. She scurried around her desk, tapping her mouth with her pointer finger and waving at the ceiling fan. She threw her arms around me and whispered, "Don't say anything." I got the message.

She took my hand and gently pulled me toward her desk where she shoved papers around until she found a pen and an empty envelope to write on. "Meet in twenty minutes at—" she paused and then scribbled "Flying Squirrel." I knew this bar. It was on University, just up the road a mile or so. They had vodka there, which was maybe a bad sign. She kissed me lightly on the cheek and pushed me out the door.

"Be careful," she whispered.

A new thought. I appreciated the sentiment.

I slipped out the kitchen door, unnoticed I hoped, and headed back up the alley. University was either a very short cab ride or a very, very brisk walk. I opted for the walk, glancing every few minutes behind me to see if anyone followed me. This time I was sure no one did, or they wouldn't have bothered to see where I was going—they would have just nabbed me up and ushered me into the world of the disappeared.

I found a table in a back room. Two minutes later, Anna joined me.

"Maggie, they ask about you."

I didn't need her to explain who "they" were.

"They come to my restaurant and threaten to deport everyone if I don't help them."

"What did you tell them?"

"At first, I say I don't know you. But they say they can check for fingerprints and DN... DNA? Can they do this?"

I mentally searched through the evening. I didn't think I'd touched anything that would have taken a fingerprint. The dishes and glasses would all have been washed. But if a single hair had fallen onto my chair, they'd have their DNA sample.

"I didn't know. So I finally say, 'Yes. Maggie was here.' I am very sorry. So sorry." Her tears were real.

"It's okay. You did the right thing. They would have made it worse for you and still would have gotten what they wanted."

"They want to know what we talk about. I tell them everything, but not about Daniel's letter."

"That was good. Do you think they believed you?" The question of the hour.

She grimaced slightly. "I don't know. Yes? Maybe not completely. They have someone at my restaurant all the time. Waiting for you, I think."

The hostess arrived with a couple glasses of water and a shot of vodka for Anna even though we hadn't ordered anything. Anna and the woman whispered a small exchange in Russian and then hugged.

"Would you also like vodka?" the hostess asked me. Her accent, although slighter than Anna's, was still filled with the hush of consonants.

"Just coffee, please." I wasn't going down that path again if I could help it. No, ma'am.

When she left, Anna lifted her glass to me in a toast. "Za Vas!" She knocked back the drink and set down the glass. It occurred to me it wasn't the first one of the day.

She began again. "Have you tried Daniel's fix?"

"We found someone to try it. He was able to get into the software just as Daniel described."

Anna's face brightened. "This is good, yes?"

"It is. Yes. But—" I didn't know quite how to ask this. "Are you certain this is Daniel's handwriting?"

She looked like she didn't understand. The optimist in me said it was because the writing was so obviously Daniel's that the question had never occurred to her. The pessimist I was becoming suspected she was buying time to answer a question she didn't know how to answer.

"The instructions? Are you sure Daniel wrote them?"

"Yes. I know his writing as my own. Why do you ask this?"

"We must be very careful that someone isn't trying to trick us, that this is the way they catch us. Could someone have forced him to write out the instructions?"

The hostess brought my coffee and another vodka for Anna and then left.

Anna pointed her chin at the vodka. "Next time you join me?"

"Sure. Next time." I smiled. "But not tonight."

She shrugged. "Too bad. Vodka make everything better." She waved her hand at the small glass. "Is much better than this Prozac."

No doubt.

I asked her again. "Did Daniel's letter sound like someone had forced him to write it?"

She tapped her finger against her otherwise-untouched water glass and finally said, "No. No, I don't think this. It is very much Daniel. He is very smart. He can write something to make me suspicious, but he don't do this." She lifted the next shot and once again drank it smoothly and swiftly.

"You loved him very much."

She nodded and grew teary. "He was my everything," she whispered. "Without him, I have nothing."

I leaned toward her. "He was a genius."

"Yes." The tears came faster. She unwrapped the silverware from the cloth napkin and blew her nose in the napkin. I was glad she was a friend of the hostess.

"Let me tell you what Daniel designed." I explained the plan for the virus. It cheered her enough to down another vodka. She was quite proud of him.

"We have a small problem, though."

She inclined her head slightly. I think it was intentional. I don't think it was the vodka.

"We need ten people to go through airport security with the virus-infected health card."

She paused long enough to make me think she didn't understand what I meant. She caught the eye of her friend and signaled for another vodka, which magically arrived a moment later.

"So you want me to do this, too? To go through security with the health card."

I nodded my head.

Anna swirled the shot glass around in her fingers. We didn't talk. I let her think. Finally, she said, "I will do this." She threw back the last vodka. "Gladly, I will do this."

Chapter
49

KAI LOANED ME HER CAR FOR WEDNESDAY MORNING. I did not fully disclose to her my history with cars and other inanimate objects, which I felt bad about. But I thought the deception was small considering the national security risks involved.

I arrived at the Baja Breeze parking lot by eight thirty. I didn't think UPS would deliver to a business before then, and I worried—justifiably so—about being the only car in the parking lot at that early hour. The parking lot was typical California. It had multiple levels and sophisticated landscaping and was as pretty as a city park.

I found a spot on an upper tier that gave me a view of the east-facing front door, and a side door on the north side. A half-dozen other cars lined the first rows. I knew without study-ing license plates that they were all Zaan consultant rental cars. The parking lot slowly filled. The CEO arrived around nine. I flipped him the bird, but he didn't see me.

The UPS man didn't seem to have the same sense of urgency that I did. He arrived at 9:55, which technically made him within the time limit but did not impress me otherwise with his punctuality. He carried a single envelope into the building. I assumed it was addressed to me. I opened my car door to get out since I wanted to intercept the package at the front desk. But before I made it to the steps of the parking tier, I spotted two other men getting out of a car and heading toward the main entrance as well.

I decided Mario Seneca really should lose a little weight.

My sinuses cleared. Only three people in the world knew when that package was arriving and where: Eddy, me, and Pete Kawalski.

I slipped back in the car and dialed Eddy. Unexpectedly, he answered. "Eddio," I said. "We asked the wrong question. It's not, 'Who has the most to gain?' It's 'Who has the most to lose?'"

The answer was Pete. Pete was our betrayer. He had the most to lose. If he didn't help the government, he'd never get Tina back. I couldn't believe we'd been so blind. He'd bought Eddy's Porsche and then sold him the Audi. And now he so conveniently managed to get the health cards and vaccinations.

"No kidding. I'm glad you called, Karen," Eddy said.

Shit. Using his sister's name instead of mine was our signal. He was in desperate trouble.

"I gotta know where you are," I said.

"Call me back on a land line: 650-555-149—"

The line died. Double shit.

I dialed 650-555-1490 and watched Mario and the bald black guy make their way through the parking lot.

The phone rang four times and voicemail picked up. "Hi. This is Jack and Mark—"

I pressed the end button and dialed again, this time making it 650-555-1491. The UPS man entered the main doors and headed to the front desk. Mario was halfway through the parking lot. The number rang twice and an energetic voice on the other end said, "California Tile and Carpet. How may—"

I pressed the end button again and dialed 650-555-1492. My neck tingled. Mario Seneca was going to follow that package to find me, and Eddy was in trouble. The phone rang and rang and rang. Who were these people who couldn't spend even thirty dollars on an answering machine? I hung up.

Mario reached the edge of the parking lot. I dialed the next number in line, which was no longer in service.

Damn.

And then a little angel appeared out of nowhere. I'd never thought of Keri, the brainless Baja Breeze project manager, as an angel. I'd only known her as the queen of incompetence. But she reached the front door at the same time as Mario Seneca. They smiled and did a little after-you dance. Keri shook her head and the sun caught her color, which came in a bottle, but Mr. Seneca obviously didn't care. I could have sworn he was staring at Keri's generous breasts. His hand froze on the door handle and they seemed to be chatting.

Our tax dollars at work.

Inside, the receptionist, a distant cousin to Cruella de Vil, handed the package off to a guy, who took the stairs three at a time.

The UPS man exited. Mario Seneca barely noticed.

I dialed Michael.

"Michael speaking."

"Hey. It's me. There's a package about to be delivered to my desk. Make sure it gets to our Russian friend."

I clicked off and dialed 650-555-1494. After two rings, a woman said, "Motel California. How may I direct your call?"

Thank you, Jesus. "What's your address, please?"

She rattled it off—some place on Half Moon Bay Road—and included the zip code, which was useless.

As I circled out of the parking lot, I saw Michael de Leon, UPS package in hand, slip out the north door and head in the direction of the Tiger Lily, my favorite Thai restaurant.

I'd thought I understood panic. That's what the whole week had been about. But it turns out that was just an appetizer, a mere taste, to the real thing. This moment was a full, seven-course meal of terror.

At first, I hit only red lights. And then I only hit slow traffic on the narrow winding road. If I'd been in my own car, I would have been more creative, but for good or for bad, I was blocked in at each stop. It took me twenty-three minutes to get to the Motel California, a quaint collection of cabins nestled in a yew forest and thick Virginia creeper. Every agonizing minute meant Pete had plenty of time to call in his DHS buddies—the ones who would have no trouble betraying him once they had Eddy and me in handcuffs.

I circled the lot until I found an old blue Taurus parked in front of a room that let out onto the parking lot.

Twenty-three minutes is a lifetime if you're worried about someone your heartbeat depends on. However, twenty-three minutes was not enough time to come up with a good rescue plan. So I did a stupid thing and knocked on the door.

"Housekeeping," I said in my best Spanish accent.

"Not now," a voice called from inside the room. I recognized it was Pete.

"Is time," I said.

The door flew open and Pete, red-cheeked with anger, stared at me.

"Hello, Pete," I said.

It took him a moment to realize it was I, Maggie Rider, wife of the man he'd just betrayed, and not Meg Ryan.

His shoulders drooped. "Maggie." With his left hand, he rubbed the graying stubble on his face. With the gun in his right hand, he waved me in.

Eddy, whose beautiful black curls were now replaced with blond-tipped spikes, was still alive. He was, however, tied to a chair––the fact that he wasn't dead and the two of them were alone in the room no doubt a sign of Pete and Eddy's undying friendship.

I crossed the room in three steps and kissed Eddy.

"Stop it," Pete said angrily. "Don't touch him."

I looked at Pete and removed the tape from Eddy's mouth.

"Be careful," Eddy whispered. "He's totally lost it."

"Get away!" Pete waved the gun at me. "Get away from him!"

"Pete," I said carefully. "Why are you doing this?" I knew. I knew more than he would ever believe, but I wanted him to talk.

"Tina. They said if I gave you to them, they'd give me Tina back."

Just like they'd promised Phil Generett.

"You'd turn us over to the very people that took Tina? Those same evil people?"

"I'm sorry, but you can't understand."

"We do. We do understand. Losing Eddy like you lost Tina would make me insane. But turning us in to DHS isn't a solution."

Pete waved the gun towards me. I'd never been this close to a handgun before. In the movies, they look sleek and scary. This one looked big and clunky, almost like a clumsy toy. "They promised me. I have to believe them. It's my only chance to get Tina back."

I shook my head. "They don't work that way. They promise you one thing, but even if you deliver, they don't honor the promise."

"Not true. You're lying."

"Pete. We're talking about the government here." I rolled my eyes even though I felt like throwing up. "When was the last time the government did what it said it would do? With anything?"

He rubbed his face again. He was tired. What had he done? Dropped the package off at UPS, hopped in the car, and driven all night?

"Don't make jokes, Maggie. They promised they'd release Tina."

"And I'm telling you not to trust them. Look," I put my arms on Eddy's shoulders. "I know you feel crazy from all this. I would too." Eddy's wrists were bound together in a layer of towels and duct tape. How ironic. He didn't want to hurt Eddy. He only wanted to turn him in to DHS.

"Move away." He motioned with the gun again. Pete wasn't the gun type. He didn't even go hunting, so all this waving around made me extra nervous.

"Pete, you don't want to do this. You and Eddy have been friends forever." I kept eye contact but started working at the duct tape.

"Maggie, you have to get away from Eddy. I don't want to hurt you, too." His finger nervously tapped the trigger.

"Pete, you don't want to hurt either of us. I know you." I said it in my calmest voice, one I didn't even know I had. I wondered if it would be safe to touch his arm, or if that would just make him totally freak out. "We're all crazy because of what the government has done."

"Stop, Maggie. Move away." Like a cornered wild animal, he paced in a zig-zag path. The gun stayed pointing at Eddy.

"I have someone I want you to talk to, Pete."

He motioned with his gun again. I moved a half step back from Eddy.

"I'm not talking to anyone. Who would understand this?"

"Someone who lost his daughter to smallpox?"

"She should have gotten the vaccination. Then she wouldn't have gotten smallpox."

I shook my head. "You know as well as we do that the vaccinations don't protect you from anything. They only allow the government to track you."

"Not true. It's just propaganda that Eddy's been posting." He had no conviction in his voice, though. None at all.

"Really? You think? Is that what Tina found out when she cut a vaccination capsule open?"

His eyes stayed steely on Eddy. "I never wanted this to happen. You're my friends."

"Then why would you let DHS get us, too? Turning us over to DHS isn't going to set Tina free."

I could see the entrance to the parking lot. Every minute we stood there gave us one less minute to disappear. We wouldn't be saved by a back door this time.

"Talk to this guy, Pete. He'll tell you how he promised the government he'd cooperate and they went ahead and exposed his daughter to smallpox. She's dead now."

The hand with the gun wilted a fraction of an inch.

"It was a horrible death and they did it out of sheer spite. He was willing to obey them. He gave up everything for his daughter, and they still killed her."

He didn't protest.

"I'm going to the phone, Pete. I'm going to call the place that can reach him. It may take a few minutes—" or a couple of weeks "for them to locate this guy, but you have to talk to him." I moved slowly toward the phone. The gun followed every step, but Pete didn't say anything else.

I had the Starbucks number memorized. A cheerful young man's voice answered on the first ring.

"Good morning. I need to speak with Frank."

"Frank?" There was a pause on the other end and then a muted conversation away from the phone.

"I'm sorry. Frank is no longer available at this number."

This wasn't an acceptable answer. "I have an emergency. One like he had." I had no idea to whom I was talking. Did Phil Generett just buy coffee there once a day? Did someone there actually know him and his story? I couldn't keep the panic out of my voice. "Please. You have to get hold of him somehow."

Again, there was a muffled side conversation and then a woman came to the phone. "I'm sorry. Frank is no longer available at this number."

A switch in people told me that it was either a no-nonsense manager who had to handle an annoying caller or the someone at Starbucks who knew Phil Generett. I banked on the latter.

"Please help me. This is Maggie Rider. My husband is Eddy Rider, who built the smallpoxscare.com website." The words rushed out so fast I wasn't sure she could understand me. In a minute, I'd start crying, and then for sure she wouldn't be able to. I talked faster. "I have someone here whose wife was taken by DHS. He's going to turn us over to DHS because he believes they'll free his wife. We have to talk to Frank. Maybe then he'll understand that DHS is lying to him."

There was only silence on the other end. On our end, Pete rearranged the gun in his hand and kept glancing out the window. Did we have five minutes before DHS arrived? Three?

"Please."

Finally, the voice on the other end said, "Put him on. I can tell him about my cousin."

I handed the phone to Pete, who said nothing. While he listened, I pulled off the last of the duck tape around Eddy's wrists and we both worked at the tape at his ankles. Pete feebly waved the gun at us once, but I knew he'd never shoot us. The second he was free, Eddy shut down his computers and frantically gathered up papers and his few clothes, pitching the things into bags. Pete ignored him.

Eddy threw me a wild look. "We've got to get out of here!"

I tossed him the keys to Kai's Toyota, probably the least likely vehicle for DHS to recognize or trace.

Pete sagged to the bed and put down the gun. He still didn't talk. The tears came too fast. Finally, he handed the phone back to me and buried his face in his hands. "She wants to talk to you," he whispered.

"Yes?" I said to the person on the other end of the line.

"Thank you for what you've done, for posting the spreadsheet to the website." The voice choked with tears.

"The rest is coming within days. I have to go."

"I know. Good luck."

I hung up without a goodbye and then took the biggest chance of my life. "Are you coming with us, Pete?"

He looked up at me. His body shuddered in another sob. "You'd still let me?"

"Do you believe what that woman told you?"

"I do. I'm so sorry. I'm so sorry."

"Maggie, come on!" Eddy grabbed my hand and yanked me out towards the car. "You have to drive. We have to get out of here!"

"Come on," I called back to Pete. "This is your chance to redeem yourself."

He stumbled to the car and dove into the back seat.

"Get down," Eddy told Pete and ducked down himself. "They won't be looking for a single woman who looks like Meg Ryan."

I tousled his surfer-dude hair and laughed. God, I'd missed this man.

I pulled out of the parking lot as a nondescript tan sedan turned in. It wasn't Mario Seneca, but the two men had that DHS look: cold and too smart for words.

"Don't draw attention to the car, Maggie. Drive slowly and carefully," I said, apparently—and unfortunately—out loud.

Eddy looked up at me from the floor. He cocked a skeptical eyebrow, "Is that strategy new? Maybe it'll work for you."

I did the hair-tousling thing again.

From the backseat, Pete kept moaning over and over, "I'm so sorry. I can't believe I was so stupid."

"It's okay, man," Eddy finally told him. "The grief made you berserk."

I didn't know at that moment if Eddy and I could ever truly forgive him, but I didn't think about it. We had much bigger things to worry about.

The sobbing eventually slowed, then stopped and was replaced by soft, rattling snores. By then Eddy was sitting up like a real passenger, and we headed toward Highway 1 and the coast.

WE ATE A LATE LUNCH AT MOSS BEACH DISTILLERY, which sat above crashing waves and under ash colored troubled skies. Pete's short nap revived him enough to keep from crying while we ate, so we were all thankful for small things.

"I don't know how I can ever make this up to you," Pete said for the fiftieth time. He'd finally stopped repeating how sorry he was but only after Eddy threatened to put him on a bus back to Colorado.

Eddy and I looked at each other again. "Well," Eddy began.

"There is one thing you could do to prove you're sorry," I finished.

"Anything. I'll do anything for you."

"How safe are those health cards?"

"What do you mean?"

"Does DHS have the numbers of the cards?"

He thought for a minute. "They could get the numbers if they went in and catalogued what was missing from Tina's stock. I took ten out randomly like you told me. I just made sure they each had a different terminal number."

"So do you think they did?"

"They're very arrogant. I think it's possible that they didn't bother," Pete said.

"But they'll be doing it now," I said, confirming what we all feared.

"We don't have much time," Eddy said. We looked at each other again, and I gave him a small nod. "Here's the deal. We need ten people to go through airport security. Ten people who will use the health cards from Tina's office."

"The risk is huge," I said.

"They have the system ready to track individuals by GPS. According to the memos, they'll turn it on in a matter of days," Eddy said.

"Even without the GPS system, though, security may flag the numbers on the cards. We won't know until we go through," I said.

"Will you carry one of the cards? Will you go through security with it?" Eddy asked.

Pete looked old and tired, his body worn. He rubbed the gray stubble on his face. "I will," he said. "I'll carry the first one."

Eddy and Pete drank more beer while I made phone calls. The sky opened up about mid-afternoon and drenched the beach and rocks that tumbled down to the water. Under other circumstances, the old rumrunner hideaway would have been a romantic spot to wile away such a stormy afternoon. As it was, the gloom at our little table matched the dark skies. Even when the sun broke out late afternoon, turning the boulders into giant sparkling ornaments, the mood didn't lift inside.

We could have sung funeral dirges as we drove down to Palo Alto, but Eddy and Pete were, frankly, too sloshed to carry a tune. I told them they'd better nap. But Eddy told me he needed to keep an eye out for mailboxes that might leap into the road, which I considered an unfair reference to a previous unfortunate incident.

We were just testy and it would only get worse.

Since it was nearly six, the traffic all headed against us, and we made good time, arriving at Stepan's apartment just after six thirty. I parked two buildings away and we split up in order to arrive at Stepan's from three different directions, although the truth was that if the DHS knew enough to watch Stepan's apartment, we were long past doomed.

Jola and Anna were already there. An opened vodka bottle, ten shot glasses, and a box of tissues cluttered the coffee table in front of them. We all introduced ourselves, whispering condolences and trying to make sense of the randomness of our connections. Stepan seemed sweeter and more humble on his own turf. He'd fixed a plate of salmon canapés, crackers, and cheese. Anna had brought two tins of Russian caviar, which Stepan opened and scooped into small crystal bowls.

I'd never figured him to be the crystal bowl type.

It seemed like a celebration—or a funeral. We wouldn't know for a few more hours.

Michael and Kai showed up about seven o'clock, arriving five minutes apart.

We made introductions around again. Eddy only introduced Pete as Tina Bastante's husband and the purveyor of the health cards. He didn't reveal the Pete we'd discovered this morning because it wasn't necessary. He'd made his choices. He regretted them. He was grateful for a chance to do penance.

"Should we begin?" Michael asked me. "Do you think anyone else will show?" The question of who would have to go through security twice if no one else came remained unspoken.

"Let's give it a few more minutes. The rain probably made traffic worse."

We tried to make small talk, but given the diverse motives that had brought us together, it wasn't easy. The rain started up again outside and rattled against the window. The longer we waited, the more anxiety filled the room. At seven thirty, I told Michael to start. I didn't think we were going to get the help we needed.

"First, a toast," Stepan said solemnly. He poured ten shot glasses to the brim with vodka. We each took one, the two full ones left on the table an uneasy reminder that this very danger-ous plan would be even more dangerous now.

"To freedom," Stepan said.

"To *individual* freedom," Jola said.

"To individual *and corporate* freedom," I said.

"To back doors everywhere," Eddy finished.

We clinked glasses, said "Cheers" in our five languages, and tossed back the vodka in unison. It burned all the way down and then began to add heat in my stomach.

The doorbell rang. We all jumped. Stepan went to the door and looked out the peephole. He unchained and unlocked the door.

Phil Generett and, I presumed, his niece Lisa shook the rain off their jackets and stepped inside. I could have burst into tears at that moment. I would have blamed the vodka.

Once again, we made the introductions around, this time with hugs, handshakes, and fresh Kleenexes. Phil and Lisa toast-ed us with the two remaining vodka glasses. And then we were able to get down to business.

"I have made the fix in the software," Stepan began. "And I have programmed the health cards to match the ten new people. The information on the health cards is the same on each one, even the DNA. I swipe a friend's health card and copy the infor-mation. If you get caught, this will be a grave problem. But I did not have time to make them each different."

"*If* they work," Eddy said, "only the number and your picture will show up at airport security."

"Yes," Stepan said. "It is the last thing I must do. I must take your pictures to add to the health card and to make the new driver's license."

"Driver's license?" Kai asked.

Jola nodded. "They're asking for two picture IDs, your health card and one other one."

"Where did you come up with those?" Pete asked.

Stepan smiled and shrugged his shoulder. He was clearly proud of what he'd done. "Is easy for Russian." He winked at Anna. "You are all now from the Great State of Wisconsin, the illegal state license du jour."

"I've always wanted to go there," Eddy said. "And now I'm from there."

"It is very important that you do not mix up the vaccination capsules. The correct one must go with the correct card. Otherwise," he wagged a finger at us, "they will grab you the instant you walk through the metal detector."

"But we don't need to have the capsule implanted, do we?" Michael asked.

"No. Is simple. Detector cannot tell if RFID is under the skin or just under the shirt. We will tape them to inside of arm. The RFID detector will read it."

No one needed to be reminded that if we were caught, an RFID taped to one's arm was the only clue even a sleepy TSA agent needed to recognize a con game.

One by one, we went into the tiny second bedroom, which was Stepan's office. He took our pictures with his digital camera, entered the obvious height and weight information, and switched out a few digits on the social security number. While Stepan worked, Michael got on Stepan's computer and booked a full-fare round trip ticket to Milwaukee, Wisconsin, through Zaan's web travel system, which automatically charged the ticket to the Zaan account. Early in the morning, he would print off the e-ticket, and then cancel the ticket an hour or so later. Nothing would get charged to the Zaan account. No red flags would pop up.

Stepan would scan the e-ticket into his computer, change it ten times to match the names on the health cards, and we would have our paperwork to get through security. The e-tickets would be useless beyond security. But it didn't matter since once we went through security we could turn around and walk right back out again. We had only a single goal: to swipe our cards into the system.

Well, two goals: not to get arrested being the second one.

WE FINISHED AROUND MIDNIGHT with a final vodka toast and then dispersed. Only Stepan stayed in his own place. Pete slept on Stepan's couch. Anna and Jola crashed at the house of a friend of Anna's. Michael knew someone from Zaan at whose house he and Kai could spend the night. Phil and his niece headed for Sunnyvale to find a cheap motel, and Eddy and I found a funky little motel in Mountain View.

It was the first night we'd spent together since I'd left Colorado Springs a week earlier. Since then, the world had unraveled. The night would have been sweeter if so many "what ifs" hadn't joined us in bed, not the least of which was "what if this is our last night we'll ever spend together."

"Regardless, you may not drink vodka ever again, Mz M," Eddy said. "It makes you weepy."

I couldn't argue that because I was looking around for a tissue to blow my nose with. Once I collected myself, I recited the litany that looped in my head. "What if they have the numbers flagged? What if Stepan didn't get the cards coded right? What if one of us gets pulled aside for an extra search?"

"Then we'll be caught and arrested," Eddy said simply. "There are an endless number of things that can go wrong, Maggie. And the one that does is one we haven't even thought of." He wove his fingers through mine and kissed me on the forehead. "We just have to have faith."

"Tell me again why you're waiting to post the rest of Phil Generett's stuff. Isn't that our insurance?"

He sighed, but he didn't sound upset. "You know what posting that Excel spreadsheet did. Within hours, our pictures were plastered everywhere. What would they do if we let all that other information loose? They'd shut down the state looking for us. Security would be even tougher than it is already, and we'd miss this chance to sabotage the database." He squeezed my hand. "This is the right order."

We made love that night with the passion of the first time and the comfort and familiarity of the thousandth time. The words stayed unspoken that it could be our last time.

We lay wrapped in each other's arms, unwilling to let sleep take these last hours away from us that were truly ours. We didn't talk for a long time, and I thought he was asleep until he said, "I love you, Maggie. No matter what happens, I'll always have you in my heart."

I nestled myself into him and wiped my tears. "I love you, too, Eddio. More than life itself."

He kissed the back of my head.

SOBER, SUBDUED, AND SILENT, we gathered again the next morning at six. Michael had already printed off his boarding pass and Stepan had scanned it into his computer. Now they fiddled with it, changing names and seat assignments. While they worked, the rest of us drummed our fingers. Anna stepped outside and smoked a cigarette two different times.

Our flight was scheduled for a 10:17 departure, so we plotted our times, staggering our passage through security and allowing two hours to go through the security checkpoint. With the fifty minutes we needed to allow for the drive to the airport, park, and get to the checkpoint, we didn't have a lot of time to kill.

Michael got online one last time and canceled the trip, effectively erasing the connecting thread among us.

Stepan finally handed out the e-tickets, which looked like the real thing to my practiced eye. We taped the vaccination capsules to the inside of our arms. Kai stepped into the bathroom and threw up one last time. And we were ready to go.

Ready is always a relative term.

Eddy and I drove Kai's car. We held hands most of the way and didn't talk. There wasn't much to talk about unless he let me recite my litany one more time, which he'd made clear was the one thing I was *not* allowed to do.

The security line snaked back at least two hundred feet, winding back towards the ticket counters that had their own winding lines of people checking in with bags to check. The two lines appeared to merge at one spot and then divide again. Whatever the confusion, I would have bet my house that tourists were the problem. They had no idea how to stay alert. My heart sank when I realized part of the mess was because the TSA pre-check line didn't exist anymore. If I'd been traveling for real, I would have burst into tears.

Pete got in line. Ideally, the line would have been short enough for him to make it all the way through security before the rest of us got in line. If he got pulled out because his card didn't work or he triggered suspicion, how much more suspicious would it look for nine people in line behind him to leave? But we didn't have the luxury of waiting.

In that awful moment I realized we should have spread out over several airports or at least booked flights on different airlines and stood in line at different terminals. We could have had some kind of a cell phone signal if one of us got stuck.

What else had we missed?

Lisa, Phil Generett's niece, got in line five minutes later and Phil five minutes after that. Jola followed, then Stepan, Anna, Kai, and Michael. By the time I got in line, Pete still had at least another thirty feet to go before the first TSA agent swiped his health card and checked his credentials. In between the first checkpoint and the checkpoint at the metal detector, the airport had set up a maze, which gave the illusion that the line moved faster, but it still took at least twenty minutes to move from point A to point B. I said a silent prayer of thanks that this would be the last airport line I'd ever have to stand in again. I tried not to think about how that was a mixed blessing.

My heart kept pounding away. I casually glanced around and tried to find the security cameras. I'd read that was an important part of the TSA surveillance process. If they spotted someone suspicious in line, it didn't matter what the ticket said, the person got pulled out for extra security. I wondered if the camera could pick up the sweat on my forehead. The real test should be to shake hands with the TSA. At the moment, my damp palms would be a dead giveaway. I tried not to fidget.

We inched forward. I caught a glimpse of Kai up ahead. I wondered if she was wishing for a restroom right now. She looked a little green. If the surveillance camera took color photos, she'd be pegged.

I focused on my breathing and tried not to think about the odds of all ten of us getting through without a problem. Pete was now within five people of the first TSA agent. I stared at his back, willing him to stay calm, willing me to stay calm. I turned and caught Eddy's eye. He smiled and winked. Would the cameras catch that?

This felt like I was in one of those dreams where I tried to run but my legs wouldn't move and tried to scream but couldn't make a sound. Everything moved in molasses-slow motion.

Now Pete was two people away from the TSA agent. I didn't dare look at Eddy. Pete stepped up to the TSA agent and handed her his papers. I wondered if the edges shook. She studied the e-ticket, compared it to his driver's license, compared that to his health card, swiped the health card, checked her screen against the driver's license, and waved him on.

I would have been in a puddle on the floor at that moment, but Pete was still standing. The line crept forward. Lisa's documents checked out, then Phil's, then Jola's. Four down, six to go. I let myself relax slightly. Stepan was the genius he claimed to be, or Daniel had left amazing instructions. Or the fat lady hadn't sung yet.

I couldn't see Pete in the maze until I had nearly reached the first TSA agent. He was taking off his shoes, watch, and belt. It could still fall apart here if the health card and the vaccination didn't match. Worse, all but Eddy would be inside the maze. There would be no going back. I forced myself to breathe slowly. In, out. In, out.

"Next." The TSA agent actually smiled.

I handed her my papers and my health card and smiled back. It took the concentration of every cell in my body not to shake. I'd be sore the next day from the tense muscles.

She compared the e-ticket to my driver's license and frowned. The floor moved slightly up and down, or maybe it was my knees. "I know. Milwaukee is the worst destination this time of year," I said and smiled.

"Well, actually, the name on the ticket isn't the exact same name as on the driver's license."

I said, "No?" Oh, Lordy. Had I given her the wrong driver's license accidentally? I leaned over to look at the two. Stepan had spelled my name as "Stephanie Morghan" on my driver's license, but the e-ticket had "Stephanie Morgan," a very careless, stupid mistake.

"I can't believe that. Me and my fat fingers." I rolled my eyes.

"I'm sorry to tell you, Miss, but the names have to match exactly, including the middle name. I'm not supposed to let you through if they don't. You'll have to go back and have them reissue the ticket with the correct name."

I didn't have to act the part of a panicked traveler. "But I'll miss my flight. It's a typo. That's it." I couldn't believe I hadn't caught it.

She glanced over to her supervisor and motioned her to come. The supervisor, a heavyset black woman with a solidly gelled hairdo helmet, waddled over. The TSA agent handed her my driver's license and the e-ticket.

"The names don't match exactly."

The supervisor looked at the documents. She had a no-nonsense grit to her. "How do you spell your last name?" She asked me.

"M-o-r-g-h-a-n. It's an unusual spelling," I said. Actually, the night before, I'd told Stepan, "It's the wrong spelling." He pointed out that at least both the health card and the license were spelled wrong. "You Americans," he said, "See? Two wrongs do make a right."

The supervisor swiped the health card and studied the screen. She handed it back to me and waved me through. "Next time make sure your ticket name is correct. We're cracking down on those kinds of things." She turned and strolled back to her corner.

I shuffled into the line, which now had a gap because of all the time my papers took. I glanced back at Eddy, who looked ready to bolt. His eyes stayed locked ahead and steady. I tried to peer through the maze at the metal detector that Pete had gone through. I didn't see him, but I saw Lisa taking off her shoes, so I could only assume he made it through without incident.

I counted noses: Phil, Jola, and Kai were nearly lined up in the maze. I spotted Stepan. Under his armpits, large damp circles had grown on his shirt. That would be a trigger for the camera. I grimaced.

Anna appeared two rows over in the maze and then I saw Michael a single row over. He caught my eye. He was biting his lower lip and very slightly tilting his head and jerking his eyes toward the line behind us. He looked like he might be having a small seizure until I finally connected that he was trying to direct my attention to Eddy, the only other one of us in line behind me.

The blood rushed from my head; for a long moment I really thought I'd pass out. I tried to ever-so-casually look in the direction his head tilted, expecting to see somebody in jackboots slapping handcuffs on the only man I'd ever loved. The moment confused me, though. Eddy stood a few paces ahead of where he'd been, hands clasped in front of him, eyes straight ahead.

I glanced back at Michael, who tilted his head again in the direction of Eddy. This time, I studied the people around Eddy.

And there I saw him. Two people behind Eddy stood Sanjeev Srivastava, arms crossed and bored look on his face. He pushed his computer bag forward with his foot.

Ohmygodohmygodohmygod.

Out of the corner of my eye, I watched him creep along. He kept looking at his watch and looking toward the metal detectors. His line faced the same direction as mine, so I safely watched him crawl along for a few minutes. When he turned the corner in the maze, I studied the person in front of me. Out of the corner of my eye, I saw him look in my direction, but I couldn't tell if he was studying me or just not staring at how far he had to go to the metal detector.

Eddy approached the TSA agent.

In, out. In, out. I breathed as deliberately as I could.

I turned the corner of the maze and once again followed the back of Sanjeev. Michael approached and we made eye contact.

"He saw me," Michael muttered. "I'm sure he did. What do I do?"

"You're fine. You can belong in this line. I'm the one who will trigger suspicion."

Particularly if Sanjeev sees Michael talking to me.

Would Sanjeev recognize me? He saw me one night over dinner and one night with a baseball cap on and a pizza box. My hair looked entirely different, but my profile hadn't changed. Given the stakes, if Sanjeev were smart, he'd know my face as well as the back of his hand.

"He's looking now," I said, trying not to move my lips.

I glanced back at the TSA agent and Eddy, who'd moved into the maze. There was no going back now. Sanjeev approached the TSA, papers in hand.

My neck tingled.

We traversed back and forth, back and forth like giant rats. We'd quickly learned to be patient and polite and tolerant of this demeaning exercise. We'd learned that if we challenged the TSA, we'd get sent to the extra security line. Most of us only needed one zap to behave. Complacency and cooperation were rewarded. Challenges and individual spirit were punished.

How quickly we learn.

Each time Michael and I passed, he grew more agitated. "Sanjeev keeps looking at me," he'd mutter. I would have felt better if Sanjeev weren't looking at me, too. At every turn, he stared in my direction.

"It's okay to look back. You're not doing anything wrong. Give him a wave like you're surprised he's there." My lips barely moved. The camera wouldn't be able to read what I was saying, nor would Sanjeev.

Michael either didn't hear me or was too panicked to process what I said. He kept looking at Sanjeev but never gave him a nod of recognition.

We were screwed.

Phil and Jola reached the metal detector. Jola stepped through without a problem. But the TSA agent stopped Phil and had him walk through the arch a second time. I noticed he raised his arm and brushed back his hair. It exposed the inside of his upper arm a bit more.

One more thing we should have thought about earlier. We should have put the capsule on the outside, not inside of our arms. It was taped. Would it really have made any difference if we'd taped it to the outside instead of the inside?

The agent let Phil proceed.

Stepan cleared the second checkpoint. In all their security detecting, apparently the TSAs hadn't paid any attention to a profusely sweating person on a cool January day. So much for the billions we'd spent on homeland security. Even I could have figured that one out.

I watched Sanjeev out of the corner of my eye. He watched Michael. It could only be minutes before he saw me and recognized me. I had to stop looking at Eddy. I felt nauseous and my chest constricted. Weren't those heart attack symptoms?

Anna reached the second checkpoint. She took off her shoes and placed everything in a bin. The line edged forward. She handed the TSA agent her health card to swipe and stepped through the metal detector. The TSA agent stared at the top of the detector. He nodded her toward the extra screening section where she sat on a chair while they rummaged through her bag. The only good thing about the moment was that it took my mind off Sanjeev, who could do nothing but create problems for us.

Even from where I was in the maze, I could see that Anna had tensed up. She talked to them. They talked to her. They produced their wand and had her do the spread eagle stand so they could wand each appendage and her body. If they were just checking for metal, no problem. She wasn't even wearing earrings. If the metal detector also looked for RFIDs, it would find this one in the wrong place.

I tried not to watch.

Kai entered the metal detector and was waved on. It looked to me like she made a beeline for the nearest restroom. That would be another security giveaway: who immediately heads for the bathroom and throws up?

Now Anna sat in the security booth. They took her documents again and ran them through the scanner. They wanded her left arm again, the one that was supposed to have the vaccination.

Behind us, Sanjeev finally truly woke up. "Michael!" He called in our direction.

All Michael had to do was look back at Sanjeev, wave, and smile. But he wasn't thinking straight. He ignored Sanjeev and kept shuffling forward.

I prayed Sanjeev would only look at Michael. I prayed to be invisible. I prayed that Sanjeev was just headed out to a client site. Nothing unusual about the morning would enter his brain.

Let me go on record: none of my prayers were answered.

In the next moment, Sanjeev's voice cut through the airport buzz. "Maggie?"

I desperately needed an airline sickness bag or a restroom. Neither one looked likely.

"Maggie Rider!" Sanjeev called out. Out of the corner of my eye, I saw Eddy—two places ahead of Sanjeev in the line to hell—stiffen.

It was one thing for Michael to be in line to head off to yet one more project in one more city. For the two of us to be in line and one of us to have short-cropped bleached hair shouted suspicion.

"Maggie Rider?" Sanjeev called again. He voice sounded anxious, disbelieving.

I breathed in. I breathed out. Only five more minutes. I couldn't believe Sanjeev would draw attention to himself in line like that. It could only mean one thing: calling out a so-called terrorist held greater reward than shuffling along in line, head down, attitude compliant.

He had to be brainwashed into believing he could keep his family safe. If he called Michael and me out, the Feds would truly believe they could trust him. They'd leave his family alone. Forever. Maybe. Not a chance.

But he didn't know that.

Michael stepped into the next line over from the one Anna had been in for the metal detector. He took off his shoes and his belt.

He walked through the metal detector. The TSA agent in his line looked at his e-ticket and said something to him. Michael pulled out his wallet, and the two had a brief discussion. The TSA waved him on. He put his shoes and belt back on.

It wasn't just my imagination. I could see his knees knocking together from where I stood. I intended to write my congressman as soon as I got home. Those security cameras were worthless.

I didn't dare look, but I could hear a scuffle a few rows over.

"You have to let me through. I have to stop the terrorists up there," Sanjeev's voice rose over the murmurings of other passengers. "Maggie!" He shouted my name now. "You, in the brown coat and scarf."

I thought I was blending in, but all around me, people tilted their heads at my coffee-colored jacket and peach scarf.

"An old boyfriend," I muttered to the people around me. "He's nuts. Really nuts." My eyes shifted as I said it, a dead giveaway I was lying.

The people around me started their shuffle again. I hoped they knew someone nutty too. They eased along carefully, maybe giving me the benefit of the doubt. Maybe just not wanting to draw attention to themselves.

"Stop her!" Sanjeev's voice came through again.

The three rows between us grew anxious. You could feel it and hear the chatter.

And then Eddy's voice rose over the noise. "Excuse me? Are you missing a flight? We're all worried about our flights, sir."

"No! We have to stop that woman up there. She's a saboteur." He pronounced it "sah-BO-tee-er," like someone who had read the word "saboteur" but had never heard it pronounced.

"Sah-BO-tee-er?" I repeated his odd pronunciation. "Nuts. He's totally nuts," I said again softly to the people around me.

I breathed in; I breathed out. Three more minutes. I just needed three more minutes before Sanjeev got someone's attention. I'd be home free—or arrested and detained depending on whether my health card and capsule matched. I inched a few more feet in the maze. Anna still sat in the glass booth. She was alone for the moment, thinking, sweating, praying, no doubt wishing she had a bottle of vodka. A TSA agent had reentered her booth. He held her documents in his hand.

"Stop her!" Sanjeev's voice reached a high panic level.

I carefully glanced back. Eddy physically blocked Sanjeev with a wide stance. All around us TSA agents ignored the noise.

"Her!" Sanjeev shouted again.

I shook my head and repeated the nutty boyfriend line to the agent carting the bins to the front of the conveyer. The agent, a woman thank goodness, rolled her eyes and shrugged her shoulders.

Really? I couldn't believe these people were so gullible. We didn't have a chance against real terrorists if this was the level of critical thinking we had to stop them.

I took off my shoes and put them in the plastic tub. My heart pounded. I laid my purse flat beside my shoes. My heart pounded harder. I handed my health card to the TSA agent who swiped it and then signaled me to come through the metal detector. My heart exploded.

Nothing happened. The TSA agent looked like he was watching the eighth inning of a scoreless baseball game. He handed my health card back to me. I put my shoes back on and picked up my purse.

Behind me, Sanjeev stupidly kept calling out my name. He'd reached the conveyer belt, and I melted through a crowd of people into a gift shop. I picked out some reading glasses, a Giants baseball cap, and a plaid tote bag. After I dropped the cash on the counter, I stuffed my coat and scarf into the bag, put on the hat and glasses, and strolled back to the security area. It might have been the dumbest thing I'd done in my lifetime. But it would also be the least likely thing that Maggie Rider, terrorist and saboteur, would ever do.

Two TSA agents collected Sanjeev on the other side of the metal detector and escorted him into a small glass cubicle. He pointed frantically toward the direction I'd disappeared.

I don't know why he thought anyone would believe someone with his skin tone. After all, America knew all this started with someone just like him, at least those who couldn't tell the difference between an Indian and someone from the Middle East.

I made eye contact with Anna. Her eyes were wide. Mascara tracked small rivulets down her cheeks.

"Alicia?" I said. "Alicia Bukowski? Is that you?"

She brightened. "Stephanie Morghan?"

The TSA agent looked at me.

"Oh, my God. I haven't seen you in years," she said.

What an actress.

I stepped toward the security booth. That very act could get me arrested. The TSA agent held up his hand to halt me.

I paused. "It's so good to see you!"

"You know each other?" the TSA agent asked skeptically.

"We were in college together." It was a huge stretch. But I hoped I looked young, and I knew she looked old.

The TSA agent sighed. He paused a fraction of a second too long. Anna gently pulled her documents from his hand, grabbed her bag and stepped into her shoes and out of the booth. "We're finished here, right?" she said. Her boldness was ridiculously crazy.

I held my breath.

At that moment, another TSA agent called to Anna's TSA agent. The other TSA agent was directing another passenger into the glass cubicle and handing papers off to Anna's agent, who stared at Anna a moment longer, then turned and went into the booth with his new victim. As if he had a second thought, he shifted his body around and watched us again.

Anna and I hugged each other, but not for the reasons the TSA agent thought. Arm in arm, we left the security area. I glanced back to see Eddy put his shoes back on. A TSA agent stood next to him. I could hardly watch. We'd made it this far. What were the odds all ten of us would make it?

Anna squeezed my arm. "Thank you," she whispered. "You saved me."

I shook my head. If the TSA agent suspected her, they certainly wouldn't have let her go just because an old college friend spotted her.

"It was nothing," I whispered. "They were going to let you go anyway."

I looped my arm through Anna's and we strolled off toward the restroom. My last glance back at the security area told me the one thing I didn't want to know: Eddy now sat in the extra security booth.

It was my turn to throw up in the restroom, which at the moment, was packed. Anna stood in line in front of me. We whispered to each other as we patiently waited.

"What was the holdup?"

"I got pulled over for a random search. Then they say my vaccination isn't in the right place. I say to them, 'What difference, this vaccination place? I have it. Why do you stop me because it's not in the right place?'" She shook her head. "I think to myself. My Daniel make this all possible. To track all these people. Is not good."

"But he also made it possible to stop it. And we just did." I hoped.

"Yes. This part is good." She didn't sound convinced. Maybe she needed this for her grieving process.

Her turn came to take a stall. I took the next one, but all I did was lean my head against the inside of the door. I didn't know what they were doing with Eddy.

The toilet flushed behind me. I hated automation.

Anna waited for me while I washed my hands, and we walked back towards security. Two agents were escorting an irate Sanjeev out of the area. What did he not understand about keeping his head down?

Unfortunately, Eddy still sat in security. He was leaned over, his forearms resting on his knees—his basketball bench stance. He caught my eye and gave a half smile.

If only he'd had an ounce more of charm.

"You can go," I said to Anna. The longer we waited on this side of security, the more we stayed at risk.

She shook her head. "I am with you until is over." She'd looped her arm through mine again. I felt Russian.

A second TSA agent joined the first one. Eddy looked relaxed. He stood up and talked some more. It was a good move because sitting people who talk to standing people are at a psychological disadvantage. He motioned with his hands and shrugged his shoulders.

I really needed a chair. My knees wouldn't survive this.

Finally, the TSA agent stepped back and waved Eddy out of the security booth. Anna and I strolled towards baggage claim where the others had gathered next to a carousel with a fresh load of circling luggage. We hadn't planned to rendezvous, but after the intensity of the last two hours, I don't think any of us could just walk away. We'd been changed forever. Hopefully, we'd changed things forever.

A hand touched my arm. This time it was Eddy.

I turned and hugged him and tried not to cry.

"We're safe."

"Thank God we made it."

"I love you."

"What happened?"

"Later. Not here."

We shook hands and hugged all around, promising to keep in touch. And then we left so we could disappear for the next twenty-four hours.

Eddy and I grabbed a cab to take us to the bus station. The adventure never ended with this guy.

Chapter
53

The bus station seemed downright primitive by comparison. We paid cash for our tickets and then stood in line with an exceptionally motley group, not for security, but to get a seat. The bus company took "first come, first served" as a Biblical commandment. Ten minutes before the bus was scheduled to leave, they opened a door to the outside. We patiently filed out to the platform and climbed up the bus steps to find our seats.

"They thought I resembled a terrorist named Eddy Rider," he whispered as we pulled out of the station.

"Sweet Jesus."

"I kept saying they had my fingerprints and my DNA. I could look like Hitler, but it would only take a minute to prove I wasn't."

"I can't believe you were so bold."

"It wasn't that. I just know that no matter what the technology is, as long as people are making the decisions, it'll never be foolproof."

"I hope you're right."

I fell asleep in Eddy's arms before we crossed the Oakland Bridge and didn't wake up again until we'd passed into Nevada. We got off the bus in Reno and found a cheap motel with a high-speed Internet. Eddy worked feverishly to finish getting the documents ready to load on the website. I rounded up some deli sandwiches and a six-pack and then spent the rest of the night trying not to say over and over, "I can't believe we did it. I can't believe we're okay."

At least not out loud.

We both watched the clock. At twelve o'clock midnight, the moment the server backed up the data, we toasted each other with the last of the beers. I fell asleep again around one, waking only briefly when Eddy crawled in bed around four. At nine, the alarm blared. A trumpet sounding would have been more appropriate. If the virus had done what Stepan said it would, it should have just released into the system.

We sat up in bed and Eddy hit the power button on the TV remote control. He flipped through the channels until he found CNN.

We waited.

Bland news blips scrolled across the bottom. There'd been a small earthquake in Turkey, a car bomb in some unpronounceable place in Iraq, and a nasty snowstorm developing over the Great Lakes region.

The longer we waited the more I worried something had gone wrong. Maybe it was the ultimate scam and the instructions didn't release a virus after all. Or maybe Sanjeev convinced someone that Maggie Rider, of all people, figured out how to destroy the system, and they figured out that they shouldn't back up the data.

"Just wait. These things take time," Eddy said, completing our transformation of me becoming the pessimist in the family and him the optimist.

I took a shower and got ready for the day. Eddy followed and then once again we were in front of the TV.

Finally, close to noon, the first headline scrolled across the bottom of the screen. It was a simple message: "Long delays occurring at all major airports due to a computer problem. TSA expects to resolve by 3:00 Pacific Standard Time."

"Sorry, friends. It ain't likely to get fixed in three hours," Eddy said to the TV. He turned on his computer, connected to the Internet, and began uploading the new pages with Phil Generett's information to smallpoxscare.com.

I stayed glued to the TV. The news ticker tape gradually swelled in urgency: the computer glitch appeared to be a virus, impacting the entire Homeland Security database. The DHS suspected a terrorist attack on the database. The White House reacted and raised the terrorist threat level to red, the highest level possible.

By four o'clock it was the only news story CNN or FOX talked about.

We ordered pizza, which seemed innocuous enough except that as Eddy was paying the delivery guy, CNN chose to report breaking news in the next level of the crisis. They flashed pictures of Eddy Rider and his lovely wife Maggie as the terrorists who had temporarily brought down the database.

The pizza guy's eyes flicked from the TV to me to the TV to Eddy back to the TV again and then back to Eddy.

My stomach flopped over. Eddy handed the pizza guy another hundred-dollar tip and smiled.

The pizza guy paused. His bulk blocked the door and his eyes shifted around the room one more time. Eddy's computer purred in the background.

I was a second away from throwing myself at the pizza guy's chest so Eddy could at least have a thirty-second escape lead. To where, I didn't have time to think about.

But the man in the door just shrugged his shoulders. "That's really something, huh? How just those two people could bring down Big Brother all by themselves." He handed back all of Eddy's money, including the tip. "This one's on me."

Eddy's hand shook slightly as he took the money back. "You know what they'll do if they think we're eating pizza in a cheap motel in Reno," he said.

The pizza guy gave a tiny salute. "My lips are sealed, no matter what size the reward is."

It turned out to be ten million dollars, for each of us. It might as well have been a billion dollars. There was no knock on the door.

All evening we watched the talking heads debate what had happened, how, and why.

Eddy snorted at that. "Why? Why would someone want to take down a national database that contains the DNA and fingerprints of every person on US soil? If that's the best question the media could ask, it's no wonder they couldn't put this story together before it was spoon-fed to them."

The White House held a press conference late evening to shriek about how this attack against the freedom of the American people on US soil by terrorists was unparalleled. Even the 9/11 attacks on the World Trade Center and the Pentagon paled in comparison. The president echoed those famous words of another day: "We will hunt you down and we will kill you."

But the words already had a tinny sound since Eddy's website information had started seeping into the news reports as well.

The president might as well have been repeating the famous line from the Wizard of Oz: "Don't look behind the curtain. There is not a man behind the curtain."

Already the next morning, plastic card shredding machines started appearing on street corners across the country, placed there by private citizens whose hearts beat like our own.

Epilogue

I'D NEVER DREAMED OF GOING TO HONDURAS, but when a person needs to disappear, it's hard to find a sweeter place. Eleven bus rides and a ferry later, Eddy and I landed on one of the English-speaking Bay Islands just off the mainland coast, a tranquil spot surrounded by the most undiscovered coral reefs for a thousand miles. The guidebook described the place as the Caribbean in the fifties.

We found a comfortable little house perched on stilts right on the water. I hung out for hours on our dock that jutted out over the water and watched the daily rhythm of the sea life that circled through our piece of the bay: angelfish, barracudas, tiny squid, and a small school of silky manta rays that always flew through at dusk.

The island had electricity from 6:00 a.m. till midnight every day, except on the days it didn't, and running water the hours they had electricity. There was a simple mechanical reason for this that I never learned. The supply boat regularly chugged into the bay and stocked the two tiny grocery stores with anything you could want from the mainland, except—for some unknown reason—butter. The boat also brought Eddy slightly stale copies of *The New York Times*, which cycled through a dozen hands— sans all the articles Eddy ripped out of them—before they ended up in the trash.

Some day we'd return to the US. Or maybe we wouldn't. It depended on whether the new administration could prove itself trustworthy and whether the country had the guts to make the prison sentences stick for the old administration. I was a little nervous that all those guys who had formerly run around the White House might end up on our little Honduran Island.

If they did, we didn't recognize each other.

Where They Ended Up

Keri, the useless Baja Breeze project lead: Without Michael at Baja Breeze, Keri was totally exposed—well, at least figuratively. The CEO zipped his pants and fired her for incompetence. She filed a sexual harassment lawsuit but lost, probably because she wore a see-through blouse on the third day of the trial. Currently, she's bartending at a sleazy place on El Camino. Surprisingly, she's been a faithful pen pal to Mario Seneca and promises to wait forever until he's up for parole in 2025.

Sanjeev Srivastava: He moved his family back to Bangalore but kept his job at Zaan and probably his same salary. It took him over a year, but he eventually emailed Michael and apologized for not having more courage. Better late than never.

Lisa, Phil Generett's niece: She went back to her Starbucks, having only taken off the morning. No one ever realized she'd played such an important part in saving the country.

Stepan the Dishwasher: Brilliant though he was, he was more brilliant if someone gave him the hacking instructions to follow. Still, he leveraged his part in the drama into a mega salary with a startup antivirus company.

Phil Generett: Even for the major media, it didn't take much sleuthing to figure out he was the source of the information on Eddy's website. He testified at various trials and eventually published a book about his experiences, which did almost as well as Eddy's book. Both books stayed on the *The New York Times* bestseller list for over a year. Most people treated him as the hero he was, although—as in any event of this sort—there were those who claimed he was the one who had betrayed the country with his revelations. Go figure.

Jola Pavelkavich: She worked for Zaan for a few more months, but finally quit in disgust when they asked her to work on another Homeland Security project, one that would require no cards but would scan and capture irises. She returned to Poland and started up a small company that built anti-spy gizmos. Although she was three decades too late for when Poland needed the technology the most, she made a bucket of money selling to Americans and Western Europeans.

Anna Denisov: Her Russian restaurant in Palo Alto continued to win awards and hold a devoted following, but her heart just wasn't in it anymore. Eventually, she sold out and built a small distillery that made boutique vodkas.

Michael and Kai: Michael cashed in his huge portfolio of Zaan stock and turned in his resignation to Zaan the same day as the database failure. Michael and Kai got married and moved to Southern Louisiana, where they opened a fabulous Thai restaurant in New Orleans. They occasionally visit us in Honduras, where they too hang out on the dock and watch the manta rays.

Tina Bastante: The DHS released Tina twenty-four hours after the database crash, as she'd become the ultimate lightening rod. Although they'd exposed her to smallpox, she was still well within the incubation period. The Center for Disease Control provided a true smallpox vaccine, complete with needle pinpricks. Not even a single pustule emerged. If it had only been so easy to undo the other scars the government had inflicted. She eventually returned to El Salvador, where she continued to practice medicine.

Pete Kawalski: He carried his guilt in betraying his friends forever even though Eddy reminded him repeatedly that we would have never gotten the health cards and vaccination capsules if it hadn't been for him. Pete's therapist assured him that losing Tina was a crazy-maker, but he wouldn't stop blaming himself. As penance, he took care of selling our possessions and selling our house in Colorado. He followed Tina to El Salvador, where they endured in spite of some rocky times. Sometimes love *does* conquer all.

The mole at DHS who fed Eddy his best stuff: We never figured out who it was. We're hoping he's still there, patiently waiting to discreetly expose the next Orwellian government plan.

The Reno pizza guy: We don't know. He kept his mouth shut. What a guy.

Book Club Questions

1. With nearly everything in life, we gain something and we lose something, even though it may be difficult to see in the moment. What would be the benefits of an RFID implant in every citizen? What would be the losses?

2. What role does humor play in the story?

3. What is the effect of the author's use of first person narrative? Does it make the story more or less immediate or credible?

4. How do you define civil disobedience?

5. Have you ever committed an act of civil disobedience? What did you do? Why did you do it? If you haven't, what would be the impetus for committing an act of civil disobedience? What would you be willing to do?

6. What would society be like if no one ever committed an act of civil disobedience?

7. If the government required everyone to get an RFID implant, what would you do? Why? What would you choose for your children?

8. In Chapter 28, Maggie reminds the project lead, Michael de Leon, of the old cliché of the frog that boils alive because it doesn't know when to leap out of the water that's getting hotter and hotter. Given that all the technology in the book currently exists, think about where our society is today on a scale of one to ten. One represents room

temperature water, in other words, total freedom without government control. Ten is boiling water, in other words, total control by the government. What number are we today as a society? Why do you believe this?

9. In Chapter 40, Anna compares the definition of freedom that the Soviets had until communism fell and the American definition of freedom—corporate versus individual. What do we gain with our view of individual freedom? What do we lose? What would you give up to have more corporate freedom? What would you give up to have more individual freedom?

10. The story makes numerous references to breadcrumb trails. What are the breadcrumb trails you leave every day if someone wanted to find you?

11. The story references back doors at various points, both literal and metaphorical. What are your back doors in case you'd ever need one?

12. Over the course of the story, Maggie gives up her computer because of the tracking software, her clothes because of the possibility of RFIDs, and finally cuts her hair—part of her identity—so as not to be spotted. Ultimately, she leaves her home, community, and country, maybe forever. What would you give up if you had to?

13. How have your thoughts about government control and freedom been impacted by reading The Virus? Do you view the world differently after having read this book?

If you want Janelle to join your book club by Skype,
contact her through her website at www.janellediller.com.

Coming Soon from Janelle Diller...

The Secret War:
a Mennonite Memoir

I come from a long line of storytellers, which isn't my fault.

The burden of this is that I can never just tell you something. I have to give you the context that—unfortunately for the listener—often begins with "I was born in a small town in Kansas just before the Depression." You'd be surprised how often that bit of information is important.

When we were children, you could have asked me and my brother, Aaron, what we had for supper, and he, who somehow escaped the family curse, would have told you, "Potatoes and ham gravy."

Four words.

Of course, it lacks detail, substance, and nuance, even if it does actually answer your question.

I, on the other hand, would have felt driven to tell you about the drought, the price of pork, the relatives who gave up and moved to California, and the surprising ways you can stretch nothing into not much, but enough to get full on. I'd eventually remember to circle around and tell you about the potatoes and ham gravy, but that'd be after I also told you about the piano lessons I always wanted but never got and the fact that my brother was a terrible speller and to this day spells women, "wemon." Aaron used to say, "When you ask Cat [that's me] something, you better have your knitting along."

I've speculated about why Aaron doesn't talk much. Back in the '20s, we used to have bands of gypsies that would jangle along the back roads between here and nowhere worth going. I think they stole Aaron from some dull Lutheran family up north in Pawnee County, and when they realized he was never going to be able to distract people with witty conversation, they dropped him off on our doorstep, thinking we German Mennonites would never even notice he was boring. I showed up after he did, so even though my mother always denied my version of things, I'm not convinced.

Of course, I'm only telling you this so you'll forgive me if I tell you more than Aaron would offer about those terrible times. In fact, if you want Aaron's version, here it is: "The Depression nearly destroyed us. The war was worse."

My version? Well, I think you need to know a little more.

#

I was only seven at the time, but because it was such a rare treat to go into town, I might have remembered the day even if the Sweethome bank hadn't shut its doors.

We drove into town that day in our rackety old Ford truck, just Dad and me. The seats were so low I couldn't see out the window very well if I sat like a lady should, so I kneeled on a pillow and draped my arms over the bench back and watched the world dizzily speed by just ahead of our billowing dust. The wind whipped my braids around so much that Dad called me Piggly Wiggly.

We stopped at the bank first.

"Set your fanny there, Kittycat, while I take care of some business." He pointed to a stiff leather chair. "And don't go gettin' curious."

Cats and curiosity. He'd made that point before.

The chair gave me a good angle on some old maid who worked at the bank. If she wasn't an old maid, she must've been a widow lady with ten hungry mouths to feed since old maids and widows were the only kind of working ladies in the world. She kept a tidy desk. Two sharpened pencils sat ready to attack a stack of papers, but while I sat there, they didn't move. Her mouth did, though. She seemed right glad to talk to anything that had two legs, me included. But I didn't talk back because all my life I'd been told to mind my p's and q's and this seemed like a good place to practice. Besides, if I moved my mouth, I'd most likely end up moving my fanny, too, and I knew that would come to no good.

I felt right at home there, though, because the old maid had an itty-bitty framed picture that said "Jesus Saves" on it, just like the one at church where we children had our Sunday school openings every Sunday. We used to also have a picture that said "Jesus Lives" until one of the bigger boys—probably one of the toothy Fred Miller boys—wrote, "in Enid Oklahoma and he ain't none too happy about it" underneath the picture. The very next Sunday we had ourselves a new picture, this one with Jesus on the cross and with a glass cover. It didn't have any words on it. I guess they didn't want to spark anyone's imagination.

All in all, "Jesus Saves" made more sense since we kept putting our pennies and nickels in the offering basket for him. I didn't know what Jesus was saving up for, but Sunday after Sunday like that collecting all those pennies, I figured it was going to be something big. Yessir. Most of all, though, I hoped it was gonna' be sweet and he'd share it with me. Store bought candy's what I had in mind.

Anyway, I wasn't any too surprised to find out that Jesus was saving at the bank, too.

When Dad finally came out of the office, he was laughing and shaking hands with a short, baldheaded man. I know he was in high spirits because I hadn't seen him happy very often, and I thought it was odd that a place like a bank would make him smile so much. I decided right then and there that when I grew up I'd never marry a farmer since they never laughed. I'd marry me a bankerman instead. That is, if a bankerman was in the "do" column of that long invisible list of dos and don'ts that Mennonites kept somewhere.

From the bank, we stopped at the feed mill, and Dad let me pick out the feed sack the chicken feed came in that we were buying. I picked a pretty one with teeny tiny pink flowers. I always picked one with flowers because then maybe Mama would smile a little and sew the feed sack into a dress for me. In 1933, some folks got to shop at J.C. Penny's, but not us.

We also stopped at the grocers and bought a loaf of bread. I know we must have bought some other things, too, but store-bought bread was as rare as a smiling farmer, so that sticks in my mind. Dad's last stop was at Brewster's drugstore where he bought me a chocolate ice cream cone with two scoops of ice cream. He must have thought he'd get to finish one of the scoops, but I fooled him. I didn't aim to share anything that special with anyone. Dad had a whopping big piece of lemon meringue pie and then grumbled it wasn't nearly as sweet or tart or flaky as Mama's even though he ate every last crumb of it and looked like he would have liked to lick the plate, too.

After the ice cream and pie we headed back to the truck to go home. Just as Dad was cranking the engine, Elroy Perky came running down the sidewalk, his arms flailing. With his beak of a nose and long, skinny neck, Elroy was a twin to a goose. Today, he kind of tilted forward, too, which only added to the goose look. Running like he was with his arms flapping, he could have taken flight. He seemed to be calling out to the entire street and not to anyone in particular. "They closed the bank down! They just shut 'er down!"

Dad stopped cranking and got a funny look on his face. "What'd you say, Elroy?"

Elroy stopped a moment and wheezed in some more breath. He swiped his nose with his shirtsleeve and spit on the sidewalk. "They just closed the bank down. I stopped there to get some money out, and they locked the door in my face. Wouldn't even crack it open to talk to me. Talked through the glass."

Dad pulled out his pocket watch and studied it a minute. "They'll be opening it on Monday though, right? Usual time, right?"

Elroy's face crinkled up painfully tight. "That's what I'm tryin' to tell you. They just shut 'er down. For good. You got money in there, it ain't yours no more."

Dad's face slowly took on the same painful, crinkled look that Elroy's had. He dropped the crank and leaned through the window for his zippered canvas pouch. He opened it up and flipped through his papers once, twice, and then another time. His lip started twitching, so I knew I should be scared.

"Did we have money in the bank, Daddy?"

"No" was all he said. His voice sounded thick and hoarse.

I knew that voice. My tummy turned upside down. I didn't know what was wrong since we didn't have any money in the bank. All I knew was that whatever was worse than having money in the bank and then not having it anymore, we had it.

Dad pounded on the bank door's heavy glass, with each hit jangling the welcome bell that wasn't welcoming anyone. He pounded for a long time, and even though we could see people inside, no one would come to the door. The short, baldheaded man was in there, too, but he didn't look like he was smiling or laughing anymore. In fact, even through the window, it looked like he had the same painful, crinkled look on his face that Elroy had given Dad.

Now Dad started yelling while he pounded. "Bernard! Bernard, open the door." Bernard must have been the short, baldheaded man because he scurried into a back room. "Bernard!" Dad yelled again. "You didn't sign the papers. All I need is your signature. I already paid off the loan." He pounded some more but looked like it wouldn't make any difference. "Open the door and talk to me, Bernard!" he shouted.

By now, a few other cars came flying up to the bank. Dust swirled around us. A scattering of people came on foot.

Tight, edgy voices called out.

"Open up! Just give us our money!"

"We got a right to our own money!"

"What are we going to do without our money?"

Dad finally stopped beating on the door and wove his way through the gathering group back to the truck. Someone picked up a rock and heaved it at the door, barely missing the glass. The voices grew louder, meaner. More raucous. A few more cars pulled up. Men hopped out, mad. Another rock flew. This one jangled the welcome bell and rattled the glass.

Dad cranked the engine a couple of turns and putt, putt, putted away. As we headed down Main Street, the sheriff flew past us, blowing his siren to tell people to get off the street. Since no one was on the street except for us, it was a pretty silly thing to do, but we might not have known how serious the sheriff was otherwise. My heart thumped in my ears, and I turned around in my seat to watch his dust cloud.

"Is he going to get his money out of the bank?"

"He's going to help the robbers." Dad's voice was raspy and tight.

I still didn't know what the sheriff was going to do. "Does that mean he's going to help the people inside or outside the bank?"

But Dad didn't respond. He used words like he spent dollars—few and far between. But even though he said little, his body shouted. Even at my age I could read that language as well as I could read a book. Dad's muscles tensed, his mouth twitched, and he grew deaf. I guessed the end of the world was near.

I held my breath so I wouldn't cry.

We didn't head home. Instead, Dad drove out past the grain elevator and miles out into the countryside where there were no trees, only endless fields where the wheat should've been a velvety green carpet but wasn't. I'd been this way before, but I didn't know where the road took us. It turned out that the road took us to Simon Yoder's farm. When I grew up, I eventually realized that all roads would take you to Simon Yoder's if you followed them long enough.

I knew Simon from church. He was a big man with a likable face and a happy, wide smile. When he let loose a laugh, you could see he had a shiny tooth outlined in gold. He was shiny on the outside, too, not just the tooth. Simon wore suits he bought in Dodge City at Hartley Brothers Department store and had them tailored to fit. He had more than one suit, unlike every other man I knew who got married and buried in their suits and wore them to church every Sunday morning and every Sunday evening in between. Sometimes to Wednesday prayer meetings, too. Maybe when it hadn't been the Depression they'd had more than one suit, but since I'd only known life since the Depression, I wouldn't have known those things then.

I didn't know why we'd gone here instead of home, but it was a good enough surprise. Ethel, Simon Yoder's wife, had been my Sunday school teacher when I was little—little being a relative term when you're seven. Ethel was a soft, pillowy woman with pumpkin breasts that swayed reverently and frizzy hair sticks that wouldn't stay in a bun. She seemed like tapioca pudding to me: lots of lumps but no sparkle. She was all right with me, though, because when she taught Sunday school she purchased good behavior with sugar cookies. You could buy a lot with a good sugar cookie back then.

"Wait in the truck, Kittycat," Dad said, but I climbed out anyway knowing that if he really cared, his voice would have sounded harder.

I guess I expected to walk into a cheery kitchen with racks and racks of steamy sugar cookies cooling and a smiling Ethel playing with flannel board Bible story cutouts. Instead, chaos reigned in the room. Dishes and unfinished plates of food cluttered the tabletop and sink drainboard. Ethel, looking ever so much like a fat bird on stick ankles, stood at the stove, soberly cooking up more chaos.

Helen, one of the Yoder girls, leaned against the sink, arms crossed, and lazily chatted with her mother.

My mama would have fallen through the floor if anyone had seen her kitchen look like that. So I knew that Helen was some kind of a no-good girl, even if she was a Mennonite.

Dad cleared off a kitchen chair and left me, wide-eyed and silent, at the table while he disappeared. Ethel put a couple of stale cookies in front of me and pinched her lips together to make a smile. Her eyes didn't get those sweet lines, though, so I don't think you could call it a real smile. I wondered for a little while whether it was better not to smile at all or pretend to smile but not mean it.

Helen's eyesight must have been bad because she didn't even nod her head my way but kept on chattering about her hair that she wanted to name "Bob." I didn't know girls named their hair. What I did know was that Mennonite girls didn't cut their hair. Eventually, they wrapped it up under prayer coverings like their mothers and then had lots of babies. On Sundays, Helen's hair was always hidden under her covering, so I figured it was long like God wanted it to be and she was just a short time away from baby making. But here she stood, talking about Bob and her hair, which was actually quite short, hardly to her shoulders. It was the first time I realized you could lie with your hair. Here everyone thought she was a virtuous girl and she wasn't.

I nibbled quietly, not understanding what I was doing at that moment in such a dirty spot on earth and feeling confused and maybe a little sick. Three sugar cookies and no milk later, Dad returned with Simon Yoder. Simon's only son, Harold, slouched in behind them. Simon flashed a golden edged smile at me and winked conspiratorially like we were long lost buddies. I should have felt warm inside.

"Mama," Simon said to Ethel, "Ezra and I are going into town to have a little conversation with Bernard Hibble." He tilted his head toward Harold. "You drive little blondie home and explain to Rose why Ezra's going to be late."

Harold glanced in my direction but didn't move a muscle except to smile slyly. I knew this boy from church, but until this moment, I didn't realize I didn't like him. I wanted to go home with my dad, not with this oily looking boy who wouldn't even stand up straight.

That no-good girl Helen must have stopped thinking about naming her hair because she perked up and noticed me finally. "I'll drive her." She said it fast.

I should have been relieved, but I wasn't.

"No!" I sounded more panicked than I meant to, but girls didn't know how to drive. I knew this was true because my grandma was a girl and I'd ridden with her lots of times and I knew for a fact she didn't know how to drive. I'd been in my share of ditches with that lady.

"It's okay," my dad said tiredly. "She can ride along with us. Rose will just have to sit with her worry. Won't be the first time."

So Simon, Dad, and I all climbed into the truck and headed back into town. I sat in the middle but scooched close to Dad. Simon talked while Dad drove. He said reassuring words. "Bernard will listen to me, Ezra. He owes his job to me, as well as a good share of the bank's business. I'll make him sign, or I'll see that the board votes him out." But Dad's mouth twitched anyway. Maybe he was already thinking about future debts.

Dusk fell around us, draping the fields and road in roses and ambers. The motor rumbled under my feet, steadily lulling me to sleep. I woke when Dad killed the engine. We hadn't stopped at the bank but in front of a broad brick house set back from the street. A low, wrought iron fence outlined the front of the yard and red brick front walk, nothing practical that would keep a cow in or out. A car sat on a brick driveway. It was so shiny we could see ourselves in it as we paraded past. The three of us looked like squat bugs, even tall, skin-and-bones Dad.

"Got your papers, Ezra?"

Dad nodded.

"Just let me do the talking."

A mouse of a woman with a halo of coppery brown hair opened the door. Her tummy was big and round, like she had a huge sack of feed under her dress. She rested her hands on the top of it while she talked. That seemed like a handy thing to be able to do. "Bernard's not here. He hasn't come home from the bank yet. I'll tell him you stopped by, though, Simon." She nodded at Dad and glanced at me without lowering the tip of her nose.

"Well, Alice, we'll just wait in the parlor for him then," Simon said as he opened the screen door. "I'm sure under the circumstances, he'll understand." He showed this Alice his gold tooth so it looked like he was smiling.

The mouse woman opened her mouth, but only squeaked a protest before the three of us were standing in the entryway. I thought she might stamp her foot and huff at us since that's what I'd likely do if I had that look on my face, but she didn't. Instead, she shifted into the role of a fidgety hostess and ushered us into the parlor. She disappeared while the three of us sat stiffly on a puffy davenport that was never intended to make a body feel welcome. Everything in the room that could be covered in fabric was, and none of it was the kind that had once been a feed sack. Flowers flowed everywhere: roses and peonies and dahlias twined down the heavy drapes, streamed over the furniture, and spilled onto the carpet. More than enough flowers to make me dizzy.

We waited, weed like, in the room for a 'coon's age. The fidgety mouse woman Alice came in several times to tell us Bernard hadn't returned yet. We already knew this. She didn't offer us anything to eat or drink, so I knew she wanted us to give up and leave.

Once, the front screen door slammed. The three of us twisted our necks to see if this might be the bankerman, but it was only a long, lean boy with round brown eyes who took the steps three at a time.

Dad kept taking out his pocketwatch to check the time even though the grandfather clock ticked loudly enough to keep track of every single second that passed. Nobody talked. Simon tried to a couple of times, but Dad—who never was any good at small talk even in the '40s when wheat prices improved—certainly wasn't inclined to small talk in the flowery sitting room of the man who intended to cheat him out of his farm. So mostly we just listened to the clock tick tock.

Long after the clock had gonged the hour at least twice, the short, bald-headed man finally came in the door. He took off his hat and hung it on a hall tree. He was something to stare at because the top of his head was as pasty white as his chin and cheeks. I didn't know many men who didn't make their living in the sun.

"Simon, Ezra," he said and nodded at each of them. He gave me a quick, nervous nod, too. "What can I do for you?"

Even at my age I knew this to be a stupid question. He had done business with my Dad that morning. My dad had pounded on his window at the bank and shouted to him this afternoon. And now we'd been sitting in his silly looking parlor for close to eternity with a fistful of papers.

"He wants you to sign the papers." The words just popped out of my mouth. The clock stopped its tick, tick, ticking. Dad looked at me. I waited for the floor to open up and let me crawl in, but it didn't cooperate.

Miracles never happen when you need them the most.

"That's right, Bernard," my dad said, but he looked at me first, then the bankerman. "I came because you forgot to sign the deed. I made my last payment this morning. You gave me the paperwork, but you didn't sign it."

"Well, Ezra, why don't you stop by the bank on Monday—"

"You won't be open on Monday, Bernard." Dad's voice actually sounded like Dad instead of that tight-voiced stranger I'd heard all afternoon.

Mr. Hibble cleared his throat and shuffled a small dance step backwards.

"Well, that's true. We won't be open on Monday. Tell you what, I'll take the papers with me, and I'll get someone to notarize them next week."

"No," my dad said and planted the papers in a peony patch. He took out his fountain pen and offered it to the bankerman. "Simon and your wife can witness your signature."

Mr. Hibble didn't touch the pen but took out a wilted handkerchief and mopped up little beads of sweat on his upper lip. He wouldn't look my dad or Simon in the eye. "Ezra, I just can't sign these papers here. I'm sorry about all the confusion, but you'll just have to talk to someone next week about this."

Simon sighed grandly, "Bernard—"

But my dad touched Simon's arm. "Bernard," my dad said softly, "does the bank own my farm or do I?"

Mr. Hibble cleared his throat and mopped his upper lip again. He also took a swipe at his brow and the top of his head. He didn't look very bankerly. And he still wouldn't look at Dad.

"I paid off the last dime I owed on my farm, but you didn't sign the papers. I'm askin' you again. Do I own my farm or does the bank?"

Mr. Hibble's face wrinkled for a moment. Then he stuttered, "Well, you'll need the…uh bank to sign off before… um before the farm is really uh…really yours." He still didn't take the pen.

There my dad stood, roses and peonies and dahlias swirling overhead and underfoot. Finally, Dad gently poked Mr. Hibble's chest with the fountain pen. Twice. Dad, Simon, and I shuddered ever so slightly. We're Mennonites, which I don't expect you to understand, but this was his Mennonite equivalent of throwing a punch. "Then I know you'll do the right thing, Bernard. I know you to be an honorable man." This time, pacifist that he was, he didn't poke Mr. Hibble's chest again. I watched. But he still held out the pen.

The bankerman mopped his full face and head one more time. And then he mopped the back of his milk-white neck. The part of his white shirt that was showing looked like it was doing some mopping, too. He finally looked at Simon who nodded. I think. Mr. Hibble sighed the kind of sigh I'd been hearing from my dad all my short life, and he called to his wife. "Alice. Come here please."

No one said a word as they scritch-scratched with a pen on the papers four times. Mrs. Hibble kept patting her tummy.

The entire afternoon and evening had pointed to these few minutes, and now we were done. Even with all the day's wrong turns, Mr. Hibble couldn't stop being a gentleman. So he ushered us out onto the front porch for some Kansas small talk before we left. For the few minutes the adults chatted about the weather and the wheat prices, the world wasn't teetering on the precipice of a cataclysm. But finally, Simon asked, "What's going to happen, Bernard?"

Mr. Hibble stood with his back to the corner street lamp, so I could only see the sad shake of his head and not what was on his face. "I don't know, Simon. I hadn't thought things could get any worse, but they just have." And then he lit a cigarette and let feathery strands of smoke drift around us.

We sat on the street in the puttering truck a few minutes before Dad stopped shaking enough to drive. None of us said anything. Finally, I tugged at his sleeve, and he put the truck in gear. The papers signed, we drove down the dirt street into the soft charcoal evening. Behind us, back in the direction of the bankerman's house, it sounded like a car backfired once.

Pop!

Acknowledgments

Any work of fiction depends on so many people and events. I'm grateful for the people at Bookfuel for taking my manuscript to the next level: Sam Raines, author advisor extraordinaire; Elizabeth Cameron, the editor who made the manuscript sing; and Chris Moyer, for his distinctive cover design and layout. I especially appreciate the people who read this manuscript in many forms, especially my ever-faithful sister Patrice Erickson and my ever-faithful friend Lisa Travis.

In addition, thank you to the following people for your willingness to read, give feedback, and encourage me: Teresa Barnes, Patricia Castillo, Janet and Tom Crago, Dusty Diller, Gwen Diller, Jesse Diller, Marjorie Ehrhardt, Sandy Elvington, Christie Gilbert, Erica Good, Nan Graber, Geanna Gravois, C.J. Hague, Jayne Heller, Mardell Hochstetler, Peg Hunter, Jodi Derstine Miller, Gerry Jurrens, Joseph Kolb, Yamini Natti, Ashley Rice, Meryl Roth, Cameron Smoak, Diane Sternberg, Delphine Stevens, Shannon Stubblefield Braden, Karen Valdez, Gary Van Voorst, Ingrid Wiese, Andrea Williamson, and Colleen Yoder-Andres.

And, of course, thank you to my most important critic and supporter, Steve. Lucky me that I found you.

About the Author

Janelle Diller worked for many years as a communication consultant for a high tech company. This role gave her ample opportunity to find interesting ways to say boring things. Having survived the chaos of the high-tech world for nearly a decade without getting laid off once, she knows firsthand the grinding exhaustion of the road-warrior's life. Eventually, she was able to liberate herself. Technology implementations went on without her.

Currently, she and her husband divide their time between living the good life in Colorado during the summer and sailing the Mexican coast in the winter. In addition, she writes early chapter book mysteries for the award winning Pack-n-Go Girls Adventure series. They're a ton of fun.

She's grateful she no longer has to write about technology implementations.

Janelle loves to connect with her readers in person when possible and on Skype with book clubs and classrooms. Contact her through her website at www.janellediller.com.